Take a company of misfits,
add one millionaire,
a dash of new recruits,
and stir up some trouble . . .

A Phule and His Money

A recipe for disaster

Praise for the
New York Times bestselling
PHULE'S COMPANY series

"Plenty of odd characters . . . fun!"

—*Locus*

"A winning story . . . part science fiction,
part spoof, part heart-warmer."

—*Publishers Weekly*

continued . . .

A PHULE AND HIS MONEY

ROBERT L. ASPRIN
with PETER J. HECK

ACE BOOKS, NEW YORK

A PHULE AND HIS MONEY

An Ace Book / published by arrangement with
Robert L. Asprin and Peter J. Heck

PRINTING HISTORY
Ace edition / October 1999

All rights reserved.
Copyright © 1999 by Robert Asprin.
Cover art by Walter Velez.
This book may not be reproduced in whole or in part,
by mimeograph or any other means, without permission.
For information address: The Berkley Publishing Group,
a division of Penguin Putnam, Inc.
375 Hudson Street, New York, New York 10014.

The Penguin Putnam Inc. World Wide Web site address is
http://www.penguinputnam.com

Check out the ACE Science Fiction & Fantasy newsletter
and much more on the Internet at Club PPI!

ISBN: 0-441-00658-2

ACE®
Ace Books are published
by The Berkley Publishing Group,
a division of Penguin Putnam Inc.,
375 Hudson Street, New York, New York 10014.
ACE and the "A" design are trademarks
belonging to Penguin Putnam Inc.

PRINTED IN THE UNITED STATES OF AMERICA

10 9 8 7 6 5 4 3 2 1

A PHULE
AND HIS MONEY

1

Journal #278

Even the most fortunate circumstances contain the seeds of their own destruction. So it was with the tenure of Phule's Company on Lorelei.

At first glance, a posh gambling resort like Lorelei would appear a plum assignment for a Space Legion company that until recently had been the laughingstock of the Legion. Omega Company had long been the Legion's dumping ground for incompetents and malcontents. My employer, Willard Phule (or "Captain Jester," to use his Legion name) was given command of Omega Company as punishment for a small indiscretion of his own, namely ordering a peace conference strafed. He was lucky—only his status as a wealthy munitions heir kept him from being expelled outright. The generals meant to so overload him with frustration and embarrassment that he would resign. A spoiled rich kid could find plenty of more pleasant ways to misspend his youth, they thought.

Instead he had decided to make the company the best in the Legion, and by applying unorthodox methods had come a long way toward that goal. But he had powerful enemies, and Lorelei appeared a perfect trap for the unwary. Dominated by gangsters, and given over to every sort of sybaritic entertainment, it would have destroyed most military units. That Phule's company had succeeded beyond all hopes confounded those enemies—but they were determined to find new ways to destroy him.

Now, the company was about to receive new troops—the first significant additions to its ranks since he took command. In such a tight-knit unit, any change of personnel has an impact. When the new troops have been selected by one's enemies, the impact is likely to be disastrous . . .

"They'll be docking any minute, now," said Phule, consulting his chronometer. It was the third time he'd checked it in the last five minutes. Since there were numerous time displays on view throughout the space station's arrival lounge, an observer might have concluded that Phule's preoccupation with the time—combined with his pacing and nonstop talking—was a sign of nervousness. That observer would have been right.

"A few minutes one way or the other won't make much difference, Captain," said Sergeant Brandy, who had come with her commanding officer to greet the new troops assigned to Phule's Company. "They're coming, and we'll deal with it. All of us will. I've been through this enough times before."

"Oh, I know you have," said Phule, nodding appreciatively to his top sergeant. "And I know you'll do everything you can to make them fit in smoothly. I've seen what you can do, Brandy. But this isn't just any new batch of recruits. It's a completely unique situation."

"You mean the Gambolts, sir?" said Lieutenant Armstrong, the third in the greeting party. He stood ramrod straight, almost managing to look comfortable despite the exaggerated precision of his uniform and posture. "I don't see where they'll be a problem. They're among the finest

fighters in the galaxy. It's an honor to have them in our
unit.''

"Yes, I appreciate that," said Phule. "But Gambolts
have never served in mixed units with humans before—and
these three specifically requested to be assigned to us. It's
a tribute to the good work we've done. But I can't help
wondering . . ." His voice trailed off.

Brandy shook her head firmly. "Whether the troops will
accept them? Don't worry about that, Captain. This outfit
may be the most tolerant bunch in the Legion. When you've
had to live down the reputation we've been saddled with,
you don't have room to get snooty about your barracks-
mates.''

"Losers can't be choosers, in other words," said Phule.
"I suppose that's been true in the past. Most of the companies have had to accept whatever hand the Legion dealt
them. But we've been changing that.''

"*You've* been changing that, sir," said Lieutenant Armstrong. "If not for you, we'd still be back on Haskin's
Planet, slogging through the swamps. Now we're among
the elite companies of the Legion—all thanks to your efforts.''

"I can't take all the credit," said Phule. "It's been a
team effort, and every member has contributed. That's why
I'm anxious about the new troops, to tell you the truth. The
Gambolts have always had their own elite unit in the Regular Army. Now three of them are coming to us—and I
have to wonder why. Will they fit into the team? Will they
hold themselves apart from the rest of the unit? Will
they . . ."

Whatever he was about to say was interrupted by the
blare of a klaxon and a red-lit sign flashing on and off by
the arrival door. The sign now read, SHUTTLE DOCKING:
PREPARE FOR DEBARKING PASSENGERS. Phule and his subordinates turned to face the door. Some of their questions
were about to be answered.

One advantage of building a casino on a space station is
that it can be a true twenty-four hour operation. With no

local cycle of day and night, there is no need for visitors to adjust to the local clock, or to go through what in pre-space days used to be called "jet lag". So the Fat Chance Casino was likely to have an eager crowd of gamblers at any hour. This, in turn, meant that Phule's Company had to be alert for trouble at any hour.

But Moustache, who was in charge of "daytime" security at the casino, wasn't expecting any real trouble. The tall noncom with a balding head and a bright red moustache sat at the bar sipping a brisk "cuppa" tea, scanning the early afternoon crowd with detached interest. He knew he wouldn't spot everything—it wasn't really his job, after all. Other members of the Omega Mob, disguised as waiters, croupiers, or fellow customers, mingled with the crowd, probing for the myriad signs that someone was trying to cheat. Behind the elegant-looking facade, other vigilant eyes performed the same task, aided by state-of-the-art surveillance equipment.

Of course, since the showdown with Maxine Pruett's hoodlums, there had been less trouble. Word had quickly gone out on the gamblers' grapevine to forget about trying to beat the Fat Chance. Still, there was always a handful of small-time grifters who thought they could outsmart the house security staff. Most of these were quickly spotted and quietly removed from the casino floor to a private lounge to await deportation on the next ship off-station. It was all handled very professionally—and unsuccessful grifters usually accepted their fate with a stoical shrug. After all, it was one of the risks of doing business.

So it came as a surprise when a voice spoke quietly in Moustache's earphone. It was Rose—"Mother" to the company—the voice of Comm Central, the vital glue that bound the company together. "Wake up, you old buzzard," she said teasingly. "We're about to get some rough trade. I know you senior citizens need your afternoon naps, but it'd be a shame for you to doze through the entertainment."

"Where?" said Moustache, instantly alert. He spoke under his breath, knowing that the super-sensitive directional microphone on his wrist communicator could pick up a whisper inaudible to someone at the next table.

"Blackjack tables, darlin'," said Mother. "We've got a mom-and-pop team palming and passing cards at Number Five. I've already tipped the dealer, and she's stalling."

"Good," said Moustache, standing up from the bar. "Who's covering that sector?"

"The dealer's a civilian employee. Her orders are to stay clear if trouble starts and let security handle it. We've got a couple of actors playing legionnaire stationed around the room, and they may be all we really need. But Gabriel's on the nearest exit in case they try to run. And if *he* needs help, we've got Sushi and Do-Wop undercover in that area—they're already closing in on Number Five. You might dodder over, yourself, grandpa—just to see how it all comes out. The grifters might accept you as a father figure."

"Well, Mother, perhaps I'll introduce them to you, as well," said Moustache, smiling to himself. Of course he wouldn't follow through on that threat; there was no reason to let anyone know how thoroughly the gambling tables were monitored. It might inhibit the free-spending attitude the casino wanted to encourage in its legitimate customers. And to give professional gamblers a behind-the-scenes look at security might give them ideas how to beat it.

Moustache had perfected the art of moving quickly without appearing to be in any particular hurry. If a noncom looked flustered or rushed, the troops might decide there was something for *them* to worry about. Moustache had been a career noncom in the Regular Army before forced retirement made him join the Space Legion. His crisp military bearing and his carefully polished "British Sergeant-Major" air made him the perfect front man for Phule's undercover surveillance operation in the Fat Chance. While all eyes were on him and his troop of uniformed actors (with a salting of genuine legionnaires to handle any rough stuff), the real security team could work unobserved, ready to respond to any threat before the opposition was aware of them.

That was exactly what was happening as Moustache

rounded a bank of quantum slot machines and entered the blackjack area of the casino. Do-Wop had slouched into a vacant seat at table number five, within an arm's length of a pudgy gray-haired man wearing a well-broken-in business suit over a brightly colored shirt. Beside him sat a woman of similar age, in a slightly too-tight dress and a too-elaborate, blatantly dyed hairdo. A travelling salesman on vacation with his wife, or so it appeared at first glance. But if Mother was correct—and she probably was—the outfits were sheep's clothing, camouflage to make a team of card cheats look like innocent tourists. At the far end of the table stood Sushi, looking for all the world as if he were trying to decide how the cards were running at this table before sitting down to play.

The dealer glanced up as Moustache came into view, and he winked at her. It was time to put an end to this incident. He stepped forward and put a hand lightly on the man's shoulder. "Excuse me, sir," he said. His voice was very polite but carried an unmistakable stamp of authority.

The man glanced over his shoulder, barely long enough for him to register much more than Moustache's black Legion uniform. What happened next took everyone by surprise. Both the man and the woman abruptly shoved back their chairs, knocking Moustache off balance. In the split second before he could recover, the woman had spun around and begun to throw punches, concentrating on his midsection—which, given the difference in their heights, was her most convenient target.

The woman was stronger than Moustache had expected. He had to call on all his training to fight off the middle-aged tourist. Using his superior reach, he grabbed the chair she had vacated and shoved her back against the table with it, trying to keep her pinned out of lethal range. Do-Wop was already stepping forward to help subdue her, and there were black-uniformed figures closing in from a distance, so all Moustache had to do was keep her at bay and hope the man didn't come to her assistance. With luck, he'd have nothing more serious than bruises to show for this episode.

But the woman's companion had ideas of his own. Instead of helping her break free, he leaped up on the table and launched himself in a flying kick at Sushi.

Sushi had held back from the altercation, ready to cut off either of the pair who tried to escape. So while he was caught by surprise, his reflexes and training got him out of trouble. Instead of trying to duck under the kick, he leaned backward enough to make the attacker's flailing feet miss him, then gave the flying body a hard shove in the ribs as it went past, trying to spoil the attacker's balance. To that extent Sushi succeeded, and the tourist landed ignominiously on a chair that toppled with a loud *crack* as the back legs gave way.

But the shove transferred enough momentum to Sushi to knock him off balance, as well. He spun around, bounced off the table behind him, and landed on hands and knees on the floor a short distance from his assailant. Almost at once, he sprang up, ready for action. Sushi expected the man to be halfway to the exit, or more likely, lying dazed on the floor. Instead, he was surprised to find the man already in a compact fighting stance. That made no sense at all. The man must have known he was surrounded by the legionnaires. If he wasn't going to try to escape, he should have given up quietly as soon as his cheating was discovered. Unless . . .

Sushi looked more closely at his opponent. Under the baggy suit and graying hair—which upon closer inspection appeared to have been dyed—was a man close to his prime, solidly built and obviously trained in the martial arts. His facial features showed Asian ancestry. Suddenly Sushi understood.

Sushi rose to his feet and bowed slowly. "I have been expecting you," he said to the man. He kept his voice low, speaking in Japanese. "We have business to tend to, but we should not discuss it in front of outsiders."

The other man snarled. "My family does not dicker with impostors. Our only business today is your death."

"Do not judge too quickly," said Sushi. "Look!" He made a surreptitious motion with his left hand and then dropped both arms to his sides, leaving himself open to the other man's attack.

The other man's face changed in an instant, and he, too, adopted a more relaxed stance. "Ah! I did not know! Perhaps there is something to discuss after all. But you are right—outsiders should not hear what we have to say, though I think there are few here who would understand us."

"One moment, please," said Sushi. "I will tell the others you have surrendered to me for questioning, and then we will go someplace where we may talk freely. They will not question me because they believe I am loyal to their captain. Your woman will be taken to a safe place and not harmed, and you may retrieve her at your convenience."

"That is good. I will tell her so," said the Yakuza man. The two turned to the rest of the group. Moustache had one hand on the woman's arm—she had stopped fighting when Sushi had begun talking to his opponent in Japanese; presumably she understood that language.

"I need to talk to this man," Sushi said to Moustache. "He says the woman will go with you to the holding lounge, and I don't think she'll cause any trouble now. I'll take responsibility."

Moustache looked to Do-Wop, who nodded. "Cool with me if you know what you're doing," said Do-Wop. "But be careful—just because you know that cat's lingo don't mean you want to turn your back on him."

"Don't worry, it's under control," said Sushi. He gestured to the Yakuza and together they walked out of the casino. Even before they were gone the normal sounds of gambling had resumed.

"There they are," said Brandy, and there was no question what she meant. Three human-sized cats in Space Legion uniforms would have stood out in any crowd. And while the Gambolts were famed for their ability to infiltrate an enemy position without being seen or heard, there was no need for stealth here. They bounced into the entry lounge, three oversized balls of feline energy, eyes darting in every direction. Behind them, a group of humans in similar uniform slouched into the lounge—the rest of the recruits.

The Gambolts immediately spotted the three black-uniformed humans standing together. They glided over and drew up in front of Phule, coming to attention. One of them turned on a translator and said, "New recruits reporting for duty, sir!" The Gambolt vocal equipment could make a limited range of human sounds, but communication was far smoother with a translator in place.

"Welcome to Omega Company," said Phule, stepping forward. He waited until all the recruits had moved up to join them, in a ragged semblance of a line. "I am Captain Jester, and this is Lieutenant Armstrong. Sergeant Brandy here will be in charge of your training. You'll meet the rest of your comrades and officers back at the hotel. We're pleased to have you as part of our outfit." He turned to Armstrong, who had brought out a clipboard. "Carry on, Lieutenant."

"Yes, sir!" said Armstrong, giving his usual crisp salute. He turned to face the new arrivals. "Attention! Sergeant Brandy will call roll."

Brandy stepped forward and took the clipboard from Armstrong. She inspected the new arrivals. While she'd never seen Gambolts up close, these three looked to be in excellent physical condition, and their spanking-new uniforms effectively set off their lithe forms. If the Gambolts were indeed deadly fighters as rumor said, this trio would be a strong addition to the company. The rest of the recruits looked like a perfect match for the assorted misfits and malcontents of Omega Company.

But there would be time enough to sort that out. She looked down at the clipboard and began reading names.

"Dukes?"

"Here, Sergeant," answered the biggest of the three Gambolts—a tawny six-footer, with light-green eyes and a nick out of its left ear. (Was this a male or a female? Brandy wondered idly. The Gambolts' sexual differences weren't immediately evident to the untrained human eye, and both sexes were known to choose military careers. It would probably make more difference to the Gambolts than it ever would to her.)

"Welcome aboard, Dukes. Garbo?"

"Here, Sergeant," said another Gambolt. The translator made this one's voice sound lighter and perhaps more feminine—as the choice of name also suggested—though the only outward physical distinction between this one and the other Gambolts was a slightly lighter build. Garbo had darker fur, nearly black, with a hint of a lighter colored undercoat.

"Welcome to the company, Garbo. Rube?"

"Right here, Sarge," said the third Gambolt, perhaps a few inches shorter than Dukes but even more imposingly built. Rube had gray fur, with slightly longer tufts on the cheeks, and its eyes seemed bigger than the others'. Its voice sounded a touch more jovial than the others', too, though that could easily be an artifice of the translator.

"Welcome aboard," Brandy said again. "Slayer?"

"Yo," said a scrawny human with a shaved head and a bone through its nose—it was difficult to determine its gender, as well.

This was the kind of recruit Brandy was used to. "That's *Yo, Sergeant* to you, Slayer," she barked. The recruit flinched, and muttered something that sounded like an appropriate response. Brandy nodded—she'd have plenty of time to get into the fine points of Legion discipline, such as it was. For now, it was sufficient to establish who was in charge. She turned to the next name on the list. "Brick?"

There were a dozen more recruits, all present, though none looked anywhere near as promising as the Gambolts. She finished the list, then turned to Armstrong and said, "All new troops present and accounted for, Lieutenant."

"Very good," said Armstrong, but before he could say more he was interrupted by a new voice.

"I'm a-gonna hafta take exception to that, Sarge," said a deep resonant voice. "I'm as much a member of this here company as anybody, and by the captain's own personal request, as it happens."

Brandy turned to see a pudgy human, with long, dark

slicked-back hair and even darker sunglasses. Like the others in the formation, the newcomer was dressed in black, although his jumpsuit was even more flamboyant than the version of the Legion uniform Phule's Company wore. And there was nothing at all military about the stranger's hip-shot stance and half-sneering expression.

It was Lieutenant Armstrong who broke the awkward silence. He pulled himself up to his full height and snapped, "If you're assigned to Omega Company, then fall in with the rest of the troops and report. This is the Legion, if you know what that means."

"Lordy, do I ever," said the newcomer. He sauntered up next to the Gambolts, drew himself more or less upright, and gave a passable imitation of a salute. "Reverend Jordan Ayres reportin' for duty, suh. But y'all can call me Rev."

"What the hell . . ." began Brandy, gearing up to give the new man a demonstration of how an angry top sergeant looked and sounded.

But Phule said, "Wait a minute, Brandy. Reverend . . ." Phule's puzzled expression suddenly transformed itself into a broad smile and the captain reached out a hand for Ayres to shake. "Of course! You're the chaplain I requested from headquarters. Welcome to Omega Company." He shot a quizzical look at Armstrong.

"A chaplain?" said Armstrong, staring at the newcomer. "I'd almost forgotten you'd asked. There wasn't anything about it in the dispatches from headquarters. I'm afraid you find us not properly prepared to greet you, Reverend Ayres. My apologies."

"Think nothin' of it," said the chaplain, falling back into his former posture. "And jes' call me Rev, Lieutenant. Why, the less fuss y'all make about me, the better. I'm jes' here to do a job, same as everybody else."

"Yes, that's the spirit," said Phule. "Now, I think it's time for us to get back to the Fat Chance where you people can meet your new comrades and get started on your duties. I can promise you a very interesting tour of duty with us."

"That's why we're here," said one of the Gambolts—Dukes, the biggest of the trio. His expression could have passed for a grin, although the large and very sharp canine (or were they more properly *feline*?) teeth made it far more ferocious than an equivalent expression from a human.

"Good, then let's go," said Brandy. "Follow me, on the double!"

The new members of Phule's Company shouldered their bags, and followed Brandy and their officers past the line of curious tourists at the immigration desk, out to a waiting hoverbus that would take them back to the Fat Chance hotel and their new assignment. They quickly stowed their bags and boarded, and the bus nosed out into the light traffic and headed away.

Neither they nor the tourists (who were after all most interested in getting to the casinos and spending their money) noticed the small figure in black that surreptitiously followed the legionnaires to the bus, and then set off on foot behind it, sticking carefully to the edge of the road and doing its best to avoid observation.

2

Journal #281

The unsavory elements of society look upon gambling as their private domain. Legitimate businessmen who enter that field are likely to find themselves the object of unwanted attention from those who wish to take the lion's share of the profits without having worked for it. Needless to say, this is not comfortable.

The local mob on Lorelei was led by Maxine ("Maxie") Pruett. She had greeted my employer with a well-orchestrated campaign of strong-arm tactics to frighten away customers. She also sponsored an invasion of card-sharps and grifters intended to siphon off the casino's profits. She confidently expected these tactics to force the casino into bankruptcy, at which point she planned to foreclose on the substantial loans she had made the owners.

But things did not go as Maxine had planned. Her takeover attempt was thwarted by my employer's access to the fire-power of a fully equipped Legion company—as well as to a degree of advance intelligence provided largely by my-

self. But her failure did nothing to deter outside criminals from their own forays. My employer knew that such attempts were inevitable. What he didn't know was how quickly the predators would begin to circle ... or to what extent they had Maxie's aid and comfort in their unsavory ventures.

"You're underestimating Jester again," said Laverna, looking up from the book she was reading. Out of habit, she used Phule's Legion pseudonym, although she and her boss both knew his real name by now. "Or have you forgotten how lucky you were to get away with your skin all in one piece?"

"I haven't forgotten," said Maxie Pruett. "You need a good memory to stay in this business as long as I have—or have *you* forgotten that?" Her piercing eyes glared at her chief advisor, but she knew and respected the tall black woman's talent for assessing risks unemotionally—an ability that had earned her the grudging nickname, "the Ice Bitch."

"Point taken," said Laverna, holding her place in the book with a forefinger. "But remember this: Jester's troops will eventually be rotated out. When somebody else has the post, Jester may lose interest in the place, and move his money someplace he can keep an eye on it more easily. You can afford to bide your time, see who comes in next, and make your move then. You're here for the long term—unless you make a serious mistake."

Maxie nodded. "And you think going after the Fat Chance again is a mistake."

"I know it is," said Laverna. She leaned forward in her chair. "The first time you tangled with Jester, you had all the advantages, and he still managed to come out ahead. And you were lucky, at that—all you lost was your bid to take over the Fat Chance right away. Next time, the consequences are likely to be permanent. He's got a pretty good idea who's behind any trouble that shows up at his door—and he's got the ability to hit back a lot harder than you can hit him."

"That's how I like it," said Maxie. "All the money on the table, and no backing out. It's easy for you to say 'take the long view'—you don't have to watch that joker pocket all the profits from the Fat Chance while you're waiting for him to go away."

"I'm here, aren't I?" said Laverna. "I'm here for the long run, too. It's in my best interest to keep your business healthy. That's why I'm advising you to let things take their natural course. The odds always favor the house—and on Lorelei, *the house* means you. Let the odds do the work for you, and you'll eventually win everything."

"I know that," said Maxie. She went over to a window and looked out at the streets below. The view from the penthouse suite was spectacular, with all the lights of Lorelei's casinos twinkling below her. Actually, since the hotel was on an orbiting space station, the "outdoors" was as much "indoors" as the room itself. But there was something comforting about the illusion of an actual "world" outside, and the casinos wanted their customers to be comfortable—at least, as long as they had money to spend.

Maxine looked out the window for a moment, leaning her hands on the sill. Then she said, without turning around, "But there's another problem. Success breeds success, and if Phule can keep the Fat Chance successful, it'll start cutting into everybody else's profits. Even after his unit gets transferred out, he'll leave somebody sharp in charge of it, somebody we'll have a hard time getting to. And the momentum will keep going his way. We need to stop that momentum now. That's why I've done a few things to stir the pot—things they won't be ready for."

"Yes, I hear that the Yakuza team is already on-station," said Laverna. "There was a dustup at the blackjack tables in the Fat Chance this afternoon—I think that may have been their work."

"Yes, I heard about that little ruckus," said Maxie. "I am taking your advice, by the way. None of my little plans can be traced to me—it's all going to look like somebody else's doing. I can just sit back and collect my regular percentage, and watch the sharks begin to circle around

Jester's little empire. I think I'm going to enjoy this, Laverna.''

"I hope you do, boss," said Laverna, but her expression suggested that she still saw trouble ahead. Of course, that was part of her job—anticipating trouble and finding ways to head it off. She wished that Maxie would stop finding ways to borrow trouble . . . but if Maxie had been like that, she wouldn't have needed someone like Laverna. *They give you lemons, you make lemonade,* thought Laverna, and went back to her book.

Phule stepped out of the hoverbus and into the front entrance of the Fat Chance Casino, leaving Sergeant Brandy to show the recruits to their quarters. He was followed by the chaplain, who ignored Brandy's icy stare and fell in behind the captain as if it were his place. Nothing had yet been said about Rev's nominal rank, so Brandy resisted the impulse to order him into line with the other new arrivals. There'd be time to talk to the captain when she'd finished her current job. After all, in the Omega Mob, a lot of the usual patterns of military life and protocol were—well, the only way to put it was *different*. Brandy liked it that way.

As he entered the casino, Rev cast a solemn eye upon the busy gambling tables, the scantily clad waitresses, the bustling bartenders, and the fevered patrons. Sprinkled throughout the crowd, conspicuous in their black Legion uniforms, were the guards—the ones he had been called to minister to. "This is my portion, then," he murmured to himself. "A chance to follow in the King's footsteps. Let me make the most of it." Then he said aloud to Phule, "Captain, I'll ask your permission to stop here for a while and meet the people I'll be serving. Plenty of time to find my quarters later."

Phule nodded, saying, "Sure, why not?" and Rev made a gesture that might have been mistaken for a salute before heading off into the crowd. Phule barely noticed the chaplain's departure; he had spotted Moustache striding purposefully toward him. "Yes, Sergeant, what's the situation?'' he asked, as the older man fell in step beside him.

"Sushi's disappeared, sir," said Moustache, in his clipped, British accent. "The eyes spotted a pair of card cheats at one of the blackjack tables. Sushi and Do-Wop moved in to handle it; the man turned out to be a martial arts specialist, and they put up a bit of a fight."

"That's unusual," said Phule, his eyebrows rising. "Any injuries?"

"None reported, sir," Moustache said. "A bit of broken furniture, but that was replaced in no time at all."

"Well, that's good," said Phule. He stopped, and turned to face the older man. "How long ago was this?"

"Right after you left, sir," said the sergeant. "Coming up on forty minutes ago. After the first flurry, Sushi and the man left together. Sushi told Do-Wop he had things under control, but didn't give details. And he turned off his communicator as they left. We have the woman in custody—she turned tame as a puppy after the man stopped fighting—but she's not talking. I doubt she knows where they are, anyway. We certainly don't."

"Sushi turned off his communicator, you say?" A look of concern came over Phule's face. "That's not a smart move. I have faith in his judgment, but this . . ."

"I know what you mean, sir," said Moustache, grimly. "We can't always stick to procedures, but he should have given Mother a probable destination before dropping out of touch. I didn't see anything that justified that."

"What steps are we taking to locate him?"

"Very low-profile at present, sir," said Moustache. "Lieutenant Rembrandt was informed as soon as we learned of the incident. She ordered all personnel to report any sighting of either Sushi or the other man—so far no word. We're assuming that the other man could have taken control of Sushi's communicator, so we don't want to make a general broadcast that he might intercept."

"Is there any reason to believe that's the case?" asked Phule.

"None so far," said Moustache. "But you'd best talk to

Rembrandt and Mother—they've been watching the situation develop ever since Sushi left the casino floor, and may know a fair amount they haven't passed on—the enemy may have ears.''

"Yes, of course," said Phule. "Carry on, then, Sergeant—it looks as if you've done everything you could." He turned and headed for the comm center. If anyone knew anything more than Moustache, it would be Mother.

Neither he nor Moustache noticed the small figure in black that watched them from behind a large, potted Durdanian fern, then swiftly moved to follow Phule toward the elevator bank.

"These will be your quarters, for the time being," said Brandy, opening the door to a suite on the third floor of the hotel. One of Phule's innovations had been abandonment of the normal Legion barracks system. Almost immediately upon taking over the Omega Mob, he had moved the troops out of their quarters, lock, stock, and barrel, and checked them into the best hotel in town while the quarters were rebuilt to his specifications—which were, if anything, even more comfortable than the hotel. He hadn't seen any reason to change that policy here on Lorelei. Except for a few individuals engaged in undercover work outside the hotel, everyone in the company was in the best quarters the Fat Chance had to offer.

"This is good," said Rube, unshouldering his heavy pack and putting it on the floor. Dukes made a sound that the translator turned into a murmur of agreement. Brandy wasn't surprised. In his usual thorough research, Phule had satisfied himself that human-style beds would be suitable for Gambolt use. Otherwise, he would have spent whatever was necessary for sleeping arrangements as comfortable to the Gambolts as the best hotel beds were for the human troops in his command. It was Legion policy to give equal accommodations to troops of all races, but in most units that meant equal discomfort. In Phule's Company, it meant equal luxury, from top to bottom.

The smallest Gambolt, Garbo, stood looking around the

room without speaking. Finally Garbo said, "Do all three of us have to share this room?"

"Why, is there a problem?" Brandy was taken aback. To the best of her knowledge, the Gambolts did not segregate troops by sex in their own units—Phule had been careful to determine that was the case—and in any case, they attached no social significance to males and females sharing quarters. So there had appeared to be no reason to set aside two suites for the new troops, when one large one was available. Besides, in a twenty-four-hour mission like casino security, it was common for roommates to end up on different schedules, with one needing to sleep while the others were up and active. The layout of the suite, with several separate rooms that could be closed off, took that possibility into account.

"Yes, there is a problem," said Garbo, turning to face her sergeant. "I joined this unit because I wanted to serve with humans, not to be set apart with others of my own kind. And here, at the very start, you are about to put me into quarters with the only others of my kind in your company. Isn't there anyplace else I can be housed?"

Brandy was surprised, but the request was reasonable. It *was* unusual for Gambolts to serve with anyone not of their own race. So it wasn't really surprising that a Gambolt who'd volunteered for a human outfit *didn't* want to be housed with her own kind. It was a far cry from being the strangest thing she'd run across in the Legion. In fact, to most Space Legion veterans, it would have been suspicious if there *hadn't* been something strange about a new batch of recruits . . .

"All right, I can fix that," Brandy said to the Gambolt. "But first, while we're here—Dukes and Rube, you two have an hour to unpack your things. At 1500 hours you'll report to Sergeant Chocolate Harry at the supply depot to be outfitted. At 1600 hours, you and the other recruits will report to the Grand Ballroom for orientation and duty assignments. Understood?"

"Yes, Sergeant," the Gambolts said again.

"OK. Garbo, let's see if we can find you a room before

1500—I want everybody set up with rooms and duty assignments by then. It may mean you don't have time to get completely settled in until later. Understood?''

"Yes, Sergeant," said Garbo, shouldering her pack.

"Good," said Brandy. She thought to herself, *They said these Gambolts make ideal soldiers. I wonder what's wrong with them that they ended up in the Omega Mob?* She remembered Phule's determination to make his company an example of the Legion's true potential. Maybe these Gambolt recruits were the next step toward making that determination a reality. *We'll find out soon enough*, she thought, and headed down the corridor, with Garbo close behind.

Tusk-anini was perched on a stool near the entrance of the Fat Chance Casino when two humans in bad suits stepped up to him. Even Tusk-anini, who paid very little attention to human clothing styles, could tell that the suits were bad. Not only cheap and ill-fitting, but unattractive by design. They looked as ugly as the uniforms the Omega Company had worn before Phule's arrival.

"Excuse me, friend, can you direct us to the Fat Chance Casino?" said the taller of the two humans. He wasn't that much taller, but the difference in height was the only marked distinction between them. They had nondescript faces, mousy brown hair in nearly identical unflattering short cuts, and extremely unstylish dark glasses. They also carried identical briefcases, in a sort of grayish dark material that had come out of a vat in some chemical plant. The briefcases were almost the same noncommittal color as the suits.

"You standing in front of Fat Chance," said Tusk-anini, cautiously. While neither of the humans had done anything in particular to alarm him, he had a bad feeling about them. One thing the Volton had learned during his association with humans was that feelings could be trusted. In fact, they sometimes gave you better answers than the most rigorous logical analysis.

The shorter human looked up and noticed the sign and said, "Yes, so we are." Now that he heard the voice, Tusk-anini realized that the shorter one was a female, a fact that the baggy suit and short haircut did much to conceal from the casual glance.

The man spoke again, "Are you a casino employee?"

"Yes, I am," said Tusk-anini—not quite truthfully, for while the legionnaires had been brought to Lorelei to guard the casino, they had always been freelance contractors, not regular employees. Now, of course, as a member of Phule's Company Tusk-anini was in fact a part-owner of the Fat Chance. A comparatively small part-owner, since every member of Phule's Company also had shares, but put together the Omega Mob was the majority stockholder.

"You're just the sophont we need to talk to, then," said the man. "We're trying to gather information on the operation here. We'd like you to answer a few questions."

"Asking anything you want. I answer what I may," said the Volton cautiously. He had begun to wonder whether these two humans were from a competing casino, or from one of the criminal organizations the Legion was here to guard against. His eyes narrowed, giving his warthog-like face an even fiercer expression than normal.

"Maybe I should rephrase that," said the man. He pulled a wallet out of his jacket pocket and flipped it open to reveal a holo-ID, which he held up a few inches from Tusk-anini's snout. Above his picture (which miraculously made him look even less attractive than he was in person) were the initials *IRS*; below it was written *Roger Peele, Special Agent*. "We're in receipt of information to the effect that your employer is failing to report substantial amounts of income," said Special Agent Peele. "If you impede a lawful investigation, you're guilty of conspiracy to defraud a government agency. That's a serious offense, in case you didn't know it."

Tusk-anini abruptly stood up. This brought him to his full height, nearly seven feet tall, and put his enormous barrel chest nearly at eye level for the two humans. "You ask me betray Captain Jester!" he accused. "Tusk-anini no do that! Not right to betray the captain."

"Easy now, friend—you're looking at this all wrong,"

said the woman in a calm voice. "We appreciate your loyalty to your commander—that's what makes the military work. But sometimes you have to look beyond that to a higher loyalty. Your captain has to report to his generals, and they report to civilian authorities. The Interstellar Revenue System is part of that civilian authority, a very important part of it. It's your duty to cooperate with us."

"If captain say it my duty, I do it," said Tusk-anini. "He not say it, I not do it. You go away now." He took a step forward. His powerful physique and staring eyes made him a menacing figure. The two IRS agents involuntarily stepped backward.

"Very well," snarled Special Agent Peele. "We have more than one way to find out what we want. And you'd better hope your own nose is clean—because if it's not, you'll be in the same trouble as your captain."

"You call my nose dirty?" roared Tusk-anini, and at that the two IRS agents backed off still another step. "You go away and leave captain alone," he repeated.

"We've come here to do a job, the same as you," said the woman. "We're not going anywhere until we've finished it. When we do, it'll go better for you if you're on the right side, friend."

"Tusk-anini know what side he on," growled the Volton. "You not on captain's side, you not my friend. I no like people who call me friend when they not." He took another step forward, and this time the two IRS agents turned and hurried away.

"Captain! You're just in time—you won't believe what's happened now."

Phule was hurrying down an inside corridor to the company's command and communications headquarters to learn what progress was being made in the search for Sushi and the mysterious man he had disappeared with. But he turned at the sound of Dee Dee Watkins's voice. He already knew that her problems usually required far more time and energy than they really deserved. But to ignore Dee Dee was to risk escalating the problem. "Yes, Miss Watkins?" he said, trying his best to look concerned.

The tiny blonde entertainer was standing with her hands on her hips, looking as if she were prepared to challenge the entire fighting strength of Phule's Company if it stood between her and what she wanted. Considering that she was wearing a little girl's flowered pinafore and had her hair up in pigtails, her ability to project an air of menace was no small accomplishment. Perhaps she had some future as an actress after all, Phule thought to himself.

"Take a look for yourself," she said. "Lex has me wearing this ridiculous costume for the big closing number, all because he's jealous of me, and he's trying to sabotage my career."

Phule looked at the costume more closely. While it was clearly not designed to emphasize Dee Dee's major assets, it more than made up in cuteness what it lacked in sex appeal. Even then, it fit snugly in the right places, and displayed a very satisfactory length of leg . . .

He made himself focus on the starlet's face. "I'm sorry, Miss Watkins, I'm afraid my military duties have eaten up too much of my time for me to keep up with what's happening on the artistic side of the operation. If you're asking my personal opinion, I don't think you look at all ridiculous in the costume, but of course I'm no expert."

Dee Dee's frown deepened, "Well, Captain, I'm disappointed. If you'd try . . ."

Whatever she was about to say was interrupted by a shout of "Stop him!"

Before Phule could turn to see what the commotion was about, a small, dark-clad figure dashed out of a doorway leading back to the casino and cut directly between Phule and the actress, knocking them both off balance. A pair of uniformed legionnaires burst out of the same doorway at full speed. Somehow, they managed to avoid Dee Dee, but in the process they crashed into one another. One bounced off the wall and caught his balance against a small, potted frogwood tree, but the other went down—catching Phule directly in the legs. Dee Dee let out a piercing shriek as the captain landed on the floor.

"Oh my God. Captain, I'm sorry, sir," said the legionnaire who'd bounced off the potted plant. He rushed to help Phule upright, making little brushing motions as if to clean off the captain's uniform.

The legionnaire who'd knocked Phule down looked up with a dazed expression. His gaze paused for a moment on Dee Dee's legs, but quickly moved upward when he realized whom he'd decked in his rush. He clambered quickly to his feet and stood at attention. " 'Pologies, Cap'n," he said.

"No damage done, men," said Phule, looking at the legionnaires. "Gabriel, what's this all about?" he asked the one who'd helped him to his feet.

"We spotted a spy, sir," said Gabriel. "Right here in the Fat Chance."

"Gab'l sayin' truth, Cap'n," said the other. Phule recognized him as Street, Gabriel's partner—a lean, tough man from the slums of Rockhall. He could speak fairly good Standard, but when he got excited—as he was now—his accent was so thick Phule could barely understand him. "He comin' this way when we spot him. Bet for sure be followin' you."

"He might be an assassin, sir," said Gabriel, grim-faced.

"An assassin?" Phule scoffed. "I doubt it. For one thing, whoever that was you were chasing had a perfect chance to do me in not thirty seconds ago, and didn't. What makes you think he was a spy, anyway?"

"Not so hard figurin' that out," said Street. "He the wrong species—ain't no little lizards in the company. Got humans, got Tusk-anini, got a couple Synthians, hear we got some cats now. No lizards, Cap'n."

"Maybe he was a customer," said Phule, still dubious.

"Why he wearin' our uniform, then?" asked Street. "He spyin', you bet all you money on that."

Phule frowned. He hadn't gotten a close look at the small figure that darted past him before he'd been knocked down, but it did have a distinct resemblance to a meter-high lizard—and it *had* been wearing Legion black. Perhaps Headquarters had sent an observer to keep an eye on him without letting him know . . .

"Well, he's gotten away for the moment," Phule said. "You two men return to your posts, and keep your eyes open. I'll tell Mother to alert everyone for a possible intruder, and . . ."

"Got it already, darlin'," came the voice from his wrist communicator. "Small lizardlike alien in Legion uniform on the loose—that shouldn't be too hard to spot."

"Good," said Phule, musing. Hearing Rose's description of the intruder set something itching in the back of his mind, but he couldn't quite pin it down . . . Well, he'd figure it out soon enough. Meanwhile, he asked, "Any word on Sushi's whereabouts?"

"Nothin' we can use, sweetie, but we've got other news. We found out we'd recorded his conversation with the man he fought. It's in Japanese, but we've run it through a translator. I don't want to jump to conclusions, but Lieutenant Rembrandt's all in a sweat—the poor girl thinks Sushi might be about to defect. Listen to this and see what you think."

Phule lifted the wrist communicator to his ear, and the recording started, but as he began to concentrate on it, Dee Dee stamped her foot. "Well! I come to you with a problem, and what happens? First, two of your men nearly knock me down, and then you act as if I'm not even here. I'll have you know . . ."

Phule's concentration broke, and he looked down at Dee Dee, whose frown was deeper than ever. "Excuse me, Miss Watkins, I was listening to an intelligence report. If you'll give me one moment . . ."

"Give you a moment? Why, you haven't given me so much as the time of day! Lex is trying to ruin my act, and all you have to say is . . ."

"Captain, is trouble happening," said Tusk-anini, coming around a bend in the corridor. He hurried up, ignoring the fuming Dee Dee and said, "Two humans looking for you—they try make me tell them things, but I no talk. I think they want make trouble.''

"Trouble? What makes you think that?" Phule knew that anything that worried the usually taciturn Volton had to be serious.

"They show me identification, say *IRS*," said Tusk-anini. "I don't know what that means, but Gnat tell me it big trouble, so I come tell you."

"IRS?" Phule repeated. "They can't have anything on me—my records are immaculate. Beeker knows more about tax law than the people that wrote it."

"Captain! I'm *not* going to stand here and be ignored," said Dee Dee in a voice that could have frozen the swimming pool in the hotel across the street.

"Yo, sucker, you the boss here? We been lookin' for your ass," said a gruff voice from a medium distance. Three large humans came down the corridor, practically filling it. Two of them were males, to judge from the long, unruly beards. All three were wearing denim and leather covered with metal studs, chains, and patches. Their bare arms showed a variety of tattoos, but they had in common a large red "R" with blazing jets on either side. The man in the middle was almost as large as Tusk-anini. He wore a German-style helmet on his head, a brass ring in his nose, and several more in each ear—one in the shape of a human skull. They swaggered up and stopped in front of Phule, the leader (or so he appeared to be) less than an arm's length away from the captain.

Phule pulled himself up straight and said, "As you can see, I'm speaking to this young lady. I'll be glad to listen to you people as soon as I'm done with her." He turned back to Dee Dee, who had fallen silent upon seeing the three newcomers.

"Tryin' to get it on with the fox, huh?" The big man sneered. "That jive can wait—we got serious business. You know a cheap punk name of Chocolate Harry?"

"Chocolate Harry no cheap punk," growled Tusk-anini, moving in to stand at Phule's side. "And you talk polite to captain, or you not like what happens next."

The three newcomers laughed. "Listen to the warthog," said the woman—her voice was deep and rough, but unquestionably female. "He thinks he can tell the Renegades how to talk, he got another think comin'."

"So—you're the Renegades," Phule said. He'd heard C.H.'s tale of how a rival biker gang had vowed vengeance for some long-ago injury, but had never taken seriously the likelihood that they would actually track down his supply sergeant. Apparently he'd miscalculated.

"Damn straight, soldier boy," said the big man. "Us and a few hundred others is the Renegades, and we're looking for Chocolate Harry. Sounds to me like you and the warthog just might know where he is."

"If we do, it's none of your business," said Phule. "He's a legionnaire, and you'd be better advised to forget whatever disagreement you have with him. We protect our own."

"Your own?" The woman spat on the floor, then grinned crookedly; Phule could see that she was missing several teeth. "You can call him your own, but his fat ass is *ours*, soldier boy. And you know what we gonna do when we get it?"

"We gonna slice it three ways," said the big man, leering evilly.

The third man spoke for the first time, in a rasping low voice made even more sinister by his absolute deadpan delivery. "We gonna cut it deep, wide, and often." He patted a sheath on the belt of his jeans, where the handle of a vibroblade could be seen.

"You not getting close enough to do that," said Tuskanini, and as he spoke, a loud whistle came from behind the three Renegades. They whirled to see Moustache standing there, backed by half a dozen legionnaires brandishing Rolling Thunder belt-fed shotguns. "You go now before we getting mad," said the Volton.

"Shit," said the big man, half under his breath. Then he turned to Phule and said, "We got no fight with you, soldier boy. Tell your kids to put away the toys—we're not gonna start nothin' now. But make sure Chocolate Harry knows we've got him spotted, and he can't hide no more.''

The three Renegades turned as one, and strode out past the assembled troops, managing to keep up an impressive front in the face of so much firepower. When they had gone, Phule let out the deep breath he'd been holding. If the bikers had decided to grab him and Dee Dee as hostages, the shotguns would have been of little use. But for now, the threat was defused.

''Captain! Now, about this costume!'' Dee Dee's voice snapped him back to reality. It was beginning to look like a very long afternoon.

3

Command of a military unit is no sinecure, even in the notoriously lax Space Legion. Put in command of a unit that had become a dumping ground for malcontents and incompetents, my employer knew he faced a formidable task in making anything of it—let alone an elite company. That he had accomplished as much as he had spoke highly of his determination. It goes without saying that the accomplishment was achieved at no small personal cost—especially considering that much of what he had accomplished had been opposed at every step by his superior officers.

As became apparent, his successes on Lorelei only gave his enemies more reason to hate him.

General Blitzkrieg stomped into his office. It was shaping up as another rotten day. There had been a lot of those lately—it was almost enough to make him opt for early retirement and accept the lower pension as fair trade for the aggravation. But he wasn't about to be eased out of the saddle. Not while his purpose remained unfulfilled.

"Here are your news printouts, sir," said his aide, a tired-looking major who'd held the position for three years. Being aide-de-camp to one of the three top generals in the Space Legion had looked like a brilliant career move a few years earlier: an ideal shortcut to promotion for an ambitious officer with neither political connections, personal wealth, nor military talent. But Major Sparrowhawk had been second-guessing her decision to take the assignment ever since. She handed the sheaf of customized, automatically-edited flimsies to the general. Most senior officers got their intelligence straight off the Net, but Blitzkrieg was a stickler for the ancient print technology— "good old hard copy," as he called it.

The general riffled through the printouts, and threw them into the trash. "Nothing worth a damn," he growled, and turned to go into his inner office.

Sparrowhawk cleared her throat. "Begging your pardon, sir, but I've been sorting your news printouts for you for the entire time I've been here. For the last year or so, you hardly glance at them before you throw them away. Perhaps I need to redefine the sort, or expand the coverage. What are you looking for that isn't showing up?"

Blitzkrieg stopped and scowled at his aide, who began to regret asking. "Don't you know by now? I'm waiting to see if that damned Captain Jester has finally done something I can cashier him for. You won't have to expand your coverage to find that—sooner or later, the idiot is bound to commit a blunder that'll put him in the headlines galaxy-wide, and I'll give him what he deserves. And then I can retire, knowing I've done the Legion a service for which my successors will be forever grateful."

"I thought as much, sir," said Sparrowhawk. Her brows knitted for a moment, then she said, "I think you might want to take another look through those flimsies, then. There's an article there I had to look at twice myself—it wasn't immediately obvious why your search parameters turned it up. But I think you'll find it very interesting indeed."

"Really?" Blitzkrieg bent over and retrieved the print-

outs from the trash. He flipped through them again, this
time more slowly. His expression became more and more
puzzled. Finally he looked up at Sparrowhawk and said,
"Major, if you think I enjoy guessing games, you don't
know me very well. What's the story, and why would I be
interested?"

"The third one down, sir," she said, secretly pleased that
the general had overlooked it twice. "The one about the
new government on Landoor."

"Hmmm . . ." The general scanned the article, but his
perplexity grew, and at last he held it up accusingly.
"There's nothing about Jester here, Major."

"No, sir," said Major Sparrowhawk, patiently. She knew
she'd have to explain it to him—Blitzkrieg's rise to the top
of the Space Legion had nothing to do with intellectual
eminence. "Do you remember the episode that first brought
Jester—he went by the name 'Scaramouche' then—to your
attention?"

"Damned right I remember it, Major," growled Blitzkrieg. "The ignorant pup talked a pilot into strafing the
signing of a peace treaty. Luckily there was enough warning for everyone on the ground to get to cover—or maybe
not so luckily. A few casualties, and we'd have put Jester
behind bars."

"Exactly, sir," said Sparrowhawk. "It may have slipped
your memory that Landoor is the world where that incident
occurred."

"Yes, of course I knew that," said Blitzkrieg. "So, life
goes on, and they've got a new government. Nothing to
concern us, eh, Major?"

"Perhaps not," Sparrowhawk doggedly continued.
"Nothing directly, of course. There was some information
down in the fifth paragraph I thought you could turn to use,
but perhaps I misunderstood its implications."

"Possibly you did," said the general, glancing at the
sheet of printout in his hand. "Well, not everyone has the
instinct for grand strategy, Major. But if you stick with me,
you may have the opportunity to learn the rudiments."

"Yes, sir," said Sparrowhawk. Now she was certain

he'd read the paragraph again. Perhaps he'd see how to bend it to his own ends without more prompting. He wasn't really all that stupid, she told herself. With her help, he'd eventually get his revenge on Jester—and then retire, and at last she'd be free of him.

The general took the printout into his inner office, and closed the door. When he was gone, she turned back to her computer—her stocks had been doing nicely, but recent news suggested that they might have peaked. She wanted to see if it was time to sell and get into something else . . .

She managed to read nearly a dozen screens of financial analysis before the general buzzed her on the intercom and roared, "Sparrowhawk! Get me the General Staff office, right away! No, make that a conference call—add on Ambassador Gottesman, too. I've come up with the perfect answer to our problems with Jester!"

"Right away, sir," she said, smiling. She already knew exactly what the general would want from his superiors. Sometimes, the job had its rewards, after all.

"Hey, Do-Wop, how's it going?" said Mess Sergeant Escrima, looking up from a shipment of fresh asparagus that had just arrived. The sprouts were young and tender, a miracle of hydroponic agriculture and genetic tailoring, but Escrima was still inspecting them as critically as he did every item of food that passed through his kitchens. "Any sign of that partner of yours yet?"

"Nah, Sarge—wherever Soosh is hiding, it's a good spot," said Do-Wop, stopping at the end of the counter where the asparagus was laid out. He looked around the kitchen. "We're looking everywhere we can without spooking the customers. I guess you didn't see him?"

"Haven't laid eyes on him," said Escrima, waving a hand to indicate the whole kitchen. Two assistant cooks were at work slicing something, and several large pots were already boiling atop the luxury hotel's state-of-the-art TherMaster MultiRange. "Not today, at least. Last I saw him was Sunday—I needed to borrow a few bucks until payday. Bad run of luck . . ."

"Tell me about it, man," said Do-Wop, rolling his eyes. "I thought I knew my way around a card table—especially after the captain had those pro gamblers show us the ropes. There's not a card mechanic's trick I can't spot by now. But it don't make me a winner. I think my luck's even worse than it was before I knew what to watch out for."

"Ditto," said Escrima. "Without Sushi, I wouldn't have two nickels to rub together. With him bankrolling me, at least I've got something to get back to the tables with so I can try to reverse my luck."

"Yeah, he's been lending me enough to scrape through, too. I'm gonna owe him a bundle next paycheck, though. Maybe I'd be better off if he didn't come back." Do-Wop frowned, then blurted out, "You know I don't mean that, Escrima."

"I didn't think you did," said Escrima, nodding. "But he won't be going anywhere—too many people owe him. Let's hope he's not selling our markers to the Yakuza. I hear those boys play really dirty with deadbeats. So hurry up and find him—I don't like owing *him* three months' pay, and he's one of us. I'd hate to owe it to somebody who's only in it for the money."

"Yeah, at least Soosh won't break your legs if you miss a payment," said Do-Wop. "You spot him, let Mother know ASAP, OK?"

"Sure will," said Escrima, nodding. "Good luck."

"I could use that in more than one department," muttered Do-Wop as he went out the door. Escrima didn't answer; he had already turned his attention back to that evening's meal.

"Come on, this is ridiculous," said Brandy. She stared at the harried desk clerk. Garbo stood next to her, drawing curious stares from customers standing in line at the registration desk. Everybody had seen the Gambolts on the trivid news; seeing a life-sized one standing two meters away, in full Legion uniform, was another story entirely. Especially if you knew the catlike aliens' reputation as the most deadly hand-to-hand fighters in the galaxy . . .

But dangerous as the Gambolt looked, it was the undeniably human Brandy who was the real danger at this time, with her temper edging toward an explosion. "How hard is it to find me one regular room?" she growled, as the desk clerk tried to get his computer to cooperate. "Didn't anybody teach you how to charge it to the captain's account?"

"I'm very sorry, ma'am, but I keep getting some sort of error message," said the desk clerk. His eyes slid sideways to Garbo, who had stood like a statue ever since Brandy had brought her down to the desk. It had been no more than ten minutes, but it was unnerving.

"Maybe you're entering the account number wrong," said Brandy. "You do know the captain's account number for Legion business, don't you, Junior?"

"Yes, ma'am," said the desk clerk. He was a thin, nervous-looking young man, with a tasteful gold-plated ring in his left nostril and an asymmetrical, neo-Georgian blue-powdered wig. "The system has a macro to access the captain's Dilithium Express account without entering the number every time. There shouldn't be any problem with his credit. I'm not quite sure what . . ."

"Well, you better figure it out, Junior, or there'll be a Gambolt sleeping in the lobby," said Brandy. "I don't *think* she'd eat any customers, but she might take a bite or two out of the staff. So the sooner you get her a room, the better."

"I'm trying, ma'am," the desk clerk repeated. "If this try doesn't go through, I'll enter it manually." His expression was sulky and put-upon, but by the way his fingers flew over the cyborged touchpad imprinted on the skin of his left forearm, he was taking Brandy's threats very seriously indeed. Brandy continued to scowl, although she suspected she was already getting all the mileage she could out of sheer intimidation.

So it was purely by chance that she happened to look away from the registration desk just in time to see a small, black-clad figure round the corner of the counter and sprint toward her. This must be the intruder Mother had warned everyone about!

Whether by instinct or training—after so many years in the Legion, it was hard to tell where one left off and the other began—she dropped into a defensive crouch. Her attention now focused, she registered consciously what she'd been hearing in the background—voices raised, and feet hurrying in pursuit.

"He went through there!"

"Hurry, before he gets away!"

And louder than the rest, "Spy!"

"Hold it right there," she said in a voice that radiated the authority of a veteran top sergeant. To anyone with the barest minimum of military training, that voice was nearly impossible to disobey. And sure enough, the black-clad figure came to a momentary halt. In that frozen fraction of a second, she saw a meter-tall lizard, dressed in a miniature Space Legion jumpsuit. They stared at each other for perhaps a full second.

Brandy was already in motion before the lizard broke out of its frozen stance. She dove straight toward its midsection. But the lizard was quicker than she was. It sidestepped to the left, watched Brandy sail past it to land flat on her belly, and turned to dash off toward the open door across the lobby. "Get him, Garbo," barked Brandy, sprawling at full length on the floor.

The lizardlike alien, which had appeared to accelerate to top speed in two strides, made a feint to the left, then dodged back to the right, and leaped its own height into the air. Brandy's mouth fell open just watching the alien move.

Garbo was quicker.

Without seeming to have moved at all, the Gambolt was waiting when the lizard came down, and calmly placed one paw on the lizard's collar, the other in the middle of its chest. Her claws were visible, spread wide on the lizard's chest. "Do not move," said Garbo. The look that accompanied the words was pure feline anticipation. It was difficult for a human observer familiar with cats to escape the impression that, if the lizard attempted to escape, Garbo would have a great deal of enjoyment recapturing it, and the lizard would not.

"Very good, you have apprehended me," said the lizard, in a translator-generated voice. "That is first-class work, and I am impressed indeed. Now, I wish to report to Captain Clown."

Brandy had managed to recover her breath and climb to her feet. The troops who had been in hot pursuit of the lizard had lined up behind her, waiting for her orders now that the fugitive was apparently captured. She looked at the lizard in disbelief.

"Captain Clown?" she asked, frowning. "There's no such person. Who the hell are you, anyway? You're not any member of this outfit, but you're wearing our unit patch."

The lizard assumed a more upright posture—difficult, with the Gambolt still keeping it under close guard. "I am Flight Leftenant Qual, Zenobian Space Command," it said. "I am attached to this company as military observer. Orders require me to report to Captain Clown, and I hereby request to be taken to him."

"Military observer?" said Brandy. She motioned to Garbo, who slightly relaxed her grip on the Zenobian's collar. "I do remember something about that, now. But why were you sneaking around the place and running away from my people when they spotted you?"

"I am observing," said Qual. "Part of this job is to cipher out how troops are ready for surprises, so I make a surprise. You catch on very quick, especially this one." He indicated the Gambolt who had collared him.

"I still think he's a spy, Sarge," growled Gabriel, who looked winded from the chase. There was a mutter of agreement from the others who'd been pursuing the Zenobian.

"Quiet," ordered Brandy, turning around. "We'll let the captain figure that out. You all return to your posts; we've got this under control. Dismissed."

"Right-o, Top," said one of the troops, but there didn't

seem to be much enthusiasm in it. They turned and headed back to their posts.

Brandy turned back to Qual and Garbo. ''OK, we'll bring you to the captain to report in as soon as we finish here. By the way, his name is *Jester*, not *Clown*. Garbo, make sure he stays put.''

''Yes, Sergeant,'' came the translated voice, almost purring this time.

The Zenobian seemed calm, as far as Brandy could tell, not that she had much practice reading the facial expressions of a scaled-down dinosaur. But the Gambolt was ready for anything, and that was all that mattered right at the moment.

Brandy turned back to the desk clerk, who stood gaping at the scene in front of him. He wasn't alone; so were most of the customers. They'd come to the Fat Chance looking for excitement, but none of them had quite bargained for what they'd just seen. It was hard to tell whether they were favorably impressed or not.

Brandy had other business to worry about. ''Well, Junior, have you got that problem with the room fixed yet? Or do I tell the Gambolt she's sleeping with you tonight?'' The clerk turned white, and frantically began punching keys again.

''What the hell is going on here?''

Lieutenant Armstrong looked at the supply depot, a hotel delivery bay modified to the Legion's specifications. The depot had looked perfectly ordinary when Armstrong had come by early that morning. Now, the entire area resembled an armed camp. There were cartons of field rations and heavy-machine oil piled up as barriers, with razor wire strung between them. Farther back was a bunker made of soap boxes, the peak of a helmet visible just above it.

Despite himself, Armstrong felt a touch of pride that the Omega Mob could accomplish something so quickly. It had never been that way before Phule had arrived.

''Halt and identify yourself,'' came a mechanical voice

from behind the barbed wire barricade. "Keep your hands in sight, and make no sudden moves."

"It's Armstrong," said the lieutenant, straining to see the speaker. "Louie, is that you? You know me, Louie. What's the situation here? It looks like you're ready for an invasion."

"Do not approach closer," said the voice. "What is the password?"

"Password?" Armstrong frowned. There'd been no password needed to enter the supply depot before—in fact, there'd been nothing to stop any curious passerby from walking up to it from the street beyond. Something must have changed. "Chocolate Harry, are you in there?" he called. Perhaps the supply sergeant would let him in and explain this strange game—whatever it was.

"There is nobody named Chocolate Harry here," said the voice. "Do not approach closer, and keep your hands in sight."

Armstrong raised his hands, putting his mouth within range of the wrist communicator. "Mother, there's something strange going on at supply," he said softly. "Can you patch me through to Chocolate Harry?"

"If I can't do it, nobody can," said Mother's voice. "Keep your pants on, sonny, and we'll hook you right up."

After a moment, another voice came through the speaker. "Who's there? Make it quick, I ain't got much time."

"Harry, is that you? This is Armstrong. What in the world is going on here?"

"You sound like Armstrong, all right, but I gotta be sure," said Chocolate Harry's voice. There was a brief hesitation, then "OK, who led the Galactic League in free flies last season?"

"Huh?" Armstrong thought frantically. Finally he said, "I don't know. Harry, this is ridiculous—I don't know anything about gravball."

"Hah! It's not gravball, it's scrumble. That's enough for me, though—you *gotta* be Armstrong. Ignorantest dude I ever saw when it comes to sports. What you want, Lieutenant?"

"Harry, I'm right outside the supply depot. The place looks like a fortress. What are you guarding—chips from the casino?"

"Right outside, hey? You see anybody suspicious out there, Armstrong?"

"There's nobody here except me! Tell your guard to let me in—I'm on company business."

"OK, Lieutenant, but hurry—and don't make any funny-looking moves. Louie's got an itchy trigger appendage."

Lieutenant Armstrong stood up and smiled, waving to the Synthian on guard. He moved gingerly through the hastily implanted barriers outside the door to the supply depot, uncomfortably aware of Louie's shotgun aimed at him the entire time. Finally, he reached the door; it opened a crack and he saw the muzzle of a splat gun pointed at him briefly before the door opened wider to admit him. "Come on in, man, have a seat. Fix you a coffee?" Chocolate Harry said, beckoning; his gaze remained fixed on the area outside. Armstrong dashed through the door and plopped himself onto the proffered chair.

"What the devil is going on here?" demanded Armstrong. "Are we expecting another raid from the Mob?"

"No, worse than that," said Chocolate Harry, throwing a heavy metal bar into place across the door. "They've finally found me. I knew it was comin', I knew it all along. But they're not gonna just walk in and take me, Lieutenant. They got a fight on their hands if they try that."

"What in the galaxy are you talking about?" demanded Armstrong. "Who are *they*, and why are they after you?"

"It's a long story, Lieutenant," said Harry. "I'll give you the quick run-through. You know I used to ride with the Outlaws?"

"Yes, of course, we've all heard the story," said Armstrong.

"Well, then you know the part about me dissing the Renegades, right? The part where I got in so much trouble I had to run off and join the Legion—and before the captain took over this outfit, that was a mighty desperate thing to do."

"Yes, I've heard that, too," Armstrong began. "The one thing . . ."

Chocolate Harry interrupted him. "Well, man, my chicken's done come home to roost. The Renegades are here, and they're gonna fry me good and crisp. Ain't no mistake—Louie heard 'em talkin' to the captain, and he came here and told me right away." Harry was cleaning a Rolling Thunder automatic shotgun while he spoke, nervously peering out the slit between the boards he'd nailed over his window.

"Well, if they're here, so be it," said Armstrong. "You know as well as I do that nobody can attack one of us without taking on the whole company. We're covering you, Harry. Anybody who thinks they can waltz in and take you has another think coming."

"Well, I sure appreciate that, Lieutenant," said Chocolate Harry. "Can't blame a fella for taking a few precautions himself, though, can you? These Renegades are mean mothers."

"Yes, I suppose I can't blame you—you'll have to make it a bit easier for the company to get its supplies, though. I'm sure the captain will help you figure something out. Still, there's one thing I don't understand."

"Yeah? What's that?"

"What in space did you do to the Renegades to make them pursue you halfway across the galaxy, years later, to get their revenge?"

"What did I do? Man, I did the worst thing anybody could have done. There's not a biker alive who wouldn't feel the same way, if you told 'em."

"And what was that?"

"*I messed with their bikes*," said Chocolate Harry, and his voice was like the sound of doom.

Phule burst into the Command and Communications Center like a man pursued by wolves—which, metaphorically at least, he was. "All right," he said, "I want to find out what's going on. Mother, how's the search for Sushi going?"

"mgdkjgisd," said Rose, mumbling almost inaudibly. Brazen as she was over the comm, she went into shrinking violet mode when faced with the necessity for face-to-face communication. She scrunched down, as if to make herself invisible behind the communications console.

"Oh, sorry, I almost forgot," said Phule, preparing to return to the hallway and resume the conversation via wrist communicator.

"I can answer that, sir," said Beeker, rising from a desk to one side of the room, where he'd been using his Port-a-Brain pocket computer. "I've been monitoring the situation since we learned of it. To put it briefly, security has reason to believe that Sushi and the man he ran off with remained within the hotel-casino complex."

"I heard the recording," said Phule. "It sounds as if the Yakuza have come to settle accounts with him. Somebody must have figured out that those tattoos he got aren't the real thing, and told the Japanese mob he was an impostor."

"Yes, that's the impression I get," said Beeker. "In which case he may be in very bad trouble. Those people take their secret protocols very seriously, and it's no laughing matter for an outsider to impersonate one of them. That makes it even more imperative to find him."

"They've checked Sushi's quarters, I assume? What about the other man's room?"

"Sushi's quarters are empty, sir," said Beeker. "As for the other man, we've tried to match the images of him from the blackjack room surveillance cameras against the registration desk surveillance records—as you know, every guest's face is recorded as they are issued a room key. I fear there were no matches. Either he is a master of disguise—not impossible, if he is a Yakuza—or he is not a hotel guest."

"Was the woman with him carrying any ID?"

"Nothing traceable, sir," said Beeker, with a disappointed expression. "Lieutenant Rembrandt supervised the search, and she says she's never seen anyone so clean. You wouldn't think somebody in this day and age could have bought clothes, jewelry, accessories, and a purse full of odds and ends, without leaving any traces in the vendors' computer systems, or buying anything that would give away her origins. If necessary, security can run a more thorough search, and perhaps we'll find something then.''

''It'll be a waste of time,'' said Phule, shaking his head. ''If she's gone to that length to conceal her identity, she's probably got the other bases covered. We'll do what we have to, though.''

''I agree, sir,'' said Beeker. ''But we can safely leave those details to the experts. For now, I believe there's at least one piece of good news to report.''

''Well, it's about time—I was starting to think the day was going straight downhill,'' said Phule. ''What's the good word?''

''We have identified the unknown intruder, who turns out not to be an intruder at all, but a military observer. You will recall Flight Leftenant Qual, sir?''

Phule's forehead wrinkled for a moment. ''Qual, Qual—oh, yes, the Zenobian. General Blitzkrieg said Qual was going to be assigned to us as—say, that's right! You mean he's here? Where?''

''Brandy and one of the Gambolts finally caught him, down by the front desk,'' said Beeker. ''He was observing our readiness by pretending to infiltrate. Some of our people took that amiss—as I think you'll understand, sir. They're saying he's some kind of spy.''

''Well, no worry about that,'' said Phule. ''The general sent him, so there's no question at all about his bona fides. Once our people know that, there won't be any problem.''

''Yes, sir,'' said Beeker, but he did not look convinced. ''There's one other problem, sir. When Brandy was trying to place the female Gambolt in a private room, there seemed to be a question about your credit.''

''That can't be,'' said Phule. ''We own the hotel, you know. They don't tell the owner his credit's no good—especially not when he's covering his account with a Dilithium Express card.''

''That's precisely what the difficulty is,'' said Beeker.

"It looks as if there *is* a problem with your Dilithium Express card. And unless something very unusual has happened to the financial markets while we weren't looking, that *is* impossible."

4

"The very rich," someone once said, "are not like you and me." Someone wiser than he knew replied to this, "Yes, they have more money." My employer was very rich, and in that fact lies much of the secret of his success.

Where other commanding officers might have had many of the ideas that allowed Captain Phule to turn his Legionnaire company into an elite unit—housing them in first-class accommodations, giving them training facilities of the newest and finest quality, serving them meals of which a four-star restaurant would not be ashamed—only a very rich man would have had the ability to put those ideas into action without concerning himself with the military bean counters' objections. A man who can wave a Dilithium Express card and say "Put it on my account" can accomplish many extraordinary things.

So when a junior hotel clerk, making a routine charge against the card, was told that there was a problem with the credit, it threatened to bring down the entire structure my employer had so carefully erected. Worse yet, it suggested that someone very powerful indeed had entered the field against him . . .

"To sabotage a Dilithium Express account is no small feat," said Nakadate. He and Sushi sat in a vacant cubicle in the Fat Chance Hotel's business annex, an amenity provided by the hotel but rarely used by the vacationing gamblers.

"You've seen merely the tip of the blade," said Sushi. He put down the vidphone set he had used to hack Phule's account. "Freezing the account is only the start. If I want to, I can transfer funds out, then leave the account so nobody can even tell it's been hacked, let alone how or by whom. Is this not a talent our families could make use of?"

"I have seen these things done before, but never so quickly. And never without much more elaborate hardware." The Yakuza man's face bore an expression of grudging respect. The two men spoke in low voices—though it was unlikely that anyone overhearing would understand Japanese.

"The kind of hardware you're talking about is bulky, and it is a red flag if the wrong people know you have it," said Sushi, leaning back in his chair. "Everyone's eyes are on the man with a sword, while the unarmed man draws no notice. The fools forget that bare hands are deadly, too."

"Spoken like a ninja," said Nakadate. Then his brows creased. "But why have you put yourself in my hands? Knowing that you can do this, and that you are willing to betray your own captain, why should I not kill you before you turn this skill against me and my family?"

"A wise man does not break his sword because a fool has cut himself with his own blade," said Sushi calmly. "I will assume that you—and whoever may have sent you—are wise enough to see my value. If you do not, I am in no more danger than before, when you were ready to treat me as an impostor."

"I was surprised that you knew the passwords," admitted Nakadate. "No impostor could have known the signal you gave. On the other hand, we have not been able to verify your claim to be one of us. I am still not certain what to do with you.''

Sushi spread his hands and gave a shrug. ''Is it necessary to do anything at all with me? And even if it is, why are you the one who must decide?''

''I am sent by the family on Burning Tree, which has jurisdiction over this sector. For my misdeeds, they have given me the burden of solving the enigma your existence poses. It is tempting to take the easy road—but as you note, you may be an asset not easily replaced.''

''And what if I can lift this burden from your back?'' said Sushi. A hint of a smile played around the corners of his eyes, but it did not extend so far as his mouth.

If Nakadate noticed it, he gave no sign. ''My back is strong,'' he said. ''Therein lies much of my usefulness to the families.''

''It is good to inure yourself to difficult work,'' observed Sushi. ''It is not so good to make your work more difficult than it needs to be.''

''That is often true,'' said Nakadate. ''But to put it directly, I see no way to solve this problem without causing other, perhaps worse, problems. Perhaps it is best for me to watch and wait for a while.''

''Perhaps,'' agreed Sushi. ''But what I have in mind would make even that unnecessary.''

''Perhaps,'' said the Yakuza man. ''I will tell you, though, I am nicknamed 'The Mule'. My brothers chose that name with excellent reason.''

''You are justly proud of it,'' said Sushi, not smiling at all. ''But let me tell you what I propose, and then you will be in a position to make up your own mind. First, I think you need to know that . . .''

Sushi talked for quite some time, and by the time he was done, Nakadate, who had begun listening with a very skeptical expression, was wide-eyed.

''Excuse me, son, do you have a minute to talk?''

The young Legionnaire looked up to see a man in a black

jumpsuit and dark sunglasses, his hair combed back in a thick pompadour with long sideburns. Spotting the Legion insignia at the collar, he relaxed. "Sure, I guess so," he said. "I go on casino duty in half an hour, but until then I'm free. What can I do for you?"

"Well, I reckon the shoe's on the other foot, young fella," said the newcomer. "I'm assigned to this here outfit, and I need to find out just where and how I can be of most use. The name's Rev." He extended a hand and the young Legionnaire shook it. "What's your handle, son?"

"You can call me *Gears*," said the young Legionnaire. "Mechanic's mate first class is my rating, and I'm pretty good at it, if I have to say so myself."

"Good, good, a fella should take pride in his work," said Rev, rubbing his hands together. "I take a lot of pride in my work, too. That's why I was so pleased to be assigned to this company—your captain's gettin' quite a reputation for findin' fresh answers to old problems, and I'm the same sort of guy."

"That's good to hear," said Gears. His eyes fell on the other insignia on Rev's collar, indicating the wearer's specialty—a stylized musical instrument of antique design. He seemed to remember it was called an "eclectic gutter," or something of the sort. "What's your line, Rev? I don't recall what that particular insignia means. You aren't a musician, are you?"

Rev responded with a low chuckle. "In a sense I am, son—I play sweet music for the soul. But that's just the insignia for my particular denomination. I'm your new chaplain. Now, you know that means I serve the whole company—Christian, Jew, Greater Holistic, Pagan, Muslim, Anti-Norfian—all can come to me for advice or consolation. Back home, my denomination is Church of the New Revelation, which some call Church of the King."

"I guess that makes sense," said Gears politely. "Now, what was it you said you wanted to talk about?"

"Why, I need to know what your troubles are," said Rev. He squatted down next to Gears, bringing his face level with his listener's. "Your troubles in particular, and the troubles other folks are having. 'Cause that's my mission here—to help you all with your troubles.''

Gears smiled wearily. "Well, I guess I know what my biggest trouble is, but I doubt there's much you can do to help with it.''

"You'd be surprised, son," said Rev. "The King saw more trouble than you and I will ever know, and yet he rose above it and raised his voice for the world to hear—until he had to Leave the Building. Tell me what bothers you, and if there's a way to fix it, we can find that way—you, me, and especially Him.''

"Well, I guess you could say I'm unlucky, Rev. That about sums it up.''

"Well, we're all a bit unlucky sometimes, aren't we? But anybody's luck can change. We can all make a comeback and be bigger than ever, the way the King himself did.''

"Well, I'd sure like that," said Gears. "But I'm afraid it'll take a big comeback to get me out of the hole I'm in.''

Gears paused and looked Rev up and down; evidently satisfied with what he saw, he continued, "When we came to Lorelei, all the guys were excited—not just me. We'd been stuck on a backwater world where there wasn't any real action, and now we figured we could build up a bit of a nest egg for after the service, y'know? And when the captain brought in all those professional gamblers to show us their tricks, we figured we couldn't be beat. So naturally, when we're off duty, a lot of us wander over to one of the casinos and give it a whirl—at blackjack, or craps, or poker, or magic—any game that gives a guy a chance. We know enough to lay off the slots, or superstring roulette.''

Rev nodded solemnly. "I know what you mean, son. The King Himself spent many years in the casinos, and was faced with great temptation every day.''

The young legionnaire nodded, not really listening. "Anyhow, it isn't as easy as it looks. It all seems pretty clear when you've got a pro there, showing you how to spot tricks and how to figure odds, but when the chips start piling up on the table, it's not easy to think straight. We've been here seven Standard months, and I've probably lost four months' pay. Some guys are willing to front a few bucks, so I'm not hurting too bad. Besides, the Legion covers food and housing and all the stuff you need to get along. But I sure could use a change of luck to get my head back above water.''

''Well, that's something to think about,'' said Rev, standing up straight again. ''I reckon the King would understand that kind of thing from his days as a common soldier, like any other boy called to service. I can see there's plenty of good work I can do here, and now I've got an idea where it might start. Thank you, son—we'll be talking again.''

''Thanks, uh—Rev,'' said the Legionnaire. ''If your King can do anything to change somebody's luck, there'll be a lot of fellows mighty obliged to him.''

''I'll take it up with Him,'' said Rev with a deep chuckle. ''I sure will, son.''

Journal #298

One of my employer's primary qualifications for a position of command was his ability to project absolute confidence when it was time for an important decision. He did not always possess this confidence in private. Waiting with me for a court-martial to decide on his punishment for ordering a strafing run on a peace conference, he had been as nervous as a new recruit who feared that an inspector would deny him leave because his bed-making skills were deficient.

But whatever indecision he felt in private—or in my company, which amounted to the same thing—he had learned not to show it to subordinates. And now, when there seemed to be half a dozen crises coming to a head at once, I thought the time was more than ripe for him to take the bit in his teeth.

Thus, I was not surprised when he took me aside and began to talk through appropriate responses to his current prob-

lems. What did surprise me was his perception of the relative priority to be assigned to each of them. Needless to say, it differed considerably from mine . . .

Phule looked around the room at the four others there—his brain trust, a politician might have called it. There were his three direct subordinates in the chain of command: Lieutenants Rembrandt and Armstrong, and Top Sergeant Brandy, as well as his butler and personal confidant, Beeker. Beeker was perhaps the captain's most valuable asset—not only on account of his complete detachment from military matters, but because of his ability to go anywhere and speak to anyone in absolute confidence. The troops knew he wouldn't snitch, and so they told him everything.

Phule got straight to the point. "As you all know, there's trouble brewing in several areas at once. Let me make this clear at the outset: There's nothing happening that we can't handle—in fact, taken singly, none of these problems is any great threat to the company."

"I'm glad to hear that, sir," said Lieutenant Armstrong. "It's been a very confusing day."

"Confusing ain't the word for it," said Brandy, who'd been in the thick of the action all afternoon. "Between Sushi going AWOL, the Zenobian playing spy, and the FUBAR at the hotel desk, I've had my hands full. And now I have to break in these recruits—though the Gambolts shouldn't be much trouble."

"Those aren't the worst problems," said Armstrong. He somehow managed to maintain an exemplary posture even sitting in an easy chair. "Chocolate Harry's digging in for a siege. Unless he's gone completely off the beam, I think we're going to see some fighting."

"Oh, C.H. has a phobia about those bikers," said Rembrandt, scoffing. "A few legionnaires should be enough to brush them aside."

"Take a walk down to supply depot and you'll change that tune," retorted Armstrong. "From the way Harry's fortified the place, he's not expecting us to brush them aside, and I think he knows what he's up against."

"Well, he did ride with the Outlaws," agreed Brandy. "If somebody's put a scare into him, I won't take 'em too lightly. But this isn't a street fight, here. Those bikers are on course to do battle with the best damn Legion company I've ever seen. Unless they've brought a few hundred armed Renegades onto the station with them, I can't see how they pose any real threat."

"The threat isn't to us, but to our operation," Phule pointed out. "Good as they may be at street fighting, it'd be suicide for them to meet us in a pitched battle. But we can't carry on combat operations in the middle of an entertainment complex without serious consequences. An occasional fistfight or two is inevitable in any place that serves liquor. But I don't want to try to tell a court-martial how the casino's customers—*civilians*—were caught in a cross fire between my troops and an attacking biker gang."

"No argument with that," said Brandy. "So if we can't outgun 'em, what do we do? I hear they've been nursing this grudge for years—and they wanted Harry's hide bad enough to spring for space-liner tickets to one of the most expensive resorts in the galaxy when they found out he was here. If they're that mad, we aren't going to buy 'em off just by having Harry come out and say, 'Sorry, guys, it won't happen again.' "

"Oh, I agree," said Phule. "But let's put this problem aside for a minute. It's one of several things we're looking at here, and I think we need to go after them in the right order. Once we've got the first couple of pieces in place, the rest of the puzzle will sort itself out."

"That's as good an approach as any," said Rembrandt, who had shown in Phule's absence her ability to make tough decisions under pressure. "Where do we start? C.H. and the Renegades? Sushi's disappearance? The Zenobian spy?"

"The Renegades are the big problem," said Armstrong bluntly. "If we don't shut them down, they're likely to start shooting."

"I'm not so sure," said Rembrandt, knitting her brows.

"If Sushi is collaborating with the Yakuza, he could give them a lot of dangerous information. He could be the brightest man in the company, and I wouldn't be surprised if he understands a lot of what goes on at the command level without having been told. If he decided to sell us out, he'd be extremely dangerous."

"Dangerous? Hell, I'll tell you about dangerous," said Brandy. "That Qual may be a spy or he may not, but he's got half the troops convinced he is. That's no good for morale. You'd be smart to send him off somewhere where he can't do any harm—and where the troops won't be worried he's going to stab them in the back."

Beeker raised his hand and said, diffidently, "Sir, if I may be so forward, I would suggest that the difficulties with the Dilithium Express account ought to take precedence over all other problems. The person capable of manipulating that account is by a substantial margin your most dangerous adversary."

"That's a good point, Beeker," said Phule. The others in the room nodded. Despite Beeker's admitted ignorance of military matters, his grasp of broader issues had earned him their respect. He offered his opinion infrequently, but when he chose to do so, he was listened to.

"It's a very good point," Phule continued, "but I suspect it'll resolve itself in due time. Meanwhile, you're all overlooking our real mission."

"Say again, Captain?" asked Brandy. She had long ago come to the conclusion that Phule had memorized all the military textbooks ever written, and was systematically breaking every rule contained in them. His resounding success was proof positive that all those rules were utter nonsense. But of course, every sergeant knew that already. That didn't mean they didn't have to be enforced, of course. When you'd gotten your people trained to do exactly what you said, even though they all knew it was completely senseless, then you could get them to fight for you. Military organizations had worked that way since the dawn of time. Sometimes Brandy suspected that by the time Phule was finished, even that central tenet of the military might be revised . . .

She realized that the pause had been growing uncomfortably long, and that Phule was looking at her with expectation on his face. "Sergeant, we have new recruits," he said. "Don't you think you need to get busy showing them how we do things in the Legion?"

Armstrong was flabbergasted. "Sir, do you really intend to ignore these crises? Any one of them could destroy everything we're doing here."

"I don't intend to ignore them, Armstrong," Phule said quietly. "But unless everything goes wrong at once, these crises will be over in a matter of days. Our recruits will be with us a good deal longer than that—possibly for the rest of their careers. The continued success of this company depends on how well we train them. Lucky for us, we've gotten hold of them before they've been set on the wrong path by some other outfit."

"Captain, does that include the Gambolts?" asked Brandy. She'd seen Garbo capture the fleeing Zenobian, almost without effort. The Gambolt had been uncannily agile—and faster than any human she'd ever seen. "Everybody knows they're the best hand-to-hand fighters in the galaxy . . ."

"They may be Gambolts, but they're *untrained* Gambolts, Brandy," said Phule patiently. "You should know that training is the difference between a military force and a mob. We've made our reputation by making great legionnaires out of other outfits' rejects. Now we've finally got a chance to train our people from the ground up. Why don't we all get to work turning them into legionnaires?"

"Yes, sir!" exclaimed Armstrong. His expression suggested that he disagreed with Phule's priorities, but he was too good an officer to say so out loud. Besides, Phule's decisions had a way of turning out right, despite the odds. He hoped the odds hadn't finally caught up with them . . .

"Great Gazma, it is a pleasure your acquaintance to make again, Captain Clown!"

Flight Leftenant Qual looked elegant in his custom-made black dress uniform. Except for his height—a bit under one meter tall—he might well have been a regular Legion officer. Of course, the Fat Chance Casino's four-star dining room had not had any trouble seating the diminutive alien. Their stock in trade was their ability to seat and feed a member of any known civilized race. Given that this was their first visit by a Zenobian, they had done remarkably well—a hammocklike device adapted one of their regular armchairs to fit him very comfortably.

"I have to admit it was a pleasant surprise when I learned that it was you who was being assigned to my unit as a military observer," said Phule. He did not normally eat at the casino's elite restaurant, although of course as majority owner it was his right—and would have cost him nothing. But Mess Sergeant Escrima was every bit as good a cook as the Fat Chance's master chef, and Phule could settle down to a meal of Escrima's cooking with far less fuss and expenditure of working time—he could sit there reading a report, or carry his plate over to another table to talk with his people without causing a disturbance. Nor was there any problem getting seconds . . .

But tonight was a special occasion: Phule and his officers were formally welcoming the Zenobian visitor, and it seemed appropriate to put on a bit of extra formality. The gleaming silverware, snowy-white linen, bone china and twenty-page wine list might not impress Qual in the same way they would a human visitor, but the little alien could easily recognize that he was being given a first-class reception by his hosts.

And, in fact, Qual was evidently enjoying himself. He sloshed a generous dollop of wasabi on a bit of tuna rolled in seaweed and popped it in his mouth. It had been agreed after a hasty conference that seeing the Zenobian bolting down live food—his race's normal fare—might disconcert the other customers (not to mention his tablemates). But the chef was resourceful, and Qual had been perfectly willing to compromise on raw fish for the occasion—"After all, a soldier must accustom himself to hardship," he had said, with what the translator chose to render as a chuckle. Noting Armstrong's struggles to get the food past his nose, Phule decided it was a chuckle. Lieutenant Armstrong was not an adventurous man, especially when it came to eating.

"I hope you and your troops have pardoned my little prank this afternoon," said Qual, his translated voice coming through with a remarkably polished accent for all its occasional bizarre word-choices. "One of the first things one would like to grasp about unfamiliar troops is their reaction to the unexpected, and immediately upon arrival, before anyone knows what is occurring, is a splendid opening to observe this."

"Undoubtedly," said Lieutenant Armstrong, staring at his plate with the expression of a man who was wishing for a medium-rare deluxe plasmaburger with a side of veg-e-chips. "However, it would have been considerate to alert the commander as to your intentions, if no one else."

"Captain Clown was notified that I was to be assigned to his company, is that not exact?" said Qual, looking at Phule.

"Yes, of course I was notified," said Phule. "General Blitzkrieg informed me some time back."

"And he made my mission transparent?"

Phule had to think for a beat before answering, "Yes, it was quite clear. You were coming to study our tactics . . . and ethics, I believe the general said. Now that I think about it, I'm not certain I entirely understood that last part."

"Ah, but is it not self-evident, Captain Clown? Our races seek to conclude a treaty, and of course this would be a good thing. But we Zenobians want to know with whom we are about to treat, and what they are likely to do, and even more serious, whether they are likely to do what they say they will do. So I have come to study your company to learn all these things."

It was impossible to read Qual's expression, and the translator was shaky at rendering the nuances of his tone. Phule wondered suddenly what would happen if Qual reported that the humans were untrustworthy. That was a sobering thought. Any number of very unpleasant results might follow a very simple misunderstanding with this alien envoy . . . He began to wonder if General Blitzkrieg had somehow manipulated him into this situation.

Rembrandt had picked up the same train of thought. She paused with her wineglass in midair and asked, ''Flight Leftenant, does this mean that your report on our company is going to determine whether or not your people will sign a treaty with us?''

The Zenobian gulped down another chunk of raw seafood—his teeth were undeniably formidable-looking—and said, equably, ''To be sure, Lieutenant, we place great gravity on trust and ethics. Of course, I am but one observer; there are others visiting your leaders in trade, in political realms—it is of importance that we know enough to decide wisely. Of course, it was felicitous that Captain Clown was the first of your species to meet us—his generosity opened the dining coop for what we hope will continue to be a very beneficial relationship.'' He popped a handful of shrimp into his mouth and grinned—at least Phule hoped it was a grin. Except for his impeccably fitted Legion uniform, the alien resembled nothing quite so much as a miniature allosaur. The display of all those teeth might mean anything at all.

But Qual's stated intentions were benign, and he *was* an official envoy of his species. Until there was evidence to the contrary, Phule and his officers would have to take him at his word. Even if Qual's table manners were not exactly comfortable to observe at close range . . .

The dinner had left Phule very satisfactorily fed—along with a couple of glasses of excellent wine (Boordy Grand Cru Blanc, of an excellent vintage). It would have been tempting, after his event-filled day, for the captain to make an early night of it. But he had promised his officers he was not going to neglect the looming crises. He'd stop off in Comm Central, find out if there had been any new developments, and then see if he had any bright ideas for dealing with them.

He had turned down the corridor to his destination and

gone half a dozen strides when a voice from a shadowed alcove whispered to him: "Captain!"

Phule turned and peered into the shadows, where a slim figure in civilian clothes lurked. "Sushi!" he said, anger in his voice. "What's going on? Do you know what's been happening around here?"

"Some of it, sure, Captain," said Sushi, putting a finger to his lips. "Keep it down, though—we haven't got time to get anyplace more private, and if the wrong people overhear me, I'm in deep *kimchee*."

"Some of us are beginning to think *you're* the wrong people," growled Phule, but he stepped into the alcove and lowered his voice. "Tell me everything—and it better be good."

"It is good, Captain, very good," said Sushi, but there was a worried look on his face. "You've heard about the couple that came to the casino this afternoon?"

"Yes. We still have the woman in custody, last I heard."

"Oh, yeah," said Sushi. "That reminds me, you can let her go now."

"I suppose you've got a good reason for that," Phule said, looking skeptical.

"Sure, Captain. But let me start at the beginning. You remember how when I got these Yakuza tattoos you were all worried about what would happen if a real Yakuza member showed up?"

Phule nodded. "I gather that's what happened today."

"Right. But there's more to it than a family member just showing up," said Sushi. "Somebody here tipped them off about me. In fact, the guy came looking for me, ready to rearrange my internal organs into some nonfunctional pattern if he found out I was bogus."

"Which of course you were," Phule pointed out. "Your internal organs appear still to be functioning—although I can rearrange them myself, if it seems necessary. For now, I'm still neutral on the subject. What did you say to him?"

Sushi gulped, then managed a sheepish grin. "Well, Captain, you remember how I told you that my family maintains certain business connections—strictly for informational purposes? After you convinced me that what I was doing might be more dangerous than I had anticipated, I called home and got one of my uncles to dig up some information for me. Specifically, he gave me a few names and passwords that only somebody very high in a family would know.''

''I hope he didn't have to pay too high a price for them,'' said Phule. ''That kind of information can be very dangerous to use. Especially if you aren't absolutely certain of its reliability.''

Sushi nodded, soberly. ''Believe me, Captain, I knew that. But I figured that once somebody showed up looking for me—which was inevitable if we stayed here more than a couple of months—I was already in major trouble for impersonating a member of the families. Using the wrong password couldn't get me any deader. So I had to take the gamble.''

''Someday that gambling fever's going to get you into real trouble,'' said Phule, shaking his head. ''So you had these passwords—what then?''

''Well, you probably heard that the guy started a brawl in the casino. He'd picked a spot where I'd be among the ones responding, and he and the woman with him started cheating blatantly. When Moustache tried to put the pinch on them, they went into combat mode—but I was the real target. When I realized what was happening, I showed him a password, actually a sort of recognition sign.'' Sushi made a quick gesture with his hand, then continued, ''At first the guy—his name is Nakadate, not that that'll mean anything to you—at first he was suspicious, but combined with some fast talking, the fact that I knew the sign convinced him that we needed to go off someplace to talk without the whole casino watching us. So we told the woman to wait for us, and we went to talk.''

''That's the first smart thing you've told me—at least there was some sort of hostage for your safety. Going off to someplace private with the enemy is a quick way to get yourself killed.'' Phule sighed. It was a relief to see Sushi still alive and kicking; he had begun to fear the worst. But now he had to figure out what was really going on—unless, for once, Sushi was actually telling him the whole truth.

Sushi grunted. "Captain, I hate to tell you this, but if he was going to kill me, the hostage wouldn't have made any difference. Once Nakadate turned her over to the guards, she was on her own and she knew it. Besides, I doubt she has any information that would help you if something did happen to me."

"Well, that figures," said Phule. "Security tells me she's not carrying anything that gives even a hint to her origins—unless she grew up in a spaceport convenience shop. And she's playing it like a complete innocent. All we have on her is the blackjack cheating—but we can make that stick, if we need to. Why should we let her go?"

"Because she really doesn't know anything, and because some of our people could get hurt if she decides to make a break for it. I've seen her fight. She's not worth the risk. Sir."

Phule rubbed his chin. "Hmmm—maybe that makes sense, but I'll have to think about it a little longer. Let's get back to the Yakuza. What did you and Nakadate talk about when you went off alone?"

"Well, sir, I thought I could convince him I was a legitimate member of a family he didn't know. That's the way the Yakuza is organized—there's no one central authority. But he wasn't ready to buy that without corroborating evidence. He wanted to know what I was doing in the Space Legion, instead of helping out in my family's business. And so I had to convince him I was stealing from you."

"*Stealing from me!*" Phule bellowed, grabbing Sushi by the shirt front. "Are you the one who's been monkeying around with my credit account?"

Sushi put a finger to his lips. "Calm down, Captain," he said quietly. "What if Nakadate brought along more backup than he's told me? I had to *convince* him I was stealing from you, but that doesn't mean I really was. Your money's protected better than an emperor's favorite daughter—you ought to know that."

"All I know is that my Dilithium Express account was frozen this afternoon," growled Phule. "If that was your doing . . ."

"Of course it was my doing," said Sushi. His voice was calm, but he spoke quickly, as if to forestall objections. "Look, Captain, I'm on your side—would I be telling you about this if I wasn't? I'd transfer as much as I could to my own accounts and get on the fastest spaceliner out of here. Besides, think of the possibilities. If I can hack your account, I can hack an enemy's account, too. If the other guy's troops aren't getting paid, or his supply orders aren't getting filled, that gives you a pretty big edge over him, doesn't it?"

"So why didn't you tell me about this before you went and did it?" Phule demanded.

"Because if you knew somebody could do it, you'd probably set up safeguards against it. It's what I'd have done if it were my account. And if you'd gone and done that, I might not have been able to convince Nakadate I was crooked. Besides, it's fixed, now, Captain. Check it—if there's a millicredit missing, you can take it out of my hide."

"Maybe I ought to do that anyhow," said Phule with a calculating stare. "Why couldn't you think up some less drastic way to keep the Yakuza off your back?"

"Because I saw an opportunity I couldn't turn down, Captain," said the young legionnaire. "I'd been thinking for some time what I'd do if somebody from the Yakuza ever showed up. We aren't talking a bunch of street-corner thugs here; these people take a very long view. Nakadate saw that my ability to hack your account made me dangerous to his family, too—he was thinking about finishing me off right then and there. I had to sell him the idea that I'm too important an asset to throw away. So I made him think I'm working for a super-family—somebody above everybody's head."

Phule looked skeptical. "I thought you said there wasn't any overall Yakuza organization—only the separate families."

"That's right, Captain," said Sushi. "At least, there hasn't been before now. I invented it just today."

"And you expect him to believe that? What happens when he checks back with his family and finds out you're pulling his leg?"

"I'm about to take care of that," said Sushi. "I need to use the comm center gear to get a message to my family. They're going to plant the rumor that there *is* a super-family, working to make the Yakuza more powerful and profitable than ever. As I said, these people take the long view. If they think it's to their long-term advantage, they'll play along."

Phule stared at Sushi for a moment, thinking. "Maybe they will. But when they learn your super-family is phony as a Vegan kilobuck, what then? They'll be after you again, and this time you won't be able to talk your way out of it."

Sushi grinned broadly. "Ah, but it won't turn out to be phony, Captain. You see, that's the beautiful part of this scam. We're going to *take over the Yakuza*! Now, let's go down to Comm Central and get the ball rolling."

He started off down the corridor. For once completely speechless, Phule followed him.

5

A hell of a place to hold a formation, thought Brandy, looking at the Grand Ballroom of the Fat Chance Casino Hotel. In front of her, over a dozen rookie Space Legionnaires stood at attention on the dance floor—three of them Gambolts. They had been aroused by automated early-morning wake-up calls from the hotel's central computer, for this, their first training session with Omega Company. A variety of exercise equipment had been brought in from the hotel's fitness center (an amenity that the visiting gamblers largely ignored). This session had been designed to incorporate physical training as much as basic indoctrination in military discipline.

Brandy stared at them with frank curiosity; it was unusual for the company to get recruits who hadn't already come through boot camp, learning the ropes of how to be a legionnaire—and, for the most part, convincing their drill instructors that they didn't have what it took. Or that they had an attitude that would make them a problem wherever they went. That was the raw material that had gone to make up the Omega Mob, and it had made the company the butt of every Legion joke—until Phule came, and showed that even the ugliest ducklings could grow up into something unexpected.

Could this crop of new recruits represent a change of course for Omega? Had the company's success under its new commander convinced the brass to start sending a better quality of raw material? Or had these newcomers somehow been diagnosed as likely misfits and malcontents even before they'd put on uniforms? Well, it didn't really matter. Whatever this crop of rookies had been before they got here, it was Brandy's job to make them into legionnaires. *Might as well get started*, she thought. *If it's going to be bad news, waiting to find it out won't make it any better.*

"All right, rookies, listen up," she said, stepping forward and raising her voice to a penetrating bark. "You aren't going to like a lot of what's going to happen here, but I don't care whether you like it or not. It's my job to make you into Space Legionnaires, and I'll do it if I have to kill half of you. Do you understand that?"

The troops responded with a general murmur of acquiescence, certainly nothing approaching enthusiasm.

"*What did you say?*" Brandy demanded, at the top of her lungs. This was an old drill-instructor's game. Usually somebody would get flustered enough to say something she could take as an excuse for a first-class chewing out. Even an innocent reply would do—the point was to show the recruits that they were in a new environment, where rank and discipline and the rules were what mattered. Even if the recruits thought the rules were stupid (which they often were, given the quality of the Space Legion's top brass in recent decades), they were going to have to learn to pay them lip service. Eventually they'd figure out where the loopholes were so they could get through their hitches without being miserable the entire time. When push came to shove, a clever, resourceful legionnaire who could break the rules without getting caught was better to have in your outfit than a mindless rule-follower. But to get that kind of legionnaire, you had to start off by enforcing the rules with an iron hand.

"Well, Sergeant, we all said different things," said one

man in the front row—a young, round-faced human, slightly below average height, with a bit of a potbelly. The recruit had an earnest expression, and the kind of patient smile a schooldroid might be programmed to use while teaching a slow class.

Well, it wasn't an ideal point of departure for a tirade, but it'd have to do. "You, there, what's your name?" Brandy snapped.

"Mahatma, Sergeant," said the recruit, still smiling. Brandy was disappointed that he didn't make the common rookie mistake of forgetting to call her "Sergeant," or the worse mistake of calling her "sir." But she'd have to make do with what she got. That was one of Phule's principles, too.

"And what the hell do you think is so funny, Mahatma?" said Brandy, stepping forward to confront the recruit face-to-face.

"Funny isn't quite the right word, Sergeant," said Mahatma, still smiling dreamily. "Everything here is so . . . *transitory.*"

"Transitory?" Brandy hadn't heard that one before, and for a moment it caught her off her guard.

"Yes, Sergeant," said Mahatma. "We see things in such a short perspective, don't you agree? What's here today will be gone tomorrow, and we along with it. So why get disturbed at any of it? All will pass."

"Is that what you think?" snarled Brandy, moving to within inches of Mahatma's face. This usually had the effect of making even a tough case nervous, but Mahatma didn't even flinch. "You might have on a Legion uniform, but you look like a civilian and you talk like one. Maybe you should get down on the floor and do some push-ups for me—say about a hundred, for starters. That ought to give you the long perspective. And we'll see whether that smile's still there when you finish. *Do it now!*"

"Yes, Sergeant," said Mahatma, still smiling as he got down on his hands and knees. "Do you want a hundred exactly, or will an approximation suffice?"

"I said a hundred and I meant it," said Brandy. "I want

to see that back straight, rookie. And if you stick your fat civilian butt up in the air, I promise you I'll kick it. *Do you hear me?''*

"Yes, Sergeant," said Mahatma, looking up at her. "Thank you for giving me the chance to make myself stronger."

"Get going!'' shouted Brandy, who was starting to feel as annoyed as she was pretending to be. Mahatma started doing push-ups. Very slowly and calmly, without looking up and without bending his waist. There was a patter of laughter from the ranks. Brandy glared at them. "So, you think it's funny, hey? *OK, all of you—a hundred push-ups! Now!''*

The recruits scrambled onto their hands and started doing push-ups. Most of them were nowhere near as calm as Mahatma. That was good—they would make better targets than the unflappable Mahatma. The morning was finally promising to go as she'd planned it. *"Keep those backs straight!''* she yelled, at nobody in particular, and began looking for someone to make an example of.

"Excuse me, Sergeant, what shall we do now?"

Brandy recognized the translator's intonations even as she turned to see the three Gambolts standing behind her in a group. She frowned. "Push-ups," she said. "One hundred push-ups. That order was for you, too."

"Yes, Sergeant," said Rube. "We did one hundred push-ups. What should we do while the humans are finishing?"

"You did the hundred? That's impossible," said Brandy. She looked at her watch; it had been less than two minutes since she'd ordered the squad to do push-ups. Her frown got deeper. "You must be doing them wrong. Show me how you do push-ups."

"Yes, Sergeant," said the Gambolts in chorus, and all three began doing push-ups in unison—at something like two per second, with straight backs, full arm extension, chests brushing the floor without resting there . . . Brandy watched in fascination while the three Gambolts blew off another hundred. They weren't even breathing hard. Behind them, the human recruits were floundering through the routine, most of them barely halfway to their quota. She knew from experience that most of them wouldn't be able to reach it.

A second glance showed her Mahatma, still doing his push-ups very slowly and calmly, as if he had no other concern in the world. He wasn't breathing hard either. Right then, Brandy decided that this had to be the weirdest training squad she'd ever seen. At least, the Gambolts weren't going to be a problem, she decided. And with their example, maybe the rest would shape up even faster.

She didn't realize until a good bit later that the Gambolts' example might not have the effect she anticipated.

"Live chicken?" Escrima wrinkled his nose fastidiously. "Sure—it'll cost a bit, but I can get it. What would I want it for, though? There's not a man in the outfit—me included—who can taste any difference between ClonoBird cutlets and the stuff you have to peel the feathers off of. I can even get ClonoBird with bones, if the recipe calls for it. So why stretch the budget for the old-fashioned stuff?"

"It's not a man we're looking to feed," said Lieutenant Rembrandt, looking every bit as fussy as the Mess Sergeant. "And there's no recipe. It's for that Leftenant Qual, the Zenobian. He's used to live food."

One of Escrima's subcooks looked up from the mouth of the oven, which she'd been loading with trays of croissants. "Live food?" she said. "Eeuww!"

"My reaction exactly," said Rembrandt. "But the captain wants to make a special effort for Leftenant Qual. He's here as a military observer from his planet, and apparently his word on how we treat him could make a difference in whether they sign a treaty or decide to fight us."

Escrima leaned over the counter, his hands and lower arms covered with flour. "Is the lizard going to eat his live birds right in the mess hall?" he asked. He was not smiling.

"I hope not," said Rembrandt, shaking her head. "That stunt he pulled yesterday, running around and making people chase him, made him unpopular enough."

"I heard the Zenobian is a spy," chimed in the subcook. "That's why the brass sent him here—they figure he'll get caught, and it'll give the captain a black eye."

"How will it give the captain a black eye if we catch the Zenobian spying?" said Escrima, turning around to face her. He looked down at the open oven door and said, "Better get the rest of those trays in—we want 'em all ready at the same time. Your job's cooking, not counterspying."

"Yes, Sarge," said the subcook, and resumed her task.

"She's right about one thing, though, Escrima," said Rembrandt. "The Zenobian asked to be sent here because we were the first human outfit he encountered, back when he came exploring for new worlds and landed on Haskin's Planet where we were stationed. Qual figures he'll get a friendlier reception from the captain than he would somewhere else. Maybe he figures he can spy on us more easily. He even said that part of his mission was to study our tactics. That sure sounds like spying—especially if he goes back home and gives his general staff chapter and verse on how we fight."

"Somebody could arrange it so he doesn't go back home," suggested Escrima. His fingers brushed the handle of a cleaver, perhaps accidentally, but Rembrandt noticed and shook her head.

"That kind of accident would put the captain in even hotter water," she said firmly. "Qual spelled it out plain and clear at our dinner last night. We've got to play along with him, because his report could make or break the treaty negotiations. He can saunter around and take notes to his heart's content, and we can't do a thing about it."

"So we're right between the frying pan and the heating unit," said Escrima. "Tell me again why I should go out of my way to get this lizard special, tasty food while he's spying on us?"

"Captain's orders," said Rembrandt glumly. "I don't like it much myself, to tell you the truth, Escrima—either we ruin the whole company's appetite so one alien envoy can eat as he pleases, or we risk going to war because we won't give him his favorite dish. The captain thinks we're better off treating with Qual in good faith, which is why I'm here. Get us those live birds—I'll do what I can to make sure he eats them where none of us have to watch it. And Escrima—make sure your people keep this quiet. The Zenobian's unpopular enough as it is. No point throwing more fuel on the fire.''

"You got it, Lieutenant," said Escrima. He favored Rembrandt with a crooked grin. "You know me better than to think I'm going to spread stories about how some taste-less alien prefers live bait to my delicious cooking, don't you?"

"I guess so," said Rembrandt, chuckling. "It was bad enough having to eat in the hotel restaurant last night. Maybe if this Zenobian gets a taste of your stuff he'll switch to human food and never look back."

"He will, he will," said Escrima, with the confidence of a true artist. "And the first taste is free!"

"Excuse me, do you belong to the Legion company?"

Flight Leftenant Qual looked up at the two humans. "Most assuredly," he said. "It gives me great satisfaction to affiliate myself with the notorious band of Captain Clown."

The taller human—Qual had trouble telling them apart, they were so similar—said, "It is the captain we need to ask you about. I am Special Agent Peele, and this is my partner, Special Agent Hull." He showed an identification card that meant nothing to Qual, although the Zenobian could see that the holo on the card matched the face in front of him.

"You may ask as you wish," said Qual, displaying his teeth in the friendly gesture humans called a *smile*. "Ig-norance can be remedied. Such is my reason for being here."

"Very well," said Peele, gesturing to Hull, who opened her briefcase and took out a compact multicorder. "We have reliable reports that your captain has been concealing large amounts of income. Our preliminary investigation suggests that the casino operation here generates substantially more revenue than its competitors. Is that true?"

"I certainly hope so," said Qual, looking back at the casino, which towered over the three of them out on the public street. "It is a distinct pleasure to see one's benefactors prosper. Is that a recording device?"

"Yes, regulations require us to make accurate records of all our interviews," said Peele. "Do you have any information that would indicate that the captain has skimmed off a portion of the profits for his personal use?"

"I really have not been here long enough to know that," said Qual. "Does your recorder register images as well as sounds? My people would be interested in such a device."

"It's a standard, government-issue multicorder," said Hull, somewhat defensively. "We are not authorized to discuss our equipment with civilians."

"I see," said Qual, smiling again. "But you recognize, I am not a civilian, but a soldier, hence the uniform. Is it not so?"

"The distinction is complex, and your conclusion is in this case inaccurate," said Special Agent Peele. "Besides, we are here to discuss your captain's finances, not our equipment. Now, if you don't mind . . ."

"I could utilize such a recorder in my work," said Qual, reaching for the unit in question. "Will you sell it to me? I have many of your dollars."

"It is against regulations to sell government equipment," said Hull, pulling the recorder away from the Zenobian's eagerly extended claws. A frown came over her face—the first semblance of an expression she had shown.

"Ah, regulations, of course," said Qual. "Do you always obey these regulations?"

"Be careful what you say," said Peele, holding up a hand. "It is a serious offense to solicit government agents to violate regulations. Do not pursue this line of inquiry, or we shall be obliged to report you to our superiors."

"I should enjoy very much to meet your superiors," said Qual, his teeth still on display. "Are they here on Lorelei?"

"Unfortunately not," said Hull. "This entire station is a notorious haven for tax-dodgers, and the local authorities have managed to minimize the influence of the IRS here. The casino owners are required to distribute a declarations form to bettors winning large amounts, but very few of those forms are ever filed. And we seriously doubt the accuracy of those we do receive.''

''Proof that Captain Jester—or Mr. Phule, to use his other alias—is evading taxes could give the IRS the leverage to establish a permanent presence here. Then we could begin to build cases against the other casino owners,'' said Peele. ''Our mission is the thin end of the wedge, so it is very important that we play strictly by the regulations. There's a great deal at stake here.''

''All this is most edifying,'' said Qual. ''The ones in authority among my people will be very inquisitive to know how you do such things. But I am depressed that I cannot tell you about the finances of Captain Clown. This is beyond my ken.''

Peele looked at Hull, who said, ''I think he's telling the truth—he really doesn't know anything that concerns us. We're wasting our time here.'' She deactivated her recording device.

''I think you're right,'' said Peele, grudgingly. ''Well, we'll let you go about your business, then, good sophont. But we may have further questions at another time.''

''It has been most instructive to meet you,'' said Qual, with a stiff little bow and another toothy grin. He stood and watched as the two IRS agents walked away.

Back in the casino doorway, some distance away, Tuskanini watched with narrowed eyes. He wasn't sure what to make of the little Zenobian, but he knew he didn't like the IRS agents. As far as he was concerned, that was more than enough reason to be suspicious of Qual.

Except for mealtimes, it was unusual for many of the Omega Mob to be together at once. Different assignments and different shifts (especially in the round-the-clock operation of the casino) meant that days or even weeks might go by without any occasion for the entire complement to be in the same place at once. So it was a novelty for Phule to find himself addressing a large room full of legionnaires.

Phule looked around the room, waiting for the hum of voices to die down. Catching the serious mood, the men and women of Phule's Company spoke in quiet whispers, with none of the high-spirited byplay they would have shown before an address by their captain. As the last arrivals found their way into the few empty seats in the large room, Phule stepped to the podium and cleared his throat. The audience fell silent.

"It's good to see so many of you here," he said, looking around at the assembly. "As you know, this is a voluntary meeting—there'll be another later today, for those who're on duty now and can't get away, so if you have friends who'd like to come, please let them know."

Phule looked over at Rev, then turned back to his troops. "We've had a number of new members join our company recently," he said. "Some of you have had a chance to meet them, and I hope you're making them feel at home with us. We're building a reputation as the best company in the Legion, and we want the new people to know that they're part of something special when they come here." There was a murmur of assent to this, and Phule waited for it to die down before continuing.

"I'm going to introduce a man that some of you have already met." He gestured toward the chaplain standing next to him. "Some time back, during our journey here, I realized that it would be valuable for many of you to have the benefit of wise council in times of trouble, a shoulder to lean on and a friend in time of need. And while your officers and sergeants understand your particular situation better than anyone outside our company, they can't always fill those roles. So I asked Legion Headquarters to send us a chaplain. He's been here several days, meeting people and getting a feel for the situation. Now he's asked for a chance to introduce himself to the entire company, and that's why I've called this meeting. Will you please give a warm welcome to our new chaplain—Rev."

While Phule was speaking, Rev had stood quietly to one side of the podium; his head was bowed, and his hands were clasped over his breastbone. He might have been a lawyer preparing to deliver a jury summation. Now he stepped to the podium, waited for the patter of polite applause to die, and began. "Thank you, friends. You know, from time to time in our busy lives, a voice speaks to us—a voice we can't ignore. It may be the voice of a loved one, a mother, or a wife. It may be the voice of someone in authority, like your captain. Or it may be a quieter voice that comes from way down deep inside, remindin' each and every one of us about a duty left undone. A *call*, we term it in my line of work. I have had a call to this company, and here I stand before you in response to it."

Rev paused a moment, lowered his head and took a deep breath, then looked up at his audience and continued. "I have been called here to tell you about—*the King*," he said in a voice that resonated with significance.

"The King? What king?" It was Gabriel who spoke, but the same question was in the minds of every man, woman, and alien in the chaplain's audience.

"That's a fair question, son," said Rev, stepping in front of the podium and rubbing his hands together. "A fair question—and the answer is a story that's oft been told, so many times that I know it by heart—but since y'all may not have heard it, I guess it won't hurt none to tell again. A long time ago, on old Earth, there was a poor boy. A mighty poor boy—but one with a gift, and a spirit to make the most of himself. And make the most of himself he did. Why, in a few short months, he became the most imitated man on old Earth. He was on every screen, in every printout, on every frequency—and he was takin' in money faster than this here casino. He could have had anything he wanted. And do you know what he did? He went out and became a soldier. Not an officer, now. Not even a sergeant—a regular soldier, carryin' a gun and marchin' and takin' orders."

"What for he do that, if he the king?" said another legionnaire—his name was Street, Rev remembered. "How come he don't buy hisself a 'mission, be an officer?"

"Because he never forgot what it was like to be a poor

boy, Street,'' said Rev, strutting back and forth in front of the assembly. ''Not even after he finished with the army, and went back to givin' folks what they wanted. He didn't want to forget what it was like to be just a regular fellow, and he made sure he had somethin' to remember it by. So he never lost his touch with the real people. The little people like he'd been when he was still a poor boy. And they never forgot him. But he never put his nose up in the air. He could have gone anywhere in the world, talked to anybody he wanted to—presidents and governors and ladies so pretty they could make you forget your name. But he wanted to stay close to the people. And so he went to Vegas—which was the Lorelei of old Earth—and brought his gift to folks who gambled their money there, 'cause it was the only way for them to rise above their unhappy state. That's when he really became the King—when he brought himself to where the people who really needed him could see him. You see what I mean, Street?'' He pointed at the legionnaire, his head lowered and his gaze intense.

''Maybe I do,'' said Street, noncommittally. He folded his arms across his chest and sat there, looking at Rev without quite meeting the chaplain's eye.

''*Sure* you do,'' said Rev. He clapped his hands. ''And because the King went out to the casinos, givin' the people an example of how a poor boy could rise to the top, showin' 'em they just needed to find their gift and follow where it led, I feel very 'specially at home here with y'all on Lorelei. It's the kind of place the King would have gone to do his work, before he Left the Buildin'.''

The faces in the audience usually told Rev how well his word was being received. Now, looking at the Omega Mob, he saw rapt stares on more than one face—the look that told him his words were striking home. Some of them nodded tacit agreement; others held their chins higher than usual, inspired by his story. It was time to pick up the tempo, to swing the entire crowd along with him.

''The King knows how you feel,'' Rev said, rising up on the balls of his feet. There was a rhythm to his speech now. ''He's been down low, and rose up high again. He took a walk down Lonely Street, and came back to Graceland. He went into the Army and did his duty like a man. When he had hard times, he knew how to make a comeback—and he came back in *style*. He went to Hollywood, he went to Vegas, and he stayed the same as when he was a poor boy. And he can help you make your comeback, yes he can!''

''How's he gonna do that?'' came a voice from the back of the audience.

''Well, that's what I'm here to tell y'all,'' said Rev, grinning broadly now. ''On account of he spent so many years in Vegas, the King knew how folks could get in over their heads at the casinos. Losin' money they couldn't afford to lose, bettin' on somethin' they thought was a sure thing. Takin' out loans at bad interest rates to pay off their tabs, or sellin' all their valuables. Well, I've found out that some of y'all are in that same fix. And here's what I'm a-gonna do. Every one of you who comes forward and pledges to follow the King, the Church will pay your gamblin' debts in full, one lump sum—you'll be on that comeback trail right there and then. How's that sound, now?''

''That sounds too good to be true,'' came the same voice from the back of the room. The speaker rose to his feet, and everybody turned to see Do-Wop standing there, a suspicious look on his face. ''Ain't no free rides, not where I come from. So what's the catch, Rev? I'm in far enough over my head to grab anything that floats. But I wasn't born yesterday. I want to hear the whole swindle—what do *I* have to do if the King pays off my tab?''

''Why, I'd think that's understood, son,'' said Rev. ''You would be promisin' to become one of his faithful followers. To do like he said, and bring the message to other folks, too.''

''I figured that much out by myself,'' said Do-Wop, his arms folded across his chest. ''So what's the scam? Lay it on me, Rev, so I figure out whether to bite or not.'' He stood there expectantly, and the assembled legionnaires fell silent, waiting for the answer.

''You've got to be a true follower,'' said Rev. ''That

means you have to make a pilgrimage to Graceland, back on old Earth—you can't be a full believer till you've done that. And it means making yourself in his image. His faithful often have plastic surgery to be more perfect, although it's not required right away. And . . ."

"Hold on, Rev," said Do-Wop. "Plastic surgery? I gotta change the way I look?"

"That's right, son, changing the way you look is a way to change the way you act, so you won't be cruel. After everything the King is gonna do for you, it's the least you can do to show how you appreciate him. Why, I've had the operation myself—take a look." Rev turned one side of his face to the audience, then the other, before looking back at Do-Wop and smiling. "Now, what do you say, son?"

Do-Wop looked at the chaplain, his face an unreadable mask. The room was dead silent, as everyone waited for him to speak.

Finally, he looked at Rev and said, "Man, I can't do it. Count me out—I owe Sushi enough to send *him* on that trip to Greaseland, but I guess I gotta pay it off myself."

"What?" said Rev, his jaw dropping. "Why? What could possibly be wrong with my offer?"

Do-Wop looked him squarely in the eye and said, "Rev, the way I see it, you're offering me a face worse than debt."

The crowd dissolved in laughter.

6

Journal #307

*My employer was confident that a focus on the company's
military priorities would allow his people to forget about
the external problems, which would then more or less resolve themselves. As I had feared, this belief turned out to
be over-optimistic. In fact, the problems remained on the
edge of everyone's awareness, putting the entire command
cadre into a constant state of anxiety that something would
boil over into an outright crisis.*

*The only two who seemed unaffected by the ongoing crises
were Flight Leftenant Qual, who went around the hotel
observing and making enigmatic comments; and Chaplain
Rev, who despite Do-Wop's public refusal of his offer to
pay off gambling debts, seemed to be winning a fair number
of converts. For the rest, it was chaos as usual . . .*

"OK, rookies, fall in," shouted Brandy. The new recruits
hastily assembled themselves into a formation—most with
a helter-skelter clumsiness she hoped they'd soon outgrow,
but the Gambolts flowed into position like water running

downhill. Brandy had to admit, she'd never seen anybody so natural at the things a legionnaire had to do. "Now we're going to have some fun. Today we begin unarmed combat instruction. Sergeant Escrima will assist me."

Standing on the thick gymnastics mat next to Brandy, whose physical bulk more than matched her parade-ground vocal equipment, the mess sergeant looked for all the world like a miniature statue of a human being. That was highly misleading, as the new troops were about to learn.

"OK, I'm going to demonstrate a basic move, and then you'll get a chance to try it for yourselves. Can I have a volunteer?"

The rookies looked at one another nervously—they'd already had occasion to find out how strong Brandy was. A couple of hands went up, tentatively. Brandy ignored them, and pointed to Mahatma. "Here, this isn't hard—why don't you try it first?"

The little round-faced man—his belly had already begun to lose its roundness—came forward onto the mat and Brandy stood facing him. "I'm going to show this to you in slow motion," she said to the troops. "This is a very basic move, one that lots of others are built on. Watch." She stepped closer to Mahatma.

"Now, watch what happens first," she said. Brandy reached out her hand and pushed Mahatma in the center of his chest. He stepped backward, keeping his balance. "OK, Mahatma, tell me what I did and what you did."

"You pushed me, and I stepped away," he said, smiling as always. "Would a battlefield opponent let you push him like that?" It had become almost a joke: Whatever you did to him, Mahatma took it with a smile—and followed up with a question that threatened to undercut the whole exercise.

Brandy temporized. "I'll get to that. For now, the idea is, when I push you, you start to lose your balance. You're falling backward, so you step back to catch your balance again. Sounds easy, when you explain it. But let's try that again, with a little difference."

She stepped up to Mahatma, and again pushed him in

the center of the chest. But this time, her foot had snaked out to ensnare his leg before he could catch his balance, and he fell backward onto the mat.

"You see it?" she asked the other recruits. "Keep the opponent from stepping backward, and he's got no place to go. All he can do is fall." She reached down and helped Mahatma to his feet. "Now, you try it on me."

"All right, sarge," said Mahatma. He reached up and pushed Brandy, putting his foot behind her. She fell down, twisting as she fell, and rolled back up to her feet almost as soon as she was down.

"That's the second part of the lesson," she said. "If your opponent knows how to recover, you won't have the advantage for long. So you have to be ready to follow up right away. Now, who else would like to try it?"

This was the point at which she usually got somebody who'd had a little martial arts training as a civilian. One of the new troops—the one who'd had his hand up before, she noticed—had a smirk on his face. "OK, Slammer, your turn."

Slammer swaggered out of the lineup, and took a stance opposite Brandy, his weight evenly balanced on the balls of his feet. He had obviously had training, and he looked to be in better than average physical condition for a recruit. Brandy suppressed a smile, then said, "Aw, let's make it a little bit more of an even contest. I must outweigh you twenty pounds." (It was more like fifty, but nobody had ever called her on that—not to her face.) "Here, Sergeant Escrima is more your size."

Escrima stepped forward to take Brandy's place, his face impassive. Now the recruit had the weight advantage— probably thirty pounds, and several inches in reach. "OK, Slammer, let's see you try the move on Escrima."

As Brandy had anticipated, Slammer grinned broadly and stepped up to Escrima, evidently planning on some spectacular throw instead of the simple technique she'd demonstrated. The recruit grabbed the little sergeant by one arm and began to turn so as to flip him over his hip. What happened next was hard to follow, but it ended with Slammer falling flat on his back from what seemed a considerable height, with an impressive thud. Escrima pounced on him like a hawk, one knee across a biceps, one hand on Slammer's throat, and the other poised in a fist in front of his face.

"Third part of the lesson," Brandy said to the other recruits, who stared in awe at their fallen comrade. "Never take an opponent for granted. You go into combat, there's no such thing as a fair fight. No rules, no refs, no timeouts, and no points for style. Slammer tried to get fancy with Escrima, and look where it got him."

Escrima let Slammer get up, and the recruit returned to his place in the formation, rubbing his biceps where the sergeant had kneeled on it. "OK, now you're going to break up into pairs and try the move I showed you. Stick with the lesson, and we'll show you all more moves as soon as everybody's had a chance to practice this one."

The recruits broke up into pairs, spreading around the mats and trying the technique Brandy had shown them. Inevitably, a few of them had trouble even with something this elementary—and others tried to show off, attempting more complicated moves. It was about as typical a training session as Brandy had ever seen.

Except for the Gambolts. Their feline anatomy put an entirely new twist on everything. Pushed backward, even with a leg confined, they would simply do a backflip and land back on their feet, quicker than any human athlete. Once again, the Gambolts were simply leagues beyond their human counterparts. The other recruits had noticed by now, and there was muttering among them. When the exercise was finished, there was a distinct look of resignation on a number of the recruits' faces.

As the training session progressed, there were more and more discouraged faces. The Gambolts made everything look easy, and the humans were rapidly coming to realize that they were outclassed by three recruits as fresh out of civilian life as they were. Normally, Brandy would have known what to do with a recruit so clearly superior. After all, a sergeant had the benefit of years of training—and a willingness to play whatever trick was needed to bring a recruit into line. A few quick falls with someone like Escrima, and even a fairly advanced martial arts student would be properly humbled.

But the Gambolts were so good, she wasn't sure even Escrima could put them in their place. It didn't take much foresight to see that this was going to be a real problem . . .

"Those Renegades are still snooping around, Captain," said Lieutenant Rembrandt. "I'd like to find some way to get rid of them."

"I take it they haven't done anything we can use as grounds for barring them from the casino?" said Phule, tapping a pencil on his desk. For the second or third day in a row, the daily officer's briefing was shaping up as a series of unsolved problems. He didn't like that, but for the moment, the problems remained intractable.

"Not unless we do it for general obnoxiousness," said Lieutenant Armstrong. "That's within our rights. From what I can tell, anything a casino owner wants to do—up to and possibly including outright murder—is legal here on Lorelei."

"That's one of the few benefits of the mob having made the rules for so long," said Rembrandt, nodding. "We can bar anyone from the Fat Chance for any reason we concoct. But I don't think we can expel them from the station unless we catch them cheating at the tables, or damaging casino property, or running some kind of credit fraud. And the Renegades have been careful not to do that."

"Where are they staying?" asked Beeker. "Perhaps you could call in a favor from one of your fellow casino owners."

"They're at the Tumbling Dice," said Rembrandt, a sour look on her face. "That's Maxine Pruett's home base. Not much chance of calling in a favor from *her*."

"No indeed," said Phule, glumly. "In fact, it wouldn't surprise me to learn that she had something to do with their discovery that Chocolate Harry was here with us." A frown came over his face. "Interesting that we've had so many outsiders arriving to make trouble for us all at the same time, isn't it?''

''The Renegades, the Yakuza, and the IRS,'' said Beeker. ''There does appear to be a pattern there. At least, young Sushi appears to have deflected the Yakuza for the time being. And I can certify that your personal books are in excellent order—even if the revenue agents are inclined to nitpick, I am confident that you can come out of anything except the most hostile audit with a clean nose.''

''Good man, Beeker,'' said Phule. ''I have complete faith in you to handle that end of things. But the Chocolate Harry situation has to be taken care of. Turning his supply depot into a fortified position has kept the Renegades at bay, but the hassle factor is hurting efficiency. When somebody has to go through a security checkpoint to get a can of vacuum grease or a spare battery, they're likely to go without—and that means some piece of equipment won't be working right. On the other hand, if we make C.H. dismantle all his defenses, the Renegades will have an open shot at him.''

''Which brings us back to the question of how to neutralize the Renegades,'' said Armstrong, scowling. He slapped his hand on the arm of his chair and said, ''I say we snatch them when they're off their guard, then find some pretext to kick them out of Lorelei. Let Maxie yell about it after they're gone.''

''You would risk getting people hurt,'' Beeker pointed out.

''We'll be in a sad state when the Legion can't handle a few civilian brawlers,'' said Armstrong. He raised his chin, and his chest swelled. ''I expect we'd deal out considerably better than we got, Captain.''

''I know our people can take care of themselves, Lieutenant,'' said Phule. ''But we're in an enclosed space full of civilians, and we can't go throwing our weight around every time we feel like it. I'll try your approach if nothing else works, but I want to see what other options we have, first.''

''There's another problem with that approach,'' said

Rembrandt. "If Maxine Pruett's causing all this trouble, throwing the Renegades out would be only a temporary solution. She'll find another way to harass us—and I think we can count on her to keep doing it as long as we're here."

"You're right," said Phule. He closed his eyes and massaged the bridge of his nose. "I suspect she *is* behind most of our recent troubles, though I can't prove it. If she can keep us responding to a hundred minor nuisances, she'll weaken us for responding to a really serious threat from some other quarter. It's classic guerilla tactics."

"Is there any way to go after Pruett directly?" asked Armstrong.

"Not without exceeding our authority," said Phule. "And not without risking civilian casualties. For that kind of direct action against her, we'd need a really blatant provocation—and Maxie's not foolish enough to provide one. Even if she did, General Blitzkrieg would find a way to turn it to our discredit."

"You know, I wonder if this company hasn't outgrown its mission here," said Rembrandt. "Lorelei looked like a plum assignment when we got it, and—all difficulties aside—our stint here has been very rewarding. But casino guard duty isn't exactly what I joined up for, and I'm afraid it's having a negative effect on the company's readiness for its larger mission."

"Hmmm—I'd begun to think something like that myself," said Phule. "The casino doesn't need an elite Legion company to break up bar fights and discourage cheaters. I'm afraid a lot of our people are in danger of losing their edge because nothing they do requires it of them."

"That's how I feel," said Armstrong. "A bunch of civilians could do most of this job as well as we can. If it weren't for Pruett trying to horn in, we could leave our actors-in-uniform behind to stand guard. With a cadre of trained security guards to take care of more serious trouble, the place would be as safe as it is now."

"You're probably right," said Phule, nodding. "The only flaw in that picture is that Maxine Pruett won't go away. Even if she did, some other mobster would step into her shoes.''

"Back to square one," said Armstrong. "If the place weren't so profitable, I'd advise you to wash your hands of it."

"Oh, I'd sell in a nanosecond, for the right price," said Phule. "The worst mistake an investor can make is holding on to something past time to sell it."

Beeker nodded approvingly. "Remember, though—it's just as bad to sell something too early, out of panic. Maxie Pruett would love to see you sell the casino too cheaply. She'd have control of it within six months—if not immediately."

"Yeah, I bet she'd be moving in the back door as you went out the front," said Rembrandt.

"Well, for now, I'm standing pat," said Phule. "The right time to move on will come—and when it does, we'll be ready. Until then, we'll make the best of what we have."

"Yes, sir," said Rembrandt and Armstrong. Neither one looked especially happy.

"Too much happening," said Tusk-anini wearily. "Not good—can make one little mistake into very big one."

"I know what you mean," said Super-Gnat. The diminutive legionnaire was freshly off duty, and was still wearing the cocktail waitress costume that allowed her to move among the casino crowds without attracting undue attention—except from those gamblers whose glass was empty. "This company can handle any kind of trouble, as long as we attack it as a team. But now we've got Chocolate Harry holed up because of those outlaw bikers, and it's a major expedition to get into supply depot. And you saw those IRS agents sneaking around for info about the captain. What's worse, it looks like we've got a spy in the company."

"Is method for this in military textbooks," said Tusk-anini. The giant Volton legionnaire had been spending late nights poring through books on every conceivable human subject, especially Lieutenant Armstrong's library of military history texts. "Hold position against one enemy while concentrate strength against another. *Defeat in detail*, is called. Work good in theory, maybe not so easy in practice.''

"*Not so easy in practice*," repeated Super-Gnat. "That ought to be the Legion motto—at least, the way most of the Legion runs. We're lucky to have a commander who doesn't do things the regular way, you know, Tusk?"

Tusk-anini snorted—it was a very piglike snort, which somebody not used to Voltons might have taken wrong. Super-Gnat knew it was the equivalent of a low chuckle in humans. "Is more than luck," he said. "Captain had to make some bad mistake to get sent to our company. But he no fool—and that no joke, either. He show us we can be best company in Legion, and make us work hard to do it. He got to be best commander in the Legion."

"I'm with you on that one," agreed Super-Gnat. "But remember, he didn't get here without making enemies— and not all of them are outside the Legion. Mother told me that the top brass think the captain's showing them up, and they want to put him in his place. That's bound to mean trouble for the rest of us, too. We've come through everything OK so far, but I keep waiting for the other shoe to drop.''

"I no hear shoe drop," said Tusk-anini, his eyes narrowing suspiciously. "When this happen?"

"Uh, that's not meant literally, Tusk," said Super-Gnat. "What I mean is, I keep expecting them to send the company someplace really rotten, like the middle of a war zone or something, to get the captain in trouble."

"That not going to happen, because there no wars going on right now," said Tusk-anini, patiently. "You worry too much, Gnat."

"Maybe I do," said Super-Gnat. "But remember, it hasn't been so long since there was a war—in fact, I hear tell that's where the captain pulled the SNAFU that got him sent here. I don't know whether you were paying attention to the scuttlebutt, but word was that he talked a couple of pilots into strafing an enemy position—except he didn't know that's where the peace talks were going on. And it's a big galaxy—there could be another war breaking out almost anywhere, and we could find ourselves being sent to fight.''

''Who we fight?'' Tusk-anini looked skeptical—not easy behind his specially fitted dark glasses, worn to protect his sensitive eyes from normal light. ''No enemies around to fight—plenty of room for all species, not like old Earth before space flight. No reason for wars.''

''So why's there a Space Legion, then?'' Super-Gnat put her hands on her hips and stared up belligerently at her big partner. ''For that matter, why's there Regular Army or Starfleet? Seems to me the government's paying a lot to keep fighting forces around if there aren't going to be any more wars. But that's not what I'm getting at. Even if there's not a war, there are ways the brass could try to shaft the captain—and believe you me, Tusk, they'll be trying to find them.''

Tusk-anini snorted again. ''Captain not alone. Maybe generals find some way to get captain in trouble, but we no let it happen because trouble for captain mean trouble for us.''

''You've got the right idea there, Tusk,'' said Super-Gnat. ''But there's one thing you should never forget: Generals usually don't *care* about whether they get regular troops in trouble. We're warm bodies to throw at a problem until it goes away. That's what makes our captain different—he cares about us because somehow, deep inside, he knows he's like us. So we have to take care of him, too.''

''We take care of him,'' agreed Tusk-anini. ''So let other shoe drop—we catch it before it hit the floor.''

''That's the right idea,'' said Super-Gnat. ''Now that we've got that much figured out, why don't we go down to the pub and see if we can figure out which foot the other shoe is on?''

The Omega Mob had never formally adopted the Olde English Pub, in the basement of the Fat Chance Casino, as the company watering hole. Nonetheless, at any given hour you could find legionnaires hanging out there—sipping a drink, playing games, or tossing darts, and talking about the things that off-duty military personnel have talked about from time immemorial. The legionnaires didn't keep the civilian casino customers from using the Pub—the captain would have frowned on any attempt at that—but they clearly set its tone.

The Pub was especially noisy tonight, with several groups of legionnaires, in and out of uniform, gathered in different sections. There was a serious game of Tonk going on at one table; Street was the big winner so far, but Double-X had been on a hot streak for several hands, and the banter between the two was getting louder as the stakes got bigger. At the corner table farthest from the blaring trivid set, Doc and Moustache were playing a quieter, if not necessarily calmer, game: blitz chess. Two or three other legionnaires looked on, waiting to play the winner.

In still another corner, Do-Wop was holding forth with a string of stories, most of which were of highly dubious veracity, although he swore up and down that he had been a witness, if not a personal participant, in all of them. The circle of listeners included Dee Dee, between sets on her evening show, Junior, Super-Gnat, and Tusk-anini. The latter, perhaps because of his limited experience of human ways, was the only one who didn't appear downright skeptical of Do-Wop's yarns.

"So then I say to the cop, 'Yeah, I'm the owner of this whole building,'" said Do-Wop. "Well, I could tell he wasn't buyin' it . . ."

"Why you want cop to buy building?" asked Tusk-anini, his eyes riveted on Do-Wop.

"Not the building, Tusk—I wanted him to buy the story, see?" Do-Wop tapped his fingertips on the tabletop. This was not the first interruption from the giant Volton.

Tusk-anini's frown deepened. "You want him to buy story? Was cop magazine editor?"

"Aw, gimme a *break*, Tusk," said Do-Wop, while the ring of onlookers broke into laughter. "I might as well try sellin' hooch to robots. Just let me finish the story, and then ask your questions, *capisce*?"

"But I no *capisce*," said Tusk-anini, who had spent plenty of sessions listening to Do-Wop's stories in the past. "That why I ask questions."

Do-Wop threw up his hands. "Jeez, cool it with the questions for a while, will ya? Now, where was I?"

"Probably about halfway to getting yourself thrown in jail," said a new voice, and Do-Wop looked up to see Sushi, standing there with a broad smile.

"Yo, man, long time no see!" said Do-Wop, jumping to his feet and throwing an arm around his partner. "Last anybody heard, you was kidnapped by the Yazookas."

"*Yakuza*, and there was only one of them," said Sushi, laughing as he returned Do-Wop's hug. "And the guy didn't kidnap me—we went off to transact some business. Which went exactly the way I wanted it to, I might add."

"Knowin' you, it was some kind of monkey business," said Do-Wop, who'd been a complete stranger to the subtler forms of chicanery before Phule had teamed him with Sushi. "You gonna tell us the story?"

"Hey, you no finish *your* story!" protested Tusk-anini, as Sushi plopped himself in a vacant chair, signalling for the waitress.

"Later, Tusk, later," said Do-Wop, waving his hand at the Volton. "The man's been runnin' games, and I gotta know the score. Spill, buddy, spill!"

Sushi leaned forward and began, "Well, I guess everybody's heard about the start of it. I was on duty in the casino, in the blackjack section. The dealer spotted a couple of players passing cards . . ."

"Sssst! Careful what saying, here comes spy!" said Tusk-anini.

"Spy? Where?" Sushi looked puzzled.

"Quiet, he's coming this way," whispered Super-Gnat, putting a hand on Sushi's elbow. "Let us handle him, and we'll tell you what it's about later."

Sushi nodded just as Flight Leftenant Qual came up to the table. Agile as he was when running flat-out, his normal walking gait was a comic waddle. "Greetings, comrades," said the little Zenobian. "May I join your gathering?"

"Guess we can't stop you," muttered Do-Wop.

"Ah, that must be humor!" said Qual. His translator gave out a strange sound somewhere between a hiss and a snarl, which might have been its attempt to render Zenobian laughter into human speech. Whatever the meaning, it did nothing to ingratiate him with the legionnaires.

Qual pulled an empty chair over from a nearby table and seated himself between Tusk-anini and Do-Wop, both of whom cast baleful stares at him. "So, is this how Legion spends evenings?" he asked, looking around the group.

"Who needs to know?" asked Do-Wop. His tone did not invite further discussion.

Qual's translator was not set to make fine distinctions between tones. "Pardon, did I not introduce myself? I am Flight Leftenant Qual," he said, showing his teeth. "Military attaché from Zenobian Empire."

"We know who you are," said Super-Gnat, her voice dripping icicles. "And we know what you're here for, too."

"Excellent," said Qual, slapping the table. "It is to be sympathetic, not so? Let this one purchase the next circle of drinks!"

"No want drink," said Tusk-anini, his eyes narrowed.

"Me neither," said Do-Wop, though his glass was empty. He was not often known to pass up a round when someone else was buying. The others who'd been sitting at the table all indicated their refusal.

The only exception was Sushi. "Well, I just got here, so I'm dry," he said. "If you're buying, I'm drinking."

"Excellent," said Qual, slapping the table again. "I am doleful none of your comrades are thirsty, but perhaps some different time. I like your custom of having one bring the drinks—it makes more time for mingling than when each must go to the pool for itself."

"Assuming you want to mingle," commented Super-Gnat, casting a significant glance toward Qual. "And now that I think of it, I guess I've had all the mingling I want tonight. Tusk, are you ready?"

"Tusk-anini ready," agreed the Volton, rising to his feet.

He nearly brushed the ceiling, towering over the little Zenobian. "Good seeing most of you," he said, and turned to follow Super-Gnat away.

"Time for me to get ready for my third set," said Dee Dee, standing up. One after another, the others at the table also made excuses and exited. Finally only Sushi sat there with Qual, waiting for their drinks to come.

"A shame so many had to leave," said Qual. "I will simply have to get to know them some other time."

"So it would seem," said Sushi. He pulled his chair up closer to Qual. "But there's no reason for us to be strangers. Tell me, Flight Leftenant, what kinds of things are you most interested in finding out about our people?"

"Why, almost everything," said Qual, his teeth gleaming in the flickering barroom lights. "You are much unlike my race in many ways. To begin with . . ."

The conversation stretched into the late hours.

7

Journal #310

The key to happiness in life is timing. This is certainly true in finance: Sell stock early or late, and you will always blame yourself. The same is true in military affairs: A general who commits his reserves too soon may see them beaten back by an enemy still strong, and one who delays is likely to find the battle already lost. Even a thing as trivial as entering a room can be done at better and worse times.

My employer had the knack of good timing. Perhaps it was inherited—his father had certainly been adept at timing the introduction of new products. Or perhaps young Phule had simply inherited a more mysterious, but even more useful, trait: the ability to convince everyone around that what one has just done was precisely the right thing to do at that particular time.

"Too good?" Armstrong guffawed. "Some of our troops are too good? That's the first time this company's been accused of that!"

"Lieutenant, I sincerely hope it's not the last time," said Phule, pacing behind his desk. "But if Brandy says it's a problem, I want to hear about it. Sergeant?"

Brandy had an unaccustomed worried look on her face. "Well, Captain, those Gambolts are so good that the other recruits can't keep up with them. I ask for a hundred push-ups, and they finish them before the rest have done twenty. We practice unarmed combat and nobody can touch 'em. We haven't run the obstacle course yet—it's still being set up, over in the park—but I'll bet my stripes that when we do run it, the Gambolts will make everybody else look sick."

Armstrong let out an appreciative whistle. "Great. This company's needed somebody to set an example for our people. Now the rest have something to emulate."

"Except they can't," said Brandy, shaking her head. "They might as well try to outrun a laser beam. Any time speed or strength or agility makes the difference, the cats have the humans completely outclassed. And the whole training platoon is starting to get discouraged. Unless we can figure out something, their morale's going to go straight down the pipes, Captain."

"It seems to me we had this same problem right after I came to the unit," said Phule. He pulled out his desk chair and sat down, leaning forward. "It was the obstacle course that gave us all the answer, if you'll remember."

"Sure, I remember," said Brandy. "That turned the whole company around—showing us that working as a group we can accomplish things that only a few of us can do by ourselves."

"The recruits need to learn that lesson," said Phule. "And I think the Gambolts especially need to learn it. But for it to work, we'll have to change the exercise a little. Tell me what you think about this idea . . ."

He went to the sketchboard and began outlining a variation on the Omega Mob's obstacle course exercise. At first Armstrong and Brandy were skeptical, pointing out flaw after flaw. Phule adapted his plan in response to their objections, and soon the three were working together, eagerly designing the new exercise. It was late at night when they declared it ready, but they were convinced they had the answer.

Still, the whole plan depended on the new troops rising to the occasion. So far, there'd been no sign they were capable of it. Unless that changed, Phule's Company was in danger of returning to the mediocrity from which it had risen.

"What the hell's going on over there?" Maxie Pruett gestured toward the Fat Chance Casino. The gesture was unnecessary; everyone in the room knew exactly what she was referring to.

"As far as I can tell, Boss, not a damn thing," said Altair Allie. Maxie had sent Allie to keep an eye on the Fat Chance as soon as she'd heard that her plans for Phule's Company were ripening. "There was that one day when all hell broke loose, with the Yakuza guy starting a fight, and the little lizard playing chase through the casino, and the tax collectors and bikers showing up, and then nothing. The Army guys are acting like it's all routine."

"Not Army—Space Legion," said Laverna.

"Legion, schmegion," said Altair Allie with a dismissive wave. "They got guns and uniforms, and that's Army enough for me. Point is, they're acting like nothin's wrong."

"Precisely," said Laverna. "They've announced a major training exercise scheduled for tomorrow afternoon. Open to the public—we'll be watching, of course. In fact, I plan to go see it myself. Still, they're carrying on as if they hadn't noticed any of the aggravation we've been sending them. We pulled a lot of strings to give them all that grief. Greased quite a few palms, too."

"And I expected a hell of a lot more effect," said Maxie, with a fierce frown. "They ought to be worried . . . No, more than that. Under that kind of pressure, they ought to be sweating bullets. What's wrong?"

"The Yakuza agent shipped out two days ago," said Laverna. "He and the woman who came with him left without contacting us, so we don't know what happened there. But the impostor they came looking for is still very much alive."

"That's right, I seen him in the Pub last night," said Altair Allie. "Didn't look like he'd lost any sleep lately."

Maxie's frown deepened. "What about the Renegades?"

"They're still hangin' out," Altair Allie answered. "No action yet, far as I see. But part of the hotel is closed off to outsiders now, and it didn't use to be. It could be they're hidin' some new secret weapon or somethin', but I'd lay you two-to-one that big mug Chocolate Harry—the one the bikers are after—is hidin' out there."

"Well, if he is, he has to come out sooner or later," said Maxie, nodding. "All we have to do is keep those Renegades around to nail him when he does. And that won't be hard. A free first-class hotel room and meals on the house are a pretty good incentive, don't you think?"

"I'd hang around for that," said Altair Allie. "But not gettin' any action might get to 'em after a while."

"If they get antsy, we'll stir up some action for 'em," said Maxie. "A good old-fashioned smoke bomb in the right place can scare a lot of people out of hiding . . ."

"Legionnaires aren't a lot of people," said Laverna, shaking her head. "I wouldn't bet on that kind of trick working."

"And since when did you become such a legionnaire fan?" Maxie snapped. "Is that fancy-dressing butler sweet-talking you into double-crossing me?"

"You know better than that," said Laverna. "You pay me to tell you the truth, and that's what you're getting from me. The next time I pull my punches will be the first time."

"I didn't say you were pulling your punches. I said you were taking the Legion side," Maxie retorted, standing up and walking around the table. She aimed a finger at Laverna from point-blank range, and bellowed, "If you double-cross me, you're finished. Got it?"

"I knew that a long time ago," said Laverna, still calm. Her nickname, the Ice Bitch, had never seemed more appropriate. "I'm not under any illusions; my only insurance

is being too useful for you to do without me. That's what
I'm doing now—telling you something you need to know.
I shouldn't even have to tell you—you should remember
the last time you tried to play rough with Phule's people.
You don't want to see what they can do if they get really
angry—as I'm certain they would if you flushed Chocolate
Harry out of hiding for the Renegades to catch.''

"I didn't say anything about doing it ourselves," said
Maxine. "I figured we might drop a little hint here or
there . . .''

"I know what you meant, and so do you," said Laverna.
"Do what you want to do—that's your usual way, anyhow—but don't pretend you'll like all the consequences.
You might even try not to get angry at me for warning
you.''

Maxine glowered, but nodded. "OK, I get the idea. All
right, then. We won't poke up that hornet's nest. Besides,
we still have the IRS on his tail. Allie, any report on
them?''

"They're poking around and asking people questions,
but that's about it," said Altair Allie. "That's their game,
though. Pop up out of nowhere with a piece of paper that
says you owe 'em everything you got. If soldier boy ain't
playing by their rules, he's a goner. And there ain't nobody
in the casino game can play it straight enough for them
buzzards—not and still make a buck, they can't.''

"Tell me about it," said Maxine. "Well, now that
they're on to him, we'll have to let them play it their way.
And hope they don't notice anybody else on Lorelei.''

"Present company, for instance," said Laverna grimly.
Maxine looked at her intently, but the Ice Bitch's face be-
trayed no sign of emotion. Perhaps it was only an offhand
comment—and perhaps it was a subtle hint that Laverna
might have other kinds of insurance against her boss than
she'd admitted. Whatever it was, Maxine didn't like it one
bit. But there wasn't much she could say about it, for the
moment.

"You bastards don't have any right to do this," shouted
Gears, as two stone-faced bouncers unceremoniously hus-

tled him out of the Three Deuces. Neither bouncer answered. At the doorway, they picked him up between them, gave him a couple of warm-up swings, and tossed him bodily into the street. He landed in a heap, but rose quickly to his feet, turning with raised fists to confront his adversaries. Too late: They'd faded back inside the door, not even waiting to see if he'd try to return.

Gears stood for a moment, pondering what he should do next. He wasn't drunk enough—though he was nearly angry enough—to charge back in and confront the bouncers. *That* game had only one likely outcome. He patted his jacket pocket. His wallet was still there, where the bouncers had shoved it after frog-marching him over to the cashier to collect his winnings. They'd cashed his chips honestly enough, then stuffed the money into his wallet and given him the heave-ho. But they'd made it clear he wasn't welcome to gamble in the Three Deuces again. No gambling house likes system players, especially not when their system actually wins.

What now? he asked himself. It was late—not that that made any significant difference on Lorelei, where the casinos and saloons were open round-the-clock, ready to take a sucker's money any time he appeared. But it did make a difference to Gears, who had to be ready for duty back at the Fat Chance in just under four hours. Some of that time ought to be spent sleeping—if he wasn't going to nod off on duty, and get yelled at by Chocolate Harry, which he wasn't anxious to try.

He sighed and looked down the street toward the Fat Chance, then shook his head. His luck was hot tonight—even with a system, you needed luck to win big. Tonight the dice had been coming up right. It would be a shame to quit when everything was in the groove. He turned the other way, and went looking for another casino.

Next thing he knew, he was in an unfamiliar neighborhood, with dimmer lights and fewer people than the ones he normally frequented. Belatedly, it crossed his mind that it might not be as safe, either . . .

That was when a large, dark shadow loomed from a

nearby alleyway, and a gravelly voice said, "You just found the wrong part of town, buddy."

"Who's that?" said Gears, suddenly aware that he and this newcomer were the only ones on this side street.

"I'm not stupid enough to tell you that," said the stranger, in a surprisingly reasonable tone of voice. In the dim light, Gears could see that he was dressed in workman's clothing, and muscled like a man used to heavy physical work. He was also very big. The stranger stepped closer and said, "The less you know about who I am, the less you can tell." He reached out a huge paw. "Just give me your money and it'll go easy with you."

"No way in hell," said Gears, and he spun away from the man, already breaking into a run. He remembered an open saloon at the next street corner; he'd go there and call the Fat Chance for backup.

He'd barely taken two steps before something slammed into him from the side, knocking him to the ground. His breath went out of him in a rush as the attacker landed on top of him, and the gleam of a blade in the other man's hand put a stop to any idea of fighting back. "What's the hurry, sonny boy?" said a voice in his ear. "We ain't done talkin' to ya."

"You really should have given me the money," said the big man, kneeling down next to Gears. His voice sounded genuinely sad. "Now you've got my friend involved, and he's a lot nastier than I am."

"That ain't no way to talk, Chuckie," said the second assailant. "You're likely to make sonny boy think we don't like his kind hereabouts. Truth is, we likes 'em fine."

"Long as they aren't stingy with their money, that is," said Chuckie. "OK, tourist, my friend's going to let you get to your money so you can hand it over, and then we'll all go our separate ways. Now, don't make any tricky moves. I don't think you want to find out what he likes to do with that vibroblade."

The second man sat up; this took his weight off Gears's chest and arms, but kept his legs pinioned. The blade hovered over his unprotected belly. "You heard Chuckie," he said. "Give us the money and nobody gets hurt."

Gears had won a lot of money that night—nearly enough to pay off his debt. But the blade was hard to argue with. "All right, take it easy," he said. "Just let me get to my pocket."

Gears reached for the pocket where his wallet was, but as his hand approached it, the man pinioning his legs brandished the knife and grabbed his wrist. "Hold still," the man said. "Let's see what's in there." He reached down and removed the wallet. "Well, sonny boy's a good boy after all," he said, handing it to his partner.

"You'd be surprised how many people my friend has had to cut because they thought they could outdraw him," said Chuckie. He opened the wallet and whistled. "Sonny boy's been lucky tonight."

The other man looked up at the money, and Gears saw his chance. A quick chop to the wrist sent the vibroblade flying, and Gears followed with a punch to the throat, throwing the man to one side. He pushed his way free of the choking assailant, and made a leap for Chuckie, who'd fallen back.

Chuckie held him off with a straight arm, long enough for the other man to recover first his breath and then his knife. He threw a crushing forearm around Gears's throat, and a moment later, the legionnaire felt the blade throbbing next to his rib cage. He went limp.

"Tsk, tsk. That wasn't very smart," said Chuckie, in a mock sympathetic voice. "Now we'll have to hurt you— it's bad business to let people think they can fight back without getting hurt, you know."

Gears saw motion off to one side, and then a mechanical-sounding voice said, "Great Gazma, what a curious sight! Is this a common economic transaction?"

"This isn't your business," said Chuckie, moving ominously toward the speaker, whom Gears now recognized as Flight Leftenant Qual, the Zenobian. "Walk on by before something happens to you, too."

"Oh, no, this appears to be one of my comrades," said

Qual, moving forward. "It would not be soldierly not to assist him."

"One step closer and I cut his liver out," snarled the man with an arm around Gears's throat. "Stand off and nobody gets hurt."

"I take exception," said Qual. "You are now the ones in danger of a hurt. Let the human go, if you would."

"We wouldn't," said Chuckie. "Now, we're going to back away real slow. You stay right where you are if you want your friend safe. My partner's dangerous when he gets nervous, and I'm afraid you've put him right on the edge."

"How unfortunate," said Qual, stopping and touching something on his belt. "Perhaps he needs a period of inactivity." He held out his hand and did . . . *something*. Gears felt a sudden lethargic feeling overcome him, and he slumped to the ground. He was vaguely aware of the arm around his throat coming loose, and as he fell, the other man's body dropped to the ground next to him. Idly, he wondered what had happened.

Then Qual was standing over him. "Rest, friend, and have no concern," said the Zenobian. "I have communicated to Mother to send us help—all the trouble is complete now."

I don't know what he did, but I think he saved my life, thought Gears, and then unconsciousness overcame him.

"Am I making a mistake to trust him, Beeker?" Phule pushed aside the sheaf of printouts he'd been reading during breakfast and leaned back in his chair.

"I take it you are referring to Sushi, sir?" said Beeker. He set down his coffee cup.

"Right," said Phule. "Do I continue to trust a man who can take control of my Dilithium Express account, or do I safeguard the money—and show him I don't trust him? When the lives of everybody in this unit could depend on that trust some day?"

"One always needs to strike a balance between trust and security, sir," said Beeker. "There are things that every member of your company needs to know—daily passwords, for example. But only a few are cleared to receive top secret information—and yet nobody takes that as a matter of distrust. The fewer people who know some things, the more secure we all are. It would seem axiomatic that access to your money needs to be restricted."

Phule took a sip of juice and rubbed his chin. "That's great advice, Beeker—except, what is there that's more secure than Dilithium Express? If he can hack that account, is there anything he can't hack?"

"Perhaps not," said Beeker. "But if Dilithium Express is vulnerable, obviously some alternative is necessary."

"I guess you're right," said Phule. "Too bad there's no way to keep the information quiet—but even if we captured that Yakuza agent, there's no way of knowing he hasn't already reported to his bosses. Or that any of several people have not figured out what happened."

"Yes, the genie is out of the bottle," said Beeker, his face impassive as always. "Now our goal should be to minimize the damage it can do. Or better yet, to turn it to our advantage."

"I don't see how I'm going to get any advantage from having people know my credit account is vulnerable," said Phule. He stood up from the table and began to pace. "As far as I can tell, the only person who comes out of this with any advantage is Sushi, if you get right down to it."

"Oh, I believe there may be a way to profit from Sushi's skills," said Beeker. "Sometimes, letting everyone know you can do something is as good as actually doing it. Word that one of your men can meddle with a Dilithium Express account should make its way through the criminal underworld quite rapidly. This will undoubtedly prompt many of them to turn all their efforts toward duplicating the feat—but of course, you will have protected your assets against any such attempt."

"I see," said Phule. "And while they're doing that, they're not trying to attack us in other ways. Well, it's not much of a silver lining, but I'll take what I can get. But we still need a way to protect my assets without losing easy access to them."

"As to that, sir, I have a suggestion I believe you will find of interest," said Beeker, a faint smile on his lips.

"Do you, now?" said Phule. "What do you have in mind?"

Beeker was about to reply when Phule's wrist communicator buzzed. "Yes, Mother?" he said, wondering what new crisis had occurred.

"Get yourself prettied up and don't drag your feet, sweetie," came the familiar voice from the communicator. "Your favorite brass hat wants to see you on the holophone."

"General Blitzkrieg?" Phule's jaw fell.

"Well, it sure sounded like him to me, silly boy. If I were you, I'd hurry up and talk to him. I can stall the old lizard-face as long as you need me to, but I doubt it'll improve his not-so-sunny disposition."

"Give me three minutes," said Phule. "Did he say what it was about?"

"You must be out of your ever-lovin' mind," said Mother. "Now, get your tail movin', toots—that three minutes is already started, and as much as I'd enjoy giving the general the run-around, I'm worried about what he'd have done to me if he found out I was wastin' his time." She broke the connection.

"General Blitzkrieg," said Phule, looking at Beeker. "He certainly picked an interesting time to call."

"Yes, sir," said Beeker, looking at Phule critically. "You've enough time to comb your hair before you talk to him. It would be exactly in character for the general to waste the first five minutes of a trans-space holophone call reprimanding you for your appearance."

Phule grimaced. "I wish I had time to change the whole uniform, but I doubt it'd make any difference. Let's hope the news isn't too bad this time."

"Sir, I doubt very much that even General Blitzkrieg could do very much to make the situation worse," said Beeker. He paused a beat, then added, helpfully, "Of course, if there's any way he can make it worse, I'm sure he'll be glad to do it."

• • •

General Blitzkrieg was smiling. It was not a pleasant smile, but Phule tried to ignore that and concentrate on what the general was saying. "Captain, I must admit we haven't always seen eye to eye, but it seems somebody's bought the image you've created for your unit. Your company has been requested for an assignment that might be a genuine feather in the Legion's cap—assuming your people are up to it, of course. Wouldn't want to send them if they can't deliver, you know."

"I'm pleased to hear that, sir," Phule said cautiously. He stood at attention, facing the general's holographic image across the room. He knew Blitzkrieg could see his every move, as well as he could see the general's. He would have to make an effort to keep his emotions off his face—never easy with someone as infuriating as the general.

"I have complete confidence in my people," he continued. "What sort of assignment, sir?"

The general's smile stayed on. "There's a world that just got over a civil war. Well, to tell the truth, the Federation had to step in toward the end and stop things from getting out of hand. The Legion had a part in that, I'm proud to say. They've got a new government in power, and they're making progress toward putting things back on track. But of course, there are factions that aren't happy with the new order, and so the Federation has been supplying troops to keep things in hand. A peacekeeping team from the Regular Army is being rotated out, and we've managed to convince Ambassador Gottesman to accept a Legion unit as their replacement. It took some politicking, believe me, but when the ambassador found out the Legion was available, he asked if we could send your unit."

"That sounds like a genuine coup, sir," said Phule. "What's the planet called, if I may ask?"

"It's got some silly name—let's see ..." The general frowned, then leaned over and punched a button on a computer somewhere offscreen. "Landoor. They call their world Landoor."

Phule thought a moment. "I don't recognize the name,

sir—not that it makes much difference, of course. You say they requested my company specifically?''

"That's right, Captain,'' said the general. The predatory smile was back. "I admit I was surprised—you haven't always been my idea of a model officer, you know. But you have had a knack for getting favorable news coverage, and evidently that's paid dividends. All things considered, I must admit it hasn't hurt the Legion as much as it might have. So we've decided it's time for you to wrap up the guard assignment on Lorelei and get ready to transfer to Landoor.''

"Yes, sir,'' said Phule. Then, after a pause, he continued, "Uh, as you no doubt realize, sir, my company is the majority stockholder in the Fat Chance Casino. That makes us the contract holders, and naturally we're very concerned about continued security after we're transferred away. We'll need sufficient time to arrange a replacement before we can leave.''

The general's smile vanished. "Captain, this is no time for barracks-room lawyering. There's a whole planet asking for your company to protect its people, and all you're worried about is your pocketbook. That's not the Legion way, and I'll be hanged if I'm going to stand for it.''

Phule held his ground. "Sir, with the general's permission, may I point out that the security of Lorelei is of concern to far more people than just my company? Several thousand people arrive on this station every day, staying for an average of five days, and they spend an average of three thousand dollars apiece during their stay—on hotels, food, gifts, and entertainment as well as on gambling. They come with families and children, too—and they expect a safe environment. Some of them are retired, and a lot are ordinary working people who saved up their money for a dream vacation. Any breakdown in casino security affects them more than it does my pocketbook—because from their point of view, they have much more at stake.''

"Fine sentiments,'' said Blitzkrieg. "Or they would be, coming from any other officer. Coming from you, I suspect they're a ploy to look altruistic as you protect your own interests. Quite frankly, Captain, you aren't a team player.''

"I take exception to that, sir,'' Phule said, rather hotly. "I treat my people not just as members of a team, but as a family. Believe me, these troops have very little tolerance for posturing. They'd find me out in a minute if I was merely paying lip service to that dogma.''

"Perhaps,'' said General Blitzkrieg, momentarily taken aback by Phule's fervor. Then he recovered his aplomb; he leaned forward and pointed a finger at the transmitting camera, and at the man viewing his image. "But the Legion can't permit officers to set their own conditions for accepting an assignment. If you refuse the assignment, you'd better be ready to justify that decision to a court-martial. And I can tell you now, Captain, all your headlines won't do you a lick of good if it comes to an insubordination charge. And I'll make sure it *does* come to that. Now, are you going to accept the Landoor mission or not?''

Phule didn't hesitate. "Sir, my company will go where the Legion sends it.''

"Good, that's settled, then,'' said Blitzkrieg, although without great enthusiasm. It was easy to guess that he'd wanted Phule to give him an excuse for an insubordination charge. He frowned at Phule and said, "You will ready your company for shipment to Landoor in—''he turned and looked at the readout again—''sixty standard days. That will be all, Captain!'' Blitzkrieg broke the connection.

Phule sighed, and turned to Beeker. "Well, that's done,'' he said with a weary smile.

"Yes, sir,'' said the butler. "Now you can withdraw your company from Lorelei, and no one can question your motives or impugn your honor.''

"True,'' said Phule. "But that's not the whole story, Beeker. If Blitzkrieg thought I really *wanted* this transfer, he'd break his back to prevent it. Now, he'll make sure we stay there long enough for me to get the unit back on track. This new assignment will give the company a worthy common goal—and that kind of motivation is exactly what's been missing here.''

"I suppose so, sir,'' said Beeker, skeptically. "I'd think

the opportunity to build the company's portfolio would have been enough to motivate them, but perhaps I fail to comprehend the military mentality.''

Phule cracked a wry grin. ''Military mentality? After watching my interview with the general, I'm surprised you even use those two words in the same sentence.''

Beeker sniffed. ''Sir, I suspect that the general's mental powers are beneath ordinary calculation. However, some of your troops show a modicum of intellect, albeit in my opinion largely misdirected. It was to them that I referred.''

''Thank goodness,'' said Phule. ''I was afraid it was some backhanded reference to me.''

''Sir,'' said Beeker, pulling himself up even straighter than usual, ''let me assure you that, had I wished to refer to you in a derogatory manner, I would have done so in such a way as to leave no doubt as to my intentions.''

''Good. I was afraid you might not be feeling well,'' said Phule. ''Well, that still leaves us one question to settle. Now that we've gotten something we want from the general, what are we going to do with it?''

''Well, sir, I think you had better begin by informing the company,'' said Beeker. ''Some of them, I suspect, will be a good bit less sanguine than you are about departing this station.''

''Man, I'm gonna miss this joint,'' said Do-Wop, setting his lunch plate down at a table with three fellow legionnaires. Word about the company's reassignment had gone out in midmorning. Within an hour it was the only topic of conversation among the Omega Mob.

''Are you really?'' Super-Gnat raised her eyebrows. ''I'll be glad to get back to a real planet, myself. Something about natural sunshine and fresh air . . .''

''I be happy if not too much sunshine,'' said Tusk-anini, who came from a nocturnal race. ''But fresh air good to breathe. Soft ground feel good underfoot, too.''

Do-Wop had already begun shovelling food into his mouth. But between two forkfuls he mumbled, ''I'm a city kid, y'know. I hear the place we're headed for is the real boonies—jungles and swamps. If they got any sidewalks at all, I bet they take 'em in after dark.''

''That not true,'' said Tusk-anini. ''Landoor City have more people than Lorelei, lots of buildings, too. I know—I study maps and books.''

''Yeah, but what's there to do?'' growled Do-Wop. ''I mean, here we got all kinds of entertainment, lotsa places to grab some action, y'know? What's Landoor got?''

''Not as much as here,'' said Sushi, who had done his own research as soon as he'd learned of the new assignment. ''It had some pretty lively resorts back when the mines were working, but that was in your grandpa's time. Now the main attraction is the scenery—some nice beaches and mountains, they say. And supposedly some pretty good amusement parks.''

''Hey, that could be cool,'' said Do-Wop. ''I ain't been on a good roller coaster since before I joined the Legion.''

''That's not why we're going there,'' Super-Gnat pointed out. She took another of the warm butterhorn rolls Escrima had made for that night's meal, and said, ''We've got a job to do, is all. I'm glad we're not being sent to some iceball asteroid to do it. In the Legion, you take what you can get. Could you pass the butter, Sushi?''

Sushi handed her the butter plate and said, ''Gnat's right, you know. We've been pretty lucky, since the captain took over. You watch the news, you realize how many rotten places we could've been going.''

''I don't pay no attention to the news,'' scoffed Do-Wop. ''Waste of time, if you ask me.''

''That why we no ask you,'' said Tusk-anini. ''Sushi and Gnat telling truth—plenty bad places to go to.''

''Yeah, and I'm afraid we're about to go to one of 'em,'' said Do-wop, helping himself to a roll. ''Those people just had a war, right? So some of 'em must still be shooting each other, if they need peacekeepers. Maybe they start shooting at *us*. Don't tell me that's better than what we got here.''

''You don't want to hear, so why you want us tell you?'' said Tusk-anini. ''Me, I wait and see new place. We going there whether like it or not. Tusk-anini will try and like it."

"That's the attitude I like," said Brandy, stopping to eavesdrop on the conversation. "It figures Do-Wop starts griping about a place before he even gets there."

"Ah, give us a break, Top," said Do-Wop, looking up with a hurt expression. "A guy's got a right to gripe a little bit, ain't he?"

"Sure, gripe all you want," said Brandy. "But don't expect anybody to give you any sympathy if it turns out you actually like the place." She grinned and went on her way to the dessert counter.

"What the hell's that supposed to mean?" said Do-Wop, as the others at the table laughed.

"I don't know for sure," said Super-Gnat, "but I think it means she expects you to piss and moan no matter what's going on."

"Well, sure," said Do-Wop, puzzled. "What else is a guy supposed to do to pass away the time?"

The others at the table laughed again.

"So you're going away," said Laverna. She and Beeker sat in a softly lit back booth in the Tumbling Dice Casino's Domino Bar. The other tables near them were empty; this time of afternoon, most of the casino's customers were at the gambling tables. Anybody who wanted a drink could have it delivered to the floor. That made this a perfect spot for a quiet talk.

"My job is moving to another planet," said Beeker, shrugging. "I can't very well do anything but go with it."

Laverna toyed with her glass. "I don't believe that for one minute," she said, staring at the butler. "You could retire right now and be comfortable for life. Don't bother to deny it—I looked it up after a few things you said, and I know just how much you have. You're not going to be buying a private asteroid as your retirement home, but you're not going to miss that regular paycheck, either. So you damn well *could* stay here, if you felt like it."

"I suppose so—although this place is hardly my ideal retirement home." A few bars of brassy music came over the sound system as Beeker paused, weighing his words carefully. He continued, "Since you make no secret of having looked into my financial state, I will admit having researched yours. It appears to me that there is no financial reason for you to remain with your employer, either."

"No financial reason," said Laverna. She lowered her head, then looked up at Beeker. "Still, I won't be buying that ticket any time soon. I think you know what I mean, Beeker."

"Yes, I understand what you are saying," said Beeker. "Let me point out that, if you really wish to leave, there are ways it can be done. Once you are off-station, it becomes that much easier for you to disappear."

"Yes, if I don't mind spending the rest of my life hiding," said Laverna. She shook her head. "I'd mind that less than most, I suppose—time to read all the books I've never had time for, time to try writing something of my own. I've never lived the kind of life that attracts attention. But that's not the problem. I know too much, and Maxine can't afford to let me out of her control. Even if she were gone . . ."

"Her successors would worry about what you might reveal—or might be made to reveal, if you turned against them. And the successors would have no personal ties to you to make them hesitate." Beeker leaned forward and lowered his voice so the music prevented his words from being heard beyond their table. "Still, if you wanted to try, my employer and the Space Legion have resources beyond those of any private person."

Laverna was quiet for a long moment before saying, "And why should Phule use those resources for my benefit? You don't expect me to believe he'll do it out of benevolence—or because you have asked him to help me. As for the Legion—I don't really think I'm the sort to join—not at my age, anyhow."

"Actually, there's rather a tradition of people joining the Legion because they want to escape the past," said Beeker with a thin smile. He sat back up and looked around at the garishly decorated room, before leaning forward and continuing. "In my employer's unit, at least, the food and accommodations are as good as in any luxury hotel—and the retirement plan is actually rather good. Granted, the work is sometimes dangerous . . . but you're used to that, of course."

"Stop it," whispered Laverna. "You're starting to sound like a recruiting sergeant." She peered at him intently. "You don't really mean it, do you?"

Beeker steepled his fingers. "I merely offer it as an alternative to staying here, recognizing as you do that eventually someone will decide that you know more than is good for them. As an intelligent and perceptive woman, you must have given some thought to making your escape before that moment comes. It seems to me that now, with your employer's influence waning and competitors beginning to circle, is as logical a time as any. But of course you have to judge the moment for yourself."

Laverna's eyes looked from one side to the other, making certain nobody was within hearing distance. "You know, Beeker, you might be right about that," she said. "I'm not going to make any decisions on the spur of the moment, you understand. But you have given me something to think about."

"Don't think too long about it," said Beeker. "The opportunity won't be here much longer, you know."

"I know," said Laverna, and she fell silent. The music system was playing a sinuous minor-key dance tune from two decades ago, music from when they'd both been young. An innocent time, before either had known much responsibility.

The conversation, when it resumed, moved on to other things.

8

The average visitor to Lorelei never even learned the location of Gladstone Park, let alone set foot in it. It was not one of the space station's leading tourist attractions—in fact, it was not designed for tourists at all. Its official function was to supplement the station's air-recycling system, cleaning the excess CO_2 from the atmosphere and replacing it with fresh, organically generated oxygen. The chemical processors were as close to perfect as to make no difference, but many customers persisted in believing that air "naturally" cleaned by twenty square kilometers of trees and grass was somehow better than the "artificial" stuff the recyclers produced.

Had it been their choice, the casino owners would have had no compunction about digging up the grass and trees and replacing it with a few more casinos. After all, it contributed nothing to the station's economy, which was almost entirely gambling-based. The tourists who'd come to Lorelei wanted artificial light and late hours and the frantic hustle-bustle of money changing hands. Just knowing that

the park existed was a sort of security blanket for them.
Very few tourists wanted to actually go there.

But the full-time residents—the workers in the hotels, ca-
sinos, bars, and restaurants—needed someplace to unwind,
someplace they could look at a green surface other than
the top of a craps table. A croupier might find it rejuve-
nating to ride a bicycle on his day off, and a cocktail wait-
ress might enjoy sitting on a bench and resting her eyes by
looking at flower beds. Even the bosses found the park a
great place to take the workers for a corporate outing, to
display their benevolence by setting out an opulent spread,
and to prove that they still had the common touch by getting
out on the field for a pickup gravball game with the em-
ployees . . .

Shortly after its arrival on the space station, Phule's Company had begun making regular use of Gladstone Park for
training exercises. Its variety of "natural" terrain, from
dense woods to open meadows to rocky hillsides made it
a useful simulation of conditions likely to be encountered
planetside on many worlds. After all, Phule had no illusion
that the company's assignment to Lorelei was a permanent
one. He knew that sooner or later, the Legion's top brass
would give Omega Company an assignment that put it to
the utmost test. When the call came, Phule wanted his legionnaires to be ready for it.

But today was a special exercise—not least because so
many spectators had come. It was not unusual for a small
group of Lorelei's inhabitants to observe the legionnaires'
maneuvers. Some of these, Phule knew, were spies for rival
casinos trying to spot some weakness in the troops guarding
the Fat Chance Casino. He accepted the challenge and made
sure the show was always sufficiently daunting to discourage anyone foolish enough to think about taking over the
casino by force—not that any had been willing to make the
attempt, after the convincing defeat of Maxie's bid.

Today, though, the exercise had been publicized, and had
drawn a good crowd of curiosity seekers anxious to get a

glimpse of the legendary Gambolts. The publicity had stressed the cat-like aliens' reputation as the finest troops in the galaxy, as well as their being the first Gambolts to volunteer to serve in a unit with other species. The publicity had not mentioned Phule's plans for the exercise. Since such plans were not usually announced in advance, nobody thought to comment on it.

Phule looked down at the gathering crowd from atop a portable observation tower the legionnaires had constructed to one side of the exercise field. There among the spectators were the three Renegades, peering intently at the Space Legion troops assembling below his position. *Looking to see if Chocolate Harry has come along*, he thought. Of course, the supply sergeant had been excused from today's activities. C.H. would have to deal with the Renegades eventually—that was a given—but Phule was not going to force him to abandon his defenses. The confrontation, when it occurred, would take place on ground of Harry's choosing. Phule thought he knew how to manipulate the outlaw bikers onto that territory. That was, in fact, one purpose of today's exercise.

He scanned the crowd with his stereoculars (not the mil-spec Legion-issue model, but a custom set from Optronix Ltd., with extra memory for stored images and enhancements for infrared, glare reduction, and infinite focus). Right away, he spotted two more familiar faces: reporter Jennie Higgins and holophotographer Sidney, covering the show for Interstellar News Services. Phule's Company had been hot media fare ever since the commanding officer's flamboyant style had come to Jennie's attention. The resulting attention had been a mixed blessing, but on the whole Phule was glad to have had it. Better a reputation you had to strive to live up to than one you wished you could live down.

There were other familiar faces among the spectators, too. There were half a dozen he recognized as security chiefs for rival casinos, undoubtedly here to pick up hints on his troops' capabilities. And despite her official abandonment of the attempt to run Phule out of business, Maxie had sent her assistant Laverna to view the happenings—or perhaps she had come on her own, although she didn't give the impression of being the outdoor, spectator sports type.

On the other hand, the crowd was full of the spectator sports types, most of whom had come to be entertained—and to bet on whatever was about to transpire. Several bookies had set up impromptu stands, ready to set odds and cover wagers. (It didn't matter that the exact details hadn't been announced; there was bound to be something to bet on, and somebody willing to risk a few units on the outcome.) Phule smiled; once the crowd saw what he had in mind, the bookies would be swamped with business. He was almost tempted to send Beeker over to place some bets on his behalf, but there was little point to it. Any bet large enough to be interesting would skew the odds to the point that he'd get a minuscule return—assuming the bookies were willing to cover it in the first place.

And, reluctant as he was to admit it, it wouldn't be a sure return. He was gambling—even without placing bets, he was gambling—on a system that was about to be put to its most strenuous test. It had been risky enough to pit his whole company against the Red Eagles, the Regular Army's elite company. Now he was pitting raw rookies against Gambolts, the most respected fighters known. He'd find plenty of bettors willing to go against him—and it was not going to be a sure thing.

"Everything's set, Captain," said a voice at his elbow.

Phule awoke from his musing with a start; he hadn't even seen Brandy approaching. "Good work, Brandy. No point keeping all these people waiting, then. Let's get it started!"

"Right, Captain!" Brandy turned to the small group of uniformed figures waiting a short distance away, and barked out her orders. "Gambolts—front and center!"

The three Gambolts moved gracefully through the ranks of legionnaires and came to attention.

"The obstacle course is designed to build the confidence of the entire unit," said Brandy, speaking for the onlookers' ears as well as for her troops'. "This company has its own special way of running the course, and you'll learn that in due time. But today we have a special exercise for our new members. Flight Leftenant Qual, our Zenobian military attaché, will be assisting us. Are you ready, Leftenant?''

"Ready, Sergeant Cognac," said the Zenobian's translator as the little lizardlike alien stepped forward, his teeth displayed in what Phule knew was intended as a smile, but which most of the spectators instinctively flinched away from. Those who paid attention to such details would have noticed that Qual was wearing not his regular dress uniform, but black fatigues and running shoes.

Brandy turned to the three Gambolts again. "The Leftenant will run the course, and we will give him a three-minute head start. Then you three will try to capture him and bring him to the finish line. He will attempt to reach the end under his own power. You will take every precaution not to injure one another, but short of that, all tactics are legal. Any questions?''

The Gambolts shook their heads—a gesture they'd picked up from their human counterparts since joining the Legion. "Good," said Brandy. "Leftenant, start when you're ready.''

"Bonsai!" shouted the Zenobian, and he took off down the course.

Brandy watched him take off, then turned back to the troops. "Oh yeah, we forgot to tell you one other detail about this exercise. Three minutes after you Gambolts start, the rest of the recruits will follow you. It'll be their job to prevent you from capturing the leftenant. Again, anything they want to do is legit, as long as nobody's trying to hurt the others.''

Surprise blossomed on the recruits' faces. "Sergeant, is this some sort of joke?" said Mahatma. "Of course, we're going to give this our best try. But we've seen what these Gambolts can do. They'll be at the finish, with Leftenant Qual in tow, before most of us have cleared the first barrier.''

"Don't give up before you start," said Brandy, her eyes fixed on her chronometer. Qual was barrelling down the course, showing the same agility he'd demonstrated while leading Phule's legionnaires in a not-so-merry chase through the hotel. "Two minutes to go."

"Qual may have enough of a head start to get there before the Gambolts can catch him," muttered one of the other recruits. "That's our best chance of winning." Several heads in the ranks nodded in agreement.

Meanwhile, the crowd had grasped what was going on, and was rapidly trying to place bets before the issue was settled.

"That lizard's quicker than a flash," said one spectator. "I got fifty says he gets to the end before the cats catch him."

"I'm offering two-to-one on the lizard, even money on the cats," replied the bookie he'd approached.

"No way, you gotta give me three-to-one!" Because of the Gambolts' formidable reputation—and reports of Garbo's quick capture of Qual in the Fat Chance lobby—the heaviest betting was on the Gambolts. Soon, Qual's supporters were getting odds of five- or six-to-one. Nobody seemed to consider the human recruits a serious factor.

"One minute," said Brandy. The Gambolts were stretching their muscles, limbering up for the run. Like the rest of the recruits, they would be carrying full packs for the run—a tradition Phule had insisted on, even though it apparently gave the Gambolts an even greater advantage over the human rookies. Pound for pound, their catlike bodies possessed more raw strength than even the best-trained human athlete could match.

Suddenly one of the onlookers let out a gasp. "Look! The lizard's stopped!" he shouted, pointing down the course. Sure enough, after covering approximately a quarter of the distance, Qual had come to an open area, stopped, and was now sitting down on the ground in the middle of it.

"What the devil is he doing?" said one spectator, who'd been betting heavily on the Zenobian. "Is he worn out, or has he gone plumb crazy?"

"It's a fix!" yelled another bettor. "I want my money back!"

"No way, buddy," said the bookie who'd taken his wager. "You can't afford to lose, don't bet your money. Anybody wants to hedge their bets, I'm givin' two-to-five on the cats."

"Gambolts go!" barked Brandy, and almost as if flung from a catapult, the three Gambolts were streaking down the course, making an incredible pace without showing any strain at all. All three had their eyes on Qual, who lounged almost insolently in plain sight a short distance down the course. Some bettors turned to admire the Gambolts' speed and grace, but others were waving wads of money at the bookies. Within less than a minute, the odds had dropped to one-to-ten. The bookies did their best to stall these bettors, trying to accommodate the few suckers still willing to bet on the underdog Qual.

"OK," said Brandy, seeing the Gambolts well down the course. She turned to face the recruits and put her fists on her hips. "Listen up, people," she barked. "You're Legion, now, and what's more, you're Omega Mob, and that means *family*. We run the obstacle course our own way, and you're gonna see that right now." She reached to her chest and grasped a whistle hanging from a lanyard, put it to her mouth, and blew a shrill blast.

Out of the crowd, where they'd mingled unnoticed in mufti, came the Omega Mob. Not all of them—the guard detail at the Fat Chance had to be kept up to strength—but enough to multiply the strength of the recruit's squad tenfold. "This is your family," said Brandy. "We all run together—officers, NCOs, recruits, humans, Synthians, Gambolts—*everybody*! Let's show 'em how we do it."

Nobody bothered to ask whether the Gambolts' three-minute head start had expired. The spectators watched, open-mouthed, as the Omega Mob, with Phule and Brandy in the lead, surged forward, and the new recruits were swept up with them.

Up ahead, the Gambolts had closed to within a few dozen yards of Flight Leftenant Qual, who had risen to his feet again. Now the Zenobian began to display the same kind of speed and elusiveness he'd given the legionnaires during the chase through the casino, with half the Omega Mob in pursuit.

Dukes had decided to try a full-speed-ahead charge at his quarry, and so he was nearly within arms' reach of Qual when the lizardlike alien feinted to the left, took a sliding step to the right, and then suddenly dived under the Gambolt's grasp. The maneuver put Qual in the clear for a moment, as Dukes somersaulted, recovering quickly from his headlong dive.

Qual did not have long to think about his next move, as Rube was on him almost instantly. This time, Qual put on a burst of speed directly away from Rube—and toward the recovering Dukes, who eagerly spread his arms to contain the fleeing Zenobian.

Just as it looked as if the two Gambolts had succeeded in cornering him, Qual made another sudden change of direction, and Rube, unable to slow down quickly enough, plowed into Dukes. The two went down in a heap, and lay there stunned as Qual sprinted away. That left Garbo, who had held back a few paces from the other two pursuers, the only Gambolt still on her feet. She changed direction, following Qual as if she were attached to his tail with a six-foot wire.

Qual had taken a twisting course, changing direction every few steps, but now he straightened out and sprinted directly back toward the starting line of the obstacle course. In pursuit was Garbo, sticking close but gaining no ground. A few yards behind her, Dukes and Rube were back on their feet, in the chase again. And ahead of Qual was the Omega Mob, picking up speed as it ran the course.

By now, the spectators were in a frenzy. Perched on a hill overlooking the course, they could see all the action. The bookies were now accepting side bets on which Gambolt would catch the Zenobian, with Garbo a clear favorite, although both Dukes and Rube were drawing some support. Despite Qual's impressive show of speed, only the die-hard longshot players were still betting that he would elude all three pursuers.

And, in fact, Qual seemed to be running into a trap of

his own making. Directly ahead of him was a high wall, a much more formidable barrier for the little lizard than for his pursuers. Qual had managed to scale the wall on his way out onto the course, but nowhere near as easily as the Gambolts, who had sailed over it almost without slowing down. Sensing their quarry's predicament, Dukes and Rube spread out to either side, effectively closing off the Zenobian's escape in those directions. As if conceding defeat, Qual stopped perhaps ten feet short of the wall, turning to face his pursuers with a smile.

Then, behind him, the wall fell down.

On the other side awaited the Omega Mob—over a hundred strong.

Phule stood at the head of the company. He pointed forward and shouted, "To the finish line! All together!"

The Omega Mob moved forward like a tidal wave. As they passed Qual and the Gambolts, they picked them up and carried them along with them, chairing them on the shoulders of their comrades, cheering as if they'd won a gravball championship. There were obstacles in their way, but it didn't matter. The Mob didn't slow until they'd reached the finish line, and behind them the course was flat as a pancake.

"I'm still not sure I understand what happened out there," said Jennie Higgins, leaning back in her chair and clasping her hands behind her head. "The Gambolts chased the Zenobian around, and then the rest of the company came and swept them all along to the finish line, without settling anything—the bookies tried to argue that the Gambolts had lost, but eventually the bettors made them call off all the bets. What were you trying to accomplish?"

Phule smiled. It was easy to smile, sitting with someone as pretty as Jennie across the table from him. "There were two things we needed to do for the company, and I think we did them," he said. "And there were a couple of longer-range things I hoped we'd accomplish, although the jury's still out on those."

"And are you going to tell me what those things were,

or do I have to sit here and guess?'' asked Jennie, teasingly.

Phule shrugged. ''Oh, most of it's no secret. The first thing we needed to do was show the new recruits they're part of the company—family, is more like it. That's the basic purpose of our obstacle course exercise, really. We run the course as a company, rather than individually, to show everyone that together they can overcome things very few of them could singly.''

''Yes, that was clear,'' said Jennie. ''That strong esprit de corps has marked your company as long as I've known it. But that doesn't explain why you let the Zenobian run out first, or sent the Gambolts after him.''

''Leftenant Qual got off on a bad foot when he came to join us,'' said Phule. ''Some of the company had the impression he was spying on us. Well, a couple of nights back he rescued one of our people who got in a tough spot, which did a lot to change that false impression. But I wanted to solidify the company's sense that he was working with us, and luckily the Leftenant was willing to play the role I offered him, as a rabbit for the Gambolts to chase.''

''Willing?'' Jennie laughed. ''It looked to me as if he was really enjoying himself out there. At least, as far as I can judge a Zenobian's expression.''

''Yes, I think he was,'' said Phule. ''He has kind of an odd sense of humor, but I think he gets a kick out of being pursued. Possibly because, on their own world, his people are the hunters, and so it amuses him to play the quarry instead.''

''OK, that makes sense, but why have only the Gambolts chase him, instead of the whole company?''

''Two reasons,'' said Phule. He leaned forward and lowered his voice. ''Now we're getting to the part I don't want spread too widely—though I suppose some people will guess it by themselves.''

''I won't write anything that could damage the company,'' said Jennie. ''You should know that, by now.''

''You've been very supportive,'' said Phule. ''Anyhow,

you know the Gambolts' reputation as the finest fighting troops in the Galaxy. They've always served in their own elite units, so it was quite an honor when they asked to join my company.''

"I can imagine," said Jennie. Then, seeing Phule's expression, she guessed, "But it has its downside, too."

"You've got it," said Phule. "They're so obviously superior to our other new recruits that it was affecting morale. I had to counteract that. Chasing Qual let them show how good they are, which is important—they need to feel success, too."

"But not catching Qual right away took them down a notch, as well, I assume."

Phule nodded. "They didn't manage to get Qual cornered until they worked as a team, which was what I hoped for. They tend to be loners, and it was important to get them thinking as members of a team. That was a bit of a gamble on my part—it depended on Qual staying free until then."

Jennie put a forefinger on her chin. "And right when they got him cornered, the company swept them all up."

"Yes, that's exactly it," said Phule, smacking his fist into his palm. "I wanted the company to catch up to the Gambolts just at the moment they'd succeeded in running Qual down—to make them associate that feeling of success with being part of the whole company. The timing was tricky, but Qual carried it off—and I don't mind telling you, it was a relief that he managed to. It all fell together when the rest of the company gathered them up and treated them as comrades. I wanted to inspire them to stop thinking of themselves as competing individuals, and become members of the family—to take pride in each other's abilities. Now we can build on that."

"Well, I hope you're right," said Jennie. "After what I saw today, I'm glad they're on our side. I'd hate to have somebody that good as my enemy."

"Jennie, we count you among our very best friends,"

said Phule, smiling even more broadly than before. If her response was typical, the exercise had a chance to achieve his final, unspoken goal. Now, he had to hope the right people had been watching . . .

9

The shortest route from the officer's mess to the Comm center went through the hotel's ballroom wing. Phule and Lieutenant Armstrong, on their way to their offices after a working breakfast, happened to pass the Grand Ballroom as Flight Leftenant Qual, grinning from ear to ear, led the recruits in warm-up exercises before unarmed combat training. He was leading them through a set of jumping jacks to an improvised cadence that, after the translating circuits had mangled it, had even Brandy falling out with laughter. The recruits looked as enthusiastic as they'd been since joining the Legion.

Phule smiled at the sight. "Well, I think we've finally scotched the rumor that Qual's a spy," he said.

"Yes, sir," said Armstrong, striding alongside. "It was a stroke of genius to have him play bait for the Gambolts in that exercise. That made him the underdog, and the recruits were all rooting for him. That broke down a lot of barriers."

"Yes, that went a long way toward solving the problem," said Phule. "But we got a piece of sheer luck, when Qual rescued Gears—you know him, from the motor pool—

from robbers out in town. That stun ray of his probably saved our man's life."

"Yes, that was very lucky," said Armstrong. "He couldn't have sat down and planned things any better to rehabilitate his reputation."

Phule came to a sudden stop and looked at his lieutenant. "Hmm—tell me the truth, Armstrong. You don't think that could be exactly what happened, do you?"

Armstrong's jaw fell. "Why, that's imposs . . . No, I guess it's not impossible. It is far-fetched, but I suppose Qual could have arranged it. But if the robbers were hired to take the fall, or tricked into it, Qual couldn't be sure they wouldn't talk."

"I think you should call to Station Security and make sure those fellows are thoroughly questioned before they're sent off to prison," said Phule. "Odds are they're small-time robbers who picked the wrong victim. But if there's anything fishy about Qual's being there to make the rescue, we need to know about it as soon as possible."

"Yes, sir," said Armstrong, although he didn't look happy. "That's the way things have been lately, isn't it? Just as we think a problem's solved, it turns out there's a new twist we haven't thought of."

"I'm afraid that's the way of it, Lieutenant," said Phule, nodding sympathetically. Armstrong always wanted problems to be simple, with simple solutions. It had taken Phule a good while to learn that real life didn't always work that way. With luck, his lieutenant would make the necessary adjustment before he had a command of his own. It was one thing to go through life thinking you could ignore all the shades of gray in the world; it was another thing to stake the lives and safety of people under your command on that assumption. Well, Armstrong was learning, a bit slower than he might have, but there was hope for him.

The two officers burst through the door to the command center together. Mother shot them a panicked look, then ducked behind her console. "Good morning, Mother," said Phule. As usual, the reply was inaudible. Phule gave a sigh, and continued into his own office. He'd been working on the assumption that pretending everything was perfectly normal might keep Mother from ducking into a shell every time she had to deal with someone in person. The jury was still out on this approach.

But when he entered his private office, the light on his desktop communicator was blinking. He picked it up. "Yes, Mother?"

"Well, honey-bun, I thought you'd never notice," came the saucy voice in his ear, suddenly bold now that she didn't have to look him in the face. "Got some people want to see you, not that I can figure out why. I assume you're still not interested in talking to those pesky IRS agents."

"That's right, Mother," said Phule. "What did you tell them?"

"Your morning schedule's full, they should check back later, like ten years from now. It's close enough to true, sweetums. You haven't left yourself much time to get organized for this reassignment."

"We'll be ready," said Phule. "And with any luck, I can put off the IRS until we've left the station. That'll give Beeker time to work on my taxes. What else is on the menu today?"

"Another group of civilians dyin' to see you," she said. "You'll love this bunch—all three of 'em look like flunkouts from charm school. Act like it, too. You wanna know their names?"

"Three of them, you say?" Phule's interest suddenly picked up. "Sure, let's have the names."

"OK, sweetie." There was a moment while Mother retrieved the names. "Stonecutter Johnson, Joe the Blade, and Asteroid Annie. Representing the Renegades Hovercycle Club, they say. Shall I give 'em the brush-off?"

Phule sat up straight in his chair. "Oh, send them in, by all means," he said, suddenly alert. "But first, why don't you patch me through to the supply depot? I think the time may finally have come to solve another of our outstanding problems."

"So, Sarge, when these Renegade guys show up, what do we do?" Double-X peered through a slit between the board

Chocolate Harry had nailed over the casino loading dock, now converted to Omega Company's supply depot. The view outside was unchanged.

"We kick ass," said Louie's translator voice. The Synthian brandished his automatic shotgun, as if eager for the impending showdown. "Blow them away."

"Easy for you to say," said Chocolate Harry, "Problem is, it ain't enough to blow away the first guys they send. We finish this bunch off, there'll be others—and more after them. These dudes don't give up a grudge just because they have a tough time settling it."

"Yeah, I can get into that," said Double-X. "Back on Crumbo, where I grew up, the Slambeens and the Ratzers used to go at it like that. Those were some tough guys—steal the glimmer right off a cragbolt, and laugh about it like it was nothin'."

"Yeah, well, you never saw me back down from no cragbolt, neither," said Chocolate Harry, sneering. He asserted this with a certainty bolstered by the fact that he had never to his knowledge been on the same planet as a cragbolt. "A man's got a rep to live up to, he can't pick and choose his fights."

"I guess that's right, Sarge," said Double-X, who like most sensible legionnaires was more in awe of his own sergeant than of any potential adversary—human, alien, or monster.

"Somebody coming," said Louie, in what sounded like a hoarse whisper despite the translator's limited range of expression.

Chocolate Harry leaned over to look at the monitor screen showing the output of the security cameras he had covering the approaches to the supply compound. "Relax," he said, after a moment. "It's the captain." Then, after a longer pause he added, "At least it *looks* like the captain."

"Should I challenge him, Sarge?" asked Double-X, picking up the microphone.

"Nah, I'll hail him on his private frequency," said C.H. "The Renegades might be able to rig somebody up to look like him, but they can't jigger the whole comm system without a lot of work. That ain't their style, anyway—more likely they'd walk up to the door and call me out.'' He reached to activate the wrist communicator, but before he could do so, Phule's unmistakable voice came from the speaker.

''C.H., are you in there? I have something we need to talk about.''

''Sure, Cap'n,'' said the supply sergeant. ''Come on in— we aren't gonna shoot you.''

''Oh, I wasn't worried about you shooting me,'' said Phule's voice. ''But you might start trying to shoot the people I've got with me, and get careless.''

''What do you mean, Cap'n?'' said Chocolate Harry. Then, as he saw who stood next to Phule, his voice went up an octave. ''Look out, Cap'n! It's the Renegades!''

Phule's calm voice came back: ''They've promised not to try anything, C.H.—I think they've realized they'll get more by talking to you than any other way. Will you let us come in and talk?''

Chocolate Harry said nothing for a long moment, his face impassive but his mind racing. At last he said, ''You vouch for 'em, Cap'n? They ain't carryin' heat?''

''They're clean, Harry,'' said Phule. ''Are you going to let us in?''

''OK, Cap'n. Yo, Double-X, Cap'n comin' in, with hostiles. Keep 'em covered, but no shootin' unless they make the first move. Got it?''

''Yeah, Sarge,'' said Double-X, and he went to unbar the door.

Phule and the three Renegades picked their way through the obstacles outside the supply depot, and finally entered the door. Inside, the Renegades stopped and stared. Phule stepped over to the side of his supply sergeant, who stood with his fists balled at his sides. ''Relax, Harry,'' he said in a low voice. ''I think we're going to solve your problems.''

''I know these guys,'' said Chocolate Harry, his eyes fixed on the intruders. ''Stonecutter Johnson, ain't it? And your old sidekicks, Joe the Blade and Asteroid Annie.

Never thought I'd see your nasty faces up *here*."

"Not a bad setup you got, Harry," the big Renegade said, nodding appreciatively. "Anybody starts a rumble with you boys, he better know how to take care of hisself."

"The Legion knows its business," said Phule calmly. "You saw a sample of that."

"You put on a pretty convincin' show," said Johnson, with a grudging nod. "Them cats can *move*. And they're only part of what you got. Make a dude stop and think."

"Yeah," said Harry. "You do that, Stonecutter, and maybe nobody gets hurt. OK?"

"Hey, Harry, we *been* thinkin'. OK?" said Johnson. "When we got word that you was on this station, the club took a vote. Maybe it'll surprise you to know that some of the new guys didn't think it was worth comin' after you, after so many years. But us old-timers remembered what you done to our bikes, and payback is payback, no matter how long it's been."

"Don't matter if there ain't but two of us left alive," growled Joe the Blade. His fingers twitched in the vicinity of his vibroblade sheath, but then he remembered it was empty. He punched his fist into his empty palm, with a curse. Behind him, the Synthian guard took a tighter grip on his shotgun.

"What the hell is this?" said Chocolate Harry, turning to Phule. "Cap'n, you said they was comin' to talk!"

"We're talkin', ain't we?" said the woman Renegade, with a gap-toothed grin that conveyed very little warmth. "Didn't say we was gonna talk *nice*."

"Easy, now, all of you," said Phule. "I don't ask you to be friends after so long, but I do think we can arrive at some way to solve your problems. You Renegades have brought a grievance against Chocolate Harry, perhaps a legitimate one—I don't think he denies that there was some incident in the past."

"Damn straight there was a freakin' incident," growled Stonecutter Johnson. "Harry's a freakin' liar if he says anything else."

"I'd appreciate it if you'd do without the profanity,"

said Phule, his voice suddenly cold. "Whatever the merits of your argument, that sort of language adds nothing to it. Now, what we're here for is to find a way to end this feud, because frankly it's an impediment to the Legion's operation."

"It shouldn't be too hard to end the feud," said Asteroid Annie, sneering. "Give the three of us five minutes alone with the fat boy, and no interference. We'll settle it right fast."

"Harry might surprise you," said Phule, calmly. "But that's not how we're going to solve this. The Legion looks after its own. If you attack my sergeant, you'll find out what it means to take on a full Legion company. And the same goes for any other member of my command."

Stonecutter Johnson put a hand on the woman's shoulder. "That's right, Annie, the Cap'n told us that before, and I believe him. It's the same way we'd be if somebody came after one of our own—or at least, that's how it was in the good old days, before all the snot-nose kids came into the club and let all the biker traditions go to hell."

"A-men, Stony. Things ain't like they used to be," agreed Joe the Blade. His face took on a wistful expression, and he added, "It must be five, six years since I last cut somebody's ears off." He scratched his scraggly beard, and gazed speculatively at the supply sergeant.

"*Cap'n!*" Harry squawked. "You gonna let 'em threaten me like that?"

"Kick ass!" came Louie's translated voice, and the little Synthian brandished his shotgun. "Blow them away!"

"Now who's makin' threats?" snarled Stonecutter. "Cap'n, I didn't think you was lurin' us into a ambush, but if that's how you're playin' it, I'm ready to snaggle." He struck a defensive martial arts pose, and his cohorts followed suit.

"Everyone calm down," barked Phule. "Louie, put that weapon away. These people came here unarmed, in good faith, and that's how we're going to play it. Now, Chocolate Harry, if I understand the situation, these people accuse you of tampering with their hovercycles."

"Well . . ." Harry began.

"Tamperin' ain't the word for it," shouted Asteroid Annie. "He reversed the wires on the hover circuit, so they flipped over when we went to ride 'em."

"And he poured Insta-Stick glue on the seats, so we couldn't get off without taking off our jeans," said Joe the Blade, shaking his fist.

"And he put helium in the reaction tanks and burned out the mass converters," said Stonecutter Johnson. "Any man that'd do that to somebody else's hawg . . . well, he ain't fit to ride, Cap'n. He ain't . . . fit . . . to ride."

"Is this true, Harry?" Phule turned to his supply sergeant.

"Well, Cap'n, it was like this . . ." Harry began again.

"The explanations can wait, Harry. There's only one thing I need to know right now: Is what they're saying true?"

Chocolate Harry pulled himself up to his full height and saluted. "Yes, sir!" he barked.

"That's all I wanted to know," said Phule. "At ease, Sergeant. I told you the Legion protects its own, and I meant it. But these people are entitled to some recompense for what you did to them, and I mean to see that they get it. It's the only way to end this standoff, and to get back to our real business."

"What you gonna do, then?" asked Chocolate Harry, his gaze shifting warily between Phule and the Renegades.

"Yeah, man, what you gonna do to him?" said Stonecutter Johnson. He and his fellow Renegades cast suspicious looks toward the Legionnaires.

"Nothing," said Phule. Then, as the others' mouths opened in protest, he held up a hand. "Nothing to *him*, that is. We're going to follow an old maxim: 'Let the punishment fit the crime.' Sergeant, where is your hovercycle?"

"*Cap'n!*" Harry dropped to his knees like a felled ox. "Cap'n, let 'em cut my ears off! Let 'em tattoo me paisley from head to toe with a dull needle! Let 'em throw me out the airlock, but Cap'n, please don't let 'em have my hawg!"

"Cuttin' them ears off would be fun," said Joe the Blade, grinning evilly. Asteroid Annie's eyes lit up.

"Yeah, go ahead, cut 'em off," bawled Harry. "Cut 'em both off, and shave me with a ripsaw, and then boil me in Chinese mustard. But don't mess with my hawg!"

"Where's the hovercycle?" repeated Phule. "No more delays, Harry. I'll have the cycle or I'll have your stripes."

"Sure, bust me back to buck private, Cap'n," said Harry, still on his knees. "Bust me all the way back, and throw me in the stockade, and dump the key in a black hole, and feed me on sawdust and battery acid. I won't complain, no sir, not one word, long as you don't let 'em have my hawg."

"Hey, man," said Stonecutter Johnson, stepping up to Phule. "We don't care what you do with his fat ass. It was our bikes he screwed with. Give us the hawg and we don't care what else happens to him."

"Is that so?" said Phule. "Will you stick by that? If I give you the hovercycle, will you drop your grudge against Harry?"

"Let us have the hawg, to do whatever we want with it," said Stonecutter, leering. "After that, it's over. Stonecutter Johnson says so, and what Stonecutter says, no Renegade's gonna go against it. That right, dudes?."

"Nothin' but right," said Asteroid Annie, grinning. Joe the Blade nodded his assent, as well.

"Very well, then," said Phule. "Harry—the bike."

Sobbing incoherently, the supply sergeant pointed to a door in back of the supply office. Phule strode over and opened it, to reveal a shining hovercycle—a machine gorgeous enough to make any rider drool. The Renegades let out a collective gasp at the sight. "It's yours," said Phule. "Take it and go—and I'll hold you to your word. The Space Legion will hold you to your word."

"No need for that," said Stonecutter Johnson. "We got more than we ever expected. Chocolate Harry, the feud is off. You don't got nothing ever to fear from us again."

"Thanks a million," said the supply sergeant bitterly.

"I'd rather you'd cut my ears off. Don't stand there and rub it in—take the hawg and go."

"You ain't gotta ask me twice," said Johnson. He gestured to his cohorts, and the three Renegades walked the cycle out of the supply depot, grinning broadly. The door closed behind them.

There was a moment of silence, as they all stared at the door. Then Harry said in a near-whisper, "Great god-a'mighty, Cap'n—I think it worked!"

"Of course it worked," said Phule. "As far as they're concerned, they've got their revenge. And they've got what they think is the single thing you valued most in life. Great acting job, by the way."

"Thanks, Cap'n. Once you called me up and told me what was comin' down, I saw it was the only way to play it. And I really did have a qualm or two seein' 'em take away my good ol' hawg. Even if I couldn't really use it here, that there cycle was my oldest friend. Had a lot of memories connected with it."

Phule clapped him on the back. "Well, I told you I'd replace it, and you know I'll stand by that. You pick the model, and it's yours—soon as those Renegades go back home."

"Sounds good, Cap'n," said Harry, smiling. Then his face turned wistful, and he said, "Maybe there ain't no real hurry, though. There wasn't a whole lot of chance to ride it here, and that ain't good for a hawg. We're gonna get planetside again before long, where I can really crank it up and run—I guess I can wait till then to get a new hawg."

"That makes sense," said Phule. "I'm sorry to see you lose that old one, though. Do you really think they'll destroy it?"

"They ain't that crazy," said C.H. "More likely, they'll take it back home as a trophy—maybe they'll do somethin' to mark it, but no real rider would ever really hurt that bike. I bet they keep it in good shape, break it out and ride it every now and then, to show off how they got their revenge on me."

"And do you think they did?" asked Phule.

Harry thought for a moment. "Yeah, I guess they did—at least by their lights. And I got somethin' I wanted, too—somethin' I never thought I'd see again."

"What's that?" said Double-X, who'd started taking boards off the windows.

Harry's smile was beatific. "Peace of mind, dude, peace of mind. Ain't nothin' in the galaxy to match it."

From his seat at the head of the table, Phule looked around the conference room. For once, he was addressing a group of civilians: the managers and department heads of the Fat Chance Hotel and Casino. He reminded himself that he couldn't take their obedience for granted, as he would with his Legion subordinates. This time, he'd actually have to convince them he was right.

On the other hand, as majority owner of the Fat Chance, he carried considerable authority here. That had its downside, actually—it could mean that a major loophole in his plans might go undetected because nobody had the nerve to call the boss on it. Well, he'd had that trouble with his Legion command at first, too. The people he was leaving here were good enough that any miscalculations he made should be spotted and corrected before they got out of hand.

"Everyone's here, so let's begin," he said. The murmur died down. "You've all heard the news by now, that my Legion company has been transferred to another assignment. That means that we will no longer be available to guard the casino."

"I've heard it, and I think it's a disaster, plain and simple," said Gunther Rafael, the former owner of the Fat Chance. Phule had kept him on as a figurehead manager, and planned on putting him in charge of day-to-day operations once the company was gone. "Your people have been the only thing keeping the mobsters from walking into the casino and taking it over at gunpoint. Quite frankly, I expect them to try exactly that, the minute your ship leaves the station."

"The mobsters have had their wings clipped," said Phule, looking at Rafael. He hoped he hadn't overestimated the former owner. "I don't think you'll find them anywhere near as bold as that. We won't be leaving you without security, you know."

"You might as well," said Rafael. "Everybody knows it's the Legion that's protecting this place. That's kept us safe. When you go, it'll be like leaving babies to guard a bank vault."

"No it won't," said Phule. "As many of you know, most of the 'legionnaires' in the casino are actually uniformed actors. The real Legion guards are out of uniform, undercover. So if a few uniformed personnel leave, it can be explained as normal turnover. As far as the public sees, the Legion will still be here. I'll be away, but that shouldn't affect security."

"It certainly shouldn't," said Doc. He'd been training the actors impersonating legionnaires for the last few months. He was in Legion uniform, with a set of sergeant's stripes—a "promotion" he'd been granted in anticipation of Moustache's leaving with the real Legion. Doc looked every bit the part, standing straight as an arrow at the foot of the table.

"The place was a target before," said Doc, "because the mob thought the new owners would be pushovers. The mob's been pretty quiet since they found out the Legion means business. And after the way the company tore up that obstacle course the other day, I'd guess that just having a few Legion uniforms visible will keep the hoodlums out from underfoot. I doubt we'll have to deal with anything much worse than the occasional rowdy drunk after word of that gets out."

"And we don't need a Legion company to handle that kind of problem," said Lex, who'd taken over managing the casino's entertainment program. "We can take care of that by giving some of our stagehands overtime as bouncers to back up Doc's team."

"You can go a long way in this business by putting up the right front," agreed Tullie Bascom. Phule had lured Tullie out of retirement to run the Fat Chance's gambling operations. "The Legion's rep is all the security we need."

"As far as the other operations, I'm satisfied they're in good hands," said Phule. "The entertainment is the best on the station, thanks to Lex . . ."

Lex gave his best professional smile. "Well, I have to give a lot of credit to Dee Dee Watkins," he said. "She may have the biggest case of artist's temperament I've seen since I first stepped on a holostage . . ."

"And that's longer ago than even *I* want to think about," said Doc in a stage whisper.

". . . but she has the goods to back it up, too," said Lex, grinning wryly as everyone laughed. "And with her signed to a long-term contract, we're set for the foreseeable future."

"There's one more element we'll be putting in place shortly after I leave," said Phule. "Just so my prolonged absence doesn't start the mob thinking, we're going to implement a plan I've kept absolutely under wraps until now. I urge you all not to say a word about this outside this room—because it's the heart of the plan. Beeker?"

"Yes, sir," said the butler, who'd sat quietly in a chair behind his employer. He opened a door and in walked . . . *Phule*. "Good morning, ladies and gentlemen," the new arrival said in a voice indistinguishable from the original.

"What the devil, have you cloned yourself?" said Tullie Bascomb over the babble of voices.

"Not quite," said Phule. "This is a custom model from Andromatic, set up to our specifications. It has a very limited set of functions, but they should be sufficient for the purpose. Most of the time, it'll sit behind a desk, looking busy. But it can also walk around the casino, even sit down for a drink. It can carry on a conversation, as long as it doesn't have to be too profound—and it's programmed to break it off the minute somebody strays beyond general topics."

"Good lord, Captain, you don't intend to leave this android to run the casino in your absence?" Rafael said.

"Oh, it won't be running anything," said Phule. "You and your staff will be doing that. All it has to do is show up often enough to convince people that I'm still on the job. If somebody really needs to talk to me—which shouldn't happen all that often—well, that's what communicators are for.''

''But, Captain, you have a habit of getting yourself in the news,'' Lex pointed out. ''Your company is bound to attract attention in its new assignment, and then your picture will be on screens all over the galaxy—showing you're obviously several light-years away from here.''

''Nobody believes what they see on the news,'' said Phule. ''They've seen too many stories where they used stock footage of some politician—usually, it doesn't matter a bit. Just tell people I'm back and forth all the time, taking care of details on both ends. Andromatic tells me this basic model is very popular with political leaders. It should work for us.''

''So, instead of a Phule running the place, we'll have a dummy,'' said Doc, grinning broadly.

''I can see you've got everything set up,'' said Rafael, after the laughter had died down. ''Well, then, I guess the only thing to do is to iron out the details.''

''I hope so,'' said Phule. ''And the sooner the better. Now, you'll be getting back the block of rooms the troops have been using. That's going to be good for the bottom line, of course, but there'll be some reconversion needed . . .''

The meeting got down to business, with the Andromatic Phule standing behind the original, occasionally nodding as if in agreement with some point being made. After a while, nobody paid it much attention—which was exactly what Phule had hoped for.

10

*Once a timetable had been set for the company's departure
from Lorelei, the actual preparations went ahead smoothly.
The main complication was keeping the withdrawal a secret
from the public—particularly from the local criminal elements that might try to seize the opportunity to press their
own interest in the lucrative casino.*

*I myself thought the elaborate efforts to deceive the mob
leaders, especially Maxine Pruett, were perhaps more complex than necessary. That was before I found an incentive
to take a personal role in the subterfuge . . .*

Lieutenant Rembrandt checked her communicator. Its readout showed Galactic Standard Time as 21:29—half an hour
until the shuttle carrying the last of Phule's legionnaires
was scheduled to leave. So far, everything had gone as well
as anyone could have expected—she was almost tempted
to describe it as having been done with military precision,
except she knew the military far too well. The company's
heavy equipment was already in transit, and would be wait-

ing in orbit when they arrived at Landoor. And almost all the Legion personnel were already on the transport ship.

It was the "almost" that had her worried.

She had a very good idea which members of the company would show up at the last minute. The captain was one of them—no surprise there at all. He was still at the casino, settling the last details of the withdrawal. Nor was she particularly disturbed to see that the captain's butler had not checked in. As a civilian, Beeker was of course not subject to Legion discipline or rules. Most likely, the butler was with his employer—or on an errand for him. Still, he was normally punctuality itself; it would be a real surprise if he missed the shuttle.

On the other hand, the absence of Sushi and Do-Wop was some cause for concern, predictable though it was. Whenever there was trouble, one or the other was likely to be in it up to his ears. This time it looked as if both were involved. They'd never missed a ship, to her knowledge— not yet, at least. But they were an excellent bet to come racing up at the last possible second, with someone or another in hot pursuit. She hoped she wouldn't have to slam the shuttle door in a security officer's face. She'd spent so much time building a positive image for the company, it'd be a shame to leave the station on that sort of note.

But with half an hour to go, she might as well spend the time doing something other than worrying. She pulled out the art history book she'd been reading. She'd never had much interest in the old twentieth-century "moderns"—it seemed curious to call them that, so long after they were all dead and gone—but the author was making a good case that Picasso was, after all, a very talented draughtsman. She turned to where she'd left off and began reading . . .

Maxine Pruett didn't usually answer the communicator her-self. In fact, it was fairly unusual that she even heard its summons. People didn't call her—she called them. If they needed to get in touch, there was an office number, with a secretary during the day and an answering service at night. Only very close personal friends (and there weren't many of them, nowadays) ever called her at home. And when they did, Laverna answered it.

So it took her some time to notice the persistent buzz. She had the sound on the holovision turned up loud, as always, and the comm unit was in another of the suite's eight rooms. Maxie didn't have a nagging fear of missing an important call. That was for other people to worry about. She was perfectly capable of letting the communicator buzz until she felt like picking it up, or turning off the buzzer if she wasn't in the mood. It wasn't *her* that was going to be in trouble if an important message didn't get through . . .

But the damned thing had been buzzing for at least five minutes, and Laverna still hadn't answered. Where the hell was Laverna? Finally, Maxine stomped out to her office—really Laverna's office, since Laverna was the one who used it ninety-five percent of the time—and picked up the handset—a basic, voice-only unit. Nobody in her business wanted a videophone in her private home. "Who's there?" she growled.

"Ah, Mrs. Pruett, I was beginning to wonder if you were there," said a familiar voice.

"Captain Jester," she said, although she knew perfectly well his real name was Phule. Now *this* was a surprise. "What can I do for you, Captain?" she added. She wasn't inclined to do anything for him, but it was good policy to be minimally polite to somebody who had an armed Legion company on call.

"You can tell me where my butler is," snarled the captain. "Better yet, you can send him back—all in one piece, if you don't mind."

"Your butler?" Maxine's brow furrowed. "I don't know anything about your butler."

"Don't play games with me, Mrs. Pruett," said the captain. "Beeker was near your headquarters when he disappeared, and I have reason to believe he had gone there to see one of your subordinates. Now, are you going to send him back or not?"

"I don't know what you're talking abou . . . Wait a minute," said Maxine, suddenly making a mental connection.

"Which of my subordinates was he coming to see?"

"I don't know her full name," said Phule stiffly. "Livorno, Laverne—something like that."

Maxine's teeth clenched. "Laverna? Damn! Captain, can I call you right back? I need to check on something."

"I'll be waiting," said Phule, and gave her the comm code. "Don't take too long, though—I can promise you, you don't want me to send my people over to find out what's causing the delay."

"I don't need your promises to know that," Maxine snapped at the captain. "Cool your jets—I'll get right back to you." She slammed down the receiver and went looking for her assistant.

It didn't take long to determine that Laverna wasn't anywhere in the suite. A quick phone call established that she wasn't in the bar downstairs—her usual watering hole. The last person who'd seen her was the guard at the door. That had been in midafternoon—as she was leaving the building with a conservatively dressed middle-aged man. *The butler!*

"That bitch!" Maxine slammed down the phone. Then she began to figure out what she was going to tell the captain.

"You sure we got time for this?" said Do-Wop.

"All the time in the world," said Sushi, bending over an open panel behind which could be seen complex circuitry. "Quiet, now, I need to concentrate. And make sure nobody's watching."

"Yeah, right," said Do-Wop. He scratched himself and pretended to goof off, gazing back down the little alley next to the casino offices. Night never fell on Lorelei, but it was early evening by Galactic Standard Time, which was the system observed on the space station. There were a few people on the streets—those finishing an early dinner, or casino workers coming off shift—but nobody seemed to pay much attention to a couple of men in maintenance uniforms crouching by an open panel with tools spread around. *Just act like we belong there,* Sushi had told him, and it was apparently working.

"Nobody payin' attention," he reported. He peered back to see how Sushi was doing. The job involved removing a particular chip and replacing it with a slightly more complex one designed to fit in the same slot. That sounded easy, but sometimes the installation didn't resemble the pictures in the manuals. An easy job could become impossible if you only had limited time. There was a wire from some previous repair that was going to have to be disconnected, moved aside, and reconnected when the job was done. A few minutes longer. Well, that's why they always told you to allow more time than you thought you needed to pull off a job.

And now there was somebody looking at them. "Soosh!" he hissed, and tried to act as if he wasn't nervous. "Casino guard."

"Act calm," said Sushi, snapping the new chip into place, and pocketing the old one. "Now all I gotta do is reconnect the repair wire."

"So hurry up and do it. He's comin'!"

"Oh, in that case . . ." Sushi took his soldering laser and quickly played it over the base of the chip they'd removed. He stood up and said loudly, "Look at this piece of crap."

"What the hell?" said Do-Wop, and then the security guard was looking over his shoulder.

"They had the wrong value in. No wonder the bastard burned out so soon. Some guy was too lazy to go back to the shop for the right one." Sushi took up the obligatory repairman's critique of his predecessor's shoddy work.

"You guys workin' late," said the guard.

"Yeah, Liverakos told us finish up this last job," said Sushi. Of course he'd found out the casino maintenance chief's name. "They got a new kid on next shift, and he's late already."

"Yeah, I seen him around," said the guard. There were always new kids around. "Guess he won't be here long."

"Unless he's related to somebody," griped Do-Wop.

He and the guard went on about the ills of nepotism and favoritism on the job for a couple of minutes while Sushi quietly knelt down and finished reconnecting the wire.

"OK, we can close her up," he said. "And then I can find out if my wife's gonna kill me for getting home late."

"Lucky guy, you *got* a wife," said Do-Wop.

"You call that lucky?" said Sushi, and the guard laughed. They wrestled the panel back in place while the guard kibitzed, and Do-Wop tightened the fasteners. Sushi started packing the tools.

"OK, see you boys around," said the guard, wandering back down the alleyway.

"See you," said Sushi. It probably wouldn't be too soon, though. Unless something suddenly went very wrong, they'd be in deep space less than an hour from now. They finished packing up their tools, cleaned up the small amount of debris the "repair" had generated, and walked casually out of the alley.

Across the street, the security guard was standing, looking completely uninterested in them. They walked away quickly.

Maxine was still trying to decide on her story when the communicator buzzed again. She strode over and picked it up. "Yeah?"

It was the guard downstairs. "Boss, that Legion captain's here, with a bunch of soldiers, and they're loaded for bear. The customers are buggin'. How you want me to play it?"

Maxine's reply was instantaneous. "Stall 'em—and keep your own guns out of sight. I'll be straight down." She disconnected, and headed for the door. Halfway there, she stopped and checked her gun; it was ready and loaded. For a moment, she considered leaving it behind—it would be next to useless against the legionnaires' weaponry, and more likely to get her into trouble than to get her out of it—but long years of habit overrode the prudent impulse. She returned it to its concealed holster and stomped out the door.

Down in the lobby, Phule was there with half a dozen legionnaires. From behind the nearby row of quantum slot machines, tourists stared at Phule and his men (although they kept pumping in coins). A few nervous gamblers waited at the window, cashing their chips while they still had the chance. And several bulky gentlemen—plainclothes casino security—occupied seats in the lobby area, studiously ignoring the armed invasion.

Phule turned when he saw her and said, "About time, Mrs. Pruett. I have a confirmed report that my butler was in this building. Where are you keeping him?"

"Keeping him? Are you crazy?" Maxine said, taken aback. "What the hell do I want your butler for?"

"I don't know, but I want him back," said Phule. "And I'm not going to wait very long."

"Look, I don't know where he is and I don't care. Feel free to search the place," said Maxine. She was confident that anything she didn't want him to see was well hidden; the place had been built on the assumption that search parties might occasionally come through. A few had, over the years, though none had penetrated beyond the nominally secret areas where teams of casino employees conducted surveillance and security operations, all perfectly legal and innocuous. Maxine's real secrets were much better hidden.

"You don't care?" said Phule. "Not even if he's run off with your assistant?"

Maxine stared him down. "What if he has? She's of legal age, after all."

"If she knows half as much about your business as he knows about mine, we're both in trouble," the captain hissed. Then he looked around and said, "Is there someplace we can talk? Someplace secure? There are too many people here for my nerves."

"Too many for my nerves, too," she said, seizing the moment. "Most of 'em are your troops, if you want to know the truth. Get 'em the hell out of here, so my customers can go back to playing instead of gawking at all that hardware, and I'm sure we can find a place to talk."

"We can arrange that," said Phule. He turned to his troops. "I'll be talking to Mrs. Pruett. You take up positions outside—with your eyes open. I'll be half an hour—if I need more time, I'll call you." He tapped his wrist communicator. "If you don't hear from me by then, you call me. If I don't answer, you know what to do. Understood? Do whatever you need to do.''

"Yes, sir!'' said the squad leader, a huge man with sergeant's stripes. He signalled the troops and they began to file out the door.

Maxine nodded. "This way,'' she said, and Phule followed her to her office. He took the chair she offered, and they sat facing each other across a large desk. "Now,'' said Maxine, "what makes you think I know anything about your butler?''

"You as much as said so,'' said Phule. " *'She's of legal age'*—you know they're together, or you wouldn't have been talking that way. We'll both save time if we cooperate on this. I want my butler back, you want your assistant . . . maybe for different reasons, but we both want the same thing. We both gain by working together on this.''

Maxine didn't blink. "Working together how?''

"Ah, I knew you'd get down to business when you saw the advantages,'' said Phule. "Here's the way I see it. We can't equal your intelligence sources on-station—we aren't bad, mind you, just not your equal. Yet. We do pick up items you wouldn't, and as far as our off-station sources— well, you're not in that league.''

"You'd be surprised,'' said the mob boss. "But let's say it's so—you're saying we share whatever tips we get? What's to stop somebody from keeping secrets?''

"Really, Mrs. Pruett,'' said Phule. "We aren't going to pass along sensitive information, and neither are you. But we have to trust each other to pass along anything relevant to our mutual business. Just as we have to trust whoever finds the fugitives to return them in good condition—my butler is of no use to me dead.''

"No *accidentally shot resisting arrest,* in other words,'' said Maxine. "Well, I hate to tie my people's hands that way. It's going to make things more expensive.''

"I don't know about your assistant, but I can assure you that losing my butler will make things extremely expensive for me,'' said Phule. "There won't be any accidents, will there?''

"No accidents," said Maxine. "I don't see how I've got anything to lose passing along a tip that might help me as much as it does you, if you'll do the same for us. And we'll pass along your butler if we catch him. My guarantee on it."

"And we'll send your assistant back," said Phule. "Here's what we know: My butler didn't come back from a visit to this hotel, for a lunch date. We searched his room a while ago; there wasn't much missing, just everything he'd take if he weren't planning to come back. And he took a few pieces of, uh, company property that I had issued to him for use in his work. That's when I called you."

"Right, one of our guys saw him leaving here," said Maxine, deciding she could confirm Phule's deduction. "Right about lunchtime, in fact—with my assistant. Ten-to-one those two have gone freelance. They're old enough to know better."

"That's for sure," said Phule. "I thought Beeker was . . ." His communicator buzzed. "Jester here," he answered. He put it to his ear for privacy, but Maxine could hear the buzz of an excited voice—a woman's voice from the pitch. "When? . . . I see. They're certain? . . . Well, we'd never get the authority to run them down in space, but we can grab them at the other end. Who do we know there? OK, stay in touch. Jester out."

"They've left the station," said Maxine.

"Right. Two-nineteen shuttle to the Patriot liner, which went translight three hours ago. Next stop is Trannae. We'll have somebody looking for them when they land. Do you have anybody there?"

"Maybe," said Maxine, trying to remember which family was in charge at Trannae. It was about ninety days' journey to Trannae, if she remembered correctly—which translated to what? *Three weeks shiptime,* she thought. *Laverna would know . . .*

Phule broke into her thoughts. "I'll get the arrival info sent to you as soon as I get back to my office, but it looks as if we've got them," he said. "They aren't going to get off a liner in hyperspace."

"Good," she said. "I think we've got a deal—and now, would you and your soldiers get off my property? You're frightening the marks."

21:48—a little more than ten minutes left before departure time. If the captain hadn't appeared by then, Lieutenant Rembrandt was going to have to delay the shuttle. Her orders said to leave precisely on schedule, no matter what. But she also had her own judgment, and she meant to use it. Abandoning the captain wasn't an option.

A quiet tone notified Rembrandt that someone had entered the corridor she was guarding. She put down her book and stood up to see who was coming. She didn't expect trouble, but she pulled her weapon out of its holster just in case. If trouble did come calling, she was armed with the Phule-proof adaptation of Qual's stun ray.

The broad corridor was well-lit, and so she easily made out the two figures approaching her. They wore regulation Legion black, with unit patches for the Omega Mob. But despite the familiar uniforms, she didn't recognize the faces. One, a lean, black woman, was a complete stranger to her. The other, a heavy-built man, had sergeant's stripes on his sleeve and an ill-fitting full beard . . . there was something about him, but . . .

The eyes gave him away. "Beeker!" she whispered, recognizing him through the disguise. "What's with the chin shrubbery? And who's your friend?"

"The new recruit, Lieutenant," said the butler, his voice a low-pitched growl. "Permission to board?"

"Permission granted, *Sergeant*," she said, doing her best not to let her amusement show. Beeker was the last person she'd ever expected to see in uniform. As for his companion, she was obviously a good bit past the usual age for recruits—even in the Legion, notoriously lax in its entrance requirements. The "sergeant" and "recruit" saluted—superfluous, since she herself was in mufti—and went through the shuttle entryway.

Rembrandt peered along the corridor, but there was no one else. She checked her watch. She had time to finish a chapter, so she sat back down with her book.

She'd read half a page when the alarm sounded again. She looked up to see a single figure approaching: the captain. She put down her book and rose to her feet. "Good to see you, sir," she said. "How'd it go?"

"Smooth as butter, I think," said Phule. "Lex's actors were very convincing as legionnaires, and Maxine bought my line of goods about Beeker and Laverna running off. Did they get here all right?"

"Yes, they were right ahead of you. Very well-disguised, too. I didn't recognize Beeker right away, and if I didn't, his own mother couldn't."

"Good. Then if everyone's here, let's go on board and get started. No need to wait to the last minute."

"I'm afraid there is, Captain," said Rembrandt. "Sushi and Do-Wop haven't reported in."

"That pair!" said Phule. "I should have known they'd find some kind of trouble to get into at the last minute."

"They aren't out on business?" said Rembrandt, frowning. "What if they miss the ship-out?"

Phule shook his head disapprovingly. "They might be able to get on something fast enough to catch up with us at the transfer station at Bellevue, but it'll cost them a bundle."

"And even then they might get caught in a hyperspace loop and get to the transfer point a year late—or early," said Rembrandt. "Serve them right to pay a years' room and board while they wait for us to show up."

Phule chuckled. "Well, if they do miss the shuttle, whatever it costs to get them back to the company is coming out of their pockets. Sushi's dangerously bright, but I don't think he's figured out all the ramifications of 'time is money' yet."

"This may teach him," said Rembrandt, laughing. Then her face turned serious. "What if they're in real trouble?"

"Anything those two can't talk their way out of isn't going to get fixed in a few minutes. I can spare a little more than that, but not much. We'll lift at . . ."—he looked at his watch—"22:15, whether they're aboard or not. I'm going to go give the orders. And Rembrandt . . . ?"

"Sir?"

Phule looked her in the eye. "Don't you get caught behind, waiting till the last second for them to show up."

"I won't, sir," she said, and turned back to her seat by the door. She might as well finish reading that chapter.

"Are you being followed?" said Sushi. He spoke without turning his head, and he'd turned up the volume so the microphone would pick up normal-volume speech at full arm's length. No sense in letting any watchers realize he was using the communicator. He'd have to abandon that trick if he got close enough for anyone to overhear him speaking, but that wasn't a problem yet.

"Can't tell," came Do-Wop's muffled voice through the speaker. "People around—can't talk much."

"OK, hurry—and keep your eyes open," said Sushi. Several blocks back, he and his partner had thought they spotted someone tailing them. It could have been a coincidence, or the security guard back at the casino might have gotten suspicious. They split up—as two legitimate workers would have done. Neither Sushi nor Do-Wop was a novice at eluding pursuit. And if one of them were caught—well, that was better than both.

At the next street corner was an open convenience store. A pair of shabbily dressed men stood on the corner outside the store. *Casino strandees*, thought Sushi—Lorelei had a "proof of work" requirement for residence, which meant that fired casino workers either got another job right away, or were shipped out. Strandees were more common. Usually they were luckless gamblers who'd hocked the ticket home to finance one more try to beat the house. They could survive for a while by scrounging and hitting an occasional small payoff. Sooner or later security caught up to them, and they were on their way anyhow—with a heavy lien against their credit to cover their passage and the fines for whatever offenses Lorelei security decided to charge them with. They weren't normally dangerous, but there was always a chance these two were different. Sushi couldn't spare the time to find out. He crossed the street. Almost at once he became aware that the two were looking at him.

Act like it's all normal, he thought to himself. *Keep alert—plan what you'll do if they come after you.* The store was on the corner of a broad secondary street. A couple of blocks to his left, a hard right, and he'd be at the shuttle departure bay.

He tried to hurry his footsteps without seeming to be in a hurry. The two men were *still* looking at him . . .

"Hey, you!" one of them barked.

Sushi broke into a run. There was an incoherent shout behind him, then pursuing footsteps. He glanced back to see how the pursuit was coming, then expertly flung his repairman's toolbox into the nearest pursuer's legs. The man went down in a tumble of knees and elbows, and his partner stumbled trying to avoid him. That gave Sushi a few extra steps lead, and he intended to make use of every centimeter of it.

Sushi put a little bob-and-weave into his run. He didn't know who he was running from, but the likely candidates wouldn't blink at shooting him in the back. Behind him, the pursuers were on their feet again and coming after him. Well, that ended any chance they were ordinary thieves. They could've hocked the repairman's tools for more money than a worker was likely to be carrying.

Another glance back showed him he was gaining on his pursuers. Ahead, there were only a couple of people on the street between him and the corner. Maybe they were tourists. So far neither had reacted to him. He decided to give both as wide a berth as possible.

The first man he passed flattened himself against the building to one side, clearly unwilling to get involved. Sushi swung wide of him anyhow, in case he was shamming. But the other man stood stock-still, not blocking the way, but not getting out of the way, either. Sushi had a split second to decide which way to dodge when he heard a crash behind him and voices raised in anger. The man ahead of him fell back, astonished. When Sushi saw that, he actually turned and looked back—just in time to see both his pursuers down on the street. Do-Wop was picking himself up and sprinting after Sushi.

Sushi dodged past the astonished man, and a moment later he and Do-Wop turned, side by side, into the alleyway that led to the shuttle entrance. Ahead of them, Lieutenant Rembrandt was rising to her feet, a book in her hand. They were home free. It was a moment's work to duck through the hatchway, dog it shut behind them, and take their seats. Phule gave Do-Wop and Sushi a stare, but said nothing. Minutes later, the shuttle was leaving Lorelei.

Journal #350

Departure from Lorelei did not by any means end my employer's concerns with events on that station. In fact, several of them needed resolution even before our transport ship reached its first stop . . .

Phule looked across his desk at the woman sitting next to Beeker. He wasn't quite sure how to handle this. It had never occurred to him that Beeker's personal life might thrust itself into his awareness. It was hard enough accepting that Beeker had a personal life. Well, no sense dithering; he was going to have to deal with it.

"So, Laverna, do I understand correctly that you're considering joining the Space Legion?" he began.

"I was told that it was the only condition under which the Legion would give me passage off Lorelei," said Laverna, looking at Beeker.

"Well, that's not strictly true," said Phule. "The Legion routinely gives passage to several categories of civilians. Essential staff, immediate families of senior officers . . . Um . . . those don't actually apply, do they?"

"You'd know that better than I do," said Laverna. "I can pay for my fare, if you're worried about that. I assume you can scramble the credit transaction so Maxine can't trace it?"

"Certainly," said Phule. "But I don't think we need you to pay. As company commander, I have a certain discretionary budget, and of course what I spend my own money for isn't the Legion's business, with one or two fairly obvious exceptions."

"If it comes to that, I can pay for Miss Laverna's passage," said Beeker.

"I can pay my own way," Laverna repeated. "Let's forget about that for now, all right? What I need to know is, if I do decide to join the Legion—which I haven't done yet—what kind of choice do I have as far as my assignment?"

"Quite frankly, I don't know all the regulations," said Phule. "I do know you have less choice than a recruiting officer would try to make you think. You can request anything you want, but the Legion makes assignments based on its own needs."

"I suspected as much," said Laverna, with a thin smile. She glanced sideways at Beeker. "But tell me this: If I do qualify for a particular specialty, does the Legion guarantee to train me in it?"

"Yes," said Phule. "There's no guarantee what'll happen once your training's done. Suppose you put in for training as a quantum mechanic and assignment to Altair IV. They'd give you the training—assuming you'd qualify— but you might still end up digging ditches halfway across the galaxy."

"Understood," said Laverna. "Question two: If I do decide to join, my previous identity is kept secret?"

"Yes again," said Phule. "That doesn't mean it can't get out. As you probably know, Chocolate Harry kept his gang nickname when he joined, and was a little too free with details of his past—which let some of his old enemies track him down. And of course, my own family name is an open secret. But I don't think your situation is comparable, especially if you take a few steps to cover your trail."

"You can do all that without joining the Legion, you know," said Beeker. He said it in a level tone, but Phule thought he detected a note of urgency in the butler's voice.

"I realize that," said Laverna, looking Beeker in the eye. "But what I know about Maxine Pruett's business is enough to make me a target—even if Maxine isn't in charge on Lorelei. And it's going to make anybody associated with me a target, including a certain butler."

"I am willing to accept that risk," said Beeker.

"And I'm not willing to subject you to it," said Laverna fiercely. "The only way either of us is safe is if we're apart. Then you can rely on your cover story: I tricked you into helping me escape, then robbed you and abandoned you. They'll believe that of me, so they'll leave you alone. And you won't know where I am, so you won't be able to give me away."

"Perhaps I would wish to know where you are," said Beeker. This time the emotion in his voice was unmistakable, Phule thought, though he still kept a straight face.

"There'll be time for that," said Laverna. "Neither of us is a child. We know how to take the long view. I'll finish my Legion hitch in a few years, and you'll retire from your job at some point in the future. And then we can see what there is to see. I think that is wisest."

"So you are going to enlist, after all?" asked Phule. "If you'd like, we can cut you temporary orders attaching you to this company for your basic training, while your application for advanced training is being processed. When we know where you're going, we can send you there."

"I appreciate the offer, Captain," said Laverna. "But if I am on the same world as you and Beeker for any length of time, someone is bound to come looking for me. Better if, at the next reasonable transfer point, you send me to another Legion base for basic training. That way, the risks for all of us will be minimized."

"Very well," said Phule. "That's a sensible precaution, and I'll make the arrangements for it. Meanwhile, I can put in your application for advanced training, if you know what you'd like."

"Yes, I think so," said Laverna. "I've always thought I'd be a good emergency paramedic. Do you think the Legion needs any of those?"

"I believe so," said Phule, surprised. "I'll put you in for it. Now, unless you can think of anything else we need to settle, I'll get to work on this, and you two can have a little more time together before we change ships. Good luck, Miss Laverna."

"Thank you, Captain," she said, with one of her rare smiles. "To tell the truth, I hope I won't need it."

"I want straight answers from you two," said Phule. He glared at the two legionnaires in his office, trying his best to look intimidating. He wasn't quite sure it was working.

"Straight answers about what, Captain?" said Sushi. His quizzical expression made him look fifteen years old.

"Yeah, we ain't done nothin'," said Do-Wop, considerably less innocent-looking.

Phule sighed. He should have known he wouldn't get anything out of this pair without arm-twisting. "All right, I guess I'll have to spell it out," he said. "You two made it to the shuttle by the skin of your teeth, under hot pursuit. It's a good thing nobody with an arrest warrant walked up to the hatchway before we got it dogged, or you two might still be there."

"But we weren't late, sir," said Sushi, mildly. "I don't see how it makes any difference whether we're on the shuttle an hour before it leaves or thirty seconds before, as long as we're there and buckled in when it's ready."

"Normally, neither would I," said Phule. "You know I run a loose ship, and that's not about to change. I wouldn't have said a word about it except for the latest reports from the team we left on Lorelei."

"Whatever it is, we didn't have nothin' to do with it," said Do-Wop. He had the outraged look of a Federation Senator accused of taking bribes from someone he hadn't thought to solicit.

"I suppose I should consider it a compliment that you think we can manipulate events at that distance," added Sushi, "but we really can't take credit for everything. There are a number of operatives from various criminal organizations on Lorelei, you know."

"Interesting that you automatically assume I'm referring to criminal activities," said Phule, glowering. He paced a few steps, then turned suddenly to face the two legionnaires. "What were you doing that made you so late? And why were you wearing repairmen's uniforms? What were you pretending to repair?"

"Pretending?" the two legionnaires asked almost in unison. Then Do-Wop went on alone, "Jeez, Captain, if we was gonna repair somethin', it'd be *fixed* when we finished with it."

"Fixed is probably the right word," said Phule. He looked Sushi directly in the eye and said, "There's been a very small but steady drain on receipts at the Fat Chance—a fraction of a cent from each credit card transaction—ever since shortly before we lifted off. Not enough for any one individual to notice, but quite a bit if you spread it out over the entire station for the week since we left. Now, I wonder where those odd fractions of a cent are going?"

"Gee, Captain, that's an interesting question," said Sushi. "I guess you think we had something to do with it."

"I'd think that somebody who knows how to gimmick a Dilithium Express card might be able to figure out how to do something like this, yes," said Phule. "You realize, of course, that you're skimming from your own profits here—you two being part-owners of the Fat Chance. Not to mention skimming from all your buddies in the company."

"Hey, Captain, you still ain't proved we're the ones who did it," said Do-Wop. "Just because somebody knows how to do somethin', that don't mean he did it. Lorelei station's full of crooks, y'know."

"Yes, it's been full of them practically since it opened up," said Phule. He turned his penetrating stare toward Do-Wop, who suddenly found something to look at on the floor. "But nobody figured out how to pull this stunt until you two left the station—disguised as repairmen, and running as if you had a pack of ripners after you. I'll ask you again—what were you two 'fixing' back there?"

Sushi and Do-Wop glanced at each other, while Phule

allowed the silence to stretch out. It stretched further, and Phule was beginning to wonder if it was time to abandon the tactic when Sushi shrugged and said, "All right, Captain, if you've already figured it out, there's not much point in trying to hide it anymore. We were opening up one of the hatchways that access the station's climate control system. What most people don't realize is that the same central computer controls all the credit card transactions, as well as some other stuff we weren't interested in. But it shouldn't have tapped into the Fat Chance. It was just supposed to take from the *other* casinos. You know I wouldn't rob the other guys in the company."

"Why not?" demanded Phule. "You can't expect me to believe that one without corroboration."

"Well, before that, I'd planted a chip in the Fat Chance's central computer. That was how I cut off your card when I fooled the Yakuza. Lucky for me, he didn't ask me to use your card at one of the other casinos—it would've blown the whole caper. But that chip was also a one-way filter between the Fat Chance and the rest of the system. You see, I was already planning this little prank back then. I can't understand why it didn't work."

Phule walked up to within inches of Sushi's face and snarled, "Probably because Beeker and I figured out how you had to have broken into my account, and counteracted it. We couldn't inspect the entire system, but we could insert our own override into the software. So when you pulled your *little prank*, the Fat Chance was back in touch with the rest of the system, and your chip stole from us as well as all the rest."

"I told you it wouldn't work," said Do-Wop, glumly. "The captain's too smart for us, Soosh."

"I guess he is," said Sushi. "OK, Captain, I'll tell you where the substitute chip is so you can undo the swindle, and we'll refund all the money it's taken from the Fat Chance. Will that make everything all right?"

"It'll do for a start," said Phule. "Unfortunately, you're going to have to go a step beyond that. I want you to refund all the money it's taken from all the casinos. If I let you keep any profits from this, you're likely to learn the wrong lesson.''

"Yes, sir," said Sushi unhappily. "To tell the truth, that'll actually be easier than separating out the Fat Chance's share.''

"Good. Then I want it done as soon as possible," said Phule. "Can you do it from the ship or do you have to wait till we're out of hyperdrive?''

"I can do it from your desk phone," said Sushi, pointing.

"You'll do it as soon as we're finished talking," said Phule. "One more thing. You two are going to be on a shorter leash once we get to the new assignment. Landoor is a military operation, and we're going to run it by military rules. That means no more freelancing by you two. Is that clear?''

"Yes, sir," said Sushi, and Do-Wop echoed his partner in an even more plaintive tone. Neither one looked particularly happy, but Phule didn't think he could demand that of them.

"Good," he said, looking them both in the eye. "Now, Sushi, you're going to make that comm call, and then we're going to see if you two hoodlums can learn how to work as part of the team. For your sake—for the whole company's sake—I hope you can.''

Sushi and Do-Wop both nodded. Phule pointed to the phone, and sat down to watch. There might be something more he could learn from this . . .

11

As usual, my employer carefully read his briefing materials about the new world his company was going to. Landoor had been settled two hundred years ago as a mining colony (the planet was unusually rich in certain rare earths). The Moguls, as the mine owners were called, had imported convict labor to work the mines, with the promise of land and freedom after the laborers had served a stated term in the mines. The Moguls had grown enormously rich off the sweat of their imported convicts. They built their capital city on an unspoiled tropical island they called Atlantis— which became a popular vacation spot for the wealthy of that era.

Nowadays, the mainland mines were largely owned by off-planet cartels, which found it more difficult with every passing year to derive a profit from the played-out beds of ore. The original owners had, for the most part, taken their profits and left the planet for more cosmopolitan worlds where they could enjoy their wealth unhindered. That left the government in the hands of the former bureaucrats and middle managers. They ruled a population of miners, farmers, factory workers, and small merchants, who did not have the luxury of pulling up stakes and moving to a new world at whim.

Then, a few years ago, revolutionary fervor had swept the planet, and Federation troops were imported to stem the violence. Peace had been established—placing the rebel faction in the saddle, with the former government as an opposition party within the system. (A few diehards had escaped to the mainland and set up as a resistance movement, but they were considered of no consequence.)

While peace itself was greeted with rejoicing, its imposition by outside forces had left a sour taste in the mouths of many Landoorans—especially after Federation pilots strafed the peace conference. The Legion officer who ordered the gratuitous strafing was a certain Captain Scaramouche, who disappeared from the Legion rolls shortly before Captain Jester took command of the Omega Mob. This fact was not widely known on Landoor—but it was about to become so.

And for some reason, that fact had been omitted from the briefing materials General Blitzkrieg provided to my employer.

The Atlantis spaceport on Landoor was typical for a third-rate developing world: weeds growing in cracks on the roadways, peeling paint on all the buildings, and all the other evidence that nothing very important ever happened here. But to the Omega Mob, it was gorgeous. As they piled out of the landing shuttle, the legionnaires craned their necks to look up at the first natural sky they'd seen in over a year. And off in the distance, if they listened carefully, was the muted roar of surf on a broad, sandy beach. "It's good to be back on a real planet," said Rembrandt, and there were no dissenting voices.

A short distance away stood a formation of gray-uniformed figures: the Regular Army peacekeeping force that the Omega Mob was relieving. Behind them was a local news crew, with cameras rolling. Phule beckoned to his officers, and together they strode over to pay their respects. "Captain Larkin?" said Phule to the officer in command.

"Yes, welcome to Landoor, Captain Jester," said the dark-haired young woman commanding the Army unit, stepping forward to take Phule's hand in a firm grip. "A pleasure to see you—though we wouldn't mind spending another tour here, ourselves."

The subordinate officers on either side were introduced and shook hands, while Phule asked quietly, "Anything in particular I need to know about the local situation, Captain?"

"Nothing you won't find in the briefing books we'll be handing over," said Larkin, grinning. "It's a pleasant world, and the locals seem glad to have us here—the closest we've come to action was when we had to break up an Astroball victory celebration that got a little rowdy. Gorgeous weather, no nasty bugs or beasties, and even the rebels over on the mainland seem pretty harmless. You people ought to have an easy time of it."

"Well, I hope you're right," said Phule. "I'm not one to dodge trouble, but it'd be good to deal with something straight-forward for once. Our last assignment had more than its share of hidden problems."

"Captain, if you want any trouble on Landoor, you're going to have to go looking for it," said Larkin. "I've been here over a year and haven't seen the faintest sign of it."

"With luck, neither will we."

Larkin nodded. She pointed to a group of men in civilian garb standing in front of the nearest building. "Let's go introduce you to the local authorities, then. Not polite to keep them waiting."

"Yes, by all means," said Phule. He fell in alongside the Army captain, and the two, followed by their subordinates, began a brisk stroll toward the waiting civilians. They had gone perhaps half the distance when a sharp report rang out from the roof of a nearby building and almost at the same instant, Phule heard something whiz past his head and strike the ground behind him.

"Get down! Somebody's shooting!" he shouted, throwing himself flat on the ground. He heard several other bodies hit the tarmac at the same time, presumably following his advice. He couldn't tell if the shooter had hit anyone.

The closest cover was a ground vehicle of some sort, maybe twenty feet away. Phule began a quick scuttle toward it, using his knees and elbows. He didn't know if the shot had been intended for him, but the shooter might not be particular about who he hit. In any case, he wasn't about to provide an easy target for a second try.

He risked a peek at the scene around him. The civilians were scattering like chaff, but nobody seemed to be hurt. Then another shot rang out, and he started crawling more quickly. He sensed rather than heard someone rush past him, going in the direction from which the shots had been fired: Louie, on his glideboard no doubt, with a splatgun ready at hand. Phule hoped the Synthian was taking evasive action; Louie was a small, elusive target, but the shooters might get lucky.

Moments later, something louder and larger zoomed over him; this time he did risk a look up. It was Chocolate Harry on a new hovercycle, with Spartacus riding the sidecar. Between the glideboard and the hovercycle, the would-be assassins would be lucky to escape. On the other hand, if they decided to make a pitched battle of it . . . he pushed the thought out of his mind, and quickly crawled the rest of the way to shelter.

Captain Larkin had gotten there ahead of him, and was leaning with her back against the vehicle, a drawn pistol in her hand. She watched him scuttle up, then said, "Just my luck—right as I'm about to leave, the party finally comes to life."

"You're welcome to stay awhile," said Phule. Then, when he'd caught his breath a little bit he added, "I take it you don't have any idea who might be doing the shooting?"

"Not a clue," she said. "It looks as if your people came

prepared, though. That was very quick response time." She nodded approvingly.

"Let's hope it was quick enough." There hadn't been any more shots since the first two, but that didn't mean it was safe. Phule gazed intently back at where his troops had disembarked, trying to see what was happening. Most of his company, he saw, had taken whatever cover they could find. Brandy was peering over the shuttle's hood, scanning the rooflines with binoculars and talking into her wrist communicator—presumably directing the response to the shooting. Seeing her, Phule reached down and turned on his own communicator.

"Jester here—what's the story, Top?"

"Still trying to find out myself, Captain. C.H. and the Synthians are out scouting. No sign of the shooter yet. You all right?"

"Not a scratch. How about the rest?"

"A few scrapes and bruises when people ducked for cover, but nothing serious. Rev split a seam in his uniform."

Phule chuckled. "Don't tell me where, I swear I don't want to know. Listen now, Brandy—I want you to secure the area so the civilians can get out of danger. Send the Gambolts to scout those rooftops, too. We can't stay pinned down here all day just because of one sniper."

"Will do, Captain. But stay behind cover until I tell you it's safe, OK? There might be more than one sniper out there, and they might be gunning for us."

Phule watched as a black-uniformed skirmish line moved quickly toward him, securing the spaceport and waiting for more shots. None came, but it was quite a while before they declared the area safe. And nobody found the sniper.

"I'm not used to having somebody shoot at me," said Phule, pacing restlessly. He and Beeker had been herded to a secure room inside the spaceport terminal while the Legion and Army troops made certain no shooters were waiting somewhere to take another shot at him. Somewhere else in the building, the representatives of the Landoor government—including the head of State Security, Colonel Mays—awaited them.

"If you'll pardon my saying so, sir, you might have thought of that before joining the Space Legion. It is hardly the vocation to choose if one is seeking to avoid being shot at," said Beeker. His expression showed no sympathy whatsoever for his employer.

"Well, we can't be certain they were shooting at me *personally*," said Phule in a hopeful voice. "They might have been aiming at almost anybody on the landing field."

"I would consider it highly unlikely, sir," said Beeker. "After all, Captain Larkin told you there'd been no trouble at all during her tour of duty. It is difficult not to draw the conclusion that today's shooting incident is directly related to our arrival."

"That doesn't make sense, Beeker. What could anyone on this world have against us? I've never set foot on it."

"That's rather disingenuous of you, sir," said Beeker. "You can't have overlooked the fact that this world was formerly New Atlantis. You should certainly remember how the civil war here ended, when a certain young Legion officer took it upon himself to have the peace conference strafed. I would think you might remember that incident, since you were subsequently court-martialed for it, and assigned to your present position."

Phule began pacing again. "I could hardly have forgotten *that*, Beeker. I understood all along why General Blitzkrieg had the company assigned here: It's the one place in the galaxy where I might have enemies."

"The one place in addition to Headquarters," Beeker noted dryly.

"Yes, I suppose so," said Phule. "One reason I accepted this assignment was as a way to make amends for that incident. Still, never having been to the capital, I didn't expect anyone here to recognize me—especially since I've changed my Legion name. Obviously, somebody's leaked that information."

Beeker nodded solemnly. "I wouldn't be in the least surprised to learn that the general himself had revealed your previous identity as Captain Scaramouche to certain local factions to whom it might be of interest.''

"That's the way to bet—though it's probably pointless to try to prove it," said Phule. "More important is to find out which of those factions decided to start shooting the minute I landed here.''

"I would think that would be easy enough to answer, sir,'' said Beeker. "Who suffered the most when you strafed the peace conference?''

"Other than myself, you mean?'' said Phule, with an ironic grimace. "I suppose whatever faction lost the most in the eventual peace settlement. The former government, I suppose—especially the diehards who kept on fighting.''

"My thought exactly. From their point of view, the strafing might appear as insult piled upon injury.''

"That would be very narrow-minded of them.'' said Phule. "It really wasn't at all directed at them personally.''

Beeker stared at his employer for a long moment. "That may be true, sir, but I suspect that many people would find the distinction rather esoteric. Even professional soldiers are likely to take being shot at as an invasion of their personal space, I'd think.''

"Well, that really ignores the whole context,'' said Phule. "I was trying to exploit a military situation in wartime. That's hardly the same as assassinating someone— assuming that's what they were up to.''

"I am glad you perceive a difference,'' said Beeker, mildly. "However, it seems apparent that not everyone is quite ready to forgive and forget.''

"Well, we'll have to talk some sense into them,'' said Phule. "In a way, that's what we're here for, isn't it?''

"Sir, I was under the rather distinct impression that we had come here to get *out* of trouble. I suppose it was foolish of me to believe that. I shall have to learn to moderate my irrepressible optimism.''

"I'd be just as happy if you'd learn to moderate your sarcasm,'' said Phule, "but I'd never recognize you without it. In any case, if the rebels really have taken my arrival as a pretext to reopen hostilities, it's going to jeopardize this company's peacekeeping mission. I don't intend to sit still for that.''

''Not at all a wise policy with someone shooting at you,'' agreed Beeker.

''Exactly. So first we have to find the rebels and convince them I'm not their enemy. Any idea how we go about that?''

''Given today's events, I should think the rebels may not be especially interested in negotiating.''

''Well, I'll have to do what I can to change that,'' said Phule. ''Until then . . .''

The door opened and Lieutenant Armstrong stuck his head in. ''Captain, it looks as if things are finally under control. If you'll follow me, the government people are ready to meet you.''

''Good,'' said Phule. ''Now let's hope *they* haven't decided to hold that shooting against me.''

''Perhaps they won't, sir,'' said Beeker gloomily. ''Always assuming they weren't the ones responsible for it.'' But Phule and his lieutenants had already left the room.

Phule followed Armstrong and Rembrandt down a corridor to an office complex, and into a large office, evidently commandeered for the purpose. The sign on the door read SPACEPORT MANAGER, and there were several harried-looking men and women in the outer office as the Legion contingent passed through. On the walls were framed photographs of beach scenes and sunsets, reminders that this island was a tropical paradise—at least, when there wasn't a war going on.

Inside the inner office, they were met by a big, bearded man, smoking an evil-smelling cheroot and wearing a dark green uniform with an impressive number of service stripes on the sleeve. To either side of him were two similarly uniformed men, both grim-faced. The window blinds were drawn. All three watched in silence as Phule and his officers stepped into the room.

Phule stepped up to the desk and stopped, standing at attention. ''Colonel Mays, I am Captain Jester of the Space

Legion, ordered here to supervise the administration of the peace treaty. Allow me to present my credentials.'' Lieutenant Armstrong stepped forward with the dossier and put it on the desk in front of the big man, then stepped back to a position flanking Phule.

Mays neither looked at it nor touched it. Instead, he took the cheroot out of his mouth, looked Phule directly in the eye, and said, "You are a man who requires no introduction on this planet, Captain Jester—or should I call you Captain *Scaramouche*?''

"I would much prefer the former, Colonel," said Phule. "The Space Legion has a tradition that a legionnaire leaves his past behind him when he joins—as symbolized by leaving his name behind him. Our former names and former ways of life aren't anyone's business.''

"A very romantic tradition, I am sure," said Colonel Mays, with a hint of a sneer. "I am sure it gives you legionnaires great comfort to know that you can walk away from what you have done before, just by taking a new name and putting on a black uniform.''

"I don't think anybody can escape the past," said Phule, wondering why he was bandying words with this man. "But by changing our names, we can focus on our present tasks without having to keep explaining how we got here. That doesn't mean the past doesn't come looking for us, from time to time.''

Colonel Mays nodded. "Perhaps the policy is a wise one, then. But in your case, you will find a good many people here who remember what you did. As for myself—and I can tell you I speak for my superiors in the government, here—there is no animosity to you. Quite the opposite— you are one of our heroes. Your strafing mission broke the old government's last resistance. We had heard very little from the mainland rebels until that shooting today. I think we can assume that *they* know who you are, as well.''

"You're certain that was the rebels shooting at me?" said Phule. "My people responded almost immediately, but the shooters had gone, and left no clues to their origins.

We haven't even established for sure that I was the target—though that seems to be the best guess.''

Colonel Mays took a pull on the cheroot. ''Until you came here, the rebels did nothing but camp out in the jungle and play their self-deluding games,'' he said. ''They have no popular support. When they are not half-drunk, they know that as well as I do. But today, when you arrived—you, the off-planet enemy who rubbed their faces in their defeat—somebody shows up to shoot at you. Yes, Captain, I think that is a very good guess.'' The two men with him laughed.

Phule glanced at Armstrong and Rembrandt, neither of whom seemed to find Mays's statement amusing. ''Another possibility occurs to me, Colonel,'' he said. ''What if someone in your government is more worried about the rebels than you are? Perhaps they faked an assassination attempt, hoping to convince the peacekeeping team to punish the rebels. Of course this is mere speculation, but can you deny the possibility?''

Mays scowled. ''Of course I deny it,'' he said. ''We are a peaceful government—in fact, the peace agreement completely disarmed our military. Now it is fit only for construction and police work. Your company—and the rebels over on the mainland—are the only significant armed bodies on the planet.''

''I see,'' said Phule. ''Well, if that's the case, you'll have no problem with us. In fact, the less we have to do, the happier my people will be. What kinds of work have you got your soldiers doing?''

''We are currently embarked on a project to increase tourist revenues,'' said the colonel. ''I don't know how much you know about our planet's economy . . .''

''You'd be surprised what I know,'' said Phule. He and Beeker had done exhaustive financial research on the world they were coming to, looking for opportunities to make the new assignment profitable for the legionnaires (and of course, for themselves). Nothing had struck them as quite ripe, but that didn't mean they wouldn't find something once they were on the ground.

Colonel Mays grunted. "Well, then, you probably know that our mines were played out over a generation ago, and nothing has really replaced them. Jobs are scarce. Many of our people are subsistence farmers—in some ways, they're the lucky ones. The former government tried to develop a manufacturing industry, but that didn't go very far."

"I can see why," said Phule. "Everything you make here is being made just as well and just as cheaply elsewhere, so there aren't off-planet markets for it. You're stuck trying to lift yourselves by your own bootstraps."

"Exactly, Captain," said Mays. He stubbed out the cheroot. "You've done your homework. So we're looking at a stagnant economy. The former government never could find a way to improve things. Now it's our turn to try—and I hope we can do better."

"I understand," said Phule, his financial instincts taking over. "What avenues are you pursuing?"

"We need off-world money, and one way to get that is to attract off-worlders here," said Mays with impeccable logic. "We hope to develop a tourist industry."

Phule nodded, thinking of Lorelei's tourist-generated revenues. "That's not a bad basic plan, Colonel—in fact, it's probably your best bet. But for it to work, you need something that can't be duplicated off-world. You have gorgeous beaches and mountains, but there are beaches and mountains all over the galaxy."

"Correct again," said Mays smugly. "Don't sell us short, Captain—we have our plans in place, and they are moving forward. Before you know it, Landoor will be the tourist mecca of this entire sector."

"This is good news," said Phule. "Stability depends on a healthy economy. If I may ask, what are your plans? I'm always looking to invest a few dollars—if the prospective return is sufficiently appealing, of course."

"Captain, I am not the person to answer those questions," said Colonel Mays, standing. "For that, you should speak to the Ministry of Development. I don't know whether they are looking for foreign investments—you will have to ask them. As far as I'm concerned, you can best help Landoor by insuring that the rebels don't sabotage our plans before they reach maturity. You saw today how desperate they are. They would rather bring the entire structure down around their ears rather than see us benefit from it. I hope we can count on you, Captain."

"Colonel, you can be sure I'll do everything I can to promote the safety and success of your world," said Phule. "I will of course keep an eye on the rebels, as well as on your government's activities. But now, if you don't mind, I had best get started settling my people in and determining the best ways to achieve these goals."

The two men eyed each other for a moment, quite aware that nothing had been settled; then Phule and his lieutenants turned and strode out of the room.

Journal #373

It had been a matter of concern to my employer that, for all the favorable publicity his Legion company had received, its achievements to date had been realized in a peacetime environment. The closest any of his troops had come to combat was in facing the Mob on Lorelei: an adversary not to be taken lightly, but in the last analysis a good bit less formidable than a disciplined military force. Now, after the events at the spaceport, it became clear that Landoor might be a much tougher assignment than anticipated.

Not that anyone believed General Blitzkrieg's assurances that Landoor had been pacified. A little thought would have made it clear that a world recovering from a civil war— with peace imposed by outside powers—was likely to harbor a fair number of unsettled grudges. The assassination attempt, and the cool initial reception by the local government, drove those points home very forcefully to my employer.

So, almost immediately after its arrival at its new headquarters (in the Landoor Plaza Hotel, located in a new development west of the capital city) the company began to prepare as best it could for the possibility of combat.

"All right," said Brandy, hands on hips, "you all saw what happened out there this morning." The recruits muttered among themselves. They had all joined the Legion with some notion that they might eventually be fired upon, but having that vague expectation become reality was a shock. It showed on their faces, and in their voices.

"Nobody got hurt today," Brandy continued. "We hope it stays that way. But we've got to be ready in case somebody starts shooting again. That means being ready to shoot back."

"Excuse me, Sergeant," came a voice from the ranks.

Brandy suppressed a groan. It was Mahatma, who smiled and followed orders to the letter and, every now and then, asked questions nobody could answer—and persisted until everybody had gone crazy trying to explain the unexplainable. She smelled one of those questions coming up. Well, maybe she could buy a little time. "Mahatma, I think maybe you ought to hold your question for a while, OK?"

"Is that an order, Sergeant?"

"This is a really bad time, Mahatma."

"But Sergeant, I just wanted to know . . ."

"Not now, Mahatma!"

The silence was deafening. Brandy glared at her recruits, but nobody seemed willing to risk annoying her further. As for Mahatma, he was still smiling, waiting for another chance. Brandy shook her head and went into her spiel. "OK, we're going to introduce you to a new weapon the company's been issued. In fact, we're the first in the Legion to have it, thanks to the captain's connections. We think it'll be especially useful here, where most of the people we'll encounter are going to be noncombatants."

She turned to the table behind her, which was covered with a large tarp. She pulled back one corner far enough to get a grip on one of the items lying there, and turned back to show it to the recruits. "This is the Phule-Proof Model SR-1," she said. "The factory says it's the first real advance in nonlethal weaponry in decades. I'd say it's more than that—as far as I'm concerned, it's the first nonlethal weapon I've ever seen that's worth a damn. By which I mean it's the only one you can use to stop somebody who wants to kill you without killing him.''

That wasn't strictly true: If you stunned the driver of a fast-moving vehicle, or a swimmer, or a tightrope walker, it would kill them readily enough. And of course, somebody who panicked and missed his shot at an enemy charging from close range was no better off than with any other weapon. But the weapon provided an answer to the ticklish situation where friend and foe were inextricably mingled in a mob scene . . .

Brandy raised the weapon to display it. ''Now, you'll each get one of these in a few minutes. But first I'm going to show you its parts. I expect all of you to be able to name every part of the weapon and tell me its purpose. We'll start at the business end. This is the front sight. Some of you may have fired a rifle, where you have a very tight target area. You'll see that this sight is much larger. That's for two reasons. First, the beam's effective area is the entire body, even an extremity. You can catch your target in the foot and still gain the desired effect. The second factor is the Variable Beam Spread Adjustment, or VBSA, which is controlled by the Variable Beam Spread Adjustment Control, which I'll get to in a moment . . .''

Brandy droned on, and the recruits' eyes began to glaze over as she moved through a long and frequently redundant catalog of the weapon's various parts. Normally, she would have insured their attentiveness by throwing snap questions at anyone who seemed in danger of dozing off during the lecture. But today . . .

There was a sudden flurry of movement as a masked figure with a vibroblade in one hand leapt into the pack of recruits. It threw a hefty forearm around the neck of a young woman who'd chosen the service name of Brick, although Brandy suspected her comrades had a softer nickname for her. ''Nobody move,'' rasped the intruder, waving the vibroblade inches from the captive's face. The recruits let out a collective gasp, and most of them stepped back—although the Gambolts, Brandy noted, held their position and assumed postures that suggested they might leap if they saw an opening.

"One false move and the girl pays in blood," said the intruder, turning his hostage to shield himself from Brandy. "I'm not afraid of your gun."

"Good," said Brandy, and pressed the firing stud.

The beam caught both the intruder and Brick. They fell limp to the floor, without a sound. The vibroblade clattered harmless to the side.

In an instant, one of the Gambolts had leapt on the intruder and pinned him down. Another of the recruits, Slayer, picked up the vibroblade. "Hey, this ain't even turned on." He leaned down and pulled off the stocking mask that the intruder wore. "This guy looks familiar," he said. The other recruits gathered around, puzzled expressions on their faces.

"He ought to look familiar," said Brandy. "He's one of us. This is Gears, from the motor pool—he volunteered to play the bad guy so I could show you how this weapon works. You can get off him now, Rube. He won't hurt anybody."

Rube got off of Gears and stood up. The rest of the recruits gathered around to look. While both Gears and Brick were lying limp on the floor, it was evident that both were breathing normally, and they showed no other signs of injury.

"I wanted you all to see that this weapon can be used in a tight situation, where your target is mixed in with a lot of people you don't want to hurt," said Brandy. "With a conventional weapon, you'd hold your fire—and if the target is sufficiently determined, you might end up taking casualties because you were afraid to take that risk. But Gears has been hit by this ray before, and he volunteered to let me zap him again so you could see how it works."

"That's right," said Gears, who had recovered sufficiently to raise his head and speak. "Flight Leftenant Qual used one of these things to save my life. So I'm a pretty big fan of this weapon. I let the Top zap me with it to show you how quick it takes down a target, without really harming him.''

''It'll still be a few minutes before he can stand,'' said Brandy, ''so you'd have plenty of time to disarm a real enemy. And you don't have to worry about hurting your own people, if they're in the line of fire. How's Brick doing?''

''I'm all right, Sarge,'' came Brick's voice, a bit faint. ''My arms and legs feel weird, but nothing hurts.''

''Take those two over to the wall and prop 'em up so they can sit,'' said Brandy. ''I'd hate to delay the rest of the demonstration while they recover. And now that you've all seen what this weapon can do, we're going to let you all have one to work with.''

The recruits were noticeably more interested, and the rest of the session passed rapidly. Brandy considered it an unusual success—especially since even Mahatma was so fascinated by the SR-1 that he never got around to asking his question.

12

Journal #376

A peacekeeping mission by its very nature is an admission that the local government is unable to keep the peace. Thus, it was no surprise that the government of Landoor looked at Omega Company as a necessary evil on the level of game wardens and dogcatchers. My employer's overtures to the government, offering to lend his people to various public works projects, met with blanket refusals. The government made it clear that, in their opinion, Omega Company could justify its presence only by exterminating the rebels—the remnants of the former government, and their supporters.

The ordinary citizens, on the other hand, appeared to have no animosity against the Legion. On the captain's instructions, the legionnaires went out into the local community, spent their money in shops and restaurants, and tried to make themselves a visible benefit to the people they were here to protect. This policy paid the expected dividend. Legionnaires soon found themselves as popular with the public as they were unpopular with the government.

"Hey, lookit the big guy with the funny nose," came a small voice from across the street.

Tusk-anini stopped and peered at the group of local children. A few short blocks from the hotel, the neighborhood had changed rapidly, clearly showing its previous identity as a factory district. The dilapidated building in front of which the children stood bore a sign announcing its condemnation and imminent demolition to make way for Landoor Park.

"Hello," he said. "My name Tusk-anini. You live here?"

The children were whispering to one another, as if uncertain what to do now that they had attracted this strange creature's attention. One of them, bolder than the rest, stepped forward and asked, "Are you a soldier?"

"Not soldier," said Tusk-anini. "Space Legion—we better than soldiers." He strolled across the litter-strewn street, doing his best to appear nonthreatening. For someone who closely resembled a seven-foot-tall warthog, this was somewhat difficult. But the captain had briefed the company about the importance of being friendly with the natives of this world, and Tusk-anini was willing to do his part.

"My name's Bucky, and I'm not scared of you," said the child, scowling up at him from something like half his height.

From behind her another high-pitched voice said, "Her real name's Claudia."

"You shut up, Abdul," said Bucky/Claudia, throwing a hostile glance over her shoulder, then turning back to stare at Tusk-anini. She was wearing the same ragged clothes as her comrades. From the look on her dirty face, she wasn't about to back down from anybody. Tusk-anini decided that she was the leader of this little group.

"You live here, Bucky, or you come to look at me?" he said, dropping down on one knee to put himself closer to the children's face level. He'd discovered that humans found him less intimidating if he sat or knelt to reduce the perceived difference in their heights. There were times when it was useful to appear intimidating, but this wasn't one of them.

"I live over on Hastings Street," said the girl. "My family owns our own whole house." From the way she said it, that was a distinction she was proud of.

"You got candy, mister?" asked another urchin, stepping up next to Bucky. She had a straw-colored shock of hair and intense, large blue eyes that seemed out of proportion with the rest of her face.

"What your name?" asked Tusk-anini, avoiding the question. He didn't have any candy with him, but he could make sure to have some with him the next time he came by. For now, acting friendly would have to be enough.

"That's Cynthia," said Bucky. "She's my baby sister, but she's all right." She looked at the smaller girl—there *was* a sort of resemblance, now that Tusk-anini knew to look for it—and said, "Remember Mom told you not to take candy from strange men."

"He's not a man," said Cynthia, with impeccable logic. One or two other children nodded in agreement. Tusk-anini might be a stranger, but he did not fit into any definition of *man* they considered relevant. Especially if it left open a loophole through which candy might be obtained.

"Tusk-anini no bring candy this time," he said. "Next time I come here, I bring some. But you ask Mom if it OK to take from me. No want her mad at me."

"He talks funny, too." One of the others had evidently decided that failure to bring candy was grounds for pointed commentary on the stranger's differences from local standards of appearance and speech.

"Shut up, Abdul," said Bucky. "He's an alien. Aliens can't help it if they look and talk funny."

"I don't like him," said Abdul, pouting. "Aliens don't belong here, anyhow."

Tusk-anini was considering whether it would be diplomatic to point out that, except for the miracle of interstellar travel, neither did humans belong here, and that where everyone was an alien it was best to practice tolerance, when the children's attention was distracted by a new arrival on the scene. "Wow, what's that?" said Bucky, her jaw dropping.

Tusk-anini turned to follow the children's gaze, and saw a familiar sight: Spartacus, one of the Synthian legionnaires, had come around the corner and was casually zigzagging down the street on his glide-board. Tusk-anini waved. "Friend Spartacus, come over here," he said.

"Wow, is that your friend?" said Abdul. "What's that thing he's riding?" He seemed entirely oblivious to the fact that the Synthian resembled nothing so much as a large slug in a Legion uniform.

"I am riding a glide-board," said Spartacus. The translator rendered his voice as a rich baritone, with an aristocratic accent that always surprised those meeting him for the first time. It was also an incongruous touch, considering the Synthian's strong populist leanings—but of course these children would have no notion of that.

"*Triff,*" said Bucky. "Can you show us how to ride it?"

"I think I can do better than that," said Spartacus. "If my friend Tusk-anini will help, I think the captain will let us bring several glide-boards along the next time we visit. Then you can all learn how to ride."

"Wow," said Abdul, his eyes growing round. "You guys are really cool."

Tusk-anini chuckled in his warthoggish fashion. Perhaps he wouldn't need to give Abdul that lesson on tolerance, after all. An alien bearing a new toy trumped human chauvinism every time.

Journal #378

Landoor turned out to be not only a welcome change from life on a space station, but an extremely attractive environment in and of itself. As the legionnaires began to explore the city and the surrounding region, they discovered that the nearby beaches and the mountainous northern end of the island were every bit as scenic as the tourist brochures made them appear. The local cuisine, which drew on several Terran traditions, was good enough to offer an at-

tractive alternative to the excellent fare provided by Mess Sergeant Escrima—who eagerly began to add local dishes to his own repertoire.

Escrima looked around the hotel kitchen. From the gleaming equipment on display, and the delicious aromas permeating the air, this was the kitchen of a world-class restaurant. It was a rare Legion mess sergeant who'd had the opportunity to actually prepare *food* . . .

Most of the odors were familiar. There was garlic and bay leaf, peppers and onions, tomatoes, the blander aromas of rice and beans in simmering pots. There was also meat, possibly several different kinds, being roasted, grilled, stewed, and sauteed. This last aroma Escrima could not identify, which puzzled him. Evidently it was some indigenous meat. But it was almost unheard of for humans to be able to eat the flesh of a local animal.

Well, he'd find out. He had an appointment with the hotel's head chef—who was somewhat apprehensive about turning his kitchen into a Legion mess hall. Escrima was here to cure him of that preconception.

He walked over and took the lid off a simmering pot for a closer look. The contents was a spicy stew, with savory meat and onions—and more. He was looking around for a spoon to taste a sample when a voice behind him said, "Ah, would you be the Army cook?"

"Not Army, Space Legion," said Escrima, doing his best to keep his voice from snapping at the newcomer, who was dressed in the traditional chef's hat and white apron. "I'm Sergeant Escrima, Food Preparation Specialist E-9, here to inspect the facilities. You've been told that we're going to be sharing the kitchen."

"Yes, Sergeant," said the chef. "This will be a very . . . ah, *interesting* . . . experience, I think."

"You're telling me?" said Escrima. "I got an appetite just walking into this kitchen. If the Legion won't eat this stuff, they ought to be checked for signs of life. I can see there's a whole new cuisine for me to learn. What do you call this dish?"

"Nutria jambalaya," said the cook. "One of our Creole-style dishes. We also have sweet and sour nutria with bingo beans, and nutria parmigiana on the menu tonight."

"Nutria?" Escrima was puzzled. "That must be the meat, but I don't recognize the name. Is it vat-grown?"

"No, no, you have missed it completely," said the cook, smiling. "Nutria is our most famous animal, imported from Earth by the Moguls. In their day, it was rare, and as expensive as horse or pompano. But the nutria thrived in the lowland swamps, and now the animal is so common that it has become our major indigenous source of protein."

"An Earth animal," said Escrima. "That should be good, then—when there's real meat locally, I'll almost never use vat protein. What kind of animal is it?"

"Game, sergeant," said the sergeant. "Has a very robust flavor, goes nicely roasted or in a spicy sauce. Very versatile, like chicken or cow, but much cheaper. The jambalaya won't really be ready until I add the rice to the meat and vegetables. But this will give you an idea of how it will taste."

Escrima filled a spoon and tasted. "Excellent," he said. "You're right, that meat will fit a lot of places—this dish will have 'em lining up for seconds. If it really is cheaper than chicken, the troops are going to eat a lot of this nutria."

The cook smiled. "Trust me, Sergeant, once you've gotten used to nutria, you'll be using it in all your recipes."

"Well, no time like the present," said Escrima. "Why don't you show me what else you're cooking tonight?"

Within minutes, the two chefs were comparing notes on spices and discussing the best local sources for fresh produce. The undercooks listened in growing awe to a pair of culinary artists picking each other's brains. The food was going to be even better than usual that evening . . .

Journal #381

Directly across the street from the Landoor Plaza Hotel was a large vacant area, fenced off and posted. When he inquired about it, my employer was informed that it was destined to be part of Landoor Park, a large project funded by the government as part of its economic revival plan. However, as to the exact nature of Landoor Park, the locals had nothing to say . . .

"Captain, I must inform you that stock in our projects is not being offered to off-world investors." Boris Eastman's tone and expression made it clear that he considered the question an impertinence. And both the size and decor of his office made it clear that he had no authority to change policy even if he were so inclined. But he was the only official willing to meet with the captain of the peacekeeping team, and Phule was determined to get what he could out of the interview.

"Mr. Eastman, I am not about to lecture you on economics," said Phule, with more than a trace of annoyance in his voice. He had gone into town to the Ministry of Development, a large building in the neo-Bauhaus style, and despite having made a firm appointment, had been kept waiting in an outer office while several locals were ushered in and out. The receptionist behind the desk had treated his inquiries with ill-disguised disinterest. But he had persevered, and finally was ushered into the deputy's office.

"That is good," said Eastman, "because I would not expect a foreigner to understand our local situation. We have a long history, and we have arrived at policies based on our unique experience."

"I am aware that your grasp of local conditions may exceed my own," said Phule, with more tact than customary. Given his extensive research into the economy of Landoor, he probably knew more about local conditions than the deputy. "But perhaps you will do me the favor of explaining your rejection of foreign capital. I would think that bringing resources in from off-planet would be the quickest way to give your economy the boost it needs."

"That is a superficial assessment," said Eastman, sniffing. "As you would know if you were a native, our world was originally a mining colony . . ."

"Yes, I have read your history," said Phule, losing his patience. "This world was discovered in 2521 CE by an expedition from New Baltimore. A geologist on the expedition, Alberto Belperio, found igneous formations on the northern continental mass—now named for him—bearing an unusually high concentration of several rare minerals. He and the ship's captain, Martin Landoor, returned to New Baltimore and raised four hundred seventeen million credits to exploit the deposits. Mining began in 2526 . . ." He continued from memory for several minutes, piling detail upon detail.

"Enough, Captain!" Eastman, whose face had turned bright red, finally interrupted him. "You have convinced me that you know our history." He wiped his forehead with a large handkerchief and continued, "Perhaps you also know about the collapse of the economy a generation ago."

"Yes. A series of improvements in mining technique made it feasible to extract the minerals from the poorer ore on several other planets. All of a sudden, the Moguls lost their monopoly."

"And the foreign scum, having sucked us dry, took their profits and left us to wither away," said Eastman, pounding his fist on the desktop. "We have learned one key lesson from that, Captain. Never again will Landoor be held hostage by foreign money. Landoor Park will be financed by money we raise from our own people, not from the likes of you."

Somehow, Phule kept his temper. "Mr. Eastman, you are making a mistake. If you will notice, my legionnaires and I are already pumping a fair amount of money into this economy. If your plans to attract foreign tourism succeed, you will be even more heavily dependent on off-planet money. If a little foreign seed money helps you get on your feet, why not take it? This isn't a zero-sum game we're playing."

Eastman shook his head. "Captain, we appreciate the fact that your troops are spending their money in our local businesses. You realize, of course, that this is a pittance. Your troops would be of far greater benefit to us if you sent them to the mainland to end the rebellion once and for all.''

''Really?'' Phule's eyebrows rose a notch. ''I was under the impression that the rebels were a joke—from what the previous peacekeeping troops reported, the only thing they've done in years is take a potshot at me, back when we landed.''

''They are a symptom of all that was wrong with the old government,'' fumed Eastman. ''Far from working to liberate the people, they are behind most of the crime here in the capital. They are constantly sabotaging our efforts to rebuild the economy—why, nearly one in three of our signs for Landoor Park has been defaced by them.''

''I saw that, but it seemed like petty vandalism to me,'' said Phule. ''I'll look into it, of course.''

Eastman was livid. ''Look into it? Better you should suppress the rebels once and for all.''

''Mr. Eastman, that is not my mission,'' said Phule. ''My orders strictly forbid offensive operations on this planet. If the rebels attack the city, or take other military action, we will stop them. By the same token, if your government takes any direct action against the rebels, we will stop you. Frankly, I don't want to take action against either side. I would be much happier investing my money to help rebuild this planet. That's what I came here to talk about.''

''And, as I told you, we do not want your money,'' said Eastman. ''I believe this interview is at an end, Captain.''

''I'm afraid you're right about that,'' said Phule, rising to his feet. ''It may be the only thing you've been right about all day.'' And he stalked out of the deputy's office, slamming the door behind him.

The eastern beaches of Atlantis were widely considered the choicest on Landoor. They offered broad expanses of amber sand, warm water, a gentle slope from wading to swimming depth, serious surf beyond the outer bar, as well as what most locals considered the right balance of natural beauty and such amenities as cabanas, boardwalks, and food vendors. So as soon as the new Legion base was sufficiently

set up to give a few personnel a day's leave, a rented hoverbus arrived at Sunrise State Beach and unloaded a large
pack of legionnaires in swimsuits, carrying blankets, picnic
coolers, and an assortment of beach toys.

It was early enough in the morning that only a few blankets and umbrellas were in place on the sand, so the Legion
contingent had its pick of spots to set up. Brandy chose a
large dune well above the surf line, where they dropped off
their baggage. Then, she made a beeline for the surf, with
two dozen legionnaires whooping and hollering behind her.
A riot of ducking, splashing, and other horseplay broke out
at the water's edge. The few non-Legion bathers quickly
withdrew to a safe distance, casting wary looks toward the
frolicking newcomers.

After a while, two civilians strolled up to the little group
that hadn't gone into the water. "You guys ain't from
around here," one of them said to Flight Leftenant Qual,
who was allowing Super-Gnat to bury him in the sand.

"You are observant," said Qual, flashing his allosaurus
grin.

The local drew back a pace, but then noticing the tiny
woman fearlessly dumping handfuls of sand onto the toothy
alien's torso, tried another conversational gambit. "You
talk pretty good for a foreigner."

"Oh, I hasten to assure you, everyone on my world talks,
some even better than I," said Qual, with a jovial chuckle.
"You should hear Chief Potentary Korg when he gets his
jaw wagging."

"Is that so? I reckon he's something, then," said the
Landooran, a skinny youth with an asymmetrical haircut
that needed retrimming. "I'm Okidata, by the way, and this
is my girlfriend Wandalune. We're from out South Worton,
down by Dunes Park."

"I do not know that district," said Qual. "Perhaps I shall
visit it now that I have met someone from there."

"When somebody gives you their name, you're supposed to introduce yourself in return," said Super-Gnat,
laughing. She turned to the two locals. "This is Qual—he
doesn't know human customs too well yet—and they call

me Gnat. We're staying in the Landoor Plaza, out west of town.''

''Wow, I hear that's a fancy place,'' said Wandalune, wide-eyed. ''Are you rich tourists?''

''Nope,'' said Gnat. ''We're here to do a job, is all. The boss gave us the day off, so a bunch of us decided to see what your beach was like. I'm glad we did.''

''That's a triff boss,'' said Okidata. ''Last guy I worked for, he bounced me for going to my sister's funeral without asking. He didn't warn me fair, so I managed to get unemployment, but jobs are scarce. There's a new government park hiring, but they had a waiting list longer than the Weasel. I'm still looking, but the unemployment may run out before I get anything.''

''That rots, for sure. What kind of work were you doing?'' said Gnat.

''I was a mechanic at a ride park,'' said Okidata. ''An apprentice mechanic, really—lug the tools and clean up grease spills and do the dirty work. They think you don't have anywhere else to go, the dirty work can get pretty dirty. You wanna eat, you do it, though.''

Then he grinned. ''Besides, it's what I wanted to do ever since I was a kid. My old man wanted me to be a printer, like him, but I always wanted to work in a park.'' His voice changed, and he squinted at the legionnaires. ''What about you guys? I didn't know they were bringing in foreigners to work here. There's not enough real jobs for us natives.''

''I know all about that,'' said Gnat. She dumped a final load of sand on Qual and dusted off her hands. ''Jobs were pretty scarce back on my home world, too—so I joined the Space Legion. Our job here is to keep you guys from shooting each other. Want to join up and help us?'' She grinned.

''If that's the whole job, you might get a lot of people to join up,'' said Okidata. ''Hasn't been any shooting since the war ended, which is about the only good thing I can say about this place. I'd take that chance, for a regular paycheck.''

''So would I,'' said Wandalune. ''I got out of school a year ago, and I've been looking for work ever since. I've had a few fill-in jobs, but nothing longer than a couple weeks. Same with all my friends. Most of 'em have quit looking.''

''Uh-huh,'' said Gnat. ''Well, the Legion's a steady paycheck and three squares a day, and a chance to get off-world, if you want to see something besides home. But there's plenty of dirty work here, too. Maybe you should talk to our captain—find out whether it's really your idea of what you want to do for the next few years.''

''Maybe I will,'' said Okidata, though he looked doubtful.

''It is an honorable calling,'' said Qual, from underneath the sand pile. ''Captain Clown has given his troops opportunities of great rarity. Ambitious hatchlings could do far worse.''

''We'll think about it,'' said Wandalune. Then she reached out and took her boyfriend's hand. ''Come on, Okey, let's go see if the rides are open yet.'' And the two locals wandered up the beach toward a medium-sized amusement park visible beyond the boardwalk.

As they departed, Tusk-anini came out of the surf and trotted up to Super-Gnat. He was dripping wet, with a thick pair of dark goggles covering his light-sensitive eyes. ''Who those people, Gnat?'' he said, noting her frown. ''They bothering you?''

''Not the way you mean,'' said Super-Gnat, looking after the departing locals. ''What bothers me, if they're telling the truth, is that a lot of kids here can't find jobs. That could make *our* job here tougher, if it's true.''

''You mean they think we taking jobs from them?'' said Tusk-anini. ''Not true. We come here, bring in money from off-world. More money for everyone here.''

''They're still likely to resent us if they see we've got money to spend when they don't,'' said Gnat, shaking her head.

''This may produce a problem,'' said Qual. ''Alas, our power to change that is circumscribed.''

''You said a mouthful,'' said Gnat. ''I hope this whole job isn't more than we can swallow.''

"Do not fear, small strong one," said Qual, chuckling. "My people have a saying: 'Better the swamp than the desert, but the river is swifter than either one.' "

"Huh? What's that mean?" Super-Gnat wasn't always sure the Zenobian's translator was correctly wired.

"Don't care," said Tusk-anini. "Right now we on the beach, so I not going to worry. Come on, you want to go in water?"

"Race you there," said Super-Gnat, and they took off running. Qual lay back and closed his eyes, grinning.

Journal #387

My employer's attitude toward the current government of Landoor had taken on a degree of skepticism. Despite his professed desire to help rebuild the planet, they were clearly reluctant to provide him with much useful information concerning their plans to develop a tourist industry—in which they claimed to put great stock. And they told him they did not want him investing his money in the Landoor Park project.

His suspicion of the government was only heightened by Boris Eastman's clumsy attempt to portray the shots fired at him at the spaceport as grounds to undertake operations against the rebels. However, I suspect that being balked in his desire to invest in the project made him decide to find out exactly what was going on in Landoor Park. When the usual interplanetary databases turned up no useful information, he decided to do his own research—right on the ground.

"What are we looking for, anyway, Soosh?" Do-Wop asked. He and his partner were in a former industrial quarter of Landoor City, dressed in civilian clothes. Except for the two legionnaires, the trash-filled streets were almost deserted. The few pedestrians they did encounter crossed the street or ducked into alleyways, seeking to avoid notice. It seemed clear that few honest citizens had business here, nowadays.

"The captain isn't sure," said Sushi, peering through the links of a rusting fence that bore a sign reading, FUTURE SITE OF LANDOOR PARK. The factory wall inside bore enigmatic graffiti, above a small pile of broken liquor bottles. A tall plant bearing bright blue flowers sprang from a patch of weeds. Nothing of apparent value was visible.

"Oh, great," said Do-Wop. "So he sends us out to the ugliest chunk of landscape I've seen since the swamps back on Haskin's Planet, and tells us to look around for somethin' he ain't sure about. How do we know when we find it?"

"Use your brains," said Sushi. "I know you've got some. The captain says the government here has some sort of secret project going on—he isn't sure what, but apparently they've put a lot of their resources into it. Something like that ought to be big enough to notice. Especially in this part of town—I don't think anybody could build a hot-dog stand here without it sticking out like a sore thumb."

Do-Wop frowned. "If it's that easy to spot, you'd think he could see it from the hotel roof as well as we can down here. Maybe better, with those high-powered glasses of his."

Sushi shrugged. "I know for a fact he's been up there looking, but it's not really high enough. I'd be surprised if he hasn't sent out a few spy-bots, as well. I guess he wants to get the grunt's-eye view. If he thinks we can give him something useful, I say we do our best to come up with something."

"OK, I guess you got a point, there," said Do-Wop. He kicked a fragment of shattered brick that must have fallen from a nearby building. "All I know is, whatever the captain's after, it ain't out here."

"Well, not anywhere we've been so far, anyway," Sushi agreed. "We've got plenty of time left, though. Let's go see what's down the street. Maybe there'll be a bar open, and a few local pigeons we can lure into a little game of chance, and ask them to tell us about secret government projects while we take their money.''

''Dream on, dude,'' said Do-Wop. ''We've got about as much chance of that as we do of finding a couple kilos of loose diamonds on the corner . . . Hey, what's that noise?''

Sushi stopped and listened. A muffled rhythmic pounding was coming from somewhere in the distance; the timbre of the sound suggested a heavy hammer striking a thick wooden block. He grinned and said, ''I don't know what it is, but I think we just found something worth a closer look. Which way do you think it is?''

''Ahead and to the right,'' said Do-Wop. ''Let's go check it out, then.''

They walked along the street between rubble-strewn vacant lots and decaying buildings, the sound gradually becoming louder. ''It's a mechanical sound—maybe a pile driver,'' said Sushi.

''Or a really big guy with a sledgehammer,'' said Do-Wop, feigning worry. ''Don't wanna mess with *him*.''

''Hey, he'd better not mess with us,'' said Sushi, laughing. ''Not only are we the best company in the Legion, I'm the number one man in the local Yakuza family.''

''Oh, yeah, I almost forgot,'' said Do-Wop. ''In that case, you go first.''

Sushi punched him in the biceps. ''Right, tiger. Odds are, we're going to find some local kids building a clubhouse. The only thing to worry about is them mobbing us for candy and handouts.''

''Yo, man, I grew up in a neighborhood a lot like this,'' said Do-Wop, his eyes shifting from side to side. ''Had me a vibroblade when I was eight years old, and a zapper before I was shavin'. Any kids around here, you and me could be in *real* trouble if they mob us.''

''Yeah, but we have two advantages on them, Do-Wop.''

''What's that, Soosh?''

''First, you've learned fifteen years worth of dirty tricks that no kid could possibly know. And second, I've got a whole bag full of tricks you haven't even learned yet.''

Do-Wop nodded. "Hey, that's cool, man. But there's still one thing has me worried."

"OK, I'll bite. What's that?"

"What if it ain't kids?"

Sushi grinned. "In that case, they're the ones who'd better be worried. Come on, let's go." They walked together toward the pounding noise.

Phule and Brandy sat at a poolside table in the Landoor Plaza, enjoying the sun while reviewing the new recruits' progress. They were by now far enough along in their training to perform most of the company's regular jobs, and Phule wanted to integrate them into the unit as broadly as possible.

The question was whether to pair some of the new troops with more experienced members of the company, or to leave existing partnerships intact. Brandy argued for keeping things as they were, while Phule favored creative tinkering. By now, the discussion had boiled down to individual cases. Both agreed that certain pairings ought to be considered untouchable: Tusk-anini and Super Gnat were the prime example. But what about Sushi and Do-Wop?

"I put them together because I thought they'd both learn something," said Phule. "Do-Wop was too impulsive for his own good, or anybody else's—he'd steal anything that wasn't nailed down. And Sushi was way too calculating—a classic cold fish. But I'm afraid they've learned their lessons too well. If we put one of them with Mahatma, maybe that'll give them a better sense of ethics."

"It'd turn Mahatma into a cynic," said Brandy. "Heaven help us if that happens. Leave 'em alone, I say. They're perfect together, Captain."

"Too perfect," said Phule, shaking his head. "After that escapade the day we left Lorelei . . ."

"Easy, Captain, here they come," said Brandy, looking across the pool. "Grinning from ear to ear, too."

"Trouble, I bet," said Phule, He turned to look at the two arriving legionnaires. "All right, what have you two been up to?'' he said, as they approached the table.

"Doing our job, Captain," said Sushi. "We've been scouting the government park, and guess what we found?"

"From the look of you, I'm not sure I want to know," said Phule. "But go ahead and report."

"Aww, Captain, you really oughta trust us more," said Do-Wop. "We learned our lesson, no foolin'."

"I don't think he wants to hear what we found," said Sushi, nudging Do-Wop. "He'll find out in a few months, anyway."

"Yeah, I guess you're right. He can always go over and take a look for himself," said Do-Wop, winking.

"I should have known better," moaned Phule. He looked the two grinning legionnaires in the eye and said, with all the sincerity he could muster, "I apologize for any aspersions cast on your character, and humbly request your report."

"Does that mean what I think it does?" said Do-Wop, looking at Sushi. "Are we out of the doghouse?"

"Sounds like it to me," said Sushi. He came to attention. "Sir, we wish to report our observations in the area we were dispatched to scout. We set out from the hotel entrance at thirteen hundred hours, on a bearing of . . ."

"OK, you clowns, enough is enough!" Brandy barked. "Now, what did you find?"

"Top don't want us to have any fun at all," muttered Do-Wop. "See if *I* reenlist in this outfit . . ."

"Keep it up, and you'll find out what my idea of fun *is*," said Brandy, in a menacing tone. "Spill it!"

"Well, if you both insist," said Sushi, with an offended expression that might have been convincing if he hadn't then broken into a grin and said. "We found roller coasters."

"A *roller coaster*?" said Brandy and Phule, almost in unison.

"Roller coasters," Sushi corrected. "At least three of 'em, all different designs."

Phule's jaw hung open. "Are you sure?"

"Sure as a rigged election," said Do-Wop.

"Go look for yourself," said Sushi, shrugging. "If you can think of anything else those babies could be, I'll be glad to listen, They're still under construction, but if they aren't roller coasters, I've never seen one. Anyhow, here are the map coordinates, best we could figure them out—we had to look over the fence from the roof of a condemned factory building."

"Roller coasters," repeated Brandy. "I don't get it."

"I do," said Phule. "Now I know the government's plan to turn around the local economy. It should have been obvious! They're going to build a giant theme park!"

"If it's so obvious, why the secrecy?" said Brandy, frowning. "You'd think they'd want the whole galaxy to know about it."

"Yes, you'd think so," said Phule. "The only answer I can think of is fear that somebody will find out about the idea and steal it. The government here is very suspicious of off-planet influences. They aren't used to thinking of outsiders as a source of help. Well, we're going to have to change that."

"Sure," said Brandy. "But how?"

"I'll tell you when I figure it out," said Phule.

13

The discovery that the government's secret project was a gigantic theme park answered a number of questions. Now we knew their strategy for bringing in off-world visitors: to make Landoor the amusement park and thrill-ride capital of the galaxy. The idea had its merits; with unmatched beaches, equable climate, and exotic scenery, the planet already had the makings of a tourist mecca. Supplementing these natural assets with the ultimate in technological excitement was a sound strategy, and one suited to the Landooran temperament.

Unfortunately, the government was laboring under several disadvantages. The recent war, combined with exaggerated reports of rebel activities, had made tourists distinctly leery of making the world a vacation destination. An aggressive publicity campaign could undoubtedly have overcome this, but the government had made almost no efforts in this direction. My employer, who well understood the power of positive publicity, found this inexplicable until a chance conversation put things into perspective.

"Wake up, honey-bun." Mother's voice came over the comm system, startling Phule. He *hadn't* been asleep, but he had been in a deep study about what his most recent intelligence reports meant. "We've got a local to see you," she said.

"Anybody we know?"

"Says his name is Okidata, and claims to know Super-Gnat and Qual," said Mother. "Just a young kid—I bet he'd *like* to know Gnat better. Says he's interested in joining the Legion."

"Suddenly I'm a recruiting officer, on top of everything else," muttered Phule, thinking of Laverna. For a moment he considered passing the kid on to someone with more time. On second thought, it might be refreshing to talk to someone outside the usual circle. Perhaps this local kid could give him insight for the company's mission here. "Send him in," he said.

Okidata was dressed in what, from Phule's limited contact with local civilians, seemed to be job interview clothes. He shook hands somewhat nervously and sat down in the seat Phule indicated. "I met some of your soldiers at the beach," he said. "I told them jobs were scarce around here, and they suggested I think about joining up. I don't know if they were serious, but jobs aren't getting any easier to find. So I'm here to find out what the Legion's about."

"Well, I can probably answer some of your questions," said Phule. "But maybe you'd do better by telling me what kind of job you're looking for, and I can tell you whether there's anything like it in the Legion."

"I used to be a roller coaster mechanic . . ." Okidata said. "When I lost my job, I applied to the new government park, but they turned me down because my cousin's out with the rebels. I guess I'm open to suggestions."

"Really?" said Phule, like a hungry dog jumping on an unguarded sirloin. "Suppose I show you a picture and you tell me what you make of it."

In the next fifteen minutes, Phule learned more about roller coasters and other thrill rides than he'd learned in his entire lifetime, and Okidata was still warming to his subject. Judging from the spy holos, the government park was erecting a sort of culmination of existing roller coaster design—an ultraride. "Unless you're totally wrong about the scale, that's gonna be the best ride on the planet," said Okidata, shaking his head appreciatively. "That first drop has to be ten meters higher than the Kingsnake, over in Dressage Park. Those cars will be hitting some crazy speeds—and look at those corkscrew loops! Everybody's gonna want to ride that baby."

"There's a problem with that, though," said Phule. "From what you tell me, this planet is close to fanatical about thrill rides and amusement parks. Am I right?"

"I guess so," said Okidata. "I've never been off-world, so that's hard to judge. We sure like 'em a lot, though." He turned his eyes longingly back toward the holo of the new government roller coaster.

Phule put both elbows on his desk and his chin on his folded hands. "OK, so the government has a master plan to build the biggest theme park in the planet's history— maybe the biggest in the galaxy. A circus big enough to make up for the shortage of bread. But they're keeping absolutely mum about it. You never heard of it, even though you applied for a job there. And my men had to go out snooping to figure out what they were doing with that big chunk of vacant land. Why aren't they shouting it from the rooftops?"

"Well, I sort of understand that," said Okidata. "We've got five or six ride parks, and they're all playing cutthroat against the others. Every time one of 'em has a new ride, they get more customers than the rest, until somebody tops it. So when word gets out they're building something new, all the others have spies, with hidden cameras and everything, trying to learn the secrets even before it opens. How steep is the main drop-off? How many flip-overs does it have? Are they using video enhancements? Sometimes, when a new ride opens, half the people in line are spies from the other parks, trying to figure out what they can steal for their own rides."

"So the government is acting on the same principles as the private parks," said Phule. "They think in terms of a limited customer pool, when the real game is drawing people from off-planet."

"I never thought of that," said Okidata, scratching his head. "Makes some sense, though."

"If you want to get people in from off-world, you need to tell them about it," said Phule, smacking his palm on the desk. "And if you get enough of them, you don't worry as much about the competition, because there's more business for everybody. The government's still playing by the old rules, but the game has changed. And maybe it's about to change some more . . ."

"Looks to me like maybe you could use a guy with my background," ventured Okidata. He smiled.

"I think you're right," said Phule, suddenly standing up. "Ask for an application in the outer office. I've got a job, and you're the man I want for it."

"Does this mean you want me to join the Legion?" said Okidata, watching Phule, who abruptly began stuffing holos and printouts into a briefcase.

Phule looked up at him. "Not yet, son—you'll be a civilian consultant. But I do have a job you're perfect for. Now, go fill out that application—things are about to get exciting around here, and we need you on board!"

Journal #405

To date, the rebels remained an unknown factor in our picture of Landoor. The legion troops were here, in theory, as much to protect their interests as the government's. But with the possible exception of the shots fired at my employer upon our landing—and there was much room for doubt about that incident—we had seen nothing of them. This did not sit well with my employer, and I knew that he would eventually decide to remedy the situation by meeting them face to face. Discovering the true nature of Landoor Park gave him the incentive he had lacked.

Needless to say, I considered this an overoptimistic approach to the problem. Not that I had any reason to believe that my employer would pay any attention to my doubts . . .

"So here's what they're building," said Phule. Once he knew exactly what to look for, it had been a simple matter to drop a few handfuls of tiny robot cameras in the proper vicinity. Government counter-bots had hunted them down and eliminated them, but not before they'd returned enough holointelligence to give Phule a clear picture of the government's gigantic roller coaster.

"It is quite a surprise, sir," said Beeker, looking over his employer's shoulder. "A rather quixotic undertaking, if you want my opinion."

"But brilliant, in its way," said Phule, leaning back in his chair. "If anything could attract enough money from off-world to revitalize this planet, a theme park is exactly the ticket. Why, it must be the biggest thing of its kind I've ever seen."

"You would be a better judge of that than I, sir," said Beeker. The butler was obviously not as impressed as his employer. "It strikes me as imprudent in the extreme to invest all their capital in this single project. And as you discovered, they are not interested in off-world investors."

"Well, at least not if the investor is me," said Phule. "It's too bad—the one lesson they've learned from their history is not to let off-world money control their economy. As a result, they've put all their eggs in one very precarious basket."

"The time-tested road to ruin," said Beeker, solemnly. "If this project fails . . ." He let the sentence trail off.

Phule finished it for him, "If it fails, they're wiped out." He leaned forward and pointed to the pictures. "The devil of it is, this isn't at all a bad idea, in and of itself. It's almost enough to do the job they want it to do. Almost . . ." A dreamy look came over his face.

Beeker recognized what Phule's expression meant. "Sir, if you are looking for a way to throw away money, you would be better advised to return to Lorelei and bet against the house in one of Maxine Pruett's casinos. It would be considerably slower and less frustrating than what I fear you are contemplating."

Phule chuckled. "You know my mind, don't you, Beeker? But listen to this: The only thing really wrong with what the government is doing is that they're relying on the park to restart their economy. And nobody else on the planet has either the capital or know-how to make it succeed."

"Nobody except you," said Beeker, straight-faced.

"Nobody except me," Phule agreed. His smile was the epitome of self-satisfaction.

"You were sent here to keep the locals from killing one another, not to ruin yourself trying to bail out their economy."

"Well, they aren't trying to kill each other, so I must be doing something right," said Phule.

"They haven't been trying to kill one another since the war ended," Beeker pointed out. "On the other hand, someone definitely tried to kill *you*."

"That's not proven," said Phule. "The government wants me to think the rebels did it, in hopes that I'll send out my people to suppress the rebels for them. In fact, I wouldn't put it past Colonel Mays to send one of his own men to fire off a couple of shots in my direction."

"Of course, that does not mean the rebels wish you no harm," said Beeker. "They evidently have learned of your responsibility for the strafing incident."

"Yes, well, I suppose I was going to have to confront that part of my past sooner or later," said Phule. "Nobody was really hurt, you know . . . I guess it'd be better to tackle it head-on than to keep dodging it . . . Say, that's not a bad idea, come to think of it. I wonder where the rebel headquarters is?"

Beeker's jaw dropped. "Sir! It was bad enough when you contemplated throwing away your money, but I really must advise against throwing away your life as well."

"Don't be such a nanny, Beeker," said Phule. He was on his feet and pacing, a sure sign that his mind was racing at top speed. "We're not here to work for the current government, whatever they want to think. My orders are to help all the people, and that certainly includes the rebels, if they want to take advantage of my generosity.''

''So you mean to offer them the opportunity to put a noose around your neck,'' said Beeker. ''Sir, you cannot expect me to stand aside and allow you to do this.''

''No, of course not,'' said Phule. ''I was planning on taking you along when I go to meet them. You and the chaplain, I think.''

''What?'' Beeker's eyes went wide. ''What good can the chaplain possibly do?''

Phule spread his hands. ''Why, he's a man of peace— what better symbol of my peaceful intentions? And you're obviously a noncombatant—no kind of threat. Unless everything we know about them is wrong, neither of you will be in the least danger. And you'll serve as insurance for me—even if they have a grudge against me, I don't think they'll act too hastily if there are innocent witnesses.''

''Very well, sir. You have obviously made up your mind,'' said Beeker, rising from his chair. ''I suppose I had best prepare for the journey. When do you intend to leave? And will you at least inform your officers of your intentions? Perhaps they can offer some competent military advice.''

Phule shook his head. ''Their advice would be to take along a squad of armed legionnaires, and that would be exactly the wrong thing to do. This needs to be a secret mission. I've found a young civilian who's got a cousin in the rebel camp, and he claims to know the way. And unless we want to lose valuable time, we should leave as quickly as possible.''

''As you wish, sir,'' said Beeker. ''I only hope you have some idea what you are doing.''

''Of course I do,'' said Phule brightly. ''I'm going to save the entire planet. Isn't that what we're here for?''

Journal #406

Our departure from Lorelei had left behind an unstable situation, and potentially a very dangerous one. My em-

*ployer's confidence in the android double he had pro-
grammed to impersonate himself seemed to me excessive.
Eventually, the local gangsters were bound to see through
the deception. What would happen then was anyone's
guess.*

Maxine Pruett glared at the holoscreen. "That conniving
son of a bitch!" she shouted. The scene had only been in
view for a moment, but she knew that face almost as well
as the picture on a dollar bill. In all the years she'd been
running the Syndicate on Lorelei, he was the one person
who'd thwarted her. Captain Jester, AKA Willard Phule,
the munitions heir.

There he was on some planet a quarter of the way across
the galaxy. She hadn't caught exactly what it was he was
doing. In fact, she'd only had the news on out of a sense
of guilt. Laverna had been her eyes and ears on the outside
world, the one who kept her apprised of things that might
affect her while she paid attention to running the business
and enjoying the fruits of her hard-won (albeit ill-gotten)
gains. Now Laverna had run away from her, and she had
nobody to monitor outside events for her. Phule was responsible for that, too.

What she couldn't figure out was how he'd managed to
get off-station without her knowing it. Her snoops had reported seeing him in the Fat Chance nearly every day, and
there were plenty of uniformed legionnaires on guard—so
what did it mean that he and his company were on Landoro,
or whatever that place was in the news story? The answer
must be that one of the Phules was a double. It made
sense—there'd been times she'd had the "same" act
booked in two or three of her casinos at once, with the star
making token appearances in each show, and using doubles
to make it appear he was onstage more than he really was.
Phule must be running a hustle like that . . .

So how was she going to take advantage of her discovery? There was no question that she was going to take
advantage of it—you get an edge, you take it. That was

how the game was played. It would be sweet revenge to finally take the Fat Chance away from him after all he'd done to balk her.

A lot depended on which "Phule" was the impostor, of course. She wasn't about to make an overt move against him if he was actually here to counter it. She'd already had a lesson in the Legion's brand of hardball, and didn't want to repeat it. But if the fellow over in the Fat Chance was the double . . . well, that might be a very different story.

It shouldn't be hard to figure it out. Phule could afford to hire somebody good enough to pass a fairly close inquisition. Still, there'd be things Phule hadn't briefed the double on, questions he wouldn't be able to answer if somebody caught him off his guard. She wouldn't even have to confront him in person. A phone call could tell her who she was dealing with, if she knew the right card to play. But she had to have the right card before she called.

"Holo off," snapped Maxine. The picture abruptly winked out of existence, and the room fell silent. The holo hadn't used to interfere with Maxine's thinking, but that had been when she'd had Laverna to do a lot of that thinking for her. Now she realized that she'd been an idiot to buy Phule's line about his butler eloping with her assistant. Most likely he'd taken them both with him. Well, that wouldn't be hard to find out, either. And when she'd found them, there were favors she could call in. That was one of the advantages of running the Syndicate's favorite resort. She'd been generous with free rooms, free meals, special seats at shows for visitors from other Syndicate families— paying forward in anticipation of future need. Now it was payback time, in more ways than one.

She tried to remember who she knew on that planet— what was its name again? She must not have been paying close enough attention. Well, if she turned the holo back on and watched another twenty minutes the news story would cycle back again. No—she hired people to do that. She'd order somebody to turn on the news and take notes while she figured out what to do about Phule. She picked up the comm handset and pressed a button.

Unexpectedly, it didn't ring. Instead, after a few moments, a synthesized voice came on. "There is no answer at the extension you are calling. If you wish to leave a message, please wait until . . ." She broke the connection, cursing. She wasn't used to getting recorded messages, or waiting. What the hell was she paying these clowns for, if they weren't there when she needed them? That had never happened with Laverna.

She thought a moment about trying another extension, then slammed the handset down. She felt like shaking things up, and she was going to start by finding the lazy goon who'd been supposed to answer that call and reminding him who was boss here. It had been a while since she'd had to do that, but she hadn't forgotten how. The guy on the other end wasn't likely to forget it, either, once she'd finished with him. She stepped toward the door, a grim smile on her lips.

The door opened before she reached it.

She stopped, astounded. Nobody else was supposed to be able to open that door. She was reaching for her weapon when a man stepped forward and said, "I wouldn't do that, Mrs. Pruett. We have the place surrounded, and the penalties for attacking a Federation agent are very severe."

"Federation agent?" she gasped. She recovered her aplomb almost immediately. "What the hell are you doing in my private quarters? You're out of your jurisdiction. Lorelei law says I'm justified in blowing you away for breaking and entering. Get out before I do just that."

"I'm afraid you're mistaken—this *is* my jurisdiction," said the man, and he flipped open a wallet to show a holo-ID. Below the letters *IRS* it read, *Roger Peele, Special Agent*. "The Federation allows localities a good bit of autonomy in criminal and civil law," said Peele solemnly. "But the tax code applies everywhere."

"Tax code? You can't bust me for taxes," said Maxine. "I'm the one who called and tipped you off about the Fat Chance. It's those damned Legion crooks you should be after, not me."

"We make our own decisions about whom to go after,"

said Agent Peele. "We are looking into the situation at the Fat Chance, and we will deal with it in our own time. Meanwhile, we have good reason to believe that you are systematically underreporting your income. I will ask you to come with me, Mrs. Pruett—we have quite a few questions to ask you."

"I'm not answering any questions till I see my lawyer!" shouted Maxine. "Now get out of here before I call Security."

"We have your lawyer and your security people already in custody," said the agent. "You can talk to them down at headquarters." He held out his hand, palm up. "Now, I suggest you surrender your weapon before you find yourself in even more serious trouble."

Maxine cursed. But she handed over the weapon and went quietly. She'd owned a casino long enough to tell when her luck had run out. Today, it had come up snake eyes.

General Blitzkrieg knew he was in trouble the minute he heard the commotion in his outer office. There was only one person with the chutzpa to charge into his office and demand to see him without an appointment. "I know he's in there, Major. Now, you can stand in my way and get run over, or you can step aside and let me in. Either way, I'm going to see him, whether he likes it or not."

Blitzkrieg wished, not for the first time, that he had gotten an office with an emergency exit for these situations. But that would only postpone the inevitable. Like a trip to the dentist, this confrontation could be put off only at the price of worse pain later on. He pushed a button on his intercom and said, doing his best to sound nonchalant, "Major, no need to detain Colonel Battleax. Send her right in, if you will." It sounded phony even to him.

The door opened and Colonel Battleax marched in. Through the open portal the general caught a glimpse of Major Sparrowhawk, whose expression indicated that she was no happier at being made the scapegoat for the delay than Colonel Battleax was at being made to wait. He was going to pay for both those mistakes, he realized. Sometimes he wondered what good being a general was if it afforded no protection from subordinates.

"Good morning, sir," said Colonel Battleax. That was some small relief, he thought as he returned her very proper salute. At least she was going to observe the forms of military courtesy. Beyond that, he was unlikely to find this a pleasant interview.

"Have a seat, Colonel," he said, returning the salute. "To what do I owe the pleasure of your visit?" *Keep up the fiction that you're glad to see her,* he thought, *and maybe she won't bite your head off this time.* He didn't put much trust in that notion, though.

Colonel Battleax settled into the chair facing Blitzkrieg's desk. "I've been watching the news, General," she said. "You've been pulling strings again."

Blitzkrieg feigned surprise. "What are you referring to?"

"A news story from Landoor. It seems there were shots fired at the spaceport, presumably by antigovernment rebels."

"Landoor . . . that name is familiar . . ."

"Of course it's familiar," said the colonel, losing patience. "You went horse-trading to the Joint Chiefs to get a Legion company posted there as the peacekeeping force. You don't do that so often that you're likely to have forgotten it, unless you're getting senile even faster than anyone thought. You sent Phule's Company—Captain Jester's Company—to Landoor."

"Why, yes, I suppose I did," said Blitzkrieg. "It seemed a feather in the cap for the Legion . . ."

"Don't pull that guff on me, General," said Battleax. "Jester was a complete nonentity until he ordered that strafing on New Atlantis, as it was called then. You've taken his subsequent rise as a thorn in your side. Now you transfer him to the one place in the galaxy where there are people with a bigger grudge against him than yours. You expect me to believe this is unpremeditated?"

"Why, yes . . . er, *no* . . ." Blitzkrieg turned red. "Damn it, Colonel, what are you getting at?"

The colonel stood up and leaned forward over the general's desk. "General, it's time you realized that, whether or not you like Jester, he's a rising star. If you'd accepted that all along, the entire Legion would have gotten credit for everything he's done. Instead, he's the shining exception. I can't think of another Legion unit the Joint Chiefs would've been willing to put in such a sensitive position. Now if he falls on his face, he'll take the entire Legion down with him. You may not be able to see beyond your own nose, but those of us who can aren't going to let you get away with it." She glared at him, then straightened up and added as an afterthought, "With all due respect, sir."

"This is preposterous," said the general. "I deny it all, of course." He was sweating.

"Frankly, General, I didn't expect anything else," said Colonel Battleax. "If Jester comes a cropper on Landoor, there are some of us who will see that blame for it comes back to roost where it belongs. So I suggest you do whatever you can to insure that nothing untoward *does* happen to him."

Blitzkrieg shrugged. "Really, Colonel, I don't see where this is any matter for great concern. A Legion captain ought to be able to take care of himself. If he can't, that's a pity, but ultimately no reflection on us."

The colonel nodded, grimly. "Very well, sir, if that's how you intend to play the game, that's how it'll be played. Good day, sir." She saluted and left the office.

Blitzkrieg leaned back in his chair. That hadn't gone so badly, he thought. Still, best to keep a closer eye on the Landoor situation. If Jester got in trouble there, he might be able to devise a way to burnish his own reputation by riding to the rescue. Yes, that might be a very satisfactory way to profit from his enemy's distress. He'd have to keep it in mind.

"He's gone *where*?" Lieutenant Armstrong's disbelief was written plainly on his face. He'd just poured his first cup of coffee, so his normal stiff bearing hadn't quite had time to set in.

"Here's the note he left with Mother," said Lieutenant Rembrandt, shoving a piece of paper at her fellow officer. "At least he *left* a note—I'd have liked it a lot more if he'd told us in person, though."

"We'd have tried to talk him out of it, which is why he didn't ask us," said Armstrong, glancing up from the note. "He has Beeker and Rev along, I see. Do we have any idea where specifically they've gone?"

"The rebel headquarters is somewhere on the mainland," said Rembrandt. She waved a hand vaguely. "We don't know exactly where. Mother couldn't find any intelligence reports on it. The captain had already asked her. I was glad to hear that—at least he didn't set out completely blind. But the rebels haven't been enough trouble to justify close surveillance, up until now."

Armstrong frowned. "No satellite intelligence?"

"The satellite network here is pretty rudimentary," said Rembrandt, wearily. "The captain learned that when he was looking for that secret government project. There are a couple of old weather sats, dating back to the mining days, with add-ons for GPS and communications. But nothing military."

"Nothing? Didn't these people just have a war?"

"Sure," said Rembrandt. She walked over to the coffee urn and topped up her cup. "But remember, with only one nation on this world, they didn't have an enemy to keep tabs on. When that civil war broke out, their economy had collapsed, and neither side had off-world allies. It was a low-tech war all around—no armor, no air force, no long-range missiles. And no intelligence sats. Even after the war, the Army peacekeeping team never took the rebels seriously enough to spend the money on sats."

"Well, I guess we should be thankful for small favors," said Armstrong. "At least nobody's got enough firepower to overwhelm a single Legion company if they decide to start shooting. I guess that's an acceptable trade-off for the extra set of eyes."

"I agree," said Rembrandt, adding a dash of cream to her coffee. "Except we still need to figure out where the captain's gone. If an emergency comes up, I want to talk to him before I do anything drastic.''

Armstrong looked up from his coffee cup. ''I don't see how that's a problem,'' he said. ''We can zero in on their wrist communicators, right? Or is there something else you haven't told me?''

''You got it. Everybody except the captain left their communicators behind,'' said Rembrandt. ''And he's turned his off. I think he didn't want the rebels to get their hands on advanced tech if they decided to take him prisoner. One communicator won't do them much good; they need two or more to get any advantage from them.''

''Rats,'' said Armstrong. ''So we can't get in touch with the captain unless he initiates the contact.''

''That's the story,'' said Rembrandt. ''We better hope that nothing happens until he decides to come back.''

''We better hope the rebels don't decide they've got a useful hostage on their hands,'' said Armstrong.

''Yeah, I thought about that, too,'' said Rembrandt. She drained her coffee and set down the cup. ''Maybe you better get over to the comm center and see if you and Mother can figure out some alternate way to track down the captain.''

Armstrong picked up his coffee cup and rose from his chair. ''I'll get right on it,'' he said. ''Let you know if I hear from him.''

''Right,'' said Rembrandt. She watched Armstrong leave, then turned to the day's schedule. She'd be running the company in the captain's absence—this time without even Beeker's help. There had better not be any emergencies while she was in charge. She expected to have her hands full finding the captain.

They found the rebel base by following a bayou that led deep into the mainland, passing a little trading post, and turning up a broad jungle trail that rapidly became narrower as the lush vegetation closed in. Various stinging and biting insects closed in, as well. If the trail had been a bit better, it might have been possible to outrun them. As it was, the passengers spent half their time swatting pests. Phule wondered how the rebels managed to control the insects—or whether they simply put up with them as part of the price for their freedom.

Okidata, who was acting as driver as well as guide, stopped the hoverjeep outside the camp. "I don't know what kind of electronics they have, but there must be something they can pick us up on," he said, slapping a mosquito. "From here on in, we're probably being watched."

"I've been taking that for granted ever since we left our own base," said Phule, mopping his sweating brow. It was no exaggeration. Ever since the spaceport sniper had taken two shots at him, he'd assumed that every time he came outside Legion headquarters he might become a target again. So far, it hadn't happened. But up until now, he hadn't come strolling right up to the rebels' camp, either. Well, he ought to be all right as long as the rebels respected a flag of truce. *If* they respected it . . . "See if you can open up a comm connection," he said. "Might as well do what we can to keep from startling some trigger-happy sentry."

"You folks already way too late for that," came a voice from surprisingly nearby. Phule looked up to see a large weapon pointed at him. Behind the weapon was a wiry, bearded man in jungle camouflage with a red bandanna headband. Closer inspection revealed that he was wearing gold hoop earrings to match a gold front tooth. "Guess you better put them hands up," the rebel added, almost as an afterthought.

"Hey, take it easy—I'm on your side," said Okidata, indignantly.

"I ain't got the time to figure that out right now," said the rebel. "Get them hands up and we'll settle it later."

"We're here under a flag of truce," said Phule, reasonably. "Besides, our driver can't control the hoverjeep with his hands up."

"I wouldn't put too fine a point on it, sir," said Beeker, raising his hands. "At the moment, the gentleman appears to be in a position to insist on his demands.''

"We ain't gonna worry about the hoverer," said the man with the gun. "Why don't you jes' get out so I don't have to worry 'bout you drivin' off all of a sudden? You don't wanna go makin' me jumpy, do you?''

"I reckon *not*," said Rev, his hands high above his head. "Looky here, ol' buddy, don't shoot—I'm jes' gettin' out, like you asked."

"That's a smart feller," said the rebel, nodding. He watched Rev get out, motioned him off to one side with the gun barrel, then said, "OK, next out—you with the bowler hat, there. Shake a leg."

"Very well," said Beeker. "Please be careful where you point that weapon. I'm afraid my health insurance doesn't cover acts of war, and I fear that any injury I receive under these conditions might be construed as such."

Two other armed rebels showed up while the man with the gun directed Phule and Okidata out of the hoverjeep. They gawked when they saw the Legion uniforms, but kept their weapons aimed at their captives, and managed to give the impression that they would fire if provoked. Nobody provoked them. When all four captives were standing together, hands raised, one of the newcomers whistled. "Whoo-ee, Buster, looks like you done made a real haul."

"He certainly has," said Phule. "Now, if you want to make the most of it, I suggest you take us to your superior officers."

"Suggestion noted," said Buster. He turned and spit into the underbrush, then said, "Durn if you ain't the fanciest bunch I seen in a while, though. Two of you in them black uniforms, and the other two wearin' their Sunday best, too. You all got the look of some kind o' face cards—what's your game, anyway?''

"We've come here to help you win," said Phule. "Now, will you take us to your officers?''

"Help us win?" said Buster, his eyes wide. "That's the damnedest proposition I've heard all month, and I keep some mighty strange company. What makes you think you can help us?''

''This,'' said Phule, pointing to the leather pouch strapped around his waist.

''Keep them hands up,'' said Buster. ''What you got in there, anyway? If it's some kind of secret weapon, it's a mighty small one.''

''Nothing secret about it,'' said Phule. ''But it's the one weapon every fighting force needs more than any other. Now, if you'll take me to your superior, maybe he'll let you stick around while I open it up and show him. If you don't delay us unnecessarily, I'll even put in a good word for you.''

Buster laughed. ''The day I need a good word with the brass is gonna be a long time comin'. But I like your style, mister, so I'm gonna do what you say. This here vehicle oughta be safe right where it is. If you boys will just start walkin' along that trail, you ought to come to the camp in no time at all. Don't do anything rash, though—'cause I'll be right behind you.''

''Believe me, friend, coming here was as rash an act as I'm prepared to engage in for some time to come,'' said Beeker. ''We'll be greatly obliged if you keep it in mind that we are here under a flag of truce.''

''I'll keep it in mind, long as nothin' happens to jar it out of my memory,'' said Buster. ''Let's get a move on.''

They started off along the jungle trail. Behind them, Buster began to whistle a jaunty melody. Phule trudged along, his hands held high. Perspiration had begun to soak his uniform, and the jungle flies swarmed around his face. It was inconvenient not being able to swat the flies, but Buster and his men might misunderstand any sudden notions. Off to the side, there was a droning chorus of spooky sounds—indigenous animals, he assumed. Presumably the creatures weren't dangerous. At least, the rebels seemed to pay them no mind. Then again, the rebels were armed, and he wasn't.

Faced with the reality of the jungle, Phule belatedly began to wonder if everything was going to be as easy as it had looked when he was planning it. If he'd miscalculated, he might have gotten himself in far worse trouble than he'd bargained for . . .

14

The first roller coaster on Landoor was built by an unemployed mining engineer, J. T. Dressage. Inspired by seeing youths in the mining towns taking daredevil rides on abandoned mine railroad cars, he purchased a quantity of track at salvage prices. Borrowing the money to buy a plot of land outside Landoor City, he built a ramshackle wooden trestle, and opened his ride—"the Daredevil." It caught the fancy of the public and, within a short time, Dressage had not only paid off his debts, but purchased fifty acres of adjacent land and expanded his operation to become the first of Landoor's theme parks.

The success of Dressage Park caught the eyes of several small businessmen, who pooled their savings and set up a rival operation south of the city—Dunes Park, with an even wider range of rides and attractions. Within a few years, no Landooran considered a vacation complete without a visit to one of the Atlantis theme parks. Indeed, they were the first enterprises on the planet developed without the participation of the Moguls. They (and the smaller parks that sprang up in their wake) thus became an important symbol of national pride to the Landoorans—the working people to whom the Moguls were alien princes with no roots in their world. This image was confirmed when the Moguls decamped to greener pastures and left Landoor to the Landoorans.

At that point, Landoor found itself with all the circuses it could ask for. But as they soon realized, there was a desperate shortage of bread. And therein lay the seeds of revolution . . .

The trail took Phule's group and their guards on a mildly strenuous hike through dense, steaming jungle, in which the occasional Earth-origin tree or animal could be spotted. (The original settlers appeared to have brought along a fair supply of parrots—or possibly a few escaped breeding pairs had been sufficient to start a population explosion.) The contrast between the slightly purplish local foliage and the brighter green Terran-import leaves made the walk unusually picturesque—although not quite enough so for Phule to stop worrying about his reception at trail's end.

At last, the trail crossed a little stream on stepping stones, and on the other side was the guerilla camp. Phule thought to himself that the camp was completely vulnerable to an air attack. Given the government's manifest eagerness to put the rebels out of business, the fact that they hadn't done so was proof of how thoroughly they had been disarmed.

There were a good number of two-person tents in camouflage colors—obviously off-planet in origin, since the hues clashed with the local vegetation. Open cooking fires were scattered at intervals among them. Here and there were small groups of armed men and women, sitting on the ground or engaged in various tasks, from cooking to construction of larger, more permanent buildings. There was nothing resembling a consistent uniform, although many appeared to have adopted the red bandanna as a quasi-official badge.

Buster pointed to the center of the clearing, where a large

tent stood next to an improvised pole bearing a colorful flag, different from the one flying over the government buildings: the rebel flag, no doubt. "That-a-way," he said. Phule and his group followed, drawing curious stares from the groups of rebels they passed on their way through the camp.

The main tent had an awning protecting a folding table at which sat a lean man with a fringe of stringy gray hair beneath a field cap. He wore the closest thing to a real uniform that Phule had seen so far, although it bore no recognizable insignia. He looked up as Buster herded Phule and his companions into the shade of the tent. "Who's this?" he said, squinting at the newcomers.

"Found 'em out in the woods," said Buster. "They drove right up in a hovercar, asked to see you. So here they are."

"Have they been searched or questioned?" said the man, looking at the uniformed legionnaires.

"Nah, they weren't showin' no hardware, so we just brought 'em in," said Buster. "Like I say, this guy in the front wanted to talk to you."

"This is an inexcusable lapse in security," said the rebel leader—for that was obviously what he was. "If these men had been carrying concealed weapons . . ."

"Oh, give us a break, will ya?" said Buster, with a sweeping gesture. "Look at these jaspers and tell me any of 'em has the brass to sneak in a weapon. Minute they pull it, they's gonna be buzzard meat, even if they do get a few of us. They look like the suicidal type to you?"

"Perhaps not, but we have security procedures for a reason," said the leader. "This is not the first time you have shown a lack of judgment . . ."

"I think he showed excellent judgement in bringing us directly to you," Phule interrupted. "I think you will find what I have to say very interesting—and very much to your advantage."

"And you are?" asked the rebel leader, glaring at Phule.

"Captain Jester, Space Legion," said Phule, with a little nod. "With me is Chaplain Rev, as well as my chauffeur and my personal butler. And whom am I speaking to?''

''A chauffeur and a butler, eh?'' said the rebel leader. ''And a chaplain, too. That's a first, for sure—most people who come looking for me bring along an infantry brigade or so.'' Belatedly, remembering that Phule had asked his name, he puffed up his chest and said, ''I am Le Duc Taep, Provisional President of the Restored Republic of New Atlantis.''

''Ah, then I am speaking to the right man,'' said Phule. ''Mr. President, I have come to show you how to win your revolution.''

''What did you say?'' said Le Duc Taep. He looked at Phule's uniform again. ''Aren't you from the peacekeeping team?''

''That is correct. In fact, I am its commanding officer,'' said Phule, smiling broadly.

''You!'' Le Duc Taep rose to his feet and pointed at Phule. ''You are the officer formerly known as Captain Scaramouche?''

Phule's smile didn't waver. ''Mr. President, perhaps you aren't familiar with our Legion traditions. A legionnaire's previous identity is unimportant. Even when a member has been . . .''

''You *are* Scaramouche!'' shouted Le Duc Taep. He turned to Buster and the guards and exclaimed, ''Seize him!''

''Salutations, Lieutenant Strongarm!'' Flight Leftenant Qual came bouncing into Comm Central, located in the penthouse suite of the Landoor Plaza.

Armstrong looked up from the printout he was scanning. ''Good morning, Qual. What's the good word?''

''If you mean news of Captain Clown, I am afraid the word is a bad one,'' said Qual. ''Or no word at all, to be more exact. Have you received intelligence of him?''

''Heard nothing,'' said Tusk-anini, stationed behind a bank of electronic intelligence monitors. ''Best guess is rebels holding captain prisoner.''

''This comes of acting like the hero of some holodrama," said Armstrong. He slapped the printout down on the desktop with a degree of force that underscored his frustration. "Going out to find the rebel camp was like asking to be taken prisoner. We can only hope the rebels have sense enough to keep him alive. As long as he's alive, at least we've got a chance to rescue him."

"Well spoken, Strongarm," said Qual. "With resources of this company, such should be within ready capability. But a clever plan must be made before commencing, no?"

"Before even that, we have to figure out where the rebels are," said Armstrong. "Of course, the captain went squiring off without bothering to leave an itinerary. I suppose he went out and followed his nose, so maybe we could find them the same way. But even if we find their main camp, there's no guarantee the captain's there . . ."

"No, but that a good place to start," said Tusk-anini. "We find rebel camp, then good chance we also find somebody know where captain is."

"Tusk-anini speaks reason," said Qual, flashing his allosaurus grin. "You dispatch your best jungle scouts, and when you find the rebel camp, you will find Captain Clown."

"Best jungle scouts," mused Armstrong. "Now there's a specialty we haven't had to identify before. The Gambolts would probably be good at that. Who else . . . ?"

"Yours truly was hatched and nurtured in an environment not dissimilar to this world's, I hasten to inform you," said Qual. "I would eagerly volunteer to direct such a hazarding, if you wish to make use of my native competencies."

Armstrong rubbed his chin, then said, "I'd have to run that past Lieutenant Rembrandt—she's officially in command in the captain's absence. The question would be whether a foreign officer should lead Legion troops."

"If Qual best for doing job, why he not do it?" asked Tusk-anini.

Armstrong shook his head. "That's your problem, Tusk-anini: You've never really understood why we in the military have to do things a certain way . . ."

"Understand perfectly," grunted Tusk-a-nini. "Too polite to say what think about it."

"I admire your support, Voltonish friend," Qual said, grinning. "But Lieutenant Strongarm is correct. Shackle of command must be followed. We shall request approval of this plan from Lieutenant Rembrandt. Perhaps, though, it is best to approach her with a fully realized stratagem. Oh Layer-of-Eggs, do our computers indicate which legionnaires are from planets similar to this in terrain?"

"aghidpgtie," said Mother, who had been doing her best to ignore the presence of others in her work area until addressed directly. But she began punching search parameters into her keyboard, and soon Qual and Armstrong were working on the tentative rescue plan. It was a wild idea, even for the Omega Mob, but as he reviewed the plan, Armstrong began to think it might work . . .

"What are you waiting for?" shouted Le Duc Taep, pointing at Phule. "Seize him!" There was a stunned moment of silence in the rebel camp.

"Uh, do you mean that like literally, Taep?" said Buster, scratching his jawbone below the right ear. "We pretty much got him in hand, y'know. You want us to hog-tie him or somethin'?"

"Secure him so he can't escape, you idiots!" shouted Le Duc Taep, stepping around the folding table. "This man is one of the greatest enemies of the revolution!"

The guards raised their weapons, suddenly looking alert. Buster stepped over and put a hand on Phule's shoulder. "Don't you or your friends try nothing funny, OK? If Taep's tellin' the truth, you might be in a good bit o' trouble."

"I fail to see how that's so," said Phule, returning Le Duc Taep's gaze. "Even if I admitted being Captain Scaramouche—which I haven't—my position within the Federation peacekeeping force gives me diplomatic immunity. It would be very unwise to interfere with me in the course of my duties."

"Unwise?" said Le Duc Taep. He sneered. "There is

wisdom, and there is satisfaction. I mean to have my satisfaction, and whatever follows I will take in stride.''

"Now, just a minute, Taep," said Buster, leaning on the butt of his weapon. "Your satisfaction is dandy, but so far I ain't heard what's in it for the grunts. Say we execute this bird, and the Federation sends in a battle cruiser to vamp on us. What do the kids out there get in the way of satisfaction while they're dodgin' the assault lasers and pocket nukes?''

"They will have helped punish the greatest enemy of New Atlantis!" replied Le Duc Taep, but some of the bluster had gone out of his voice.

"Really?" said Buster. The way he said it, the word rhymed with *silly*. He paused before continuing. "Seems to me there's a few guys sittin' in Government House back in Landoor City that fill them shoes better than this here fella. Then again, maybe he *has* done somethin' worth risking that battle cruiser for to get back at him. But you still ain't told us what it is."

"That's right, Taep," said a guard, and another chimed in with, "Yeah, what's he done?"

Le Duc Taep pointed at Phule. "This is the man who ordered the scurrilous attack on the peace conference, further humiliating us at the moment of our capitulation!''

"Oh, yeah, I heard about that," said Buster. "You and the other brass got your pants singed pretty good, didn't you?" He turned to Phule. "He tellin' the truth?"

"Well . . ." Phule began, "I think I should point out that nobody was killed . . .''

Rev put his hand on Phule's shoulder. "Y'know, there's more to this situation than meets the eyeball.''

"What say?" said Buster, frowning. "Seems to me, either he done it or he didn't.''

"He *did* do it," said Le Duc Taep, his confidence returning. "Otherwise, he'd simply deny it.''

"You got a good point there," said Buster. "But let me hear this other bird's point he's tryin' to make.''

"Why, thank ye, sonny," said Rev. "What I'd like to say here is, a fellow can be different things, and what he used to be ain't necessarily as important as what he *is*. You go holdin' the past against him, you might be missin' a glorious opportunity right now."

"You still talkin' over my head," said Buster, scratching his jaw again. "Taep, you got any idea what he's sayin'?"

"What he's saying is that whatever I did or didn't do back during the peace conference—and I really don't think we have to rake over those coals again—I can make up for it now," said Phule. "My orders are to bring peace to this world—they don't say one word about who governs it. It might as well be you as the other fellow. So I'm going to help you win."

"That's big talk," said Buster, solemnly. "Win the war for us just like that? I gotta hear this."

"If you're going to try to buy forgiveness . . ." Le Duc Taep began.

"Yes, of course, what else?" said Phule. He reached down and opened up his belt pouch. He pulled out a handful of banknotes in large denominations. "I know money can't buy everything, but that's no reason to turn up your nose at it. Let's put the proposition in a nutshell. You can win your revolution, and I'm going to show you how to do it. Are you game?"

Le Duc Taep looked at the money, then looked back at Phule. "And what's to stop us from taking your money and our revenge both at the same time?"

Phule shrugged. "Oh, money's not hard to get, if you have the knack. You could raise this much yourself in a few days, if you put your mind to it. Of course, this is a drop in the bucket, compared to what you'd need. And I'm willing to back you to the limit."

"You'll buy us all the weapons we need to win the war?" said Le Duc Taep, obviously impressed.

"Oh, you won't need weapons," said Phule. "I'd hardly waste my money on that. What I'm going to do is show you how to win without firing a shot. Here's what you're going to need . . ."

As Phule outlined his plan, the rebel leader began to nod his head. Le Duc Taep and Buster—evidently a very senior officer in the guerilla band—interrupted from time to time with questions. Soon Phule had laid out a sheet of paper on the folding table and started making sketches. The afternoon wore on . . .

"Yo, Remmie, you gotta let us in on this rescue operation," said Do-Wop.

Lieutenant Rembrandt looked up from her drawing pad at Do-Wop and Sushi. Even now, with command of the entire company thrust upon her, she made herself take a few minutes to keep her eyes sharp. It gave her a way to sidestep the worry about what kind of trouble the captain had gotten into, *this* time. "No," she said.

"Whattaya mean?" said Do-Wop. "We got a right to volunteer, don't we?"

"Sure, you've got a right to volunteer," said Rembrandt, putting aside the drawing pad. "But I've got to choose a team I think will do the job without getting anybody killed—and I mean the captain, in particular. You two don't fit the mission specs, this time."

"Why not?" said Do-Wop. "We're as slick as you've got—even the captain knows that. Besides, we owe him—nobody else ever cut us half the breaks the captain has."

"Well, I'm glad you appreciate that," said Rembrandt. "I know you two are slick—God, are you ever slick—but you're not jungle scouts, and that's what we need this time."

Do-Wop snickered. "*I* ain't worried about the jungle. You drop me down anywhere on this planet, I'll be the baddest thing for a hundred kilometers."

Rembrandt shook her head. "The answer is no. There'll be plenty of other missions . . ."

"Not if these guys don't rescue the captain," said Sushi. "What are they going to do, anyway? Rush in and start shooting? Or maybe something smart, like trying to persuade the rebels to let him go? That's about the only way I can think of to make sure the captain doesn't get hurt. You'll admit we're the only ones who could do that. We can sell sneakers to snakes, if you give us the chance."

"What's a snake?—oh, never mind, I get the idea," said Lieutenant Rembrandt. She stood up and planted a finger in the center of Sushi's chest. "Maybe you can, but that's not the point. This team's going out in the jungle. They'd spend so much time bailing you two out of trouble they'd never get around to rescuing the captain."

Sushi didn't budge. "They're still going to need somebody like us at the other end," he said. "What about this— the jungle scouts find the captain, then you send us in to negotiate? Once we know our goal, you can send us by hovercar, if you want. That way you don't have to worry about all the jungle thingies getting us."

"I ain't scared of no jungle thingies," Do-Wop reiterated.

"I'm sure you're not, which is another good reason you're not going to be a jungle scout," said Rembrandt. Do-Wop opened his mouth to protest, but she held up a hand and continued, "Sushi's idea has some merit, I have to admit. But I'm not going to give a thumbs-up until I know where the captain's being held. Until then I don't even know whether he needs rescuing, let alone what the best plan will be. Maybe it's sending you in to bamboozle the rebels or going in with force or something else we haven't thought of yet. The one thing I do know is that you're not going out in the jungle. Get used to it."

"Well, Lieutenant, I think you're being too cautious," said Sushi. "But if you promise you'll keep my plan in mind, we'll let you get back to work. And thanks for listening."

"I won't forget your plan," said Rembrandt. "No other promises, though. Now, aren't you two supposed to be on duty someplace?"

"Uh, like Soosh said, we'll let you get back to work," said Do-Wop, and the two legionnaires beat a hasty retreat. Rembrandt sighed and reached for her sketchpad again. Sushi had given her a potentially useful idea. She'd have to think about a way to make it work . . .

"Lieutenant, got to talk," came a familiar voice. "Rebels holding captain prisoner. Got to be on team rescuing him."

Rembrandt sighed. "Tusk-anini, I don't remember anything in your file about you coming from a jungle world," she said. She began to suspect that she was going to have a lot of discussions like the one just concluded in the time before the jungle team set out.

Eventually, Armstrong and Rembrandt cobbled together a two-stage mission for rescuing Phule. First Qual and the Gambolts would use their skills to find the rebel camp at which Phule was presumably being held prisoner, and report its location to base. If Qual's report convinced the officers that Phule actually needed rescuing, a fighting force of volunteers would go in to do the job.

After dark, a hoverjeep swooped low over the waves and put Qual's team ashore on the mainland in the area in which the rebel camp was rumored to be located. The Zenobian and the three Gambolts melted into invisibility almost before they had reached the dark line of brush a few dozen yards above the high-tide mark on the sand. As soon as they were out of sight, the hoverjeep turned back to the island, and the Legion base.

Qual watched from the shadows, then turned to the Gambolts. "Now we travel softly," he said to them, and they nodded; Qual's dark-adapted vision registered the nods, as theirs registered his silent "follow me" gesture. They followed.

They were travelling light, planning to live off the land rather than slow themselves with unnecessary food and equipment. All were from hunting races, and experiment had proven that they could eat the native wildlife as well as the earthling species introduced by the original settlers. The Gambolts, in fact, were especially fond of nutria. When Escrima first offered that dish on the Legion menu, Duke had sampled it and said approvingly, "It tastes much like rodent—but of unusual size." The others had nodded. Brandy, who overheard the compliment, had very carefully made sure it did not get back to Escrima—at least, not accurately translated.

At first the team followed a broad stream that took them west and north into the interior. Qual set a rapid pace, and the Gambolts followed him easily. Toward midnight, they came to a natural-looking log bridge across the stream, with a narrow game trail leading off in either direction. They examined both banks for traces of human passage.

"The odor of humans is stronger to the left," murmured Garbo. "There must be a settlement in that direction." She lashed her tail in involuntary excitement.

Qual pulled out a map and examined it. "The humans' chart does not illustrate a town in this vicinity," he said after a moment. "However, there are shown a few trappers' camps, and a trading post that seems more continuous."

"I smell too many humans for a camp or trading post," said Garbo. "But perhaps they hunt in large packs, like the *goulfes* of our world."

Dukes and Rube nodded their agreement. "There are males and females both," Rube added, wriggling his nose.

"Do their trappers hunt in mixed-sex groupings?" asked Qual. "Our people hunt alone, so I cannot judge humans by our customs."

"Their military mixes the sexes, as ours does. Perhaps they hunt together as well," said Garbo. "If we moved closer, perhaps we could distinguish the captain's scent."

"Gazma's tail! I find it quaint that such a meagerly toothed species hunts at all," said Qual, with a grin that brought a feline gurgle of amusement from the Gambolts. "We shall do as Garbo suggests and explore the trail to the left."

They set off into the darkness again. Along toward dawn, they surprised a small, leaping creature; Rube captured it before it took two bounds, and they breakfasted quickly before moving along. Ahead, the scent of humans grew stronger.

Lieutenant Rembrandt was toweling off from her morning shower when her communicator alarm went off. She dropped the towel and picked up the communicator. "Rembrandt here," she said. "What's cooking, Mother?"

"Hot stuff, Remmy," came the saucy voice. "Our little lizard wizard and the three pussycats have found the rebel camp, and the captain's there."

"Is the captain free or a prisoner?" asked Rembrandt.

Mother paused before saying, "Well, honey, that's the tricky part. You know how Qual talks kind of strange . . ."

"Great Gazma, do I ever!" said Rembrandt, laughing. Then her voice turned sharper. "What are you telling me, Mother?"

"Well, they found the captain. But they only saw him for a moment before they set off some kind of alarm. A patrol came out looking for them and they had to skedaddle. So they didn't see enough to figure out whether he's free. Qual said one of the rebels was always there with a gun, but that doesn't prove Cap's a prisoner, does it?"

"Not necessarily, no," said Rembrandt. "Damn—now I realize it was a mistake not to have sent at least one human in the scout party. Then we'd have a better idea whether the captain was under duress. Now I've got to read a Zenobian's mind to decide whether to send the rescue party or stay clear."

Mother's voice cut through her spoken-aloud thoughts. "Any orders, Remmie? I've got other calls coming in."

Rembrandt answered without hesitation, "If one of them's Qual, patch him straight through to me. If not, keep trying to raise him. And put the rescue team on alert. I want them ready to go on a moment's notice. I'll be over to Comm Central as soon as I get my uniform on."

"Ooooh, should I send somebody over with a camera?"

Rembrandt chuckled. "Not if you want the camera back in one piece," she said. "Remember, hook me up right away if you get Qual. Rembrandt out." She grabbed the towel again and finished dressing in a hurry.

"Sir, I am concerned that you have not communicated with Headquarters," said Beeker, coming into the tent assigned to him and his employer. "If I were your lieutenants, I would be concerned about your safety."

"This is one of those operations where secrecy is the most important concern, Beeker," said Phule. He saved the work he had in progress on his Port-a-Brain computer, then leaned back in his seat to look his butler in the eye. "If the government learns we're out here, they're likely to see what we're doing as aiding and abetting the rebels."

"Isn't that precisely what you *are* doing, sir?"

"Only in the narrowest sense, Beeker," Phule said. "I can make an excellent case that what we're doing will benefit the entire planet. But that case will look a whole lot stronger if we've made reasonable progress toward getting the project under way when somebody starts asking questions."

Beeker's face took on a faintly disapproving expression. "I expect the government to judge that case by its own lights, sir. If they can represent your actions as taking the rebels' side, they're likely to petition for your company's removal from the planet. You'll have invested a great deal of time and effort only to get a black eye. More to the point, I'm afraid that something like that would give General Blitzkrieg exactly the pretext he's been looking for to cashier you from the Legion."

"Blitzkrieg and his ilk have made the Legion the laughingstock of the Federation," said Phule. "Luckily, there *are* some good officers at the top of the Legion. Some of them must have noticed that I'm getting them favorable press coverage, which is a novelty for the Legion. I hope they'll listen to my case before they do anything they'd regret, Beeker. They've got too much invested here for them to toss me overboard at the first sign of a little rough weather."

"In fact, they strike me as likely to do exactly that if you push them too far," said Beeker. "I must caution you not to overestimate your value to the Legion, sir—the generals do not necessarily share your view of what is best for them."

Phule leaned farther back in his chair, lacing his fingers

behind the nape of his neck. "Good old Beeker, always the mother hen. Don't worry, old fellow, I know what I'm doing this time. We'll come out with flying colors."

"Perhaps, sir," said Beeker, stiffly. "Still, I feel it my responsibility to call your attention to another scenario you may not have taken into account."

"What's that?"

"Suppose that when the government learns of your involvement here, they decide not to protest to the Federation, but to launch a preemptive strike against this base? If they have managed to conceal any significant military resources, they could destroy this camp in an afternoon. You would be a regrettable collateral victim—or they might claim that the rebels killed you when they came under attack. Naturally, there'd be no one to contradict their account. The Legion could award you a posthumous medal, if it were so minded."

"Well, that confirms my belief that we need to keep this operation secret," said Phule. "Don't worry, old fellow, we'll get out of this one all right. If you want, I can have the rebels smuggle you back to Headquarters so you can get out of danger."

"Sir, I resent the implication that I am motivated primarily by a fear of danger."

Phule's eyebrows went up a notch. "You mean you're not? I'm surprised, Beeker. I thought you considered self-preservation a cardinal virtue."

"And so I do, sir," said the butler. "But protection of my assets is also a considerable factor in my course of action at any given time. In fact, I have not necessarily rejected your offer of an escort back to civilization. But it strikes me that what you are planning here, should it succeed, would be an excellent investment opportunity for me, as well. Thus, I would like to have a degree of input into its planning that my absence would render impractical."

Now Phule broke into a broad grin. "Aha. I knew you had some sort of agenda. In that case, why don't you help me look over these plans, and let's see if we can get this project under way before the government decides to try stopping us?'' He pointed to the Port-a-Brain computer, and Beeker leaned forward to examine the screen. Within a few minutes, the two were exploring the best ways to advance the project. Nothing more was said of Beeker leaving.

Journal #412

In the end, Lieutenant Rembrandt decided she would have fewer regrets sending the rescue team than waiting to hear from Phule. Flight Leftenant Qual had remained out of communication, and lacking any report from him, it was reasonable for her to assume the worst.

The rescue team was led by Lieutenant Armstrong. He had managed to hire a waterman familiar with the area of the mainland where Armstrong thought the rebel camp to be. Supplemented with what meager satellite intelligence they could gather, and armed with a mix of lethal weapons and Zenobian stun rays, the rescue party set out. Naturally, they had no idea what lay ahead of them.

The flat-bottomed boat skimmed quickly and almost silently along the waterway. ''This is how the rebels travel around the swamps,'' said the boatman, whose name was Hansen. ''They kin duck back in these here bayous quicker than a nutria jumpin' off the bank.''

''I can see how they'd be tough to catch,'' said Armstrong. ''These waterways all look the same to me—I don't see how anybody would ever find their way without GPS.'' Raised on a high-tech world, he took the benefits of a full satellite network for granted.

''GPS—huh!'' said Hansen. He spat in the water. ''Genuine Piece of Shit, you ask me. Maybe that stuff can tell you where you at on a map, but that don't mean you gonna find your way anywhere else. The swamp keep a-changin', and if the map don't show the change, GPS can't help none. You better off havin' a local boy out on your skiff.''

''Maybe so,'' said Armstrong, with a tight-lipped smile. ''But relying on locals works until the locals decide they're on the other guy's side—no offense, but it happens too often to ignore. If you wanted to, I bet you could get me so lost I'd never come back out. GPS gives me a chance— though I'd give a lot to have a few more sats up there.''

"Something up ahead," said Tusk-anini, pointing over the bow. There was an opening in the trees, and through it those on the boat could see a structure of some sort.

"Stand ready for action," said Armstrong, and the legionnaires took their equipment in hand and looked ahead at their destination—or had it been designated as a target, now? They'd know when Armstrong spoke.

"That's jes' Bobby Czerny's place, nothin' we got to worry about," said the boatman. "Ol' Bobby sells a little food, a little bait, a little fuel, a little hooch—money or trade, he don't care what he sells or who he sells it to, long as he gets by. Don't need no artillery here."

"We don't usually get worried," said Super-Gnat, who was carrying a Rolling Thunder automatic shotgun that looked bigger than she was. She grinned. "But somebody took a potshot at the captain when we landed, and now the looie thinks he's a prisoner. So maybe we do need the artillery, y'know? If we have to use it, you get down flat and stay out of the way."

"Assumin' we don't capsize from the first shot, I reckon I'll do jes' that," said Hansen. "You folks better be careful with them big ol' guns—these here flatboats flip right over, you start to skip around on deck. A warnin' to the wise."

"We hear you," said Armstrong. "Everyone make sure you have a steady position if you need to fire. Closing on target."

The legionnaires spread out around the little boat, trying to distribute their weight equally. Most crouched down, or lay prone on the deck, to reduce the target they offered any hostile observer—and not incidentally, to lower their centers of gravity. The pilot, taking Gnat's advice, flattened himself under the tiller. And so, as the boat pulled around a bend in the waterway, Armstrong was the only one standing upright.

That was when the trouble started.

15

Despite their guide's claimed familiarity with the waterways, the boat rounded the bend and plowed directly into a submerged mud bank. Armstrong, standing upright near the prow, was thrown straight over the mud bank into water deep enough for him to go completely under.

Most of the others went overboard, too, landing in the shallow water that hid the bank—perhaps a half meter below the surface. That was enough to break their falls, although Tusk-anini landed hard enough to knock the wind out of him. Even the few who managed to remain on deck got a good shaking up. By sheer luck, none of them accidentally fired their weapons. Considering the firepower they were carrying, that kept the accident from turning into a disaster. Even the stun ray, if it had hit someone in deep water, could have been lethal.

Armstrong's head appeared above the water, and he looked around in all directions before swimming back toward the bank, where the legionnaires were beginning to find their feet. "What happened?" he said, as he reached wading depth.

"Hit a bar," said Hansen, who had rushed to the prow and was looking over the side to see what damage his boat had sustained. He glowered at Armstrong and said, "You'd 'a let me stand up, I'd 'a seen the bastard. Damn near kilt my boat."

"Killed your boat? You damn near killed my squad!" bellowed Armstrong. He pulled himself upright—no easy feat in the slippery mud—and said, "OK, everybody, back on board."

"Not so fast," said Hansen, raising a hand. "We done sprung a leak here. I don't know if she can carry the weight."

"Well, we can't stay out here in the middle of the water," said Armstrong. "Can you at least get us to shore?" He pointed toward the trading post, about a kilometer away. A small group of locals had come to the bank to gawk at the boat and the floundering legionnaires.

"She's shippin' water pretty fast," said Hansen. "I take you all, she's like to sink 'fore we get there. I could maybe take a couple of you, and send the boys on shore back for the rest. They got a couple canoes along there. Or you could all hang on to the gunwale to lower the weight. You'd get wet, but you'd get to shore a bit faster."

No sooner had he said this than there was a series of three loud splashes along the bank nearest the boat.

"What was that?" said Super-Gnat, one of the few still on deck. She swivelled her head around to look, but there was nothing to be seen but a series of expanding rings on the surface of the bayou.

"Nutria," said Hansen, ominously. "They're thick around here. Maybe you better all grab the gunwale, after all. Don't want to mess with nutria."

"Hurry it up," said Armstrong. "Put your weapons in the boat, so they don't get any wetter."

"Hey, I don't know if she can take that extra weight," said Hansen. "I can only carry the guns if all of you hop off in the water."

"I'm not getting in the water with nutria," said Super-Gnat. "I don't weigh very much, anyhow."

Hansen nodded. "OK, little lady, why don't you stay on board and keep an eye out for the nutria, and the rest can put the guns on deck and just hang on. I'll get you there, all right.'' Luckily for him, Gnat was too preoccupied with the nutria to react to being called a little lady.

Do-Wop and Moustache took the weapons from the legionnaires in the water and piled them on the foredeck before grudgingly jumping over the side. Then Hansen gunned the engine—gently, so as not to open the leak any wider—and the boat limped over to the shore, where the crowd of onlookers had grown to half a dozen. There was no further sign of nutria.

At last the bayou grew shallow enough for the hangers-on to touch bottom, and they simply let go and began wading ashore alongside the boat.

Hansen pointed forward and said to Super-Gnat, ''Grab that line and throw it to the boys on shore so's they can tie us up.''

Super-Gnat put down her shotgun and turned to pick up the rope. When she turned around again, Hansen was pointing it toward her. ''Now, young lady, don't get no ideas. I'm the only one with a gun now. I'd hate to use it on somebody so pretty.''

''You tricked us!'' she said. ''I bet you ran into that bar on purpose.''

''No, ma'am, that was a mistake. But I ain't got as far in life as I have not takin' advantage of mistakes. Now, put them hands up, if you don't mind.'' The other spectators had begun swarming on board and picking up the rest of the abandoned weapons.

Armstrong stopped and stared at him. ''You're turning us over to the rebels!'' he said, accusingly.

''Not exactly, mister,'' said Hansen. ''I *am* a rebel. And I'm takin' you all to Le Duc Taep, so's he can decide what's what. You'll get your guns back the minute he says so. Till then, we ain't takin' no chances.''

At that very moment, a large rodentlike creature came waddling down the bank from the woods to the water, about ten yards away from the group. ''What the hell is that thing?'' said Do-Wop.

''Aww, that's a nutria,'' said a bystander, who was now

cradling a Zenobian stun ray. "Good eatin'. Don't mind him, they wouldn't harm a fly."

Super-Gnat turned accusingly to Hansen. "You lied about the nutria!"

Hansen grinned self-consciously. "Yeah, that, too," he said.

The dripping hostages were handcuffed, then marched along a narrow trail to the rebel base. Their captors kept them moving, but did not force the pace, and it was not much more than half an hour before the tents of Le Duc Taep's encampment came into view.

A guard hailed them as they came into view. "Who you got here, Hansen?"

"Bunch of soldiers came lookin' for the camp," said Hansen. "Don't know what their business is, but I ain't lettin' 'em come walkin' up with guns. Might somebody get hurt."

"*You're* going to get hurt if I ever get my hands on you," said Super-Gnat, glaring at Hansen.

"Them uniforms look like the ones that captain wears, the one Taep's been talking with all week," said the guard. "If they're his folks, he might not like 'em being cuffed."

"Well, if they're somebody's friends, they shouldn't come around wavin' artillery at people," said Hansen. "Taep can decide—that's his job, right? Come along, folks." And he waved them toward the command tent.

A young woman wearing a red bandanna over her thick, dark hair stood up at their approach. She was carrying an old hunting rifle. "Hello, Hansen," she said. "Taep's in a business meeting. You'll have to wait."

"In a business meeting?" said Hansen. "What the hell, Pilar, that ain't the way things used to be around here. Is Taep puttin' on airs in his old age?"

"He's getting smart in his old age," said a new voice. The newcomer wore the rebel uniform. The man who walked out of the tent right behind him wore Legion black.

"Taep!" said Hansen. "I didn't mean no offense."

"Captain!" said Armstrong, almost in the same breath. "Tell this man to set us free."

"Do you know these people?" Taep raised an eyebrow and turned to Phule.

"I certainly do," said Phule. "Assuming they haven't done anything more serious than trying to find me, I hope you *will* set them free."

"Uh, maybe you could make an exception for the little lady, Taep. At least let me get a head start on her," said Hansen, looking apprehensively at Super-Gnat.

"This is my fault," said Phule, putting a hand on Taep's shoulder. "I owe everyone an apology. It seemed important to maintain secrecy, but I can see I've carried it too far. I should have known my people would come looking for me if I didn't report back, and that it could have been real trouble when they came in contact with your people."

"I understand the need for military secrecy," said Armstrong, massaging his wrists, which Hansen had uncuffed after a nod from Taep. "If my superior officer doesn't tell me something, I have to assume he has good reasons. Whatever brought you out here to meet the rebels has to have been pretty important, or you wouldn't have risked it."

"Well, yes," said Phule. "In fact, you arrived just as we were putting the finishing touches on it. The rebels have agreed to end their rebellion! Instead, they're going to return to Atlantis and enter into peaceful competition with the government."

"They have?" Armstrong's jaw fell. "That's brilliant, sir, absolutely brilliant. How did you manage to convince them?"

"Well, it wasn't all that hard, once I understood how people on this planet think," said Phule. "All I had to promise was that I'd help them build the galaxy's greatest roller coaster."

Journal #420

My employer's decision to do business directly with the rebels appeared to be a sound one. After his initial hostility, Le Duc Taep turned out to be far more a pragmatist than

*many of his followers. My employer was pleased to discover
that Taep had a good grasp of details and a willingness to
set aside dogma in favor of attainable goals. The two of
them sat down to create a blueprint for the return of the
rebel army to the mainstream of Landoor—as entrepreneurs.*

*Having settled the project's main outlines, my employer
returned to the Legion base to begin his part in building
the rebel amusement park. He began by securing title to a
large plot of land directly across the road from the government's park. The actual owners were the rebel leaders,
now reconstituted as a corporation—a status many of them
found more congenial than camping in the jungle. Since the
laws forbade off-planet citizens from owning shares in local
businesses, my employer was constrained to act behind the
scenes, making loans to the new park's owners, and bringing in outside experts to aid their enterprise.*

Predictably, the government was not happy to learn this.

Phule had settled into a comfortable rhythm on the rowing
machine at the Landoor Plaza's fitness club when his communicator sounded. He was tempted to ignore the signal;
he'd lost several days on his exercise program during his
trip out to the rebel base, and he was in the mood for a
good workout. But the readout on his wrist said PRIORITY,
which meant that Mother judged it important enough to
interrupt him.

"Jester here," he said, dropping one oar to raise the
communicator to mouth level.

"Hate to bother you, loverboy," said Mother's saucy
voice. "A couple of local bigwigs want to see you soonest.
You put their names on the let-through list, so I'm lettin'
you know. Shall I send 'em in, or do you want to get
dressed first? They've got steam coming out their ears."

"That depends on who they are, and what their business
is," said Phule. "I assume you asked them?"

"Ah, roger, sweetie," said Mother. There was a moment's pause and she said, "The nasty one's Colonel Mays and the ugly one's Boris Eastman—they said you'd know them. As for their business, Mays mentioned espionage, sedition, and harboring criminals. Have you been a bad boy again?"

"Not exactly," said Phule. "I guess I'd better see them anyway. I'll be in my office in five minutes."

"I'll tell them," said Mother. Then, after a pause, "That doesn't give you enough time to change. You aren't going to change to meet them? Tsk, tsk."

"If they're that anxious to see me, I shouldn't make them wait," said Phule. "Besides, if I show up in skivvies, it proves I'm taking them seriously. It can't hurt. Tell them I'm on my way." He toweled a few beads of sweat off his forehead, and made his way through the hotel's back corridors to his office.

Mays and Eastman were in the waiting room. Eastman was seated, tapping his fingers nervously, but Mays was pacing, jittery as a caged predator. They both turned to glare as he strode briskly through the door. "Well, gentlemen, sorry to keep you waiting," said Phule. "We in the military have to stay in shape, and I'm afraid I haven't had much time for that lately. What can I do for you?" He indicated the open doorway into his private office.

"You've had plenty of time for meddling," snapped Eastman. He rose to his feet, his fists balled at his side.

"That depends on what you mean by meddling," said Phule, as calmly as he could manage. "Come inside and we can discuss it."

The two followed him into the office, grumbling, and he closed the door behind them. He directed them to a large couch, then perched on the edge of his desk and said, "Gentlemen, I have good news for you. I have just returned from a mission to persuade Le Duc Taep to end his rebellion. I'm sure you will be pleased to learn that Le Duc Taep is disbanding his army. Instead of trying to overthrow the government, the rebels are ready to do their part to build a strong economy."

"Build the economy? Better you should say destroy the

economy!'' said Eastman. ''We know the score. The outlaws plan a theme park in direct competition with Landoor
Park—endangering a project the government has invested
millions in!''

Phule smiled. ''Le Duc Taep's new park will create
jobs—I'd think you'd be in favor of that.''

''He will steal our workers—people we've trained!''
snarled Eastman, ''The workers should be grateful for government jobs.''

''If the jobs are that good, Taep won't be able to hire
the workers away,'' said Phule. ''I'm a businessman, Deputy Eastman. I don't expect the law of supply and demand
to suspend itself for my benefit.''

''No, but you're not above diddling with it,'' said Colonel Mays, grimacing. ''I won't deny you your due, Captain—if you have convinced the rebels to lay down their
arms, you have earned our sincere congratulations. But tell
me this, Le Duc Taep is not a poor man, but he has never
had the capital to start up a project like this. You're bankrolling him, aren't you?''

''I've extended him a business loan,'' said Phule, with a
shrug. ''I've had everything vetted by a local lawyer, and
she assures me we're in perfect compliance with your
laws.''

Eastman made a rude noise. ''You can find a lawyer to
approve anything, if you're willing to pay enough. Don't
bandy legalisms with us, Captain. You've been trying to
undermine this government ever since you arrived on-
planet—''

Phule cut him off. ''Let's get one thing straight, Deputy.
My orders come from the Galactic Joint Chiefs of Staff—
not from anybody on this planet. I'm not so foolish as to
ignore local opinion in arriving at my policies. But so far
all I've heard from the government is accusations and bluster.''

''That's the line you're taking, is it?'' said the Colonel.
''Well, I give you credit for guts, if not for common sense.
Don't think we won't go over your head, Captain—you are
a very small fish, whether you know it or not.''

"I am no egomaniac, Colonel," said Phule. "But I suggest you stop trying to intimidate me. That's already been tried. By the way, have your police found those snipers yet?"

"I don't like your implication," Eastman bristled.

Mays held up a hand. "Let me respond to that, Boris," he said. Then he turned back to Phule. "Captain, I'm sure that my police could find the sniper quickly enough, if they questioned some of your new associates. Oh, that reminds me of a quesion I had—when can we expect you to turn over the rebel leaders to stand trial for their crimes?"

"I'm not convinced they've committed any crimes, Colonel," said Phule. "You've made plenty of accusations, but nobody's shown me hard evidence of criminal acts. Lacking that, I must consider any attempt to arrest them a treaty violation by the government."

Colonel Mays rose to his feet. "Boris, I can see we're wasting our time here. The captain will whistle a different tune when his commanding general hears about his obstructionism. Until then, we have business to attend to."

"Good day, Colonel," said Phule. "Be sure to come back when the park opens, gentlemen. I'll have Taep set aside free tickets for you both."

"The rebel park will never open," said Eastman. "Good day, Captain." And he and Colonel Mays stalked out of the office.

"Thrill rides," said Armstrong. He shook his head. "They upset my stomach. Why would somebody travel halfway across the galaxy to get on something that upsets his stomach?"

"Don't ask me," said Rembrandt, leaning back in her chair. They were in the hotel's conference room, waiting for Phule to come brief them on the company's new project. "I can take 'em or leave 'em. I mean, they're fun once in a while, but you'd never get me to stand in line for half an hour to get on that UltraDragon, over at the beach."

"Half an hour? The lines were seventy minutes long yesterday afternoon!" Armstrong said, his face a study in perplexity. "For a ride that lasts ten minutes! And this is a run-of-the-mill amusement park on a backwater planet."

"Don't let any Landoorans hear you say that," said Brandy. "They kind of like this place, and they're *serious* about those rides. Besides, it *is* a burnin' hot ride—I'd say it's worth the wait, yeah. Even Tusk-anini seemed to like it, once Gnat persuaded him to try it. And Do-Wop and Mahatma got back in line to ride it again."

"Mahatma? I wouldn't expect anything else of Do-Wop, but Mahatma . . ." Armstrong paused and scratched his head. "Maybe I don't understand Mahatma," he said at last.

"Man, if you did, you could give courses in it to the rest of us," said Brandy, chuckling. "But these Landoorans really have a thing for thrill rides. The capital isn't all that big a city, but it's got five different parks with a couple of pretty good rides apiece, or so the tourist guidebook says. So I'd bet the big park the government is building will have half a dozen *really* good rides. The rebel's park has to match that—or top it, if they can. So maybe you better take your motion-sickness pills and climb on a couple of roller coasters. It looks like we're gonna be in the business."

"Oh, we're already in the business," said Armstrong resignedly. "The captain's made up his mind, and that's all I needed to know. But I'll gladly let Do-Wop and Mahatma do the ride-testing. There has to be some advantage to being an officer in this outfit!"

"Advantage to being an officer? That's the best joke I've heard all year," said Phule, sweeping into the room. He had a roll of blueprints under his arm, which he dumped on the conference table. Behind him was a tall man in a metallic silver jumpsuit, silver-tinted goggles, and silver hair. Seeing his officers' curiosity, Phule said, "I should introduce our new consultant: Maestro Mario Zipiti, the galaxy's leading expert on thrill rides."

"Eet ees ze *plaisir* to make ze acquaintance," said the Maestro, with a florid bow. "Togezzer, ve make ze most grand ride yet to be see in ze ga*lax*y!" He pronounced the last word with the stress on the middle syllable.

"Maestro Zipiti has brought designs for all the great rides from around the galaxy for us to study," said Phule. "He's also got several original designs that he assures me go beyond anything ever built. With his help, we can expect New Atlantis Park to open its doors with the most exciting attractions on the planet . . ."

"Not only on ze planet, but anyvere in ze ga*laxy*!" said the Maestro, with another sweeping gesture that forced Armstrong to duck back a pace.

"Exciting is good," said Armstrong. "I suppose we're going to make sure they're safe, as well?"

"Safe? *Pah*!" Maestro Zipiti flung up his hands. "Ze true trill riders care nozzing for safe! Ze ride, ze rush, she is everyzing!"

"The rides will be safe, of course," said Phule. "It turns out that one of the rebel leaders is an engineer with substantial experience in building and maintaining rides. He built several popular rides in the existing parks. I looked over his résumé, and none of his rides has ever had an injury except for one or two caused by misconduct by customers. I asked him to come to this meeting. I wonder . . ." There was a knock on the door. "That must be him now. Brandy, will you go let him in?"

Brandy opened the door and in came a wiry man with a grizzled beard and gold hoop earrings. He was still wearing the jungle camouflage and red bandanna that was the unofficial rebel uniform. "Hello, Buster," said Phule. "I'd like you to meet Maestro Zipiti, the famous thrill-ride expert."

"Zipiti, huh?" Buster squinted at the man in the gleaming jumpsuit. "I heard of you—never expected to see you here, though."

Zipiti drew himself up straight and said, "I haff come to build ze greatest rides ever in history!"

"Well, that'll be different, won't it?" said Buster, clearly unimpressed. "Tell you what, Maestro—you give me the drawings and the specs, and unless you're asking for something plasteel won't do, I'll get the durn things built. We got a deal?"

"It sounds like the perfect deal to me," said Phule, cutting off Zipiti, who had his mouth open to answer. "Now, let's see what we've got on the drawing board." Smiling, he unrolled the first of several plans, and the group got down to work.

It was nearly three minutes before the first argument broke out between Zipiti and Buster, and it lasted most of the meeting. But with Phule's prodding, things moved forward. It began to look as if the rides could actually be built. Quite possibly they would even be ready on schedule. That was assuming that it could be done without either Maestro Zipiti or Buster killing the other before the project got off the ground.

The first priority for New Atlantis Park was to build a roller coaster more impressive than the behemoth in Landoor Park—which Phule's troops took to calling "The Thing." This was a daunting challenge for a group that had never set up so much as a simple "spin-and-puke" ride, let alone an attraction that could impress the citizens of a planet that considered roller coasters its highest art form. But Maestro Zipiti rolled out a design for the coaster of his dreams, which was immediately given the code name "Zipper." This design offered an initial plunge five meters higher than the government ride. It also had an unusual number of rapid side-to-side shifts on its final straightaway, and what Zipiti touted as the tallest loop of any roller coaster in the galaxy. On paper, it dwarfed The Thing, and it was quickly adopted as the centerpiece of the park.

Phule was ready to build not only the Zipper, but several of Maestro Zipiti's other designs. But here he met opposition from his other local consultant, Okidata. "You don't want to do that yet, Captain. The Zipper's gonna be a triff ride, no question. But as soon as the government sees you building this ride, they're gonna try to top it. And you're gonna have to top them in turn, or look like a second-rater. Better keep a few plans held back, 'cause you're gonna need 'em.''

Maestro Zipiti nearly exploded. "Zese provincial bunglers cannot match ze least of my designs! Ve vill build zem all!''

"Maybe you should jes' set tight, Maestro," said Buster. "The kid's got the right of it, says I—and I been goin' to ride parks longer than he's been born, so I oughta know."

"We'll wait and see," decided Phule. "With all our workers concentrating on one ride, we should have the Zipper up quickly enough, and then we'll know which direction we need to go in."

"Zis is schtupid!" muttered Zipiti, but he was outvoted. And, as it turned out, he was wrong.

16

Journal #426

One who had never embarked on the construction of an amusement park would undoubtedly consider it a simple proposition. One needs to erect a few rides, set up areas where customers may purchase food and souvenirs, and then open the gates and watch the money roll in. Even I, who tend to see shoals of difficulties where others see only smooth sailing, had no idea how complex the undertaking would become. Fortunately, neither did my employer, or he might never have embarked on the project.

As always, he made it a point to obtain expert advice from all over the galaxy. His connections, augmented by those of his family, gave him access to a range of talent few others could call on. It was therefore no surprise to anyone who had seen him in action that within days of signing the agreement with the rebels, several leading lights in the world of entertainment and of amusement park design in particular had joined our camp. Of course, Maestro Zipiti was on hand to supply his expertise in thrill rides. Lex came

*in from Lorelei to oversee the plans for a series of indoor
and outdoor stages for live entertainment.*

*From within the ranks of Omega Company, Phule detailed
Escrima to draw up plans for the food service areas, with
an eye to providing gourmet treats in mass quantities. And
the rebel camp had its own array of talent—Buster turned
out to be a top-class engineer, with an uncanny ability to
turn almost any blue-sky idea into functioning hardware.
And Okidata had a surprising fund of useful knowledge.*

*And, of course, the government insisted on sticking its own
oar in, whether or not anyone wanted it . . .*

It was somewhere near midafternoon on the second day of
construction work on the Zipper that the Landooran government appeared on the scene. A small fleet of black hovercars delivered Boris Eastman, Deputy Minister of
Development, to the park entrance. Eastman had a team of
inspectors in tow. Phule was there to meet him at the gate.

"What a pleasure to see you, Deputy," said Phule, grinning as if he meant every syllable of it. "We aren't set up
to entertain visitors yet, but of course you're always welcome."

"This is no social visit, Captain," said Eastman, turning
a stony glare on the beehive of activity going on all around
him. "It has come to my attention that you have begun this
project without obtaining the necessary permits."

"Oh, quite to the contrary, Deputy," said Phule, holding
up a hand. "I made sure we had all the relevant permits
before we turned the first shovelful of earth—the military
has given me plenty of experience dealing with regulations,
and so I make it a point to fulfill all the requirements before
I find out I can't do something I want. If you'll step over
to my office, I'll be happy to let you inspect them."

"I would be very interested to inspect these permits,"
said Eastman, his eyes narrowing. "As of this morning, my
department had no record of their being issued."

"Undoubtedly the normal bureaucratic backlog," said

Phule. He made a gesture as if to usher the deputy toward the temporary building housing his office. "If you'll follow me . . ."

"Very well," said Eastman, sniffing. "We shall soon see what is in proper order and what is not." He and his flunkies fell in line behind Phule.

Chocolate Harry, who had paused from setting up the ground-clearing machines to watch the conversation between Phule and the ministers, broke into a grin at the sight. "Check it out, man—this is the first time I ever seen the chickens line up to follow the fox into his own hole."

"I wouldn't be so sure," said Buster, scratching his bearded chin. "Them government fellers got the look of career criminals to 'em. If that deputy don't at least triple his salary in bribes, I'd be disappointed in him."

"Don't you be worried," said Chocolate Harry. "By the time the Cap'n's done with these dudes, they'll swear he's got every permit they ever thought of, and a few spare, blank ones. He's even figured out how to bribe somebody so they *stay* bribed, and I thought that was against the laws of economics."

"Economics, hell—that's against the laws of *physics*," said Buster, picking up the wrench he'd set down when the inspectors arrived. "But if he's as good as you say, I guess we might as well go right on ahead with the job."

"Might as well," said Harry, and they went back to their task. After a while, Eastman and his inspectors emerged from the office building. They marched straight back to their hovercars and departed for the city. If there had been any deficiency in the permits, it certainly was not serious enough to cause any delay in the project—at least for the moment.

"Zere design—eet ees garbage," said Maestro Zipiti. He put a strong accent on the second syllable of the last word, as if it rhymed with *garage*. "Here"—he pointed to the diagram showing the first, long climb—"zey make ze quick drop, go to ze left instead of straight, zo as to zeem more the dangerous. But Pah! Eet ees a trick even a child could zee t'rough. Gar-*bage*!''

"Sure, Maestro," said Buster, very patiently. It was the fourth or fifth time he had heard Maestro Z criticize the shortcomings of the rival park's showpiece roller coaster. "We don't want no gar*bage* in our park. That's why we brought you in to design this here ride for us." He shifted another blueprint to the top of the stack and pointed. "Now, remin' me again, what's the load on these-here cross-braces?"

"Zat ees all written out!" said the Maestro, flinging his long locks of hair back over one shoulder. " 'Ave you no read ze plan?"

"Over an' over," said Buster. "By now, I may understand it better than the feller what drew it up. What I want to know . . .''

"Merde! Un'erstan' eet better zan Maestro Zipiti! Per'aps you 'ave ze eye of ze mechanic, but zat is nozzing, nozzing! Ze soul of a genius . . .''

Buster's voice didn't change. "Yeah, I know you's a genius 'cause you done told us so. Now, maybe you can tell me what's gonna be holdin' up this here stretch of track when a car full o' people's settin' on top of it. It looks real pretty the way you draw it, but I gotta build the damn thing. Figure we got twenty-four people in a car, average weight of a hundred ten kilos apiece . . .''

Zipiti was outraged. "Zat is too high! I design eet for ninety-five!''

"An' what happens if you get a fat people's convention?" drawled Buster. "We gonna shut down all the rides? I figure we gotta have at least . . . What the hell?"

The latter exclamation was prompted by a loud explosion, followed by frantic shouts. A cloud of smoke was rising from near the park gates. " 'Scuse me, Maestro," said Buster. "I reckon I gotta go see what's up." He turned and sprinted off toward the growing commotion.

Maestro Zipiti peered off into the distance, his face turning red. "Cretins!" he shouted. "*Salauds*! You sabotage my beautiful rides, I keel you! I keel you all!'' The smoke kept rising, and somewhere in the distance a klaxon began to sound. It was the start of another typical day.

The holovision picture showed men and women in hard hats in the background, running heavy machinery. A framework of girders, bent into intriguing curves and dips, loomed against the skyline. Up front stood Jennie Higgins, interviewing Le Duc Taep.

"New Atlantis Park will be the vindication of our free way of life,'' Taep was saying. "It will embody the traditional Atlantean values of self-determination, free enterprise, and hard work. And it will be a wonderful vacation experience for the whole family.''

"How would you compare it to the new park the government is building, Landoor Park?'' said Jennie.

"The government has a false vision of what the people want,'' said Taep, puffing himself up as if the additional air would add conviction to his words. "They follow the old formula of bread and circuses, empty entertainment. But they care nothing for the soul of the Atlantean people. We will present the heritage of our nation, something to inspire the people and to show the galaxy our rich indigenous culture.''

"We understand that your two parks are engaged in quite a competition to build the most exciting thrill ride,'' said Jennie. "What can you tell us about that?''

"Thrill rides are the finest expression of the art of New Atlantis,'' said Taep. "Our rides will draw on the knowledge and skills of our native craftsmen as well as the vision of experts from all over the galaxy.''

Phule's communicator buzzed. He turned down the sound on the holoset and said, "What is it, Mother?''

"Sorry to bother you, sweetie, but that Deputy Eastman and Colonel Mays are here again. Want to see them?''

"I suppose there's no point in postponing it,'' said Phule, sighing. "Send 'em on in.''

Moments later the door to Phule's office opened and the two government officials barged through. "There,'' said

Eastman, pointing to the image of Jennie, still visible in the holo-viewing area. "What do you say about that?"

"I say it's great publicity for the park," said Phule. "It's been running every half hour, in every major market in this sector. If it brings visitors from off-planet, your park will benefit, as well."

"I expected some such impertinence," said Eastman. He pointed his finger at Phule. "What do you have to say about publishing state secrets? That's espionage, no matter how you slice it."

Phule raised his brows. "State secrets? I can't imagine what you mean."

Mays leaned forward over Phule's desk. "Do you deny tipping your journalist friend about Landoor Park?"

"Of course I deny it," said Phule, leaning back in his desk chair. "Jennie is a good reporter—she can find things by herself, and I suspect that's all she did here. I won't deny telling her about New Atlantis Park. Publicity is a big part of the game plan, Colonel. If Taep's going to repay my loans, his park's got to get off-planet customers. We've got to let the people on other planets know it's here. What better way than talking to a reporter?"

"And in the process, you force our hand," said Mays. "If we copy your tactics, we undergo a radical increase in expenses. If we ignore them, you gain the edge in publicity."

"It doesn't cost anything to talk to Jennie," said Phule. "If you hadn't turned down her interview requests . . ."

"We are bound by government regulations," said Eastman. "I would risk a jail sentence for disclosing state secrets. At the very least, I could lose my position."

"If I were you, I'd get the regulations changed," said Phule. "The planet's future depends on it."

"It is you who have put us in this dilemma," said Eastman. His face was red, and his voice had risen in pitch. "You will force us to take extreme measures, if you are not careful."

"Do what you have to," said Phule. "I'll do what I

believe is best for the entire planet, not just one faction. Now, gentlemen, is there anything else?''

''Not for the moment,'' said Colonel Mays, taking Eastman by the elbow and steering him toward the door. ''But I can promise you there will be.''

There are any number of phrases no executive wants to hear, but most of them boil down to ''Boss, we got trouble.'' Which is what Okidata said as he burst into the Landoor Plaza's dining room. Phule was halfway through a delicious plate of oysters Landoor—a dish Escrima had happily adopted from the local cooks. Bluepoint oysters had been one of Earth's most popular exports to developing worlds. They had done especially well on Landoor.

Phule wiped the spicy sauce from his lips and said, ''We've had surprise inspections and smoke bombs and wildcat picket lines and power outages, and we've survived them all. So unless this new problem is incoming missiles, I suspect it can wait while I finish these oysters. Sit down and have a drink. What kind of trouble are we talking about?''

''The government's starting a new ride,'' said Okidata, sliding into the seat opposite Phule. ''And from the look of it, they're aiming to top the Zipper.''

''Well, you predicted as much,'' said Phule, sighing. ''We'll have to see what else the Maestro has in his portfolio.''

''He'd better have something pretty triff,'' said Okidata. He was interrupted by the waiter's arrival. After ordering an iced coffee, he turned back to Phule. ''We can't tell much about the design yet, but the main drop is five meters higher than the Zipper, and they've got what might be a double loop, the second one an inverse—that's gonna be a serious ride.''

''We'll have to do better,'' said Phule. ''Learn as much about the new ride as you can. We'll call in Buster and the Maestro and see what we can come up with. We're not going to let them have the last word.''

"Yes, sir!" said Okidata, his enthusiasm returning. "This is going to be fun!"

"I suppose it is," said Phule. "I can tell it's also going to be very expensive."

"Why, sure," said Okidata, beaming. "Isn't that what fun's all about?"

Phule shrugged. Whatever it cost, his Dilithium Express card would cover it.

The new government ride was dubbed the "Beast." After studying spy-camera holos of its emerging superstructure (partly concealed behind a security screen), Phule's advisory team began to design a ride to eclipse it: code name "Topper," developed from one of Maestro Zipiti's designs. The ride featured an initial drop ten meters higher than the new government ride—insuring an even higher speed and a longer duration than the Beast. With Okidata suggesting enhancements and Buster troubleshooting potential problems, construction began even before the final touches were put on the Zipper. And in accordance with Phule's conviction that publicity was imperative, press releases went out even before the ground was broken.

Shortly after the framework was begun, a government delegation arrived at the park gate, headed by none other than Boris Eastman, with a team of safety inspectors in tow. "Now, Deputy Eastman, we've already obtained permits from the Department of Parks," said Phule, greeting them at the gate. "There's really nothing to be discussed."

"I'm afraid there is, Captain," said Eastman, smirking. "It has come to our attention that you are building a ride that violates safety regulations."

"Safety regulations?" Buster was livid. "I'm compliant with every damn safety regulation you can think up, and then some. Tarnation, we doubled the load-bearing specs on every single stress point of this bugger. You show me in the books where I'm violatin' your regulations."

"You may not have kept up with current legislation while you were out in the jungle, playing revolutionary," said Eastman, smirking even more nastily. He handed

Buster a thick sheaf of printout. "But now that you are back in civilization, you will have to conform to our laws. The relevant passage is on page fourteen, I believe."

Buster quickly flipped to the page in question and read it. He looked up and passed the sheets to Phule. "You bastards! You've set the maximum legal height for a ride right at the height of your new coaster. And you did this just last week!"

Phule quickly scanned the printout, which verified Buster's statement. "This is obviously aimed at preventing us from competing with you," he said, frowning at Eastman. "This is nothing short of restraint of free competition."

"Call it what you will," said Eastman, looking down his nose at Phule. "The law is the law. If your ride's in violation, we intend to shut down your whole park. Now, are you going to comply with the regulations, or shall I send my inspectors to start measuring?"

"I reckon we could beat this in court," muttered Buster, balling his fists. "Problem is, it'll take months, and the ride'll sit there unfinished while we fight the case."

"We'll beat it without breaking the regulations," said Phule. "Deputy Eastman, I thank you for your advisory. But if you think we're going to let this stop us, you're dead wrong."

"Perhaps so, Captain," said Eastman, grinning. "But remember, we'll be watching you. Build one centimeter over the legal height, and we'll padlock the place. Good day, sir!"

"A bad day to you," growled Buster, but Eastman had already turned on his heel and left.

Phule slapped Buster on the shoulder. "Don't worry, we knew what we were up against when we started this game. We can still top them—and they'll find out that all they've done is make it harder for themselves to come back and top us!"

"I sure hope you're right," said Buster. But when Phule explained what he had in mind, a grin spread across his face. "Yeah, that ought to do the trick," he said at last.

"Good," said Phule. "Now, all we have to do is turn it into hardware. Come on, we've got work to do!"

Two weeks later, Colonel Mays was at the gate. He brandished a copy of Phule's latest publicity release. "We've got you now, Captain! This park's being shut down today!"

"Colonel, I suggest you have your inspectors measure the height of the new ride," said Phule. "You will find that it's entirely within legal specification."

"Then you're guilty of false advertising," said Mays, He dropped his cheroot on the ground and crushed it under his heel. "Your brochure says the drop on this ride is fifteen meters higher than the law allows! If you can't deliver on that, we'll expose you for the fraud you are —and believe me, Landoorans take these things very seriously. The entire management of Dunes Park had to resign several years ago when one of their rides turned out to be ten seconds shorter than advertised."

"I've heard that story," said Phule. "But take a look— you'll see that we've cut the top ten meters off the framework, to comply with the new laws. But that's not all." He beckoned the colonel, and led him over to the work area.

"I'm afraid you'll have to put on a helmet to come any closer," he said, pointing to a rack of hard hats hanging outside the plywood curtain wall surrounding the lower stretches of the Topper's superstructure. He plopped a helmet on his own head, and waited while the colonel found one that fit. Then he led Mays through a door in the curtain, nodding to the uniformed legionnaire standing guard outside.

Inside, the colonel blinked for a moment as his eyes got used to the dimmer illumination. Then his jaw fell. "This is a travesty! You can't get around the law this easily!"

"On the contrary, Colonel, we studied the law very carefully before adopting this design," said Phule. He pointed to the enormous pit into which the tracks descended, adding at least twenty meters to the initial plunge. "The law explicitly limits the height above ground level, but it says nothing about the total height of the drop. This ride is legal, Colonel.''

''You scoundrel. We'll find some way to stop you,'' sputtered the colonel, but Phule continued to smile.

''We want to thank you for making this necessary,'' said Phule. ''We'll have a plunge into pitch darkness at the very end of the ride—so they can't see how far they're going to fall. We'd never have thought of that without your regulations. Maestro Zipiti considers it his greatest inspiration, all thanks to your government.''

''You've won this round, damn you, Captain,'' said Mays, snatching off his helmet. ''But you haven't seen the end of us. Good day!'' He stomped out of the enclosure, slamming the door behind him.

''Well, wasn't that special?'' said Buster, who'd been watching the tour from a distance. ''We'll see what new wrinkles they come up with now. I reckon we've got even more fun in store for us.''

''Buster, you may not believe this,'' said Phule, ''But there *is* such a thing as too much fun.''

''I'll believe it when I see it,'' said Buster, and he went back to work. Phule sighed, but he knew he'd pay the bills when they came.

A new ride was rising inside security screens at Landoor Park, and the spy cameras had soon reported on its salient features. It copied the Topper's underground plunge, increasing the initial drop by another three meters. At that point, the excavation hit bedrock—locally, an extremely tough basalt. Phule's engineers had already determined that going deeper would be prohibitively expensive. The new ride was given the code name, ''Monster''. And unless the government decided to rescind its new regulations, it seemed to establish an untoppable record (at least in this district) for the height of the initial plunge.

Maestro Zipiti was livid. ''Zey are creeminals, nozzing bot creeminals!'' he roared. ''Zey zink zey can fix ze law zo zey have ze field to zeirselfs! Pah! Zipiti showing zem!''

''Well, Maestro, you better pull somethin' pretty triff

out'n yer pockets," said Buster. "They got us beat up and down, and now all we gots to work with is sideways. Got'ny hot ideas?"

"Just you vait!" howled the Maestro. "Ve vill show zem!" But he didn't offer any triff ideas, and it began to appear that he was not about to.

Okidata cleared his throat. "Well, there is one idea we haven't used yet," he said. "I suppose a real ride purist would call it cheating, though, so maybe we shouldn't . . ."

"I'm no purist," said Phule. "Right about now, the only thing I care about is beating those bureaucratic rule-mongers. If we can get a better ride than they're offering, I say we do it whatever it takes. What do you think, Maes-tro?"

"Vot ess zis idea?" Zipiti said, scowling.

"Antigrav," said Okidata.

"Oh, zat has been done," said Zipiti, with a flip of his hand. "Eet vas ze grand sensation, until everybody go on ze ride and discover ees boring. Ze riders, zey vant to feel as if zey are falling, not floating."

"Right," said Okidata. "We had a ride here that tried it, back when I was a kid. Flopperoonie. *Nobody* went on it twice. But they did it like you said—floating instead of falling. There's another way to use it."

"Eempossible!" said the Maestro, but nobody was lis-tening to him.

"Go ahead, kid," said Buster, propping his feet up on the empty chair opposite him. "We gotta top the gov'ment's ride, and they done rigged the game agin' us. You got a better idea, I'm itchin' to hear it."

"OK, here's the deal," said Okidata. "The old way was to use antigrav at the top of a hill, to make the riders feel as if the car was flying off the track. Except it didn't really work—it was too smooth. The way I think we can use it is subtler. We put it on as the car's going uphill, just enough so the car doesn't lose all its speed, That way, we can make the later hills just as high as the first, and we get a lot more really steep drops. And we can keep the ride going longer, 'cause it doesn't slow down as much. You're using the antigrav not as an effect, but as an enhancement.''

''It oughta work,'' said Buster. '' 'Course, the proof of the puddin' is in the tastin' . . .''

''That's what our ride-testers are for,'' said Phule. ''Draw up the design and let's see it. We've got nothing to lose, so let's give it our best shot.'' Privately, he was beginning to wish that the rides could be opened, to help defray the growing cost of construction. But until all the park's facilities were finished, the gates would have to remain closed—and the bills would continue to mount.

As with any work of art, a ride was nothing without an audience. Until it had rattled down the track (and it had better rattle—too quiet was no good) with riders aboard, it was still an unproven entity. The ride-testers were there to prove that pudding.

The team included Omega Mob's two hardcore thrill ride addicts, Do-Wop and Mahatma, as well as Tusk-anini, who had an uncanny ability to spot minor imperfections in the trackwork just by riding over it. The Gambolts, especially Rube, also proved to be good testers; if Rube made it to the end without howling, the ride was far too tame. And to lead the group, Phule chose Brandy, who kept the group focused on analyzing the ride, rather than simply enjoying it.

It was shortly after ride-testing the Topper that Mahatma raised his hand and said, ''Sarge, may I ask a question?''

''I doubt I'll get any peace until I let you,'' said Brandy. ''What is it this time, Mahatma?''

''The reason we're testing out rides is to find out whether they're better than the government's rides, isn't it?''

''Got it in one,'' said Brandy.

''But Sarge, how can you compare two things when you only know one?''

''Say what?'' Brandy's face took on a particular puzzled expression that Mahatma's questions often seemed to elicit.

''Listen, Sarge,'' said Mahatma. ''If you want to compare apples and oranges, you have to taste an apple, and then an orange, not so?''

"*Nobody* can compare apples and oranges," said Brandy, furrowing her brow. "You can't do it . . ."

Mahatma interrupted her. "Then why does everyone say to me always, *You're comparing apples and oranges*, if I don't do it? If I do it, you can't say nobody does it."

"Brandy, Mahatma making sense this time," said Tusk-anini.

"I'm supposed to take *your* word for that?" scoffed Brandy. Tusk-anini's intellect was highly respected by the Omega Mob, but his approach to logic didn't always match the human model.

"Listen, Brandy," said Tusk-anini. "We only test *our* rides. How we know if they better than other rides unless we go on other rides?"

"Oh, I get it," said Brandy. "Well, I guess the question does make sense, after all. Except we can't go on the government's rides until they open the park. Which is a shame, come to think of it . . ."

"Yo, Sarge, I got a great idea," said Do-Wop.

"Now we're really in trouble," said Brandy, covering her eyes in mock horror. "There's probably no way I can stop you from telling me this brilliant idea, so maybe you better tell me now. But don't expect me to do anything about it, OK?"

"Ahhh, Sarge, you ain't gonna hafta do anything about it," said Do-Wop, grinning. "Leave it to me and the guys . . ."

"Right," said Brandy. "I'm not leaving anything up to you until I know the whole story. Spill it, Do-Wop. I expect I'm gonna regret this . . ."

The idea was exactly what she would have expected. The only problem was, the more Do-Wop explained it, the better it sounded. Almost against her will, she found herself nodding in agreement . . .

The fencing around New Atlantis Park was designed to let the public follow the progress of construction, while maintaining a reasonable degree of security. The idea was to whet the public's appetite, without giving the competition anything useful. This went against local custom, which treated every detail of a new ride, from its overall height to the color of the seats, as a trade secret. So when Okidata and Do-Wop pulled their hovercar up to a side entrance for Landoor Park, they were met by a pair of government security guards. The park's fence was ten feet high, topped with razor wire to prevent anyone stealing a peek inside. Harsh floodlights illuminated the area in front.

"Let me do the talking," Okidata whispered as the guard approached. "I know most of these guys, and I have the right accent."

Do-Wop seemed dubious. "OK, man, but if it gets rough, let me take over. I can talk my way out of anything."

"Yeah, and where's that gonna leave me?" said Okidata. He elbowed the legionnaire playfully and turned to meet the guards. "Hey, it's Footsy and Annie! Long time no see."

"Long time is right, Okie," said the woman, a tough-looking brunette in a dark green uniform. "Sorry we can't talk, but this is a restricted zone. You gotta move along."

"That's too bad, Annie, because I need to talk to you guys," said Okidata in a conspiratorial voice. "I got a proposition for you."

"Okie, you *better* move along," said the other guard, presumably Footsy, but he said it with a deep chuckle. "Last time you came to me with a proposition, it nearly got us both thrown out of school."

"Yeah, but it was fun while it lasted," said Okidata, and Do-Wop could *hear* the grin in his voice. "Here's the deal, guys—how'd you like a free preview of the triffest ride on the planet?"

"We've got the triffest ride on the planet right inside," said Annie, her eyes narrowing.

"Sure you do," said Okidata. "But you know what's goin' on down the street, don't you?"

"Rebel park," said Footsy. "You workin' for them?"

"Yeah, their money's as good as the government's," said Okidata. "And their rides might be even better than the government's, but of course, I only know one side of the story. Same as you, I guess.''

"Let me guess," said Annie, leaning on the hovercar's window frame. "You can sneak us onto the rebel rides. Same as you used to sneak us onto the Weasel when you worked at Dunes Park."

"I can," said Okidata. "It won't even get me in trouble with the boss, this time. He wants people to know how good his rides are, and the best way is to give out a few free samples, just to get talk started."

"And how do we earn this so-called free ride?" said Annie, her eyes narrowing even more.

Okidata belatedly remembered the repayment he'd gotten from her for the free ride on the Weasel, but it was too late to back out. "Well, maybe me and my friend could watch the gate here while you were getting your free rides . . ."

"Su-u-ure," said Annie. "And you're gonna pay our salary after we get bounced, too, huh? No deal, Okie. Jobs are still scarce."

"We could sweeten it a little bit," said Do-Wop, leaning across to smile at Annie.

"Who's this?" she asked, drawing back.

"That's my friend Do-Wop," said Okidata, inwardly cringing.

"That's right, and baby, have we got a deal for you," said Do-Wop. "For you and any of your friends who'd like a look at New Atlantis Park before it opens."

"Don't get me wrong, I'd love to check out them rides," said Footsy. "But this is the government we're workin' for. And it ain't only us involved—there's other guards, and supervisors, and all kinds of electronics . . ."

"No prob, we can take care of everybody," said Do-Wop.

Footsy was dubious. "We'd get a look at a jail cell if we mess up, and I sure ain't interested in that."

"Not to sweat," said Do-Wop. "We got all the angles covered. But we oughta park this hover so it don't attract attention, and then talk somewhere out of sight. Any ideas?"

"You go ahead two blocks, turn right, and park there," said Annie with a decisive tone. "Come back to the guard shack—and make sure nobody follows you."

"Don't worry, nobody's gonna follow us. We'll be right back," said Okidata. He put the hovercar in gear, and pulled away, smiling. Like any good fisherman, he knew when he'd got his quarry hooked.

"What this ride called?" asked Tusk-anini, looking up at the towering framework. Here inside the government park's security screens, they could see that it was a stand-up ride, with padded shoulder harnesses that came down automatically to hold the riders securely in place.

"This is the one we code-named the Beast," said Okidata. "I don't know what they're calling it. Suppose it doesn't matter."

"We will ride them all," said Mahatma, jotting something on a notepad. "But we need to distinguish one from another for the debriefing. It is too bad you don't know their name for it."

"That's the one thing I couldn't get my friends to tell me," said Okidata. Everything else had gone well so far. Annie and Footsy had let the crew through the gates, and given them "borrowed" plans showing the various controls they'd need to run the rides. And, unless the schedule had been changed, the inside guards weren't due to visit this area until the legionnaires were gone. They hoped the security screens would keep the light and noise from being noticed at any distance.

"Well, let's crank her up, then," said Do-Wop. "Are you sure you know how the controls work on this thingie?"

"I've been running rides since I was a snot-nosed kid," said Okidata, who was possibly twenty Standard years old. "They all work the same way. Don't worry—not even the government could build something I can't run."

"Think you could run the welfare department?" said Do-Wop, but Okidata had turned away and gone into the nearby cabin housing the controls. Do-Wop shrugged and followed his fellow ride-testers into the lead car.

After a minute or so, Okidata's voice came over the speaker mounted near the load-on area, "Everybody in position?"

Do-Wop looked back at the other testers: Tusk-anini, Mahatma, the Gambolts Duke and Garbo, and half a dozen others standing there. "All on board," he said, with a thumbs-up gesture.

There was a soft mechanical noise, and the shoulder harnesses descended to secure the passengers. "Everybody comfortable?" asked Do-Wop. It wasn't just a courtesy; if the harnesses didn't fit right, a rider could be thrown loose on a curve or inversion. Everyone answered affirmatively. This was expected; even on a mostly human world, the rides had to be able to accommodate a wide range of sizes and shapes. If a Volton and two Gambolts didn't fit properly, there would be other customers who wouldn't be able to ride, as well. That would mean lost fares, something that horrified park operators even more than accidents. They made sure the restraints fit.

"OK, here we go," said Okidata. He threw the start switch. The cars began their long climb up the first steep slope. When they rose above the security screens the riders got a glimpse of the still-unfinished park below them. Off to one side were two other roller coasters, one of which the legionnaires planned to test tonight. The other was still under construction, but if all went smoothly, they'd ride that one, too, before the park opened. In the distance were the buildings that would house restaurants, shops, and other attractions, built to resemble a mining camp from Landoor's early days.

The cars reached the top of the climb, and paused a moment to heighten the tension. Then they dropped into a nearly vertical dive, and the ride was on. With the part of his consciousness that wasn't wrapped up in a sheer adrenaline rush, Do-Wop heard Mahatma inhale sharply. One of the Gambolts let out a shriek. Yeah, this ride was gonna be a good one . . .

The drop seemed to last far longer than the laws of physics allowed. Abruptly the car leveled off, and the change of vector hit the passengers with crushing g-force. A series of quick S-turns rattled them, and the next thing they knew they were into the first loop. Standing upright while travelling upside down was strangely exhilarating. As they came out of the loop, Do-Wop could see a second loop straight ahead.

He also saw, out of the corner of his eye, that two security guards were standing by the let-off area. They had pulled Okidata out of the cabin and were holding him by the arms. Suddenly the end of the ride looked a lot different than it had when they'd gotten on. *Were we double-crossed, or just unlucky?* he wondered.

Then the car swept into the second loop, and Do-Wop forgot all about the guards for another couple of minutes.

The guards were standing by the track as the car slowly came to a smooth stop, and the padded restraints automatically lifted off the passengers' shoulders. One of the guards, a big man with biceps the size of Do-Wop's waist, strode forward and said, "All right, you guys have had your fun. Now you're gonna come with us, and this part ain't gonna be fun at all." His frown made his brow look even lower than it was.

"But this is not the plan," said Mahatma, brightly. "We still need to go on the other rides."

"I'll give you a ride," snarled the big guard, stepping forward.

Tusk-anini put out a hand. "You talk nice to Mahatma," he said, glowering down at the guard. The two Gambolts sidled up to flank him. The sight of an angry-looking seven-foot warthog and two six-foot felines was sufficient to stop the guard in his tracks. That gave Do-Wop time to maneuver around to the front of the group.

"Yo, man, let's not jump to conclusions," he said, trying his best not to look as if he'd been doing anything the guards might object to. "We can explain everything, OK?"

"You're trespassin' on gov'ment property, which you better start explainin'," said the guard. His swagger had returned, now that he was confronting somebody he thought he could intimidate by sheer size.

"Well, we weren't exactly trespassing . . ." Do-Wop began.

"Don't give me no mouth," said the guard. He raised a ham-like hand and stepped forward to slap Do-Wop.

The slap never landed. There was a brief electronic sound, and the huge man slumped to the ground. Anyone paying attention might have noticed Mahatma pointing a small device toward the guard, but nobody except the legionnaires would have recognized the device as a model SR-1 Zenobian stun ray.

Do-Wop looked down at the guard and shrugged. "I was gonna tell him, but he didn't wait," he said. He turned to the other guard, who stood staring at his fallen comrade. "He'll be OK in a little while, but we gotta talk fast. You guys can still get in on the deal. Here it is . . ."

A short while later, the legionnaires were stepping onto the Monster, ready for another roller-coaster ride. This time nobody interrupted them.

Journal #435

As my employer discovered, the construction of thrill rides was only one aspect of helping the rebels build their park. A variety of other amusements needed to be provided: strolling musicians, pageants, parades, concerts, various credit-operated games—all at least nominally related to the park's broader theme, a fantastic re-creation of the rebels' jungle encampment. Computer simulations of native wildlife had to be created, artificial bayous dug and flooded for boat trips to "trading posts" offering a variety of merchandise, from camouflage garments to red bandannas to toy guns.

Food service and sanitary facilities were also necessary, as was quick transportation from one part of the park to another for those customers disinclined to walk. And of course personnel to sell and take tickets, oversee the shops and restaurants, operate and maintain all these various facilities, and clean up after the park had closed. In the end, the park's payroll numbered into the thousands. And while by now there were several affluent local backers providing capital, the bulk of it came out of my employer's pockets.

"I think it would have been easier to invade the planet and overthrow the government," said Phule, looking up from his computer screen, currently displaying a spreadsheet detailing his Dilithium Express card balance. "It certainly would have been cheaper."

"No doubt you should have considered that some time ago, sir," said Beeker, who was standing looking over Phule's shoulder. "Besides, you already had a hand in bringing down one government on this planet. Or have you forgotten the strafing incident again?"

"How could I?" said Phule. "Le Duc Taep drops it into his conversation every now and then, just to remind me that I owe him, I think. I'm hocked up to my eyeballs, Beeker. If this amusement park doesn't make money, I'm going to spend the rest of my life paying it off."

"Well, sir, there are a few positive signs," said Beeker. "The local hotels are booked solid for the opening dates, mostly by off-planet visitors. Your reporter friend, Miss Jennie's publicity stories seem to have been effective."

"Don't ever tell Jennie she's been giving us publicity," said Phule. "Those are hard news stories, as far as she's concerned. But you're right—they've been invaluable. Let's hope it translates into customers."

"Any influx of money would be a very good thing, sir," said Beeker. "If the rebels had the wherewithal to repay your loans themselves, they wouldn't have needed the loans to begin with."

"I'm all too aware of that," said Phule, staring at the numbers on the screen. He punched a series of commands into the computer, then said, "At a rough calculation, the park needs to average four thousand visitors a day— roughly one and a half million visitors annually—just to pay the basic running expenses."

"The entire population would have to visit the park at least once a year," said Beeker, nodding. "Actually, sir, given the local popularity of such attractions, that would seem to be within reach.''

"I suppose so," said Phule. "But I'm not going to see any money unless they do better than that—at least double it, I'd think. Otherwise, my cash flow is going to do a fair imitation of a waterfall.''

"I'd expect Dilithium Express will stand by you, sir," said Beeker. "After all, you have an excellent record . . ."

Phule's communicator buzzed. "Yes, Mother, what is it now?''

"It's Le Duc Taep now, sweetie," said Mother. "He's got a sheaf of blueprints and that gleam in his eye that says you'd better get ready to spend some more money. Makes me think I should've started building my own park instead of joining the Legion. Or maybe you'd like to give me the money directly?''

Phule groaned. "I guess you'd better send him in," he said. The totals on the spreadsheet were about to change again. He wondered if they'd ever get back in the black.

17

Journal #442

Despite all setbacks, the day finally came when there was nothing more to do but open New Atlantis Park and see how many people came inside. As Le Duc Taep had planned, both the rebel park and the government park were to open their gates on the same day. It became increasingly evident that the dual opening day would be a landmark event in the recent history of Landoor. Schools and government offices were given a holiday to help swell the attendance at Landoor Park, and many businesses followed suit. Naturally, this was expected to give New Atlantis Park a significant boost in attendance, as well.

Off-planet tourists began arriving in a steady stream during the week before opening day. These tourists gave an immediate boost to local business, filling the hotels, restaurants, and shops as well as the beaches and existing parks. It began to appear as if my employer's heavy publicity campaign had paid off handsomely, at least as far as initial interest in the two amusement parks.

What he hadn't expected was the arrival of an entirely different kind of visitor . . .

"Uh-oh," said Rembrandt.

"Now, that's an encouraging statement," said Armstrong, looking up from a printout of political commentary culled from the net. The two officers were catching up on their news reading over breakfast, and neither had said a word until now.

Rembrandt threw her printout on top of his pages. "Take a look at the story on the lower left, and see whether it encourages *you*," she said.

"*Diplomats arrive for park openings*," read Armstrong. "Hey, that can't be all bad. Bigwigs coming means more publicity for the park."

"Keep reading."

"*Ambassador Gottesman and the peacekeeping verification team made Landoor Orbit on the* Pride of Durdane *. . . A spokesperson said their visit had been planned several months ago, but they were pleased to learn that their arrival coincided with a planetwide celebration . . .*" Armstrong looked up. "So?"

"Keep reading."

"*Also on board was a military delegation headed up by . . .*" Armstrong blanched. "Holy mackerel!"

"You see what I mean," said Rembrandt. "The captain needs to see this right away." She stood up from the table and grabbed the printout from Armstrong's hands.

"Hang on, I've got one piece of bacon left," said Armstrong, reaching for his plate.

"Eat it on the run, this is a red alert," said Rembrandt. She turned and headed for the captain's office without looking back.

Several legionnaires turned to look as the lieutenants—Rembrandt in the lead, with Armstrong gaining rapidly—hurried through the dining room out toward the company offices. Just as the rear door closed behind them, Moustache, who was sitting near the front door, leapt up and shouted, "Ten-*hut*! General Blitzkrieg, sir!"

The assembled legionnaires straggled to their feet, their mouths gaping open. The sight of any high-ranking officer was a rarity at Omega Company, and the troops' demeanor showed it. Moustache and Mahatma managed to snap off salutes that might have satisfied a moderately lenient drill sergeant. If any of the others had ever known how, they had long since forgotten it.

It hardly mattered. Looking neither to the left nor to the right, General Blitzkrieg stormed through the dining room toward the company offices. Even those who didn't know of Phule's previous run-ins with Legion brass had no difficulty figuring out that their CO was about to get his head chewed off.

"Jester, you've overstepped every trace of your authority," roared General Blitzkrieg. "You've allied yourself with the damned rebels, and put your troops to work to overthrow the very government you were sent to protect. Hmpfff! This won't just get you drummed out of the Legion—you'll be in the stockade, if I have my way."

"Sir, I can explain everything," said Phule, standing at rigid attention behind his desk. He was maintaining his aplomb remarkably well, considering that he'd had perhaps two minutes' notice of the general's arrival.

"I'm sure you can," snarled the general. "You're good at making your schemes look harmless, but I can see through them. This time, you're going to pay the price. And it will give me great pleasure to watch it!"

Seizing the pause in the general's rant, Phule broke in, "Sir, I have done nothing that isn't within my orders."

"Within your orders? Hah! We'll see about that," said Blitzkrieg. He walked around the large marble-topped desk and wagged a finger under his subordinate's nose. "But I'm not going to waste time arguing with you. I'm relieving you of your command, effective instantly. You will go directly to your quarters and consider yourself under house arrest. Do you understand me?"

"Yes, sir," said Phule, standing his ground. "Do I have the general's permission to have visitors? I will need to see my butler. I also request permission to speak to my officers, with a view to preparing a defense.''

Blitzkrieg waved a hand, knocking an empty plastic coffee cup off the desk. He didn't seem to notice. ''Permission granted,'' he said. ''It'll do you no good, but never let it be said that I denied you the right to counsel. I warn you, though—don't try to enlist your officers in any conspiracy against me, or you'll all be charged with mutiny. Dismissed!''

''Sir!'' Phule saluted and turned to make his way to his quarters. He'd get out of this, he knew. He'd been in plenty of trouble with the brass before, and he'd always gotten out of it. It might be a little tougher this time, with both his commanding general and the government of the planet he was supposed to be protecting lined up against him. But he'd figure it out. At least, he hoped he would.

Journal #445

Those who, like my employer, are accustomed to taking matters in their own hands are prone to forget that some matters don't want to be taken in hand. Alternately, these active souls prefer to put recalcitrant matters out of mind and concentrate on problems they can deal with directly. As a result, they are often surprised when something they have deliberately neglected jumps up and bites them.

Phule was about to turn down the corridor to his hotel room when he was stopped by two people in civilian outfits so identical that they might as well have been uniforms. ''Mister Phule?'' said the taller of the two.

''Yes,'' he said. ''I am Phule. I'm afraid I can't really stop to talk, though.''

''Captain, it is your decision whether or not to talk to us,'' said the man who'd spoken. Phule could now see that the other was a woman. ''However, we are here on important government business, and it would be very wise of you to make the time.'' He opened a wallet and displayed an

ID card: Special Agent Roger Peele of the Interstellar Revenue System.

Phule struck himself on the forehead and said, "I knew there was something I'd been forgetting! You were looking for me back on Lorelei, weren't you?"

"Yes," said Peele. "And after what we've found there, we're even more anxious to talk to you."

"I guess we might as well do it now as later," said Phule with a sigh. "At this point, there's nothing you can do to make my day any worse."

"Perhaps not, Mr. Phule," said the other, female, IRS agent. "However, I must warn you—it's our job to try." Her thin smile made it clear that she was not joking at all.

"Well, come with me, then," said Phule, and they followed him to his quarters.

"Well, sir, which shall we tackle first—saving you from the stockade, or from bankruptcy?" Beeker sat calmly at the keyboard of his Port-a-Brain computer, watching Phule pace nervously across the room and back again.

"Getting this house arrest lifted would be a good start," said Phule. "The park opens tomorrow morning, and I want to be there. I can work on the rest of my problems from a jail cell, if need be, but I think I've earned the right to be at the opening."

"Your priorities astonish me, sir," said Beeker. "However, I am certain we can find a way to persuade the general to give you your freedom for the day—possibly you'll have to put up with a guard, but that should be a minor inconvenience."

"Good, I trust you to explore all avenues on that one," said Phule. "As far as the rest—well, I told the IRS you had the figures to prove I'm in compliance with the tax laws, but they didn't want to hear it. I think they're so used to dealing with criminals that they can't imagine anyone actually obeying the law."

"More likely, the laws make it impossible to file a tax return without some sort of violation," said Beeker, dryly. "How much do they claim you owe?"

"Including penalties and interest, it's something like twenty million," said Phule. "That's absurd, of course—I can't possibly owe them penalties or interest if I'm not guilty of any violations to begin with."

"Your faith in common sense is quite inspiring, sir. I regret to inform you that the IRS operates on some entirely different system, as appalling in its way as anything the military can conjure up."

"Well, if you can't find me a way out, I doubt anybody can. You've got all the records here, don't you?"

"Yes, sir," said Beeker, nodding in the direction of his Port-a-Brain. "I'll set up a meeting to show them the relevant figures—that will take a good while, though. And we may still have to drag it through a couple of levels of appeal before we satisfy them. It might be easier to agree to some token payment, say a couple of million, to get rid of them."

"Blackmail!" said Phule. "I won't do it!"

"As you wish, sir. Unfortunately, they can tie up your assets rather thoroughly pending appeal. Not even Dilithium Express can entirely shield your money from the IRS, although I suspect you'll be able to pay your personal bills."

"I'll need more than that, if I'm going to keep running the company," said Phule.

"General Blitzkrieg seems bent on preventing that, sir," Beeker pointed out. "It might be prudent for you to give some thought to counteracting the general's plans, while I'm saving you from the IRS."

"Believe me, Beeker, I'm trying." Phule paused, then said, "Well, to be honest, keeping me from going bankrupt is of some urgency, as well. But I'm going to leave that in your hands, Beeker."

"I appreciate your confidence, sir," said Beeker.

Phule smiled. "It's been well-earned, Beeker. This won't be the first time you've saved my assets."

Journal #448

Obtaining my employer's release from house arrest turned out to be easier than anticipated. All that was really

necessary was Le Duc Taep petitioning Ambassador Got-
tesman to allow Phule to attend the opening of the park he
had done so much to bring to fruition. The ambassador,
recognizing the former rebel leader as a significant player
in the Landooran political arena, conveyed to General
Blitzkrieg that keeping my employer confined would have
undesirable political consequences. Surprisingly, even the
Landooran government agreed that preventing him from
attending the opening would be excessively cruel punish-
ment for someone not yet proven guilty of anything. That
was enough to get my employer his freedom—at least, for
the day.

Le Duc Taep stood looking out a tower window at the
customers standing in line outside the park. It was quarter
to eight in the morning, and some people had been standing
in line since before sunup. A few had even camped out
overnight so as to be among the first to enter. They would
have camped out longer, except the Legion security guards
had made it clear they wouldn't allow them to.

He looked back at Phule and said, "My compliments,
Captain. There have been times I despaired of this park ever
opening. Now, we have come to the crowning moment—
and look: The people have turned out for us in over-
whelming numbers. The triumph of our cause is imminent."

"Don't get too enthusiastic," said Phule. "We'd have
gotten a big crowd for opening day no matter what, with
the half-price tickets. Our publicity campaign can't have
hurt the crowds—we've beaten the government's pants off
in that department. The real test will be how many people
we have in line after the novelty wears off." Despite his
cautious words, Phule smiled. It was hard not to smile,
looking at the lines snaking through the turnstiles, and
stretching as far back as the eye could see.

"I wonder how the lines are for Landoor Park," said
Rembrandt.

"They've got huge lines, too," said Phule. "We think

we've done a little better, but it's anybody's guess until we have real numbers. And the day's barely begun.''

''We're still working to build attendance,'' said Rembrandt. ''Our people will be handing out flyers at their exits, offering anyone with a ticket stub from their opening day a half-price ticket for our park, valid for one full year.''

''That's a brilliant idea,'' said Taep. ''Once the park has shown them the superiority of our principles, not many will endorse the government's sleazy operation.''

''I'd hope they keep coming to both parks,'' said Phule. He put his hand on Taep's shoulder. ''It's important for your park to succeed, but it's even more important for all your world's people to do well. And that's going to depend on drawing off-planet visitors. Your people will support the parks, but they can't revive the economy all by themselves. It would be like two men passing a dollar back and forth every few seconds and claiming they were each taking in ten dollars a minute.''

''We're not reduced to that,'' said Okidata, chuckling at the image. ''We'll see how well the off-planet attendance holds up in the long run, but we've got a great start.''

''Well, if Jenny's opening day report gets broadcast widely enough, that'll be a big plus,'' said Phule, pointing to the reporter and her cameraman, working the crowds. There were other reporters there, too—the press had sensed a good human-interest story. ''The only thing better than publicity is free publicity,'' he said. ''I think I'll go down and mingle with the crowd some—I haven't even tried any rides yet.''

''That's the spirit,'' said Le Duc Taep. ''We'll make a proper New Atlantean of you yet!''

''I'll come with you,'' said Rembrandt. ''I've got to check on our attendance monitors.''

The stairs led down to the park's main street, where groups of tourists were surging forward toward the newly opened rides. Others were more leisurely looking into the souvenir shops along the way.

Rembrandt stopped outside the door and said, ''All right, Captain, I can tell something's eating you. What is it?''

Phule turned to her and said, "The IRS has decided I owe them some enormous amount in back taxes. I mean to fight it, of course, but that'll take time away from running the company. You may be in charge a lot more—assuming I'm not replaced entirely."

"Replaced?" Rembrandt stopped in her tracks. "That's going to happen over our dead bodies, Captain!"

Phule responded with a thin smile. "I appreciate the support, Remmie, but General Blitzkrieg is trying to get rid of me. Knowing him, he'd probably enjoy wiping out the entire company in the process—he considers its very existence a blot on his record."

"And making it a success is probably a deadly insult," said Rembrandt. The two of them began walking, sharing the street with the ebullient crowds. "The brass hats couldn't make this company effective, but you came in and did it in a couple of years—mainly by scrapping their system. And in the process, showing them up as incompetents who couldn't recognize good legionnaires if they fell over them."

"Don't say that where the general can hear you," said Phule, smiling. "Actually, as much as I appreciate the compliment, you know as well as I do that everybody in the company deserves the credit. It's a shame it's all going down the drain, now that we've finally accomplished something worthwhile."

"Sir, I'm going to do my best to make sure it doesn't go down the drain," said Rembrandt. She stopped at the corner of a little cross-street leading off to more shops and attractions. "Why don't you enjoy the fruit of your labors? If this park doesn't cheer you up, we've done something very wrong. I'd stay with you, but I've got work to do."

"Thanks, Lieutenant," said Phule. "I suggest you take your own advice and enjoy the park, too."

But Rembrandt was already striding purposefully away.

Phule strolled around the park soaking up energy from the crowds for most of the morning. He returned to the central offices to have a working lunch with Taep, who had attendance figures for the morning. Both parks had been thronged with patrons, but the best estimates indicated that New Atlantis Park had drawn a larger crowd—so far. The difference seemed to be in the off-planet visitors, a testimony to the effectiveness of Phule's publicity campaign. And the lines outside to buy tickets were still impressive. Phule and Taep drank a champagne toast to the clear-cut success. Phule privately hoped that it could continue on the same scale. It had to.

He strolled around the park some more after lunch, watching hoards of local children patiently waiting to board rides ("Stop shoving, Abdul! We'll all get on when it's our turn."), and happy riders emerging from the exits of one ride to go immediately to join a line for the next. He ate an ice-cream cone and took his own turn on the Skipper—a ride that gave the illusion of piloting a small boat through rapids, out in the jungle by the rebel camp. It was thoroughly unauthentic, but great fun.

Finally, despite his worries, he realized he was actually enjoying himself. With a smile, Phule headed back to get the latest attendance figures from Le Duc Taep. But as he entered the little cul-de-sac leading to the park offices a familiar voice addressed him, "About time you got back, Jester."

It was General Blitzkrieg, rising from a bench outside the park offices, where he'd evidently been waiting for some time. He shook his finger under Phule's nose and bellowed, "You've outdone yourself, Jester. If this is your notion of following orders, I don't want to see your idea of mutiny."

Blitzkrieg was literally trembling with anger. Phule had never seen his superior so disturbed. It almost made him hold his tongue. But he knew he had to make one more attempt to make the general see reason.

"General, I don't think you understand my position," said Phule. He looked around nervously, but this area had nothing to attract the fun-seekers. At least there were no witnesses to the chewing-out he was undoubtedly about to receive.

"There's not much to understand," said Blitzkrieg, backing him toward a corner. Somewhere in the distance, incongruously, Phule heard a brass band playing. "What's your excuse for aiding and abetting the enemies of the government you were sent to protect?"

Phule did his best to keep his voice calm. "Sir, I have done no such thing. In fact, I've insured a lasting peace by persuading the rebel forces to adopt a peaceful program instead of trying to overthrow the government. Stamping out the rebels would have pleased the current government—someone tried to push me in that direction by shooting at me when I arrived on-planet. They probably figured I'd blame it on the rebels and send out a punitive expedition. But that would have started a new war—and my orders were to protect the peace."

The general loomed over him. "You can't make an omelette without breaking a few eggs, Jester. Not recognizing that is your single greatest failing as an officer."

"I disagree, sir," said Phule. "I can't see how the Legion is hurt by a solution that minimizes the expense of life and property."

"Minimizes expenses? You gave the rebels millions of credits!" shouted Blitzkrieg. "Now every bandit in the galaxy will be trying to hold us up for business loans!" The general strode forward, backing Phule up against the wall.

"Sir, I gave them nothing until they had declared an end to the rebellion. Once they agreed to work within the system, it was consistent with my orders for me to offer them a private business loan. After all, a successful businessman is the last person who wants to overthrow the government."

"That's an excellent point, Captain," said an unfamiliar voice. Phule and General Blitzkrieg turned to face the person who had come out of the park offices; he was an impeccably dressed man with a cleft chin and an ample mane of gray hair, parted in the middle.

"Ambassador Gottesman!" said the general. He stepped back a pace, so that Phule was no longer cornered. "I didn't know . . ."

"That I was listening? Please pardon the eavesdropping,'' said the ambassador, bowing his head. Then he turned to Phule and smiled. ''I came to speak to Le Duc Taep, but I was hoping to find Captain Ph . . . er, Jester, too. A pleasure to make your acquaintance, Captain. We at State have followed your progress on this assignment with great interest.''

''The pleasure is mine, Ambassador,'' said Phule, shaking the diplomat's hand. ''I hope our progress has been satisfactory as well as, uh, interesting.''

''Amply satisfactory,'' said Ambassador Gottesman. ''No offense to you gentlemen, but we diplomats tend to feel that when we have to send a peacekeeping team in someplace, we're as good as admitting that we've already made a botch of things. The military is rarely our implement of choice. So we're always pleased when the military can find a way to pull the situation back over the event horizon without shooting.''

''Well, sometimes you do have to shoot a few people,'' the general growled, with a significant glance toward Phule.

''Oh, no argument with that,'' said the ambassador, affably. ''But it's a lot harder to restore the status quo ante, once you start doing that. We like to exhaust the other options first. Which is why we're impressed with the captain's performance here. Even the government is now admitting that the competition has made their park better. But that's all by the bye—there's other business afoot. If you two gentlemen will join me in a drink, I've got a proposition I think will be of benefit to you both.''

''Yes, sir,'' said Phule, puzzled. He would have agreed to almost anything that offered a momentary truce with the general. He would have to continue his argument eventually, but now was clearly not the time. He certainly had nothing to lose by listening to the ambassador's proposition.

The general grumbled his assent as well, although he was obviously skeptical that anything that benefited Phule could be of interest to him. They followed the ambassador down the theme parks's main street to a little bar. The sign over the door read JOE'S JUNGLE JUICE, and the building was decorated to look like a grass hut from a jungle-movie set. Children ran by squealing with excitement, heading for the next attraction on their list.

Inside, the bartender was dressed in camouflage, and the menu was full of fruity concoctions served in glasses shaped like voonga-nut shells. The piped-in music was heavy on percussion. A few other customers, off-planet tourists in newly purchased straw hats, sat at other tables, chattering brightly. Neither Phule nor the general was in the mood for small talk, but the ambassador kept up a well-practiced line of easy banter until the drinks came. Then, after a ritual sip of his Planter's Punch, he folded his hands and leaned forward. "Now, gentlemen, the real reason I'm here has to do with the Zenobians."

"The Zenobians?" General Blitzkrieg's puzzlement was obvious.

"Do you mean Flight Leftenant Qual?" said Phule, and he was suddenly even more apprehensive than he'd been when the general was chewing him out.

"Right-o," said Ambassador Gottesman. "As you know, Qual has been observing your unit as part of his government's decision-making process whether or not to ally with the Federation. Naturally, he's been sending back regular reports all along."

"He has?" said Phule. "Oh, of course he has—it only makes sense, but he's been such a part of the company that I didn't think of trying to intercept them."

"I'm not surprised," sneered Blitzkrieg. "This is typical of your slapdash methods."

"He wouldn't have had much luck at it anyway, old fellow," said the ambassador. "Qual was using some ultrasecret comm equipment their military has developed. I don't understand how it works—of course, that's not my bailiwick—but our tech boys have been on top of it since the beginning. Anyway, we've been able to monitor his messages all along."

"Oh, that's good," said Phule, looking from the general

to the Ambassador, and back again, "At least, I hope it's good . . ."

"Well, as you know, Qual came here to make a detailed study of our tactics and ethics. Apparently he's learned a great deal about both by watching your company."

"I knew it!" said Blitzkrieg, slapping his hand on the table-top. "You've delivered us into the hands of the enemy, Captain! The lizards have stolen all our secrets. I knew you were the kind who'd do anything for a few dollars, but selling out your own species . . . There'll be a court-martial on this, I guarantee you, and this time you won't get off with a slap on the wrist."

"General, you're off-target," said the Ambassador, tiredly. "Qual confessed that he found the company's tactics utterly baffling—he said several times that it would be suicide to fight a race so unpredictable."

"Really?" said the general, sniffing. "Well, perhaps Jester's security breach may not cost us as much as it might have. But I can't exonerate him on that count. These things have a way of changing, once the enemy's had a chance to absorb their stolen knowledge."

"I know the historical precedents, General," said Ambassador Gottesman, swirling the artificial voonga-nut shell holding his drink. "But you haven't heard the whole story yet. Flight Leftenant Qual's comments on our ethics were even more telling. He told his people that our race is utterly unprincipled, except for loyalty to our friends. He evidently considers this the best possible reason to forge an alliance with us. In fact, we received a formal proposal to that effect just before I was dispatched here. So I think we have the captain to thank for making the alliance possible."

"To *thank*?" The general's jaw dropped like a lead weight. "Are you telling me . . ."

"I'm pointing out that the captain has done a good deal to forward our concerns at State—both here on Landoor and in the Zenobian alliance. Some important allies might take it the wrong way if the captain's broad interpretation of his orders were taken as grounds for punishing him, especially in view of how things have turned out. State doesn't like to meddle in the Legion's business, but a word to the wise . . ."

"Ambassador, I'm old enough to know better than to spit into the wind," said Blitzkrieg. He picked up his gin and tonic and drained it in a gulp. Then he stood and said, "Since State intends to stick an oar in, we'll let the violations of orders slide—this time. But it would be in the captain's best interests to learn to do things the Legion way. Ambassador, thank you for the drink."

"You're welcome, General," said Ambassador Gottesman genially. "The Legion will profit by this in the long run."

Phule watched the general go out the door—a beaded curtain that concealed a low-level force field that kept the cool air inside from escaping—then turned to the ambassador. "Sir, I don't know how to thank you. If there's anything I can do . . ."

The ambassador smiled. "Captain, State will take its quid pro quo sooner than you think. In fact . . ."

"Excuse me, gentlemen," said an unfamiliar voice.

Phule and the ambassador looked up to see two humans dressed in identical bad suits: the IRS agents, Peele and Hull. "Why, what a surprise to see you here," Phule said, not meaning a syllable of it. "Somehow, I didn't expect to see you here in New Atlantis Park. I hope you're enjoying yourselves . . ."

"Not in the least, Mr. Phule," said Agent Peele, with no trace of humor. "We had been at the park office on business—looking for you, as a matter of fact—and were on our way out when we ran into your superior, General Blitzkrieg. We inquired as to your whereabouts, and he directed us here."

"A stroke of luck," said the ambassador. "Will you have a seat and join us in a drink?"

"You know, I think for once I will," said Special Agent Hull, pulling back a chair and plopping herself into it. Peele's mouth fell open; then, shrugging, he pulled back another chair and joined his partner. The ambassador signalled the waiter, and after they'd ordered drinks—unsweetened iced tea for Peele, and a tequila and tonic for Hull—Phule sat back and waited to hear what the IRS agents had to say.

Peele looked at the ambassador, then shrugged and said, "It's not customary to talk business in front of a third party, but I suppose this time there's no reason not to. Mr. Phule, I'm disappointed in what we've learned, and there's no two ways about it. You've set up your affairs at the Fat Chance Casino so as to minimize your personal profits, and we can't find any irregular practices at all. This is anomalous."

"Not at all," said Phule. "It's simply good business. My butler set up the programs himself."

"Yes, there's a sharp character," said Hull, staring into her drink. "We had no luck at all dealing with him. You'd think he'd written the regulations himself, with your personal benefit in view. Every time we thought we'd spotted a few million, he'd find a way to make it vanish. I wish we had somebody like that on our team, to tell you the truth."

"To tell *you* the truth, I'm glad you don't," said Phule. "So does this mean I don't owe you anything, after all?"

"Worse than that," said Peele, gloomily. "That rascal of a butler found a loophole giving double deductions for investment in undeveloped worlds, for which of course you are eligible."

"Well, that's a relief," said Phule, suddenly sitting up straighter.

"To you, perhaps," said Peele. "But it goes on. As you may know, Mr. Phule, when you travelled here, by a peculiarity of hyperspace, you arrived on Landoor before you left Lorelei. Your butler discovered a precedent that allows you to apply the deductions to last quarter's income despite the fact that you didn't loan out the money until after you arrived here."

Peele slumped in his chair, glaring across the table for a moment. At last he said, "Mr. Phule, unless we can find an error in your butler's figures, I am afraid that we owe you a damned *refund*!"

18

After the IRS agents left Joe's Jungle Juice, Ambassador Gottesman took Phule back to the park offices, where a rollicking party had broken out to celebrate the opening. Le Duc Taep was playing bartender, pouring chilled Aldebaran champagne for all.

There was a cheer when Phule came through the door, and Le Duc Taep handed him a water glass full of champagne—they had run out of proper flutes early in the festivities. "Speech, speech!" shouted Rev, and the legionnaires took up the chant until Phule mounted a chair and raised his hand for silence.

"I'm going to make this short, because there isn't very much to say, and I'm sure you'd all rather be drinking than listening to speeches," he said. This brought another cheer.

"Ambassador Gottesman tells me that both New Atlantis Park and Landoor Park have been doing spectacular business all day long," he continued. "As far as I'm concerned, this means we've accomplished even more than we hoped to. By making this the best park we could, we forced the government to keep making its park better, and now, thanks to all of you, this world has the *two* best theme parks in the galaxy!"

"I've also found out that the casino back on Lorelei has been even more profitable than expected, which means that each of you will be earning approximately twice what we projected. I hope all you legionnaires have taken advantage of the tax shelters we've set up for you—I just got an excellent lesson in how important good tax advice can be."

"And finally, I want to thank Flight Leftenant Qual, who's been with us as an observer—and a good friend— for the last several months. The ambassador tells me that Qual's mission is complete and he's been recalled to his home world—but he'll always find a welcome if he visits Omega Company." Another cheer went up, amid cries of "Qual! Qual!" The little Zenobian stood in the corner grinning, holding a tall glass of water—his race didn't use alcohol, but he was clearly as happy as anyone in the room.

"One last thing, and then I'll let you get back to the party. Ambassador Gottesman tells me that in part because of our good treatment of Leftenant Qual, the Federation has signed a peace treaty with the Zenobian Empire. That's one more feather in the Omega Mob's cap! So let me offer a toast: To the Omega Mob, the best outfit in the Legion— and I'll fight anybody, right up to the commanding general, who tries to tell me anything else!"

"Hear, hear," cried Moustache, and the assembled legionnaires broke into cheers. Out in the park, a band was playing a syncopated dance tune, and from somewhere a little farther away, there came the rumble of a roller coaster and the involuntary squeals of passengers as the lead car dove into the steep plunge that began the ride. Phule raised his water glass and took a deep draught of ice-cold champagne, then threw back his head and laughed. It had been a very good day after all.

Robert Asprin's
magikal mirth 'n' mayhem

THE MYTH SERIES
The wildest, most frolicking fantasy series around. Join mythfit Skeeve on his magical mythadventures, with Aahz, the pervert demon, Gleep, the baby dragon, and a crazy cast of mythtifying characters.

__M.Y.T.H. INC. IN ACTION	0-441-55282-X/$5.99
__ANOTHER FINE MYTH	0-441-02362-2/$5.50
__MYTH CONCEPTIONS	0-441-55521-7/$5.99
__MYTH DIRECTIONS	0-441-55529-2/$5.99
__HIT OR MYTH	0-441-33851-8/$5.50
__MYTH-ING PERSONS	0-441-55276-5/$5.50
__LITTLE MYTH MARKER	0-441-48499-9/$5.99
__M.Y.T.H. INC. LINK	0-441-55277-3/$5.50
__MYTH-NOMERS AND IM-PERVECTIONS	
	0-441-55279-X/$5.99
__SWEET MYTH-TERY OF LIFE	0-441-00194-7/$5.99

Enter the wondrous medieval world of

CHRISTOPHER STASHEFF

_QUICKSILVER'S KNIGHT

0-441-00229-3/$5.50

Geoffrey Gallowglass, the Warlock's son, is a young man bewitched by love. And he must make a choice—between the beautiful and brave thief called Quicksilver and the sultry, subversive Moraga, a witch who will do anything for the throne of Gramarye.

_M'LADY WITCH

0-441-00113-0/$5.99

Cordelia Gallowglass has inherited awesome talents from her father, the High Warlock of Gramarye, and her mother, a powerful witch. On top of that, Prince Alain, heir apparent to the throne, has come asking for her hand. What more could a young woman—witch or not—want? Plenty.

Enter the world of the Warlock

_THE WARLOCK UNLOCKED

0-441-87332-4/$4.99